The Last Day
of the Last Spring

BY

L. OLIVER DANIELS

L. Oliver Daniels
to my Best friends
Linda & Jim.

Acknowledgements

I could not have finished this work without the help of my friend Mary Churchill, my brother Greg, my sister Judy, my daughter Laura or my wife, Judy. Mary's challenging critique forced me to re-think much of what I was trying to accomplish with this story. Greg's logical assessment helped me restructure some continuity within the plot. My sister Judy provided the reaction of the readers I am trying to attract. Laura's critique turned my ending in a completely different direction than I originally envisioned. My wife Judy suffered through many changes in direction over our past forty-five years and took this project in her usual stride. I am truly fortunate to have such family members and friends, and I am deeply grateful to all of them.

Preface

The vast woodland is silent now. Its hills, piled up on top of one another for countless miles, etch a jagged silhouette against the sky. Its valleys descend into deep mazes where sunlight never penetrates to cast a shadow. The mist is gone too, and in the winter, snow is permitted to stack up against the mighty wooden pillars that support the heavens above. But don't let the pristine image lull you into a sense of serenity. The place they call the Midlands, or Highlands, is simply at rest; gathering strength until it is needed again. Then, the mist will return and those who have forgotten it will rush into its comfort. Some who enter the mist will come out of curiosity. Others will go to the Highlands to find hope. Many will arrive to meet their fate. Another number, familiar with the legends, will come to survive. Only one will come to the Midland-Highlands because it was his destiny.

The Legend

Before men noted their deeds in pictogram and prose, they struggled to live each day. They hunted animals, gathered roots and herbs and made war with others. During the times of the "killing winters", one tribe pondered ways to escape the frigid onslaught. Each winter seemed to grow longer, and each spring, fewer tribesmen were left to see the spring warmth flower the heaths. Realizing their potential demise, the tribal leaders called a council to discuss ways for the tribe to survive. One of the best hunters and warriors suggested the people move south, where he speculated, the sun would stay in the sky longer and keep them warm. This was a disturbing concept for the elders, for they were reluctant to leave the traditional hunting lands of their forefathers and strike out toward new lands that were unknown to them. Others argued that they needed only to wait for the winters to become milder, which was the memory of the eldest members of the group. The men and women couldn't agree, and the beliefs among them were so strong, that they divided. Those who wished to go south followed the hunter who had suggested it. The others chose to stay where they were.

The group that chose to go south believed they could hunt as they migrated, so they left right away to get a head start before winter returned. But, in spite of their hasty move, they were still overtaken by the severe winter. In addition, their journey had taken them out of the forest lands they knew, and put them in rolling grasslands that had little game they could hunt or shelter to protect them. After a time, starvation loomed as likely an end as freezing to death. The leader of the wanderers however was convinced he had made the correct choice, and he prodded his group forward. Heavy snows slowed their progress, and people began to die from the harshness of the weather.

One morning, the leader strained his eyes to see if he could spot anything over the vast, white, wasteland stretching out before him. Suddenly, in the distance he saw a strange sight. It appeared as if a cloud had settled to earth on the southern horizon. The chief took the sighting as a sign from the gods that they wanted him to move his people to the place where the cloud had landed. With renewed vigor he pushed his people forward through the snow and frigid air. At first, no one else could see the vision, and they balked at the chief's urging. But, after a short while, others began to see the fluffy, grey image in the distance. They began to push forward at a stronger gait, and soon everyone could see the vaporous mass that had fallen to earth. Now, they were plunging headlong through the snow, as they were certain their salvation was at hand. When they came closer, they could see that the smoky air was actually a thick mist that hung close to the land. They approached the mist with caution since they could not see into it. Then, they watched their chief disappear into the grey air and they followed. The depth of the snow began to lessen, and the travelers were able to walk with more ease. Soon, great towering trees appeared in the mist as black towers with invisible peaks. As they entered the forest, the snow was gone. The air was even warm, and green plants seemed to abound. Awed by the majesty of the forest, the people moved slowly into the green labyrinth until they came to a small spring. Steam rose from the rushing water as it gurgled its greeting to the tribe.

Suddenly, the unexpected shriek of a young woman pierced the majestic silence. The chief ran to the woman to see what distressed her, but when he saw her breathless child, his heart sank. He looked hurriedly about for something, anything, to help. Concluding the child was suffering from the effects of the cold weather they had suffered through; the chief plunged the infant into the hot spring. Everyone gathered around the chief to watch. In a moment the child's color returned to normal, and a moment after that, the baby bellowed a loud cry. The chief rose from the bank of the spring and handed the screaming child to its mother, who now wept for joy as she cradled her offspring tightly in her arms. The chief turned to his people and told them, "This is the heart of the earth," he paused as he pointed at the hot spring, "and this is its living blood."

The Nightmare

Two men huddled close together in the darkness of a spring night. They were tired, nearly exhausted, but they knew they could only rest for a few moments before their pursuit caught up with them. The two men gulped short, silent breaths of the cold pre-dawn air as they pushed themselves up the steep incline of the mountain. Both men were heavily armed and were dressed in the green, brown, yellow cotton clothing that made them nearly invisible during the daylight hours in the forest. At night however, their clever color scheme would provide no such help. Now, they had to rely on silence and stealth. They had to watch each step and each breath they took. The slightest sound could bring a torrent of gunfire upon them and end their delaying tactics. They had to survive the night and see the dawn if they were to escape their hunters.

This was not a new game of cat and mouse for these two comrades. Countless times, over the past several years, they had narrowly missed death. In that time, they came to know instinctively what they could expect from each other and they trusted their shared knowledge of one another. The taller man rose slowly to his feet. Carefully he adjusted the pack on his back before slinging a long, telescopic-sighted rifle over his left shoulder. Next, he made certain his revolver was in its place on his belt, then, he grasped an automatic weapon with both hands. The shorter man went through the same ritual, though he carried a pistol in preference to a revolver.

The taller man tugged at the sleeve of his comrade, and then started up the inclined slope with a controlled gait. The shorter man followed. They took slow, short, cat-steps. Carefully they would place a foot forward, then slowly shift their weight onto the new step before deliberately bringing the other foot forward. Six inches, twelve inches at a time, the two moved ever slightly up the slope. Fortunately, the forest canopy was so thick, that there was nearly no underbrush for them to deal with, and they relentlessly ascended the tilted earth. When they had ascended to half way up the steep land, they stopped to rest again.

Both men sat down so they faced the way they had come. Their ears strained to analyze every sound. Moments later they could hear an occasional rustle of leaves or a muted snap of a twig. They were uncertain about the number of pursuers behind them, and unsure if there were others already atop the ridge waiting for them to emerge. Many thoughts struggled to enter the minds of the two warriors as they listened to the enemy draw nearer, but the one thought they kept repeating to themselves was the need to hold the enemy at this ridge until daybreak. If they could just hold out until daybreak, it would be too late for their enemy.

The taller man pulled a hand grenade from the left strap on his heavy pack and handed it to his comrade. He located a second grenade, and then touched his comrade on the shoulder. The two men struggled to see each other in the darkness with no avail. Finally, the taller man gently poked his mate three times on the shoulder. Both men removed the safety pins from the grenades, and then the shorter man touched the other man's arm; once, twice, a third time. A second later the two grenades rolled down the slope of the ridge. The twosome waited several seconds, then watched as the two grenades flashed and roared their fury. An instant after the explosions, injured men cried out in pain, and the two warriors resumed their climb to the top. Several more times they stopped and listened, but they heard no sound of pursuit below them.

Just below the peak of the ridge, the two men stopped again. Both were surprised to see stars visible above the high canopy of the forest, and they quickly realized that the mist they had grown accustomed to, no longer shrouded the forest. They also realized that the gap in the canopy indicated they were near the wide trail running along the top of the ridge which had separated the trees enough to expose the star path. Both also were aware of the deep blue of the sky above and the even brighter blue that glowed in the east. Daylight, their salvation, was just another hour, or so, away. All they had to do was stay alive another hour.

The shorter man was the first to crawl on his stomach up to the path. His movements were slow and very quiet. He made his way to a tree on the far side of the trail. Once there, he slowly rose up alongside the tree's thick trunk. He watched carefully, with his eyes darting left and right into the brightening darkness. His ears listened for the slightest sound. When he was certain it was safe he returned to the edge of the ridge where his comrade joined him. Now, the two began a stealthy walk along the ridge trail following the star-path above them. Again they took the slow, short, cat-steps they relied upon, as their eyes flickered through the dimness and their ears filtered every sound.

As the darkness turned to gray and the two fighters began to see a short distance, they instinctively moved apart from each other. The taller man was near the left side of the trail, while his shorter comrade stayed as far to the right as he could. They still kept using their peculiar walk even though the brightening light increased their view.

Then, the unexpected happened. The man on the right of the trail took a step forward but his heel caught a round stone. He stumbled. In order to catch himself, and stay upright, he quickly brought his trailing leg forward. The hastily planted foot crushed a dry piece of wood with a loud crack. At that instant, the two, armed men dashed to the trees on either side of the trail, but the enemy was already there and gunfire burst out from the woods to their right. After only a few paces, the shorter man was felled with a wrenching pain in his right leg. He forced himself to turn and fire his automatic weapon at the flickering flashes which sparkled a short distance away. Behind him he heard his comrade open fire, but the pain was too intense, and the shorter man fell into unconsciousness.

The tall man was caught in a standing position beside a tall tree with tremendous girth, but he was still on the trail and mostly out in the open. He tried to move slowly away from the trail and behind the tree, but the land fell away too quickly for him to find a place to stand. All was quiet now, as the lone man by the tree wondered what fate his friend had met, while his eyes peered into every dark shadow in the twilight. He moved back to his original position beside the tree hoping the emerging daylight would make his camouflage clothing more effective. He carefully exchanged weapons as he allowed his telescopic rifle to slide off his shoulder then re-slung the automatic rifle. He waited several minutes before raising the long rifle into position. He glanced up at the star-path, but only a couple of stars were visible in the blue sky. Then, he sighted through the scope on his long weapon. The rubber extension on the telescopic sight cupped his right eye as he slowly scanned the forest. The optics provided better vision than he had with his naked eye and it only took a few seconds before he spotted his enemy and fired.

A split second later he heard gunfire from his left. Shards of wood splintered from the tree he stood near, then, a powerful force struck him, spun him around and tossed him down the steep slope. Over and over he tumbled until he came to rest on a small flat piece of land which jutted out from the face of the slope. He got up onto his feet, but only for a second before falling face first into the deep carpet of rotting leaves. He rolled onto his back and loosened the heavy pack. He realized now that he had been wounded. It was strange. There was hardly any pain. There was just a sense of exhaustion and he wanted to close his eyes and sleep. The sound of footsteps racing through the leaves snapped him back to a state of alertness. He searched frantically for his weapons, then, he realized that he had lost them in his fall down the hillside. The revolver! Yes, it was still in his belt. He pulled the handgun free and gripped it firmly in his right hand. Again, he managed to stand up. He even walked for several feet before he felt faint and crumbled into the leaves upon the forest floor just beside the hulk of a once mighty oak tree. He lay there waiting. The sounds of the man walking through the leaves seemed faint and distant now. He tried to reach up with his left arm, but it wouldn't obey him. The limb just hung there, lifeless and indifferent to his need. He rolled over on top of the dead arm and placed his pistol back into his belt. Now, he reached up with his good hand and with a mighty surge of power, pulled himself atop the fallen trunk of the tree. Again, he re-gripped his pistol and propped it on its butt in front of him. Carefully, with the barrel traversing his line of sight, he surveyed his surroundings. The small patches of sky above the treetops seemed bright, and blue. He could see everything clearly. Small beams of sunlight shot straight across the small flat land illuminating the tree tops.

He heard the footsteps again and his eyes locked upon a huge, white, limestone boulder balanced on the far side of the flat, just twenty feet away from him. He pointed his weapon at the boulder and listened and waited. He was aware of the sunlight descending the tall trees, and he heard the footsteps behind the massive rock grow closer and closer. He felt faint, then nauseous. He tried to keep himself from coughing, but the impulse was too strong to be contained. He coughed, and gagged. He could taste his blood in his mouth and he coughed again. This time the cough seemed to clear his airways and he relaxed upon the tree trunk. He watched as wisps of morning mist began to rise from the warm earth into the cool morning air. A slight breeze came up as if uncertain that it should, and the rising mist was swirled into a column. The wounded man watched the misty column grow and rise. He had never seen such a sight and it both fascinated him and kept his mind off his mortality. The column of mist began to spin faster and faster and it seemed to grow darker and darker in color.

The snap of a twig, just beyond the great stone on the other side of the little ridge, took the dying man's attention away from the mist. He readied himself again and pointed his revolver at the center of the rock so he could quickly move it toward either side when his enemy came into view. Small shafts of sunlight stabbed through the trees turning the white stone to gold at its top. The footsteps drew closer and closer, then, abruptly, the footfalls stopped.

Slowly, the enemy soldier peeked from behind the stone. He was unaware of the pistol pointing at him; waiting for him to come into full view. Inch by inch, the soldier edged from behind the rock. Frantically, he switched his eyes from right to left searching for his quarry. He noticed the fallen tree a short distance away, but before he could scrutinize the dead fall, a beam of light from the rising sun shown directly into his face. He moved to avoid the beam and a blow struck him square in the chest. He staggered, clawing at the great rock for support. A second blow stuck him, knocking him hard against the rock. With eyes wide open, he fell forward and died.

Now, the wounded man, lying across the tree-hulk, let go of his revolver and slumped over the rotting wood. Once again the column of mist caught the dying man's eye. But the image had changed and no longer looked like mist. It took a shape that the dying man thought he recognized. He raised his head and spoke to the shade in the mist.

"Have you come for me?" The dying man asked.

"No," the image replied softly. "I will come for you another day, in another spring, and that day will be your last."

Part One

Listen to the Wind

Chapter 1

The bar was crowded and noisy. Smiling faces opened to swallow alcoholic drinks to preserve their smiles and dissolve the realities of life while loud music stifled conversation. It was a place for fun; a place to escape the everyday problems of life and simply let go of whatever ailed a person. That's why Barbara came to the bar, to forget her years were overtaking her, and spend some time, perhaps the night, with a man who longed for a brief respite from loneliness and who could share a moment of affection. But, Barbara seldom succeeded in her quest, and now, as she surveyed the unattached men around her, she feared the worst. She knew most of the faces in the place. Most patrons were young, restless men, with little regard for anything but their next ejaculation, and the rest of the customers were women; women like her, desperately longing for attention. It was pathetic. Barbara knew it. But, for her, it was hope; no matter how shallow or unrewarding. Carefully, slowly, she glanced into the mirror behind the bar in hopes of spotting the "right" kind of guy. She studied the couples on the dance floor as they sensuously writhed against each other. Then, she perused those just standing and watching the dancers. Finally, one man caught her attention though she couldn't figure out why. The fellow was really quite average in appearance. He was nicely dressed, but seemed to be pre-occupied with his own thoughts. Still, Barbara found herself continuing to watch the man in the mirror.

Several times she considered approaching the fellow, but each time, her courage failed her. Then, after she saw him take no particular notice of the attractive waitress who thrust her breasts nearly out of her blouse when he paid her for his drink, she was able to push herself toward his table. She smiled as she walked toward the man, hopeful that he would prove to be the kind of guy she wanted him to be.

"You're lucky she didn't rape you," Barbara quipped to the man.

The young man looked up at Barbara as though he was confused at what she meant.

"The waitress," Barbara explained with a smile, "the one that can't keep her tits in her blouse."

The man paused as if trying to recollect the event he had obviously missed. "I didn't notice," he smiled apologetically.

"Wow, you must have a hell-of-a-lot on your mind," Barbara grinned.

The man smiled, but didn't comment.

"Do you mind if I join you?" Barbara asked as she pulled up a chair to sit across the table from the man. "Do you want to talk about it? Is it a woman; your wife; girlfriend?"

"No," he said softly. "It's nothing like that."

"Do you want to tell me about it? They say it helps to talk about things that are troubling you," Barbara smiled compassionately.

The man stared into his drink momentarily, before looking up into Barbara's green-brown eyes. "Actually, I have been sent here to see you, Barbara."

Barbara was taken aback by the man's knowledge of her name and a little frightened. "Have we met before? I don't recall meeting you," she smiled to hide her apprehension.

"No," the man said softly, "we haven't met before. I have been sent here to deliver a message to you."

Barbara giggled nervously. "A message? What message?"

"I am just a messenger," the man replied. "I am to tell you, that soon, you will be called to the Blessed Virgin who will appear to you near your home."

"What!" Barbara gasped in utter surprise. She was about to break into laughter, when the serious expression on the face of the man altered her response. "This is …I mean, why…I'm just a woman. I haven't been to church in years. Why…"

"Our Lady has chosen you. She will visit you."

Barbara turned her head, looking away from the man, as she scooted back in her chair. It was then; that she realized that everyone around her was motionless. All was silent. She jerked her gaze back to the man, but now he appeared only as a bright, blurred image. She was afraid. Her pulse pounded at a frantic rate. Tears of fear trickled down her face. "I don't understand," she blurted in panic. "What am I supposed to do?"

The Last Day of the Last Spring

"The Lord has forgiven you your sins. Go now, and sin no more. Our Lady will appear to you."

Barbara sat alone at the table. She was sobbing; shivering with fear. Then she heard the loud music. People in the bar, now animated, were casting curious glances at her, but she was frozen in her seat. Then, she felt an arm around her shoulders. She turned and looked into the face of the waitress with the gaping blouse.

"Are you o.k. honey?" The woman asked Barbara.

"Yes, I think so," Barbara guessed tearfully.

"It's a man, isn't it?" The waitress asked.

Barbara began sobbing and couldn't answer.

"I can't tell you how many times I've been hurt by men," the waitress volunteered. "But, I can't live without one. It really sucks, but that's the way it is."

Barbara found the unsolicited compassion of the waitress comforting. "I think I'm all right, now," she sighed. "Thanks for the help."

The waitress hugged Barbara. "Any time honey; us girls have got to stick together."

Barbara smiled, "Thanks again," she said. She started to leave, but something abruptly stopped her. She turned to the waitress again and words came flowing, uncontrollably from her lips. "I happen to know that the bartender is crazy about you," Barbara said.

"Really?" The waitress gushed. "Go on!"

"He's shy," Barbara said.

The waitress glanced at the bartender and stared into Barbara's eyes. "Thanks honey," the woman said as her face glowed with hope.

Barbara walked quickly out of the bar. Once outside she rested against the brick wall and drew in deep draughts of the night air. She wondered if she had been hallucinating, but she feared that she had not. She wondered if she was drunk, but that too, didn't seem likely. Still, she was frightened by what had happened to her. It all seemed so real a moment ago, but now she wasn't sure. She hailed a cab and the car instantly swerved to a halt at the curb. She got into the vehicle and instructed the driver to take her to her home.

When she reached her houseboat, which was moored on the western bank of the Old River in Portston, she walked to the square, open, bow and looked at the cliffs nearby. Steadily, she scanned her surroundings.

5

Everything looked normal, but she wondered if things would stay that way and for how long.

Hundreds of miles north of Portston, an old woman swept the wooden porch of her cabin, when suddenly a familiar feeling came over her. She swept harder and harder, hoping she could ward off the oncoming event, but she knew it would happen anyway. Soon, her sweeping stopped and she stood silently. Her glazed eyes saw only what her mind would show her, and her ears heard only what her mind would allow her to hear. A minute passed and the old woman stood statue-like in her trance. Then, just as suddenly as it began, the vision ended. The old woman gazed at the porch trying to unravel the experience she had just had. She searched for meaning to what she had seen, but there was not enough information. Now, she was uneasy. She never had these things happen, unless it pertained to her, and she was frustrated that she could not understand it all. She placed her broom against the wall and went inside the cabin. Carefully, she reviewed the event she experienced; then, she saw the photograph of her grandson smiling at her from the mantle. She approached the photograph and took it gently into her bony hands. Her eyes locked on the image in the photograph. Once again the feeling washed over her. A second later, she returned the photograph to the mantle and went back out on the porch to continue her chores. The broom effortlessly moved over the porch as the old woman concentrated on her task. She was so involved in her sweeping that she was unaware of having been observed by her husband during her episode.

The old man sighed. He had seen his wife act like this many times throughout their long relationship, but it always unnerved him. In time, when she knew, or thought she knew what the vision meant, she would tell him about it. He knew that. She always did. Still, he had a difficult time accepting her "power", or "curse", or whatever it was that happened to her. Yet, he also knew that her predictions were always true.

In Capitol City, the Sylvan family enjoyed the summer in their spacious estate. John Sylvan, known as JJ, which was short for John Junior, was deeply entrenched in the political world. Indeed, there were more than a few "insiders" that considered JJ a serious candidate for the number one job in the nation. JJ of course guffawed at such assertions in public to maintain his tailored sense of humility, while displaying a much more philosophical behavior behind closed doors.

JJ's marriage to Margaret Woodburne was one reason why JJ had ascended the political ladder. Sole heir to the Woodburne fortune, Margaret spared no expense or effort on her own to enhance her husband's career and her own social position among the "better" families in the nation. They were nearly a perfect match, and were widely regarded as the "model" couple in the country. The truth was that they adored each other. Margaret was always surprised and proud at JJ's ability to think on his feet, even during a heated debate. She had always feared public speaking. JJ was equally enamored by Margaret's persuasiveness with the wealthy and powerful. Together, they both believed, they were invincible.

Filling out the family, was JJ and Margaret's son, John Michael Sylvan. The boy's middle name was added to prevent the inevitable label of John III, or the Third, which JJ feared would ring as some aristocratic title that didn't fit his political philosophy. So, at the suggestion of his father, John Senior, the name Michael was added.

John Michael Sylvan was a gifted child. But, he was also very much his own master. As he was growing up, he frequently asked to visit his grandparents in the Midlands. Neither Margaret nor John could understand their son's fascination with the wilderness. JJ had never felt comfortable in the Highlands and was eager to leave it when he became a teenager. Still, they agreed to let the young boy stay with JJ's parents who lived in the heart of the forest on Long Ridge. As the boy grew, his visits became more frequent. Michael, as everyone began to call him, insisted on spending his entire summers with his grandparents. Then, he wanted to spend other holidays and weekends in the forest.

Michael's protracted stays with his grandparents ended, however, one cold day in late fall. JJ and Margaret arrived early to pick-up Michael and visit with John and Ann Sylvan, JJ's parents. Shortly, after they arrived, Margaret glanced out a window and saw her 12 year-old son dragging the carcass of a dead animal toward the cabin. Her shock was enhanced by his camouflage clothing and face paint. His hands were bloody halfway up his arms.

Margaret shrieked for her husband. JJ leapt to his feet and joined her at the window. JJ's father also rushed to the window. Old John grimaced at Margaret's pain.

"I taught him to hunt," old John volunteered sheepishly. Margaret could only stare at her son.

"I'll go talk to him," JJ offered hastily.

"I'll go with you," old John added and quickly followed JJ out of the cabin.

Ann Sylvan put an arm around Margaret's shoulder. "All boys hunt out here," she said.

"Not, my Michael," Margaret hissed. "I'll not allow him to learn to enjoy killing."

Young Michael watched his father and grandfather approach him. He smiled triumphantly. "Boy I'm glad to see you. I can use some help."

JJ looked into his son's cheerful face, and for the first time in his life, could find no words for his son.

"That's a fine deer," old John complimented.

"Eight pointer!" the boy beamed.

Old John dropped down on one knee to examine the kill. "I see you field dressed him. Did you get all that stuff out of the chest?"

"Sure did, grandpa. You always told me to do a thorough job."

"One shot," John observed out loud.

"Just like you taught me grandpa."

JJ was uncertain how to react to his son's exuberance, so he remained silent, and offered a smile.

"I'll help you hang your kill in the shed," John suggested as he reached for an antler.

"Grab a hold JJ," John grinned.

JJ secured his grip on the other antler and soon the carcass was pulled into the shed and hoisted to the rafters by a rope.

"My guess is he weighs over a hundred pounds," John surmised.

"I'm not surprised," Michael said. "I've been dragging him a long time."

"You'd better wash up out here before you go inside," John suggested.

"O.K. Grandpa," Michael agreed cheerfully.

The Last Day of the Last Spring

As JJ watched his son washing the blood off his hands and arms, he recounted his own youth. John would always ask him if he wanted to go hunting or fishing and he would always refuse.

As they entered the cabin, Michael's exuberance ignited again. "Hi mom! Did you see the deer I killed?"

"Yes dear," Margaret smiled. "I can see you're very proud of yourself."

Margaret took a long time to forgive John and Ann for teaching her son about firearms and hunting, and she resolved to keep Michael out of the forest. When Michael reached fourteen, she sent him off to a private boarding school thereby making Michael's opportunities to visit his grandparents very limited.

Events at the boarding school also showed Michael's trend to become a different man from his father. Michael loved sports. He threw himself into soccer with more than passion and played it at a fever pitch pace. But, he was also quick to get into brawls with those who would be bullies at the school. At one point the headmaster had him enroll in boxing, a decision which he later regretted. But the rising fame of the Sylvan name and the wealth behind the Woodburne name, prevented Michael's expulsion, and he actually earned high scholastic scores.

Preparatory School at Rockford Hall was thought best for Michael as he approached the more turbulent adolescent years. His mother, Margaret, was certain that the co-educational environment with some of society's "better" young women would help Michael become the gentleman she wanted him to become. She didn't expect his prowess with athletics to extend his horizons to more amorous pursuits with the co-eds, but that's what happened. Margaret was withering under the constant reports of "improprieties" generated by Michael. Brawling too, became more frequent. Finally, Margaret and JJ approached the headmaster of Rockford Hall at the beginning of Michael's last year at the institution.

Doctor Wainwright welcomed the parents to take seats in front of his imposing desk. Margaret studied the tall, thin man who resembled an assemblage of humanity that had been strained and drained of any human emotion. Wainwright appeared to Margaret as a man who saw "joy" as merely another word in the dictionary. But to both Margaret's and JJ's surprise, Wainwright offered his personal services in helping

9

"contain" Michael's rampant libido. In fact, he even had a plan. He would introduce Michael to another student at Rockford, a female, who came from a "proper" family that also needed to find someone to "focus" her attentions upon.

Margaret and JJ left Wainwright's office with renewed hope and thanked the tall, unsmiling man for his help. The next day, Wainwright introduced Michael Sylvan to Deanna Bartlett.

Michael had met his match in Deanna and enjoyed the company of her twin sister, Dianna. Deanna was as athletic as Michael was and just as amorous. They began dating each other with great frequency and notices of their behavioral miscues stopped flowing from Rockford Hall. Of course, Dianna kept her mouth shut about what was really happening between Deanna and Michael. The seemingly quiet relationship was welcomed by the young people's families who were thrilled not to be getting calls from the school administrator.

Now, Michael Sylvan is twenty-one. In a few days, he will begin his last year at prestigious National University. After that, he'll take his position in management with Woodburne Industries. The job would be more educational than challenging, as he would one day assume the CEO spot currently held by his mother. He would probably marry Deanna Bartlett. Deanna was a tall, buxom blond who could easily be a movie star. With the exception of Dianna, Deanna's identical twin sister, few women could match her beauty. The fact that Deanna and Dianna would split the Bartlett Hotel fortune, also added a layer of icing to an already sumptuous, social cake. Yet, in spite of all these things waiting for Michael to take, he was thinking of something else.

Margaret Woodburne Sylvan smiled at her son's thoughtfulness. "Are you planning your future, Michael?" She asked cheerfully.

"Was I far away?" Michael grinned.

"Only one galaxy away," Margaret teased. "Are you a little apprehensive about your last year at National?"

"No, I will be glad to have school behind me and you and dad have the future under control for me. I was just recalling the times I spent with grandpa and grandma in the Highlands. I was thinking of taking Dudley with me to visit them before the start of next term."

Margaret turned her back toward her son so he couldn't see the frown on her face. "Do you think that's wise? I mean, John and Ann are way up there in years. Do you think they'll want company?"

"I don't think they'll mind," Michael guessed. "Besides, Dudley has never been in the wilderness. He needs to see it."

"It's just," Margaret hesitated, "it's so primitive out there. There's just that one, narrow, curvy road. If you run off the road, no one would ever find you."

"Well, that's true," Michael agreed. "You have to pay attention while you're driving on the Old Road. But, it's still the most beautiful place I've ever seen. I've been thinking about the Midlands a lot lately, and I think Dudley will find it interesting. If not, he'll enjoy talking to grandma and grandpa."

"That's for sure," Margaret smiled. "Those two make great conversation." Margaret paused. "I guess I'm also curious why you have become such a close friend with Dudley. It's not that I don't like Dudley. It just that…"

"He doesn't come from one of the 'right' families," Michael finished the thought Margaret hesitated to say.

"Well, yes," Margaret confessed.

"I like Dudley because he is going to be the patriarch of his own 'right' kind of family," Michael grinned. "He's smart and focused on success. More importantly, he knows he will be successful. He will tell you that it is only a matter of time. Besides he is challenging me for the number one position in our class," Michael concluded.

"I'm being a snob again, aren't I," Margaret smiled sheepishly.

"Yes you are mother," Michael beamed, "that's what we love about you. I think I'll give Dudley a call to see how he feels about the trip," Michael concluded.

"All right, dear," Margaret said without a hint of her true feelings. She watched Michael go off toward his room. When he was out of sight, she went into her husband's office. She wanted to talk, but seeing that J.J was busy she picked up a book and waited for a chance to speak to her husband.

Margaret glanced up from her novel several times to see if JJ had finished writing his speech, but she could see that he had not. JJ on the other hand, was very much aware of Margaret wanting to talk to him,

11

but he knew she would never think of interrupting him until he had finished. He looked at her and smiled. When, Margaret looked up again JJ went over to her and sat beside her on the couch.

"You have something on your mind," he said with a warm smile.

Margaret nodded and closed her book. "I think I'm just being silly,"

JJ could see that Margaret was very concerned. "What's worrying you?" He asked softly.

"Michael seems to be changing, somehow," Margaret said. "He's more reflective, less outgoing and fun loving than he used to be."

"It could be a process of maturing," JJ offered.

"It probably is," Margaret scoffed at her worry. "After all, his hair is nearly completely gray."

JJ laughed as he pushed his fingers through his own gray hair. "The gray hair runs in the family," he chuckled. "This is his last year at the university," JJ reminded her, "he could be a bit worried about his future."

"I asked him about that," Margaret revealed. "He told me that he was reminiscing about his visits to the Midland-Highlands to see your parents. Now, he wants to take his friend Dudley there for a visit before starting the fall term."

"Michael always loved the forest," JJ recalled. "Perhaps he just wants to relax before starting his last year of schoolwork."

"It's a frightening place," Margaret blurted. "I simply don't want him to go there."

"I agree with you about the wilderness being frightening," JJ said. "Growing up there as a child was particularly scary for me. But, Michael never seemed to have the fears I had. He always seemed very much at home there. In fact, he reminds me more of my father every day."

Margaret sighed. "He does resemble old John quite a bit; especially with his hair turning gray so soon."

"Family trait," JJ said again with a wide grin.

"I guess I'll have to let him go, won't I?" Margaret asked

JJ took his wife's hand. "I suppose so," he smiled. "Remember what I said. Michael is very much at home in the forest. My father taught him a great deal during his visits with him. He'll be fine."

"I hope so," Margaret said. Still, in her heart, she felt something awful was waiting in the forest for her son.

The Last Day of the Last Spring

The ringing telephone brought a quick response from Michael as he snatched the receiver off its cradle. "Sylvan residence," he answered.

"Michael, this is Dudley," the voice from the phone announced. "Sorry, I missed your call."

"No problem, Dudley. I just wanted to know if you would like to go with me to visit my grandparents for a week, before the next term begins. They live in the Midlands."

"The Midland-Highlands? I didn't think anyone lived there," Dudley disclosed.

"You're such a city-dweller, Dudley. Of course, people live in the Highlands. My grandparents have lived there all their lives."

"I've heard a lot of weird stories about that place. Radios and compasses won't work there. People get lost and are never found. Besides, there are no roads there. All the highways go around that place."

"It's true about radios and compasses," Michael said, "in some areas they don't work. There are a lot of ore deposits there that cause that. The rest of the things you've heard are just plain tales. But if you're afraid…"

"Who said anything about being afraid," Dudley interrupted. "I'm just being prudent about a place I know nothing about."

"Trust me on this one, Dudley. The Midlands is nothing more than a beautiful forest. I won't let you wander off. Besides, if you get bored, my grandparents are great conversationalists."

"Really? How old are they?"

"I'm not sure exactly, in their nineties though."

"In their nineties; living alone in the wilderness? That's incredible."

"My grandparents are pretty resourceful people. You'll like them."

"All right, Michael. I'll try anything once. When do you want to leave?"

"How about the day after tomorrow? Be sure to pack everything you want to take to the university, so we can leave my grandparents and go directly to the campus."

"Will do. Do you want me to drive?"

"That'd be great. Your truck will be perfect for the trip. We'll need three or four ten gallon gas cans though."

"Three or four ten-gallon cans?" Dudley asked with surprise.

"There aren't any gas stations out there," Michael chuckled.

"No, problem, I'll borrow some from my dad. Any particular time?"

"Let's make it 8:00 a.m."

"All right, Michael. See you then."

"Thanks, Dudley. We'll have a great time. See you Tuesday morning."

Michael hung up the phone and noticed his mother standing nearby. "It's all set," he announced to Margaret cheerfully. "Dudley will pick me up Tuesday to go to see grandma and grandpa."

Margaret forced herself to smile. "I'm sure you'll both have a wonderful time."

"It'll be great, mom. I can hardly wait."

"Do you think we should try to contact John and Ann to let them know you're coming?"

"No, mom I want to surprise them."

"Very well, dear." Margaret held her smile until Michael left the study, then, she slumped into an over-stuffed chair. She toyed with ideas to try to divert Michael to another endeavor, but nothing she thought of seemed practical to her.

"Was that Michael who just left?" JJ asked as he entered the study.

"Yes," Margaret sighed. "He and his friend Dudley are going to visit your parents for a while, then go on to the university from the Highlands."

JJ smiled. "They'll be fine. They are two intelligent young men." He consoled Margaret with a squeeze on her shoulder. She looked up at him and nodded her head in agreement, but in her heart, she was very uncertain.

JJ sensed Margaret's apprehension and decided to confront it. "What is it about the Highlands that causes you so much concern?"

"I don't know," Margaret sighed. "Maybe I'm jealous. Michael always loved to stay with your parents. Maybe, I think that he would rather be there with them, than with me. I know how silly that sounds, but I feel as if there is something there in the wilderness that is calling him away from us."

"The call of the wild," JJ teased.

"No," Margaret said solemnly, "I fear it is something more than that."

"They'll be fine," JJ reassured Margaret again.

Chapter 2

When the day came for Michael and his friend Dudley, to leave for the Midland-Highlands wilderness, Margaret kept her fears under control. In fact, both young men felt that Margaret was encouraging them to make the journey. JJ was his usual, non-committal, self, and he simply told the two men "to have a good time". Moments later, Dudley started the powerful engine on his pick-up truck, and the trip began.

For the first few hours, the travelers made good time on the wide and spacious highway. Dudley wondered if they could complete the trip in one day, instead of spending the night outside a small town called Riverton. Michael explained that they didn't want to drive the Old Road at night and it would be easy to double back from Riverton to the Old Road in the morning. Dudley quickly accepted the plan and the two friends continued the first part of the trip.

"I've been reading about the Midland-Highlands," Dudley disclosed. "There are some great tales told about the place."

"Those are just stories to frighten children," Michael scoffed

"I'm not so sure," Dudley cautioned. "Professor Draco is obsessed with the Highlands."

"Why?" Michael laughed. "It's just a forest."

"You'll see when you take his class," Dudley warned. "His favorite tale is the one about the Highland Mist."

"There's almost always a mist around the Midlands," Michael pointed out.

"Let me tell you about the mist that Ivan Draco talks about," Dudley said patiently, "then, you can make up your mind."

"Why don't you save that story for my grandparents," Michael suggested. "They'll probably get a good laugh out of it."

"All right," Dudley grinned, "I will."

The trip continued in silence for a time, then, Dudley brought up an issue that had bothered him about his friend.

"Do you think it was wise to postpone Professor Draco's class until your last year," Dudley asked.

Michael smiled. "Ivan Draco can't be as bad as everyone says he is."

"Oh boy!" Dudley gasped. "They don't call him 'Ivan the Terrible' for nothing. He's going to tear you apart. I'm telling you to believe everything you hear about him. Remember, the number one class position is between you and me. I don't want anyone to say you ended up number two because I didn't warn you about Draco."

"You're pretty sure you're going to beat me out of that number one slot, aren't you?" Michael challenged his friend with a wide grin.

"I'm only a fraction of a point behind you," Dudley reminded Michael. "The grade you get from Ivan Draco will be the deciding factor."

"I'm more worried about Deanna and Dianna Bartlett, when they find out we've gone on this outing without them," Michael noted.

Dudley rolled his eyes back in his head. "Didn't you tell them?"

"No."

"You realize that you may have put us in a position to have a very lonely social life this term," Dudley admonished Michael.

"I'm betting they get over it," Michael laughed. "Besides, they wouldn't have gone into the Highlands for any reason."

"You're right about that. Dianna's idea of out-of-doors is a pool side bar-b-cue."

The two fellows laughed heartily at the last remark, and continued their chatter until well past mid-day. Finally, they stopped for lunch at one of the more fashionable truck stops on the highway.

After lunch, they continued their drive, but their conversation began to ebb, and they both fell into silence. It was late afternoon, before either spoke.

"There it is," Michael announced with a soft voice.

Dudley glanced at the rising terrain in the distance toward his right front. "Wow! Pretty impressive!"

"It dominates everything around it," Michael added. "But if you think it looks impressive from here, wait until you're in it."

"It's much larger than I thought it would be," Dudley commented.

"Hundreds, and hundreds of square miles," Michael said, "and there are only two things which cut through it. The Old River is the west central boundary and the Old Road is the east central boundary. In the middle, dividing the wilderness north from south is Long Ridge. That's where my grandparents live."

Dudley peered out through the windshield at the enlarging vista before him. "I've never seen anything like it." Dudley declared. "I've seen photographs, but they don't give you the perspective that I'm experiencing now."

Michael stared at the gnarled topography rising up from the earth. There was something familiar to him about the wilderness. He had a feeling of warmth and comfort, as if he had been away and now he was coming home. His mind raced with pleasant memories from his childhood. He remembered his grandfather teaching him about edible plants and how to find water to drink. When he got older, the old man taught him how to fish and hunt. Also, he was taught how to navigate the forest when a compass might not be reliable. All those lessons came flooding back to him, and Michael smiled confidently.

In order to get a better view, Michael rolled down his window. Now, he could smell the scent of the Midlands; the scent of the wild. He looked over at Dudley and grinned. "This is going to be great, Dudley."

"Yes," his friend responded, "I believe it is."

A short time later, the two young men checked into a small hotel just north of Riverton. While registering, Dudley noticed that a very old man, who had been seated in the hotel lobby when they came in, was staring curiously at them.

"Do you know that guy?" Dudley asked.

"No, I don't think so," Michael answered. "He's looking at me as if I should though. I think I'll talk to him."

Before Dudley could object, Michael was already addressing the old man. "Do I know you?" Michael asked the old timer.

"You remind me of someone I knew a long time ago," the old man answered. "Sorry, I guess I was staring. You sure do remind me of him though."

"What was his name?" Michael asked.

"I never knew his real name," the old man paused thoughtfully. "He was a ..." The old man stopped himself as if he was about to disclose something he shouldn't. "It was a very long time ago. Sorry, if I annoyed you. I've got to go now."

Michael watched the old man walk away. When the old man was gone, he turned back to Dudley. Michael looked at his friend and shrugged.

"An old friend?" Dudley teased.

"Maybe, he couldn't remember," Michael grinned.

After having a few beers and a wonderful meal, Dudley and Michael went to their rooms. Before retiring, Michael stood on the small balcony outside his room and stared at the Highlands silhouetted in the distance. He stood there for a long time before finally deciding to go to bed.

It was not a restful night for Michael. He tossed and turned most of the night as strange images passed through his subconscious. When morning finally came, Michael was relieved. He showered quickly, and then rushed to Dudley's room to wake him. The two comrades ate a hearty breakfast before paying their bill and returning to the pick-up truck to resume their journey. They filled the gas tank and all the extra fuel cans, and then began the last leg of the trip into the wilderness. A short time later, they took an exit marked "Old Road North; Midland-Highlands". A short distance from the highway they came upon a larger sign which made Dudley wonder. "WARNING" the sign blared in bold, red letters, "No services. Continue at your own risk."

Michael noticed the apprehensive look on Dudley's face. "That's for the tourists," he chuckled. "That's why we brought the extra gasoline."

"Four, ten gallon containers are in the back," Dudley replied.

"Are they full," Michael teased.

"Of course," Dudley scowled.

"Then, we're in great shape," Michael reassured his friend. "Just take it slow and easy. You'll only be able to drive about 25 or 30 miles per hour around the curves."

For the next several hours, Dudley's driving skills were put to the test as his truck crawled up steep hills and swayed from side to side in the curves. Skillfully, Dudley shifted gears and applied his brakes to avoid plummeting through the down slopes. He was pleased, however, when Michael advised him to make a left turn onto a gravel road.

"This is Long Ridge," Michael explained. "It's up hill all the way."

Dudley had gained confidence while driving the "Old Road" so he simply smiled and concentrated on his task. It was well after noon, when a large, rustic cabin with a huge porch, came into view. An old woman was sweeping the porch.

"This is it," Michael smiled. "That's my grandmother on the porch." Michael opened the door of the truck as soon as it came to a stop, and rushed to the old woman on the porch.

"John!" The old woman called out with a strong voice. "Come here! It's Michael. He's come to visit."

"Hi, grandma," Michael beamed. "I thought I would surprise you and grandpa with a visit before going back to school."

"My, how you've changed in just a few short years," grandma sighed. "You're a man. And, I'm afraid to say it, but you are the spittin' image of your grandfather."

"I consider that a compliment," Michael laughed.

"Hell, Ann, I was better looking than that when I was his age," Michael's grandfather teased as he joined his wife on the porch.

"Hi, grandpa," Michael grinned as he shook hands with, and then embraced, the old patriarch. "It's good to see you again."

"And who is the friend you forgot to introduce?" Ann asked with an impish admonishment.

"Oh, I am sorry," Michael blushed. "This is Dudley Carpenter. Dudley and I are very good friends and classmates at National University."

Dudley shook hands with Ann first, then, John. After all the introductions were made, Ann asked the two young men to carry their luggage to the upstairs bedrooms while she prepared a quick snack. Michael and Dudley quickly complied, and soon all four were seated in the spacious kitchen. Ann had a hard time keeping her eyes off her grandson. His resemblance to his grandfather, John, was most striking. Even Dudley noticed the likeness of Michael to John, in spite of the many years which separated them, and he commented on it as well. John, of course, easily brushed it off, though it pleased him to think that once he was as handsome and athletic as his grandson.

"Well, now that you're here, what do you plan to do?" Old John asked.

"The first thing we're going to do is watch the sun rise from that old, rocky outcrop on the west-end of the ridge," Michael announced.

"That would be a fine start," John said. "I'd go with you, but these old legs won't carry me as well as they once did."

"How far is it?" Dudley asked.

"About three miles," Michael answered. "It's mostly uphill though, so we should probably give ourselves at least an hour to get there."

"This is a real adventure for me," Dudley explained to the old couple. "I'm a pure city boy."

"You'll enjoy the forest," Ann reassured the young man.

"I'm very curious about the Highlands. I've heard so many tales about it though; I must admit I'm a little apprehensive."

"What kind of tales?" John asked.

"Well, I've heard that it is very easy to get lost," Dudley answered.

"That's not a tale," Ann added. "Almost every place looks like every other place."

"It's not that bad," John argued. "You just have to take care to stay in areas you're familiar with, or, be smart enough to mark your trail. It's when people start taking 'short cuts' that they get lost."

"I have also heard that radios won't work in the Midlands," Dudley added. "Is that true too, Mr. Sylvan."

"Yes, it is true," John replied. "There are many areas in the wilderness where radio signals just seem to get lost. It's a peculiar thing. You can switch on a radio and get nothing, then, suddenly you pick up a transmission from a place well outside the range of the radio you have."

"It's because of the mineral deposits," Michael explained. "There are scattered, dense ore deposits all over the Midlands."

"There are also electromagnetic fields which seem to grow in intensity from time to time," John added.

"What else have you heard, Dudley?" Michael asked.

Dudley hesitated. "Well, just strange things," he dodged clumsily.

"Such as?" Michael prodded.

"Well," Dudley took a deep breath, "my history professor, Ivan Draco, told us this story about the Highland Mist."

Michael noticed his grandparents exchange quick glances, which made him quite curious. "Go ahead and tell us the story," Michael prodded his friend while he carefully observed his grandparents for a reaction.

"O.k." Dudley grinned. "It goes like this. Many, many centuries ago, the Forest stood on gently rolling terrain. There were people that dwelled in the forest who prospered from its bounty. Then, one day, another tribe came. This group came from the west. They were very strange to the forest-dwellers that had never seen people plant crops or herd animals. So, the forest dwellers hid from the newcomers. It was a short time later, when they saw the new people were eager to cut the trees down and take them from the forest that they realized they would have to fight if they were to keep their home. But the people on the plains were too numerous for the forest tribe, and soon the people of the trees had to plunge deep into the forest for survival. The chief of the other tribe, however, was enraged by the attacks of the forest people and he insisted they all be destroyed. While the plainsmen set about slaughtering the forest-tribe, the earth began to rumble, then, it shook violently. Great chasms rent the land and molten rock spewed forth. The land rose and fell. Great jagged mountains thrust upward toward the sky and the forest ceased to exist, and became, instead, a gnarled wasteland devoid of animals or vegetation. It became a place of terror and those who lived afterward told of the evil spirits that ruled the burnt lands."

"A strange mist settled over the area and shrouded the evil lands for many decades. Finally, one day the mist lifted, and a vast forest had sprung up on the sharp hills. Although its appearance had changed from wasteland to forest, the ghosts of the forest tribes still haunt the land," Dudley concluded proudly.

John laughed at Dudley's story, but Ann only smiled. "Ann and I have been haunting this place for years," John quipped heartily. Then, after the laughter ebbed, he added his views. "The forest is a strange place sometimes," he began. "In the twilight, it's easy to mistake things that come into view for something they are not. Even during the brightest daylight in the summer, the forest subdues the light and shadows move with the wind and clouds. Take it from me," John paused for emphasis, "the only things in the forest are those that belong here."

Dudley smiled. There was a tremendous confidence that flowed from old John. It was almost as if he was part of the forest himself, being unable to survive outside its perpetual shadow. He was also struck by Michael's obvious admiration for the old man. Dudley also felt a strong similarity in personalities between Michael and his grandfather. They were very much in tune with each other in humor and manner. And, as he watched the interaction between the young man and the old man he also noticed the satisfied look on Ann's face. She seemed content just to watch and listen to the two men banter and joke back and forth. There was a warmth in the elder Sylvans that Dudley had not experienced with Michael's mother and father, and he found that the love they had was easily extended to include him as well. He smiled. He was comfortable with the Sylvans of Long Ridge.

The afternoon passed in a flash, and Ann jumped up and apologized for not paying more attention to the time as she rushed everyone from the kitchen to prepare dinner. Both Michael and Dudley offered to help, but Ann quickly dismissed them from her kitchen kingdom.

After the evening meal, John poured whiskey for the young men and himself. Ann was content with a glass of wine. Conversation was soft, warm and mostly small talk.

"How long have you and Ann lived here?" Dudley asked.

"Oh gosh," Ann paused to recollect, "sixty-four, no, sixty-five years."

"That's a long…" Something clicked in Dudley's memory. "Then you lived here during the War of Liberation," he concluded enthusiastically.

"We settled here just after the war ended," Ann corrected.

"That's amazing," Dudley declared. "There is this professor at National that I'd bet would like to talk to you."

"Which one?" Michael asked.

"Ivan Draco," Dudley replied. "He's obsessed with the War of Liberation. You'll see when you take his class."

"Why would he want to talk to my grandparents?" Michael asked.

"Because this is where the War of Liberation began and your grandparents were here."

"No, Dudley," Ann smiled. "We didn't build this cabin until after the war ended. I'm afraid we wouldn't be much help to your professor."

"Well," John announced, "you can stay up and talk about professors if you want, but I've had too much to eat and too much to drink, so I'm ready for bed."

Michael laughed, "Me too, grandpa."

"Yes," Ann agreed cheerfully, "us old people need our rest."

"I doubt that Michael and I will be up much longer," Dudley said. "Goodnight."

The Last Day of the Last Spring

"Goodnight boys," Ann said, as she got up and followed her husband to the bedroom. A moment later the door closed and Dudley and Michael were left alone.

"Well, what do you think so far?" Michael asked.

"You were right, Michael," Dudley admitted easily. "Your grandparents are really special, and I'm anxious to start exploring the forest."

"Then we had better get to bed ourselves. I want to show you the sunrise in the morning," Michael said through a yawn.

The old couple could hear the young men as they ascended the stairs and entered the bedrooms upstairs. Although, they were both in bed, they were not asleep, and each knew that the other was awake.

"It doesn't end, does it Ann?" John asked with a sigh.

"No," Ann answered, "it don't seem like it will ever end."

"Dudley has obviously studied the history of the Midland-Highlands," John added. "Several times throughout history the mist has covered the Highlands to save the people who gathered here looking for its protection. It has never let them down."

"The mist is always associated with war, suffering and death," Ann said in disgust. "I hope it never appears again."

John saw Ann's response to their small talk as too emotional. Now, he opened the topic that he really wanted to know about.

"I've noticed you..." John searched for words, "I've noticed that you seem distracted lately. Is it...is it happening to you again?"

"Yes," Ann said unhappily. "I've tried to stop it, but I can't. It just happens to me."

"Can you tell me about it?" John asked tentatively.

"I can't make much of it," Ann said. "There's this restlessness in the forest and I can hear whispering in the wind, but I don't know what it means."

"What do you hear?" John continued his questions.

Ann felt tears begin to build and she blinked them back. "They say, 'He will come. He will be told. The mist will rise over the Highlands'."

"Oh my God!" John hissed. "Oh my God!"

Michael fell into a deep sleep almost immediately after going to bed. Then, just after moon set, his eyes popped open. A gentle breeze wafted through the open window and caused the curtain to swish against the wall. When he got out of bed to close the window, he paused, believing he had heard something. He strained his ears, but all he heard was the gentle rush of the night wind swirling through the trees. He closed the window and went back to bed. After a moment of tossing about in the bed, he began to fall asleep, but he heard the sound again. It was as if someone was calling for him he thought, but after listening again and hearing nothing, he fell asleep.

In the bedroom below Michael's, Ann listened to wind also. She strained to hear the whispering sounds, but she couldn't make them out.

Ann and John stayed in bed until they heard Michael and Dudley leave the cabin. Then, they too got up. The old couple said little to each other as they dressed and went into the kitchen for breakfast. Ann could see that John was deeply disturbed about her "experiences" occurring again, but she felt there was little she could do to comfort him. She busied herself with preparing food, but it did little to help diminish her sadness. She reached for a skillet, but her hand never touched it. The event occurred so rapidly that it frightened her and she called out, "John!"

The old man sprung to his feet and placed his arms around her before she fell. He looked into her open, glazed eyes and knew that she couldn't see him. All he could do was hold onto her and wait for the thing to pass. After a moment of complete rigidity, Ann began to relax in his arms. "Are you all right?" John asked tenderly.

Ann's eyes flickered with life. "Yes," she said. "I'm fine now. It's over for now."

"I thought you were going to fall down," John said, "so I grabbed onto you."

"I have never been struck like that before," Ann said hoarsely. "It nearly did knock me down."

"Can you remember what happened?" John asked.

"Yes," Ann gulped. "I saw a woman walking along a river bank near high, limestone cliffs. She was very sad about something. I don't know what it was. She was also very lonely. Then, a voice said to the woman, 'She will come to you soon'. I don't know what that means. Then, her sadness seemed to lift, and she looked up. A young man was standing on top of the cliff looking down at her. That's when it ended." Ann shook her head in dismay. "I don't understand it."

The Last Day of the Last Spring

"Don't try," John said as he held his wife close to him.

Michael and Dudley were slowly descending the trail that ran along the top of the ridge after viewing the sunrise from a high outcrop of granite on the western end of the ridge. "Well, what did I tell you, Dudley? Was that fantastic?"

"It was," Dudley quickly agreed. "Are all sunrises as dramatic as that one?"

"No," Michael chuckled. "We were lucky."

The two men walked along in silence as they savored the memory of the sunrise. A gentle breeze nudged them along the trail. Michael listened to wind flow through the trees, then, he heard someone softly call out his name.

"Michael."

"Yeah, What is it Dudley?" Michael responded.

"I didn't say anything," Dudley answered.

"The wind is playing tricks on me," Michael grinned, "come on, I'll show you the hot spring."

As Dudley and Michael left the wide trail on top of the ridge for a small foot path just west of the Sylvan's cabin, Ann and John noticed them from the porch where they were enjoying a cup of coffee. Ann smiled as she watched Michael deftly traverse the path.

"They're headed toward the hot spring," John correctly surmised.

"Yes," Ann acknowledged. "It's good to have Michael here. He reminds me so much of you when you were his age."

"You've mentioned that before," John said. "Do you really think the resemblance is that pronounced?"

"If you held up that old photograph of us…" Ann stopped herself. She had almost broken an old promise to John, and violated a vow of silence. In more than seventy years she had never made a slip like that, now, she wondered why she had failed.

John didn't react to Ann's sudden mention of the unmentionable, but he knew the photograph that she was about to refer to. It was the one in the old green trunk under the cellar stairs. The box of secrets, that had been unopened for more than six decades, contained the only photograph of the young John and Ann Sylvan. John smiled at Ann. "Would you like some more coffee?"

"Yes, thanks," Ann replied.

John got up from the wooden bench and started for the cabin door. Suddenly, Ann took him by the wrist and looked up at him.

"We should have told them about us," Ann said firmly. "JJ, Hank, and Joan have a right to know."

John shook his head. "We gave our word," he reminded her. "We gave our word that we would be silent forever. We have kept that word all these years, and I will not change my mind now." He patted Ann's hand as she let her grip slide away. Then, he entered the cabin and went into the kitchen.

Ann closed her eyes and wished that she had not made the promise, but John was right. It was too late to do anything about it now. They would take their secret to the grave, just as they had sworn they would.

A strong breeze swirled along the ridge. Ann ignored it a first, then, she noticed something strange. It was the sound of a voice, or voices. Her head began to spin and she felt nauseous. The sound grew louder and clearer. She saw a river running past limestone cliffs. It was the sound of the water she heard. There was a woman walking along the narrow beach between the river and the bluffs. On top of the bluff, Ann saw a young man looking down at the woman. Ann tried to see who the young man was, but she couldn't see him clearly. He was hidden in a gray mist. Then, a voice said "he will be told".

"Ann? Ann. Are you all right?" John said urgently.

The old woman took a deep breath. "I'm all right now."

Chapter 3

"Damn! That is hot!" Dudley announced as he pulled a pink hand from the spring.

Michael chuckled. "Grandpa says it stays at 105 degrees year 'round. If you get in slowly, you can bathe in there. It's very relaxing."

"We'll have to try it later," Dudley said. "Right now, I'm hungry."

"Yeah," Michael agreed. "I forgot that we hadn't had breakfast. Let's head back to the cabin."

"Is it far?"

"No, it's just over there. You can just make out the cabin through the trees," Michael pointed with his right arm extended.

Dudley quickly spotted the cabin and grinned. "Let's go," he said.

Ann and John questioned the two young men about the sunrise they had witnessed and Dudley and Michael relived the experience in great detail.

"Damn I wish I could walk that far," old John lamented. "Age takes away the little things in life you love to do."

"Well you can make it to the kitchen and help me with breakfast," Ann quickly quipped, "you still love to eat."

John laughed heartily. "Indeed, I do."

"We'll help too," Michael added.

Soon all four were working in the kitchen under Ann's expert supervision. They had strips of ham and sausage, biscuits and gravy, and preserved fruit that Ann had canned in the spring. Dudley called it a feast.

After breakfast, Michael and Dudley went on a short hike. Michael led his friend northward through the tall forest, then, he began zigzagging westward. As they walked through the wilderness, Dudley began to appreciate the silence and the splendor of nature. Birds, of many species, called and fluttered past them as they approached. There were hot springs and cold springs bubbling from the earth at frequent intervals. But most of all, Dudley was impressed by the lack of light and the sharp topography. In fact, Dudley was so absorbed by the newness of his experience, that he lost track of time. The two men had been walking for nearly four hours, when, they both heard the sound of rushing water. Dudley gave Michael an inquisitive look.

"It's the Old River," Michael answered the silent question. "We're not far from where we watched the sunrise this morning."

"Why is it so noisy?" Dudley asked.

"It's called Broken Falls," Michael replied. "When you see it, you'll understand why it's so loud."

Once again, Michael took the lead, and Dudley eagerly followed. Soon, they emerged from the forest and stood upon a gravel bank of the river. Just to the south, they saw the surging water plunge through a labyrinth of granite and limestone gorges and pinnacles that had been sculpted for eons by the crushing flow. Dudley was awe struck as he looked at the steep descent filled with smooth stones and rushing water.

From Broken Falls, Michael took the hike northward along the river until they found a shallow, slower current, where they could wade across. They followed the river downstream along the western bank in a southerly direction, slowly passing the falls so that Dudley could see every detail of the natural work. Again, they found a suitable place to cross the river and strike out on an easterly path to return to the cabin. This time the going seemed more difficult. The forest on the south side of Long Ridge seemed to be more filled with trees. But, the real chore came when they had to climb the steep southern slope to return to the cabin. The sun had already set when Michael and Dudley huffed and puffed up the final path to the trail on top of the ridge. And, it was a very short time after supper when both young men opted to go to bed.

The remaining few days went well. Ann was not visited by her "experiences", and Michael and Dudley were able to explore far and wide from the cabin. Still, when the time came for the two students to return to National University, there was a sadness that seemed to overtake everyone. After, brief, but very warm good-byes, Michael slid behind the steering wheel of Dudley's truck and started driving down the ridge to the Old Road. The two men said little to each other as they each savored their memories of past few days. They bumped and jostled along the ridge road, then, they came onto the hard surface of the Old Road and turned north. The road continued to sway and turn, rise and fall just as it had south of Long Ridge. Before long, Dudley fell into a deep sleep. Michael smiled at his overly citified friend and continued to drive.

After an hour, or so, Michael began to feel drowsy too. He started to wake Dudley, but then, suddenly, there were men in military uniforms, carrying weapons, walking in single file on both sides of the road. Taken aback by the sight, Michael slammed on the brakes of the truck and skidded to an abrupt stop. Dudley flew forward and caught himself with his hands on the dashboard before he struck the windshield.

"What happened?" Dudley gasped in surprise.

"Sorry," Michael said, "There are…" he paused. The soldiers on the sides of the road were nowhere to be seen. He looked back at Dudley who was obviously awaiting an explanation. "There was a deer," Michael said hurriedly. "It ran out in front of me."

"Wow," Dudley sighed. "I'd better stay awake to help keep an eye on things."

"Yeah," Michael quickly agreed, "that's a good idea."

The drive north, on the Old Road, seemed to take forever. Twice they had to stop to fill the tank on the truck. But once Dudley and Michael reached the modern highway that would carry them to National University, they made better time. That evening, as they unpacked their belongings near their campus apartment, the Midlands seemed very far away. The experience of the wilderness adventure had been very stimulating for Dudley, however, and he spent the next few weeks telling people of his experiences in the great out-doors. In fact, the Bartlett twins would grow weary of hearing about it.

Just before classes began, Michael and Dudley took the customary walk to Prominence Hall to see their names posted on the appropriate professor's roster and thereby verifying their schedules. As they walked along the wide, marble hallway, a wiry man with black, curly hair, walked directly toward them. Dudley had no time to warn Michael that Professor Ivan Draco was approaching them.

"Well, well," Draco sneered, "if it isn't two of our most successful students."

"Good afternoon Professor Draco," Dudley greeted.

"Good afternoon, Sir," Michael added.

Ivan Draco locked his cold, black eyes on Michael. "I see you've evaded my class again this term," Draco said. "Is it fear, Mr. Sylvan? Or do you simply dislike history?"

"Neither, sir," Michael returned.

"Really?" Ivan opened a sarcastic grin on his face. "I'll find out next term, won't I?" Draco laughed as he turned and walked away.

"What's wrong with that guy?" Michael asked.

"I'm not sure," Dudley replied. "But it looks like he's ready to single you out when you get into his class."

"What do you mean by 'single me out'?" Michael asked.

"You'll see for yourself soon enough," Dudley said. "All I can tell you is to enjoy this term. Next semester is going to be hell."

Michael found the episode with Ivan Draco very intimidating. He couldn't understand why the young teacher had anything against him. He couldn't understand why Draco would care if a student delayed a class until his last year.

Classes began, and before either Michael or Dudley knew it, they were preparing for mid-term exams. When the exams where over, they had a long weekend with the Bartlett girls, and then plunged back into school work. The only thing that changed was the weather. In fact, it appeared that there would be an early and long winter. At least that's what Michael surmised as he stared out the window of his and Dudley's room and watched as people snuggled into heavy coats to block out the cold wind. The antics of the people below brought a smile to Michael's face. "I'm happy I don't have any more classes today," he said. "It looks like it's absolutely frigid out there."

"I'll bet it is," Dudley agreed. "The temperature has been falling all day."

Michael continued his surveillance from the window. Then, without warning, he felt his body temperature rise abruptly. He felt weak and sick to his stomach. Dizziness struck him, and he braced himself on the windowsill to keep himself on his feet. He closed his eyes to re-establish some equilibrium, but his pulse raced. His temples began to pound with each surge of blood from his heart. He took a deep breath and opened his eyes, but he was no longer in his room. He was standing at the edge of a limestone cliff overlooking a mighty river. Far below him was a narrow, pebbled beach. On the beach was a woman. She rocked back and forth on her haunches and wept. Occasionally she would look up at the cliff as if she was speaking to someone. Then, she would catch her head in her hands and weep uncontrollably. Michael wanted to help the woman, but his confusion as to how he had got to this place held him fast in his footsteps. Now, the woman looked up and saw him. She wiped the tears from her face with her hands causing dirty blotches to appear on her fair skin. She beckoned for Michael to come to her and her sorrow faded into a weak smile. "Michael." A voice called out, but Michael was unsure if it was the woman who called to him or…

"Michael?" Dudley questioned with a concerned tone in his voice. "Are you all right? You're very pale and perspiring. Are you ill?"

Michael didn't know what to say at first. Suddenly, he was back in his room, and apparently, had never left it. He stumbled through his thoughts for a reply. "It must be some kind of flu bug or something," he said with a trembling voice. "I'd better take some aspirin and lie down for a moment."

"Good idea," Dudley supported. "I'll get some water."

It was unusually warm for December 4th even in the southern city of Portston. Here, a great, natural harbor, formed by the Old River and Portston Bay, was crowded with ships of every kind. It was only a short distance upstream from the bustling west-bank of Portston where Barbara lived. She had a small, flat-bottomed houseboat that rarely left its pier, but to Barbara it was Cleopatra's barge. She enjoyed the privacy of walking along the usually vacant, pebbled beach, and tonight was no exception. She found herself alone, walking, sometimes staggering a little, along her "private" beach. She giggled at her tipsy gait, and then threw back her head to let the fresh breeze flow through her hair. The cool breeze was not strong enough to cool the sun-heated gravel bar, but it seemed to help Barbara sober up some. As she walked, she didn't pay much attention to the soaring, limestone bluffs that jutted up into the night sky. At least, she didn't notice anything different about them at first. Then, suddenly, a soft, blue-white glow appeared in the side of the cliff. It was strange. Barbara had never seen anything like it before and her curiosity drove her closer and closer toward the glow. Now, she stood directly below the steady brightness and as she wondered what it was she was seeing, the light took shape. It was a woman. She was dressed in white, with a light blue shawl over her shoulders. Barbara fell to her knees and covered her face with her graceful hands. She trembled with fear.

"Do not be afraid," the woman in the light said softly.

Barbara burst into tears. "Holy Mother? Why have you chosen the likes of me to see you?"

"My Son has forgiven you for your sins. Can you not find it in yourself to accept his forgiveness?"

"I am not worthy Blessed Mother," Barbara cried out.

"You are worthy to me and my Son, accept our faith in you."

Barbara found unexpected strength to check her remorse at her life. "Why do you come to visit me?"

"I have come to give you a message. You are to tell the Bishop in Portston that a great trial will be thrust upon his people." Tears slowly broke from the eyelids of the holy lady. "I am saddened at the horror which will come and I weep for the many that will fall into darkness. Tell the Bishop that all that may perish will not be forgotten. A great champion will rise from the devastation to reap carnage on the destroyers that will come." The lady knelt down on the niche on the cliff and held out her hand. Barbara slowly rose, approached the vision and took the Lady's hand. Now the Lady's tears turned to blood and dripped onto her fair garments. "We will weep together for what is to come," the Lady said.

After an hour, Barbara found herself kneeling alone on the sharp pebbles. She had lost her shoes and her knees were nicked and bleeding. In spite of her appearance and her minor wounds, she ran barefoot across the stones. She hurried up a long, wooden staircase that ascended the cliff. She hailed a taxi and insisted the driver rush to the Cathedral in Portston. Frantically, Barbara leapt from the vehicle as it slowed to stop in front of the basilica. Barbara ran up the stairs and burst through the large wooden doors toward the altar. A young, surprised priest intercepted her.

"Where are you going?" The priest asked.

"The Bishop," Barbara gasped, "I have a message for the Bishop... from the Blessed Virgin."

"It's late," the priest explained, "the bishop is surely in bed..."

"I must see him," Barbara blurted hysterically.

The priest grabbed Barbara by the arm. "You cannot see..."

"It's all right," a deep, rich voice boomed from the darkness.

"Your eminence, I thought…"

"It's all right, father" the voice echoed from the marble, "I'll talk to the young lady."

Barbara felt the priest's grip on her arm fade, as a very large and imposing shape of a man moved slowly toward her. As the hulking figure came into the light, she could see that the man was very old, but still appeared to be very strong. "Are you the Bishop?" Barbara asked tentatively.

"Yes," the huge man answered as softly as he could. "Now, what brings you to me at such a late hour," the Bishop said as he extended a large hand toward the woman.

Barbara took hold of the strong hand, fell to her knees, and then wept in terror.

Michael stood at his window and stared downward. He didn't see the students crossing the quadrangle. In fact, he was standing on the limestone cliff again, and below him, was the woman lying on a rough, pebbled beach. The woman wept uncontrollably. Michael wished he could comfort the woman, though he didn't know the source of her sorrow. He felt as if he should do something, but he didn't know what that something should be.

As the image of the woman on the beach faded into the campus at National University, Michael shifted his gaze upward toward the horizon. Once again his gaze was fixed and he stood there motionless. Dudley noticed the statue-like pose on Michael and waited to see how long it would last. After several minutes, Dudley approached his friend and looked into Michael's eyes. It was alarming to Dudley to realize that Michael didn't know he was there.

"Michael! Michael!" Dudley pleaded with his friend. "What is it? What's wrong?"

Michael slowly turned toward Dudley and stared at him with a glazed, distant stare. "The mist will return to the Highlands," Michael said, then, he turned back toward the window.

Dudley glanced out the window and saw only a vacant horizon. "Michael, the Highlands are too far away to see them from here," Dudley argued.

"Yes," Michael agreed as he turned back toward Dudley with a smile, "of course they are."

Michael cast a quick look at his watch. "You'd better hurry, Dudley, if we're late again we won't have any women to date."

Dudley was confused by the sudden change in Michael's behavior. But, since the change was for the better, Dudley happily accepted it. "You are absolutely right about that, my friend. The Bartlett ladies have little forgiveness for the tardy."

The two men rushed out of their apartment and arrived at the street just as a long limousine pulled up in front of the building.

"Good evening, Robert," Dudley greeted the driver.

"Good evening Dudley, Michael" The driver smiled cheerfully as he got out from behind the steering wheel and opened one of the rear doors.

The Bartlett twins, stunning in their appearance, were sitting in the back seat of the vehicle. As usual, Dudley quickly commented on their beauty.

"They know they're beautiful," Michael teased his friend.

"It's still nice to hear it," Deanna smiled as she pulled Michael beside her.

"At least my guy has manners," Dianna declared as she took Dudley's arm.

"It must be nice to be associated with a gentleman," Deanna bristled with mock anger.

The driver closed the door and returned to his position to put the vehicle into motion. Dianna and Dudley locked in an intimate embrace as soon as the car began to move. Deanna snuggled up to Michael and squeezed his arm. "Why do you have so much self control," Deanna pouted.

"I don't have any self control as far as you're concerned," Michael said. "I'm just slow and clumsy around you."

Deanna kissed him passionately. "You may be as slow and clumsy with me as you like," she hissed provocatively.

The chauffeur smiled as he closed the privacy screen behind him. Twenty minutes later he stopped the vehicle in front of an exclusive restaurant. The doorman opened the doors so the passengers could get out. Robert was told to be back at 9:30 to pick them up.

The Last Day of the Last Spring

In spite of the lavish food, the promise of sex in the immediate future made the meal seem commonplace. It was nothing more than an expensive nuance and neither of the four really seemed to enjoy the food. The dinner ended on schedule, to the delight of everyone, and soon Robert was letting the two couples out at the Bartlett sisters' off-campus apartment. Nothing was said as the four entered the spacious apartment and each couple went their own way.

A short time later, Michael and Deanna sat on a couch in Deanna's room. They had exhausted their passion, and now, they just sat on the couch cuddling each other.

"Have you thought about what we're going to do after graduation?" Deanna asked.

"My parents have everything mapped out for me," Michael smiled.

Deanna rolled her eyes. "I know what you mean. Our mother has become a real pain in the ass lately."

"That's the curse of being born into families such as ours," Michael explained. "One doesn't have much to say about one's own life."

"Dianna and I are going to change that," Deanna grinned devilishly.

"Had anyone else made that comment, I wouldn't have believed them," Michael said. "I know how determined you and Dianna are in pursuing your own goals."

"All Dianna wants is Dudley and a bunch of kids," Deanna disclosed.

"Dudley will probably be happy to keep her pregnant," Michael quipped.

"I'm not ready to let child bearing destroy this," Deanna stated while her hands washed over her naked body.

"Pregnancy would definitely have a devastating effect on you," Michael teased.

"What's your real reason for objecting to Dudley," Michael challenged.

"Well, it isn't me," Deanna said.

"I take it your mother doesn't approve of Dudley," Michael surmised.

"Does your mother?" Deanna asked the embarrassing question.

Michael sighed. "She hasn't come right out and said so, but she wonders why I picked Dudley for a friend."

"I've always been curious about that myself," Deanna confessed. "I would think you would be rivals."

"It's true we compete against each other for class standing," Michael said, "but I simply like Dudley. He knows what he wants, and I believe he'll get what he wants."

"Dianna is just as determined. They'll make a great couple," Deanna concluded. "Now, if you'll excuse me for a moment..." Deanna left the comment unfinished as she got up from the couch and entered the bathroom.

Michael gawked about the apartment while he waited for Deanna to return. Finally, he noticed the newspaper on the coffee table in front of him. He picked it up just to kill time, but the large photograph on the front page nearly sent him into shock. He stared at the picture for several moments; then, he got up and hurriedly dressed. The image in the photograph was burned into his mind. He had seen this scene before, in his "dreams", and now, it was real. He picked up the paper again, just as Deanna returned to his side.

"What's wrong?" Deanna asked; instantly aware of the change in Michael.

He turned toward her and looked at her with a vacant stare, as if he were looking at her from a great distance.

"I've got to go to Portston," Michael said softly.

"Portston? Why? What's going on in Portston?" Deanna was totally confused by Michael's sudden change in mood.

"I... I can't explain," Michael stammered. "I've got to go. Will you take me to the airport?"

Deanna didn't quite know what to do. "Yeah, sure," Deanna blurted, and then began searching for her own clothes. She quickly pulled on a blouse and skirt, then, her coat. Michael started for the door, and abruptly stopped. He went back to the coffee table and picked up the newspaper. He glanced at the picture once more; then, he folded the paper and placed it under his arm.

"I'll tell Dianna and Dudley that we're leaving," Deanna said.

"There isn't time," Michael said firmly. "I must get to the airport."

Deanna was frightened by the tone in Michael's voice as much as his sudden impulse to go to Portston. "O.K." She responded.

Chapter 4

It was a cool, drizzling morning when the taxi stopped. Michael got out of the cab and looked back at the driver.

"Over there," the driver pointed at a small crowd just off the road. "You'll be able to see her from there."

Michael handed the driver some currency in payment, then walked hesitantly toward a small group of people huddled nearby. It was well past sunrise, but the dark clouds and mist made it seem darker than it really was. Michael made his way slowly through the crowd until he could stand at the edge of a limestone cliff. Below him, a woman knelt in prayer. He locked his gaze upon the woman, just as the others around him were doing.

Barbara kept her gaze upon the light blue aura in a cleft in the cliff face. The light began to flicker, growing brighter. "What?" Barbara said. "He's here?" She looked upward at the curious onlookers atop the cliff. "Oh yes, My Lady, he is here. I see him."

Michael could feel the woman's eyes capture his image. He stared back at her. She seemed elated. Her face seemed to have a glow of its own. Michael wanted to talk to the woman. He reluctantly looked away from her and searched for a path to the beach. In the distance, he spotted a long, wooden, staircase that descended the bare rock.

In an instant, Michael was pushing his way past the people around him. He walked back to the road and hurriedly made his way to the stairway. He darted down the stairs as fast as he could, but when he arrived at the beach, he was once again in the midst of a crowd. He began pushing through the curious throng, politely at first, but then, his need to emerge from the crush of humanity became urgent.

A policeman approached Michael when he broke into the clear and grabbed him by both arms. The policeman stared into Michael's eyes.

"I must speak to her," Michael said softly.

The policeman, for unknown reasons, forfeited his grip, and Michael strode uncertainly toward the woman kneeling on the pebbles. As he approached her, he realized that her clothing was too lightweight to provide any warmth. Still, the woman showed no sign of being cold. She was barefoot, and her knees were nicked and bleeding from kneeling on the stones. Yet, she showed no discomfort. Michael felt confused and frightened, but he was determined to meet the woman who had spent so much time in his thoughts.

Unexpectedly, the woman turned toward Michael and smiled. Tears trickled freely down her cheeks. "Our Lady told me you would come," she said. "You are Michael."

"Yes," Michael answered with a slight tremor in his voice.

"Stay here, beside me," she said. "I am Barbara and I have much to tell you."

Michael began to lower himself onto his knees and removed his overcoat and placed it around Barbara's shoulders. "It's cold," he offered lamely.

"Our Lady's warm heart has protected me from the cold," Barbara said, "but I am grateful to you for your kindness."

Michael searched for words, but they were difficult to find. "I have seen you several times," he hesitated, "in visions, or dreams. Everything that is happening now, I have seen before, yet, I am experiencing these things for the first time."

"Do not seek explanations to these things," Barbara said. "There are other things you must learn."

"Are you the one who will teach me?" Michael asked hopefully.

"I am to remind you about an ancient tribe of people who wandered through the dead of winter to find eternal spring."

"I'm familiar with that legend," Michael acknowledged.

"I am also to remind you of the mist that has fallen upon the Highlands to protect those who come into it."

Barbara jerked her head suddenly toward the cliffs. "Yes, Holy Mother," she said, then, she was silent, listening to the voice from the stone. Several minutes passed, as Michael watched the strange woman receive her instructions. Without warning, Barbara burst into tears.

"Oh, Holy Mother, must these things happen? Can't we avoid this horror?" Barbara listened for a reply, and wiped the tears from her fair face. Her soiled hands left dark smudges on her cheeks. Michael pulled a new handkerchief from a pocket in his suit and dabbed at the smudges on Barbara's face. The woman turned toward him and a fresh supply of tears cascaded from her eyes.

"You are so young, so handsome..." Barbara sobbed momentarily, then, she regained her manner. "The Archangel, your namesake, is by your side," she observed casually. Barbara smiled through her tears. "Come with me."

Michael helped Barbara to her feet and the two made their way toward the base of the cliff. Barbara stared intently at a niche just a couple of feet above them. Michael strained his eyes to see what Barbara saw, but he saw nothing. All he could do was tremble in the cold, or his fear.

"Our Lady says from this day on, you will not fear anything," Barbara smiled warmly. "She says 'the hand that would pull a rose from the garden of victory will prick itself on a gray thorn and the wound will bring death. You are to listen to the voices of the past, and if you heed them, the spirits of the dead will rise up from the earth to protect you. You will suffer great sorrow, as will many others. Do not languish in grief. You will encounter overwhelming odds, but do not despair. Have faith in your judgment and courage in your deeds. Have no fear of the gray mist it will bring you comfort'."

Barbara turned back toward the face of the cliff. "Yes, my Lady, I understand. I will tell the bishop. Yes, my Lady, I will tell them all to pray." She stood silently for a moment, then, turned toward Michael.

"She's gone," Barbara said. "Will you help me to my home?"

Michael caught Barbara as she collapsed and prevented her from falling on the rocks. He swept her up in his arms; then, he carried her through the crowd, where the policeman assisted by leading him to Barbara's houseboat.

The two men carefully placed the unconscious woman on her couch. Michael grabbed the telephone and called for a doctor, while the policeman tended to Barbara. After Michael hung up the phone, he realized the feelings the policeman had for Barbara. He patted the man on the shoulder. "She'll be all right," Michael said.

"Oh, I'm sure she will," the policeman grinned. "Look," he said as he pointed at Barbara's knees.

Michael looked in astonishment. Barbara showed no signs of cuts or bruises. Suddenly, Michael felt a cold chill slice through his spine but he seemed to grow strong from the sensation rather than afraid.

A moment later, Barbara became aware of the two men that hovered over her. Her face was calm, but her eyes flickered with a blue flame. She looked into Michael's face and smiled.

"Your fear has left you," Barbara correctly observed. "Go now. Remember the words of the Blessed Mother." Barbara turned her eyes on the policeman next.

"I must talk to the Bishop again. Will you take me?"

"Yes," the policeman answered.

"Good bye, Barbara," Michael said. "I am uncertain how our lives have become entangled, but I will remember you and your words."

"The Blessed Mother's words," Barbara corrected with a smile.

Michael remained silent, and then he turned and left the small house-boat. He pushed his way through the curious onlookers and was oblivious to the newsmen and photographers.

The semester ended, and Michael returned home. He was quieter than he had been in the past, and he seemed to lose his interests in sports. Margaret and JJ had learned of his quick sojourn to Portston to see the "crazy woman" on the river bank, but since it had been kept out of the newspapers, there seemed to be little reason to chastise him for his actions. The family reputation was still intact, and JJ's political career was not impacted. Still, Margaret could sense that something was wrong with her son. She waited until JJ was involved in an overnight trip so she could talk to Michael alone. The opportunity arose just prior to Christmas.

Margaret watched her son toy at his food, then, she decided it would be a good time to bring him into discussion. "Not hungry?" Margaret asked.

"No, it's very good, but I'm just not interested in eating at the moment," Michael replied with a strained smile. Margaret accepted the response, with a nod, and decided to be more direct.

"Do you mind talking about the woman in Portston?"

"No, not at all," Michael said.

"Did you go see her, because of religious convictions?"

"No, I went to see her because I thought she could explain some things to me."

"Did she give you the explanations you wanted?"

"She gave me all she could," Michael smiled.

Margaret was uncertain about how to proceed, so she tried another approach. "This woman…"

"Barbara," Michael interjected.

"Do you believe that, Barbara is talking to the Blessed Virgin Mary?"

Michael considered the question for a moment. He had been so self-centered with his own concerns that he had not considered what Barbara must have been going through. Now, as he thought of Barbara, he became aware of her loneliness. "Yes, mother," Michael said softly, "I believe she is."

"Michael, do you know anything about this Barbara? Do you know what kind of woman she is? She is a woman of questionable morals. She has the reputation of a prostitute. That's the real Barbara. Now, she's suffered a mental breakdown and has invented this story about the Blessed Virgin." Margaret stopped talking. She could tell by the look in Michael's eyes that he wasn't listening. She waited a moment, but Michael just sat there. "Michael did you hear me?"

Michael didn't look at her. "I must listen to the voices of the past," he mumbled to himself.

Margaret was confused by Michael's words. She got up, walked toward him and gently raised his face to look at her. She instantly was aware of the fact that Michael didn't know she was there. She was overcome with emotion and slowly allowed her son's face to lower as she stepped back from him. She felt as if she had looked into the face of madness and was helpless to do anything about it. Tears exploded down her cheeks and she slumped into a chair and waited for her son to return to her.

Deanna looked enviously at her sister as Dianna slipped her naked body into a luxurious sheath gown made of very expensive satin. "Is that for Dudley?" Deanna asked.

"Of course," Dianna beamed, "it'll drive him crazy."

"I'll bet."

"Why don't you call Michael and go with Dudley and me?"

"No, you two go ahead without us for a change. I may call Michael later."

"Well, all right," Dianna quickly agreed. "I can hardly wait for Dudley to see me in my new dress."

"He's going to rape you," Deanna quipped.

"If he doesn't I'm going to be very disappointed," Dianna sneered. "See you later. Give Michael a call. I think he needs you."

"I will," Deanna answered, but she doubted that Michael needed her and that thought hurt more than she thought it would.

Deanna angrily plopped down on her bed and stared at the ceiling for a moment. Then, she rolled over and slapped the receiver off the telephone. She listened to several rings, then, finally Michael answered.

"Michael, this is Deanna. If you don't come over here and make love to me, I'm going to kill myself."

"I'll be right there," Michael replied with a chuckle, then, he hung up.

Deanna smiled as she placed the receiver of the phone back in its cradle. Then, she thrust her legs toward the ceiling and propelled herself into a standing position. She would have just enough time to shower, put on a little make-up and meet Michael, naked, when he knocked on the door.

Margaret seemed more relaxed as Christmas passed. Michael appeared to be "normal" and spent a great deal of time with Deanna Bartlett, her sister and Dudley. His spirits seemed to be very high, as well, and Margaret passed off his previous behavior as just a passing phase.

Michael too, seemed to believe that whatever had happened to him before was now just a bad dream. He and Deanna were very romantically involved, and he had only three courses to deal with in his last term at National. After school ended, he could get on with the rest of his life.

When he and Dudley returned to their familiar room on the campus, everything seemed to be back to normal. The weather was crisp and cold, but both young men seemed oblivious to it as they prepared for the final effort in their formal education.

"I'm going to beat you out of the 'first in class' ranking," Dudley announced flatly.

The Last Day of the Last Spring

"How did you arrive at that conclusion?" Michael challenged.

"It's simple," Dudley said. "We both have three classes left. I'll easily obtain honors grades in my classes, and you will receive honors in two of your three. The best you can hope for in 'Modern History' is a passing grade."

Michael smiled. "You don't think I can get an honors grade from Ivan Draco?"

"No way," Dudley said in a matter of fact tone of voice.

"We'll see," Michael smiled.

"Yes, we will," Dudley beamed as he donned his coat. "Good luck."

Michael reached for his own winter overcoat. "Good luck to you Dudley."

The first two classes went just as Michael had expected, and he was confident when he took a seat in his third class that it too would go as he thought it would. He glanced up at the clock on the wall in the front of the classroom. As the minute hand clicked into position at ten minutes before eleven, Professor Ivan Draco entered the room and strode directly toward the rostrum. He was a young man, wiry and athletic looking with jet-black hair and fiery, flashing, eyes. He placed his notebook on the lectern then, stood in front of it.

"On your desks, you will notice a placard with a number on it. Look at the placard and memorize your number. When I call on you to participate, I will call your number. When you respond to a question, you will announce your number prior to presenting your answer. You will refer to your classmates by their number. To help you know who is what number; number one is the desk in the front row, on my far right. Number seven is the desk on my far left. In the second row the desk on my far right is number eight. Is there anyone who does not understand the numbering?" There was a dreadful silence. "Excellent!" Ivan shouted. "We have unanimous understanding. I am truly fortunate." Draco returned to the other side of the lectern. He extended his arms out on either side of the lectern and surveyed his class. One by one he gazed at each student. When his eyes fell upon Michael, his lip curled in a cruel grin. Then, he continued until he had locked his glare on each student. When he had finished his observations, Ivan Draco plunged into his lecture.

Michael concentrated on listening to the lecture, until he heard the wind rush past the window beside him. Instinctively he turned and glanced out the window. Instead of the campus below him, he saw Barbara kneeling on the rocky beach at the base of the limestone cliff. He snapped his head away from the window and stared at the professor. The wind hummed as it washed over the window. "Michael," a voice called to him, but he was determined not to listen to it. "Michael," the voice called again, "you must listen to the voices of the past." The wind rattled the window, but Michael refused to look at it. "Michael, Michael, the mist will come to the highlands."

When he returned to his room, Michael collapsed in a heap on his bed. He lay there for several minutes trying to regain his composure. He didn't understand what was happening. Why was he hearing voices? Was he going mad? Why was he seeing visions? Was the supernatural toying with him? Barbara was real. He spoke to her; touched her. Was she as bewildered as he was? Or, did she understand what was happening to him? Michael sat up and drew in a deep breath, then, exhaled slowly. He got up and left his room. He was uncertain where he was going. He just needed to be up on his feet, moving. He paced frantically across the campus with no destination in mind, when he found himself standing near the entrance to the library. He stopped and stared at the building as if he had never seen it before. Then, not really knowing why, he went inside. He approached the title card files and opened a drawer labeled "H". His finger came to rest on one card. "Highlands, Myths and Legends", was neatly typed on the top of the card. Michael pulled the card from the file and started searching for the book.

It only took a minute for Michael to locate the old; leather bound text with gold leaf lettering. He grasped the book gently, almost reverently, and took it from the shelf. He touched the leather cover with the tips of his fingers, then, carefully carried it to an empty table. Michael sat down, opened the book, and didn't look up until a young woman touched him on the shoulder.

"I'm getting ready to close the library," the young woman said timidly.

Michael looked up at the plain, be-spectacled girl. "What time is it?" Michael asked hoarsely.

"It's almost nine o'clock," the girl replied.

"The time slipped past me," Michael acknowledged. "May I check this out?" He held the book up with his right hand.

"Sure," the girl smiled. "Come with me."

Michael followed the girl to a counter. She stepped behind it and he went on the other side. Michael pulled his identification card from his wallet and handed it to the girl. "I'm…"

"John Michael Sylvan," the girl said without looking at the ID card.

"You know me?" Michael asked.

The girl shot a quick glance at Michael as if he were trying to be glib, then, her gaze softened when she realized the sincerity of his question. "Everyone knows you," the woman answered.

Michael didn't understand why everyone would know him, but he decided not to argue the point. "What's your name?"

The young woman seemed surprised by the question and she hesitated with her reply. "I… I'm Jane Linden," she said.

"I'm very pleased to meet you, Miss Linden," Michael smiled.

"Jane," the girl said with emphasis.

"I'm keeping you here too late, Jane," Michael said. "Check out this book for me, please." Michael pulled the sign-out card from the pocket in the back of the book. He glanced at the card at first, then, he stared at it. Nearly every signature on the card belonged to one person. "Ivan Draco," Michael said aloud.

"He's our best customer," Jane said.

Michael signed the card and handed it to Jane. "Thanks," he said.

Michael left the library and returned to his room. He found a note on his desk from Dudley. "We're at the 'Waterhole'. Join us if you can." Michael pushed the note aside and re-opened the book that had captured him at the library. Several tales about the Mist were included in the book. It seemed that people from each era of history were affected by the mystical fog. There was one tale that he read over and over. It was nearly identical to the one that Dudley had told him at his grandparent's cabin. Now, he had to figure out what the legend meant to him personally. He forgot about Dudley and the Bartlett girls at the bar.

The next day, Michael was up very early. He quietly dressed and left the room before Dudley woke up. After a brief breakfast, Michael sat in the cafeteria and read his book. At one point, he looked up and saw Professor Draco enter the cafeteria. He expected him to join with the other members of the faculty, but was somewhat surprised to see Draco turn toward an empty table and eat alone.

Once again, at precisely 10:50 a.m., Ivan Draco approached his lectern. He wasted no time. "Yesterday, I presented you with an overview of this course. Are there any questions?" Ivan surveyed the room with a cold stare, which was met only with silence. Then, unexpectedly a hand shot into the air. "Yes, number eighteen," Draco acknowledged.

A young man stood up beside his desk. "Sir," the student began, "I resent being referred to as a number. I have a name, a very proud name, and I demand that you address me accordingly."

Draco stared at the student for a very long time. Unexpectedly, he started to laugh. His laughter became louder and louder, but finally ebbed as the professor engaged his self-control. "You are truly amusing, number eighteen," Draco said softly. The professor shook his head, but his smile faded. Now, his voice thundered. "Do you truly believe that a random sexual event qualifies you for social standing?"

The young man was uncertain how to answer the question, but Draco was on the attack, and he would show no mercy. "Answer me, number eighteen," he hammered at the student.

"No sir," the young man hissed angrily.

"You're right," Ivan shouted triumphantly. "My god, I am proud of you," Draco added with a high degree of mockery. "It is true brilliance for a man to recognize his shortcomings, and true humility for him to acknowledge them openly. When you accomplish something on your own, you will earn the respect you think you are entitled to have. Until then, however, you will remain a number. Do you understand number eighteen?"

"Yes sir," the student answered with anger in his voice.

"You may sit down number eighteen."

Draco returned to his lectern. "Is there anyone else who wishes to advance an argument in number eighteen's defense?" Draco taunted the class. "Surely, there are others of you privileged personages who share number eighteen's feelings in this matter. Have you nothing to say?" Draco glanced at each face. Then, he walked toward Michael and stood beside him. "How about you number fourteen? The others are probably looking toward you for leadership. Would you defend number eighteen? I am certain that he is accustomed to having others do his bidding for him. Are you accustomed to having others follow your commands, number fourteen?"

Michael stood beside his desk and looked directly into Professor Draco's eyes. "Sir, I believe number eighteen, as well as I, is quite capable of earning our place in society with our own skills. I am quite confident, that we will succeed in earning our own names."

"Indeed," Ivan Draco smiled. "We shall see number fourteen. We shall see."

The professor turned away from Michael and resumed his stance at the lectern and continued his lecture on the importance of studying history. Michael listened carefully as he expected Draco to call upon him, but Draco seemed to ignore him.

Chapter 5

Barbara knelt on the rocks and stared at the image in the cleft in the cliff. Behind her, a throng of believers and the curious watched her in silence. Between the crowd and Barbara was the policeman. On the top of the cliff were more onlookers and reporters.

"My Lady, I have spoken to the bishop. He is kind, but the priests around him think I am insane," Barbara said.

"Remind the bishop of the wisdom of the heart," the Lady said. "He is an educated man and he seeks answers to questions which are logical to his mind. Tell him that his mind can be misled but his heart will be true to him."

"His aides and consultants have told him that I am a drunk and a woman with no morals. I can't deny my drinking or my many relationships with men."

"The bishop understands sin and the forgiveness of sin. Remind him that the power of forgiveness is a product of the heart."

"There is one other thing, my Lady. The young man, Michael, has much to endure. Must he suffer all that you have shown to me? Can he not be spared some of his fate?"

The Lady smiled and opened her arms. "Come into my arms."

Barbara got up and walked toward the cliff as the image of the Lady glided toward her. "I am not worthy of your embrace," Barbara said.

The bright light swirled about her as the Lady held her in her arms. To the onlookers, Barbara seemed to vanish for a moment, then re-appear.

"You have great compassion, and love in your heart," the Lady said. "Few men would be able to endure what is in store for Michael. His success is dependent on his determination. Tell him nothing of what you have been shown, for he will learn of it soon enough."

Barbara felt great calm come over here as she left the Lady's embrace. "I will speak to the bishop again," she said.

"I will come to you again," the Lady said. "Go and speak to the bishop."

Barbara knelt and prayed again, until the image faded from her view. Then, she sprang to her feet, and walked back to the small houseboat she called her home. The policeman went with her to keep the crowd from her.

"I must see the bishop in Portston again," she said to the officer.

"I'll take you," the policeman said softly.

Michael sat in the library alone. He seemed to be staring out the window, but it was dark and there was nothing to see. Jane Linden noticed the statue-like posture and approached Michael to make sure he was all right. She called to Michael but he didn't hear her. He just sat there, staring at something she could not see. Jane called to him again and again. Still, he didn't hear her. She held one hand in front of his face, but he didn't seem to see it. He remained wide-eyed and motionless. Jane was about to call for help, when Michael suddenly began to speak.

"They sit around her and scoff," Michael said. "They are wise and she is simple. Yet, for all their wisdom, they cannot understand her simplicity."

Jane tried to understand what Michael was talking about, but before she could establish another question, Michael returned to reality. "Oh! Hello Jane. Is it time to close the library?"

"No," she said. "I just wanted to see if you found everything you were looking for."

"I haven't found everything," Michael smiled, "but I'm certain I'm on the right track. The only other person to have consistently checked out these books is Ivan Draco."

"I told you he was our best customer," Jane smiled, "and you are rapidly becoming number two. I would have expected you to be more socially involved with Deanna Bartlett rather than spend your time in the library."

"Deanna is very angry with me right now," Michael admitted. "I haven't been paying much attention to her."

"Because of Professor Draco?" Jane asked pointedly.

"No, not because of Draco," Michael paused and Jane waited patiently. "It's because of me," Michael sighed.

For hours, the bishop had listened to scholars, psychiatrists, sociologists, canon lawyers and consultants. He was old and he was tired of listening to long-winded explanations. "I want to speak to the woman alone," the bishop announced.

There was an instant chorus of protests, but the bishop held up his hand to silence the voices. "Please bring her to me," he said.

A few moments later, Barbara was escorted to the bishop. She fell onto her knees and kissed his ring. The bishop quickly asked her to rise and sit beside him. "Perhaps, it is I who should fall on my knees and kiss your hand," the bishop smiled.

"Oh, no your eminence, I would never be worthy of such a thing as that," Barbara said.

"If Our Lady has chosen you to see her, you are the most worthy person of all," the bishop grinned. "Tell me more about your visits with Our Lady."

Barbara easily repeated her encounters with the Holy Mother. The bishop stopped her only to ask her to provide more explanation or description of what she saw and what she heard. Barbara complied with his every request until she had related all she could remember of her experiences.

The bishop was silent for several moments, then, he asked her a few more questions. Again, Barbara answered completely and directly and waited for the next set of questions. Once again the bishop grew silent as he considered her words. The long silence eroded Barbara's confidence and she felt compelled to add more explanation. Finally, she couldn't hold back her feelings.

"I know what the other priests think of me," Barbara said. "They think I'm a drunk and a trollop."

The old bishop took Barbara by the hand and smiled. "Perhaps they don't understand loneliness," he said softly.

The simple truth of the bishop's statement brought tears to Barbara's eyes. "Thank you," she said.

The bishop nodded, then, returned to Barbara's encounters with the Holy Mother. "Our Lady has brought us ill tidings with only a slight glimmer of hope," he said.

Barbara nodded her agreement. "She spoke of the ancient mist."

"Yes," the bishop smiled, "that's the glimmer of hope."

"I spoke to a young man who also seemed to be familiar with the old legends about the mist," Barbara disclosed. "I pray for him."

"When you go home tonight, will you pray again?" The bishop asked.

"Oh, yes," Barbara replied.

"Will you pray for me?" The bishop asked softly.

"Yes, yes I will," Barbara smiled.

Dudley cupped one hand over the mouthpiece of the telephone and glared at Michael. "She knows you're here, Michael. You must speak to her."

Reluctantly, Michael nodded his agreement and took the phone from Dudley. "Hello mother," he said. "No, I haven't been avoiding you. I have been very busy. My classes are more difficult than I thought they would be." Michael listened to Margaret for a moment. "No mother, I won't be home this weekend." Again, Michael listened. "All right, mother, I'll call you Sunday. Good-bye." Michael passed the phone back to Dudley, who placed the device in its nook.

"Deanna is going to be disappointed if you don't go home this week-end," Dudley said.

"Next week Draco is going to start talking about the Great War, and the War of Liberation," Michael said with more than a hint of despair in his voice. "I've got to be prepared for him."

Dudley nodded his head. "The War of Liberation is an obsession with Draco. I don't think anyone can prepare for him on this topic, but I understand why you need to try. I'll explain it to Deanna. She's been through his class. She'll understand too."

"Dudley, when you took this course, did you find anything in the library dealing with events leading up to the War of Liberation?" Michael asked the question with a look of desperation on his face.

Dudley wished he could give a better answer, but he couldn't. "No," he said.

"I don't understand why there are no books about this event. It's the single most important happening in modern time," Michael lamented.

"You have just discovered Draco's obsession," Dudley said. "You could easily spend the rest of the term on this one area of history."

Michael considered Dudley's statement, but couldn't accept it. "There has got to be something written by someone, somewhere," Michael concluded. "I'm going to find it," he announced as he grabbed his coat and left the room. He rushed down the stairs and bolted out into a winter storm. A frigid wind swirled around him as he crossed the campus, but he ignored it.

When he entered the library he went directly to Jane Linden. "Jane, I need to ask you a question," Michael said. "I'm looking for books concerning the events just prior to the War of Liberation. Can you direct me to any books like that? I've scoured the subject cards and can't find anything. I thought, perhaps, there was something by author you might know of."

"Michael, do you think you are the first student of Professor Draco's to come here looking for those books?" Jane's question plunged Michael into a state of confusion.

"I can't believe that," Michael said. "There are tons of books on conditions before the Great War. There are numerous books on the surrender and occupation. Once the War of Liberation ends, there are dozens of books again."

Jane shrugged. "I know," she said coldly.

Michael turned from the librarian and left the building. He stood in the cold for a time trying to gather his thoughts. He heard his name called out which caused him to turn left and right but he saw no one. Then, he heard a voice call to him again. "Listen to the voices of the past. Listen to the voices of the past." The words echoed again and again in his head as he walked back to his and Dudley's room.

It was 10:49 a.m. and Michael's eyes were glued on the minute hand of the clock on the wall above the lectern. He heard the clock click and saw the minute hand twitch as it prepared to be moved forward. Then, silently, the minute hand moved to point at the large dot near the number ten. Draco's footstep could be heard as he approached the lectern. Michael felt like a doomed man and he waited for the verbal onslaught to begin. But again, Michael had failed to anticipate the teacher. Draco delivered his lecture as if he had no interest in badgering his class.

"So, the Great War ended," Draco concluded. "We were defeated. Our, country was occupied by our enemies. We were enslaved. Our governments had been dismantled. Our soldiers had been killed or captured. We had no means of production. We had no way to feed ourselves. We had to beg our captors for food. We stood by helplessly as the occupation troops had their way with our women. We toiled silently under their cruelty. We bowed under the humiliation of defeat." Draco paused as he stepped in front of the lectern. "For four years and ten months, our nation languished under occupation. Then came the mist; the mist that had protected our ancestors in times past blanketed the Midland-Highlands. For more than two millennia the mist has appeared to fill our people with hope when threatened by invasion and occupation. This occasion was no different." Draco paused.

"Then, on April 6th, the Occupation Force Commander in a small village on the southern fringes of the Midlands sends a communiqué to his commanding officer." Draco reached back and removed a piece of paper from the lectern. "This is addressed to the Commanding Officer, Occupation Forces Central Region. It was sent by the Commanding Officer Riverview Garrison." Draco paused again, then, began reading the paper. "'Zero-Six-Forty-Three hours: Riverview Garrison under attack by a large force...'", Draco stopped and glanced up at the class. "That's all the commanding officer had time to transmit before his communications were disabled. The professor walked toward Michael's side of the classroom.

"This was the start of the War of Liberation. The small town of Riverview was wiped off the face of the earth. More than five thousand occupation troops died in less than an hour. Two hours later, the Occupation Army in and around Riverton comes under an intense artillery attack followed by a ground assault. The occupiers fought a retreating battle for two hours before being routed. Shortly after noon, the Occupation Army – Western Region marches into a devastating ambush on the way to the besieged Central Region and is forced to retreat southward onto the open plains. At the same time, Occupation troops in Capitol City are attacked from the north and west by what they called a 'well planned, orchestrated' infantry assault." Draco looked at Michael. "Why were these attacks successful, number...?" Draco hesitated and Michael rose from his desk in anticipation..." four." Draco smiled as Michael sat down again.

Number four rose from her desk and offered a possible reason. When she started to add another possibility, Draco stopped her. "Number four says the Liberation forces were successful because of the element of surprise. Do you agree with that assessment number seventeen?"

The young man with the number seventeen sprang from his desk. "Yes sir," he answered.

"Why?" Draco challenged.

Student seventeen offered his reasoning, and then Draco jumped to another student, then another. So the class went on. Draco orchestrated a rapid-fire questioning of the entire class. When the class was finally over, everyone was exhausted. Most of the students sat in their desks for a moment to rest from the onslaught they had endured. A few minutes later, however, Michael sat alone in the room. He wasn't sure why he sat there. Perhaps it was because he needed the solitude. Then, to his surprise, Ivan Draco re-entered the lecture room.

"You're still here, number fourteen," Draco observed the obvious as he drew nearer to Michael. "What is it fourteen? Is there something that overwhelmed you in today's lecture?"

"I've been going to the library," Michael began, "in hopes of finding information on the events leading up to the War of Liberation."

"That's very commendable," Draco sneered. "And what did you find?"

"Nothing," Michael replied.

"What did you expect to find?" Draco asked curtly as he sat down in the desk beside Michael.

"I didn't have a specific expectation, but I thought there would be something."

Ivan Draco shook his head in obvious disgust. "That's the problem with you children of privilege," he said. "You always expect 'something' and when what you expect isn't there, you want to give up. Go find your friends and have a party or 'something'," Draco said with disappointment as he gave a wave of his hand.

"Professor Draco," Michael was angry but he was able to check his emotions, "why are there no books about the build-up of the Liberation Army?"

Draco considered the question for several seconds. "I don't know," the teacher said softly. "We'll begin exploring that question in the next class. Good day number fourteen."

Michael rose from his desk. "Good day, sir," he said as he walked toward the door. He was unaware of Draco watching him as he left the room.

Late that afternoon Michael stood at the window of his room looking toward the southern horizon. Dudley kept glancing at his friend, who had been standing at the window, motionless, for nearly an hour. Growing more concerned with each passing moment, Dudley finally went to his friend. "Michael?" Dudley asked with a gentle nudge on his friend's shoulder. Michael stood silent as if he was unaware of Dudley's presence. Dudley was becoming alarmed. "Michael," he said a little louder, "are you all right?"

Michael didn't move, or blink an eye. "There is a mist on the Highlands," he said in a soft monotone.

Dudley felt helpless and a little frustrated. He made up his mind that he would ask for help. Finally, Michael stepped away from the window.

"I'm going to the Library," Michael said.

"All right, Michael. Will you be back in time to have dinner with Dianna and Deanna?"

"No, I'm going to cancel. Tell Deanna for me."

"I'll tell her," Dudley said as he watched Michael walk lethargically toward the door.

Next, Dudley waited until he was certain Michael would not see him leave the building, then, he headed directly to Doctor Henley's apartment. Dudley was certain the head of the psychology department would be able to help him.

Michael wandered aimlessly across the campus as he wondered what was happening to him. Was he experiencing some psychic event? What did all this mean? Why was it happening to him? He walked and wondered for a long time. Finally, he realized that he had wandered into the city that curled around National University. In spite of the cold he sat down on a bench in a small park. He had never been to this part of town before, and wasn't really certain where he was. All he knew for certain was that he was tired. These things he was seeing and hearing were wearing on him, and all he wanted to do was rest and to be free from it all.

Doctor Henley had listened patiently to Dudley Carpenter's description of the sudden changes in Michael Sylvan's behavior. Now, he tried to formulate a reply. He made several attempts to begin, but each time he started to say something, he stopped himself. Dudley was beginning to get frustrated with the psychologist.

"Well, what do you think is causing this change in Michael?" Dudley prompted strongly.

"I'm not sure," Henley answered. "We must move very carefully here. With Michael Sylvan's social position, we cannot afford to act imprudently."

Dudley bit at his lip to constrain his frustration. "Doctor Henley, I'm trying to find out if my friend is ill. I see nothing imprudent in that."

"No, you're right to come to me for help," Henley stumbled, "but these sudden changes in your friend might be the result of some other, physical, malady."

"He's hallucinating," Dudley said. "Isn't that what hearing things and seeing things that aren't there are called?"

"Let's not jump to conclusions," Henley said. "It takes a very skillful clinician to be able to make such judgments."

"I'll bring Michael here to see you," Dudley said.

"No, no." Henley gasped. "Think of the potential scandal. Michael Sylvan seeing a psychologist is politically volatile. No, we'll have to find some other way for someone to interview him. This calls for a great deal of discretion. Let me think about this. I'll contact you when I have figured out a way to have Michael talk to someone about his problems. He must be willing to go along with it though."

Dudley reluctantly accepted Doctor Henley's cautious reasoning, and went back to his room. On the way, he wondered if his own education, indeed, if truth itself would be as sterile for him as it was for Doctor Henley. He ended up deciding that he would have to wait and see.

Later that evening, Dudley tried his best to entertain both the Bartlett twins. He was doomed to failure from the start, and finally gave up and shortened his visit with the two women. When Dianna dropped him off at this apartment, Dudley entered his room and found Michael fast asleep.

It was a night of torment for Michael. He tossed and turned as he struggled for sleep. And, when he finally did doze off he dreamed about strange things. Finally, even his dreams seemed to ebb. He dreamt that he was atop the granite stone at the end of Long Ridge waiting for the sun to rise. In his dream he saw his grandfather emerge from his cabin and ascend the wide trail a short distance to a narrow footpath down the steep southern slope of the ridge. Next, he saw his grandfather sit on the hulk of a great, fallen oak, as if he were waiting for someone. As the sun edged over the horizon, Michael's dream focused on the celestial marvel. When Michael saw his grandfather again, the old man was lying, face down, in the thick carpet of leaves. Michael knew he was dead, but shouted "NO! NO!" over and over again. Finally, he opened his eyes and looked into the face of his friend Dudley.

"Michael, I think you need to see a doctor," Dudley suggested softly.

"It was just a nightmare," Michael offered lamely.

"I'm not talking about what just happened," Dudley said sternly. "I'm talking about all the things you have been experiencing the past several months."

Michael looked his friend directly in the eye. "I need to work through this myself," he said. "I don't know all I need to know yet, but I'm sure I'll be able to manage it all in the end."

Dudley shook his head as he acquiesced to his closest friend. "Damn it Michael, I should take you to the emergency room right now, but I always give in to your wishes."

"Stick with me Dudley," Michael implored. "I need your friendship now more than ever."

"Michael, it's not just me that's noticed a drastic change in your behavior. Other people have asked me what is going on with you. I don't know what to tell them."

"I need time Dudley."

"How much time? Do you want me to just wait until you go completely insane?" Dudley waited for a reply.

"I don't know how much time I'll need," Michael admitted. "I just know that I'm certain I'll unravel it all."

Dudley sighed. "Will you let me know when you figure it all out?"

"You're my closest friend, Dudley. I won't keep anything from you."

Reluctantly, Dudley gave up trying to persuade Michael to see a doctor. "Go back to sleep, Michael," was all he could say.

Michael stood at the window of his room the next morning. He stared out the window, but all he could see was the image of his grandfather lying on the floor of the forest. In spite of his mental aberration, he was aware of Dudley's presence. "I don't know what the hell is happening to me," he said.

Dudley stumbled for something appropriate to say, but in the end, he remained silent and clasped his friend by the shoulder.

"I'd better get to class," Michael smiled as Dudley let go of his grip.

Michael stared at the clock. He wanted desperately to have the mental power to prevent the minute hand from advancing, thereby, incarcerating Professor Ivan Draco forever in his office. The fantasy was short lived, as the old clock clicked loudly in anticipation of its next move. Michael sighed, then, he heard Draco's footsteps approach the lectern. Michael looked up, just as the young professor began to speak.

"Seventy years ago, the greatest Army this nation has ever had, sprung out from the Midland-Highlands wilderness to lay carnage to a victorious invasion force which had overwhelmed the nation just a few years earlier. The War of Liberation lasted nearly five years and in the sixty-five years since, there is not a single shred of information about the formation of the Army. Indeed, even the men who served in it only wrote of battles after the destruction of Riverview. We know nothing from the original surrender until the assault on Riverton."

Draco paused to look around the classroom. "Today, we will explore hypotheses on the simple question which has tormented historians for more than sixty-five years. The question is "Why?" Ivan closed the lecture text and stepped in front of the lectern.

"Why is history silent on this great moment?" Draco continued. "How can we learn what happened? Who was involved?" Draco grinned. "I anxiously await your brilliant theories."

Michael listened with all the concentration he could muster. Then, something drew his attention toward the window. Slowly, reluctantly, he turned to look out the pane. In the distance on the horizon, he saw what appeared to be a billowing cloud.

"Michael," a voice called to him. "Michael, the mist has come to the Highlands. Come here Michael. Come to the Highlands."

"Do you agree number fourteen?" Draco asked.

Michael struggled to regain his composure. "I'm sorry sir, could you repeat the question?"

"Do you agree? That's the question," Draco responded with his usual annoyance. "Perhaps, if we begin again you will be able to participate." Draco paused, then, he redirected his question. "How about you, number two? Are you paying attention?"

Michael was embarrassed and he felt his neck fill with blood. He had never been caught unaware in class. This was the first time, and he didn't like it. He spent the remainder of the class boiling in his embarrassment.

Chapter 6

Professor Draco carried his tray toward the faculty lunchroom. He cursed at himself for not waiting until later in the day to take lunch when Doctor Henley approached him. He was uncertain why he disliked Henley, but it didn't matter that he was unable to come up with a reason. He turned to avoid the oncoming Henley, but it was too late.

"Ivan?" Henley smiled his well-practiced smile. "Could I have a word with you?"

"Why certainly, Doctor Henley," Draco demonstrated his political prowess, "it's been quite a while since we've had a chat."

Henley motioned Draco to a nearby table and both men took seats on either side. "This is a very delicate matter," Henley said softly. "It has to do with John Michael Sylvan. Have you noticed anything peculiar about him lately?"

"He's just another wealthy, influential lap dog like most of the other students here at National," Draco said. "The fact society tolerates him is the only peculiar thing I've noticed about him." To Draco's surprise, Henley was not bothered by the social commentary as he usually was.

Henley propped both elbows on the table and looked directly into Draco's eyes. "Dudley Carpenter came to me the other night and made some rather startling statements about his friend Michael."

"Hmm," Ivan mumbled softly. "Carpenter is very intelligent. I would put a lot of credence in what he says."

"Really?" Henley seemed taken aback by Draco's complimentary manner about Dudley Carpenter. "I'm surprised to hear you say that."

"Why?" Draco grinned. "Carpenter has my vote for number one in his class."

"You're overwhelming me," Henley confessed. "When Carpenter was in your class, the entire campus was bristling with rumors of your verbal exchanges with him."

Ivan smiled proudly. "Yes, we had some great dialogues, he and I. He earned his name quicker than anyone ever has in my class."

"Good lord," Henley gasped. "You're not doing that number thing in your classes again."

"Oh yeah," Draco said without a hint of apology.

Henley sighed and shook his head. "Carpenter seems to think Sylvan is hearing things. Now, after talking to you, I can understand why. The pressure you're putting him under may be responsible."

Draco chuckled. "You don't believe that anymore than I do. Have you talked to Sylvan?"

"Of course not," Henley hissed. "Think of the potential scandal that could result if I spoke to him. You know how people exaggerate these things."

"So you want me to do it for you," Ivan guessed correctly.

"You have a good background in psychology," Henley said, "and Sylvan is one of your students. No one would suspect anything unusual if you had a private discussion with him."

Draco smiled. "I'll see what I can do."

"Please, Ivan, don't bully him," Henley asked softly. "He may be going through a difficult time."

With that final comment, Henley got up from the table and took his still full tray toward the kitchen. Draco watched Henley toss his food into a garbage container and leave the cafeteria. Then Ivan enjoyed his own lunch in solitude.

Michael felt good the next day as he entered Draco's class. He felt he had gained new insight into the War of Liberation, and had even formulated a thesis, of which, he was quite proud. He smiled at the long faces of his classmates as he took his own place next to the window. He glanced up at the clock, and the minute hand moved forward to launch Professor Draco toward his lectern. The professor plunged immediately into the task at hand.

"You were asked to formulate a thesis about the origins of the Liberation Army and present it at this class. I can hardly wait to hear your learned presentations. Number fourteen, please begin."

"Yes sir," Michael smiled as he rose to stand beside his desk. "I propose that the government anticipated a defeat and concealed enough men and equipment in the nation's wilderness areas for the Liberation Army to be formed."

"Really?" Draco beamed pleasantly. "You suggest that the government deliberately planned to surrender so this clandestine army could rise from the ashes and overwhelm the occupation troops? Please, tell us all what led you to this scheme."

"The nation was convinced that a settlement could be negotiated with the enemy. Subsequently, wartime preparations were slowed. When war finally did come, the country was simply not ready. Defeat was only a matter of time. I propose that high-ranking government and, or, military persons, began hiding caches of material to keep them out of enemy hands. When defeat could no longer be denied as a predictable outcome, someone, or some group, implemented a plan whereby partisans could locate and use these supplies."

Without taking his eyes off Michael, Draco called for student twelve to respond to Michael's premise. "Don't hesitate number twelve," Ivan scolded, "do you accept number fourteen's premise or not?"

"No sir," the young man replied. "I believe the invasion and subsequent victory by the enemy so enraged the people that they began fighting against the enemy from the very beginning."

"How do you respond to that, number fourteen?" Ivan prodded with a smile.

Michael didn't hesitate to reply. "Sir, it's true that there was resistance to the enemy in nearly all the occupied areas, but the passion of the partisans was not enough. There had to be weapons and munitions available for them. Also, they needed tactical planning and coordination. The will to fight sustained the Liberation Army during the war, but I believe it was a pre-planned strategy that led to their success."

Draco approached Michael until he was standing within an arm's reach of him. "Tell me number fourteen, how did you arrive at this hypothesis? Did you formulate this idea on your own?"

"I came across this thesis in some papers in the library," Michael admitted freely. "After reading them, I realized that this was a strong theory and supportable from a logical point of view."

Draco turned to the rest of the class. "Has anyone else found these enlightening documents in the library?" Ivan Draco waited for a reply, but there was only silence. He returned his gaze toward Michael. "Please tell us about these 'papers' you found, number fourteen."

"Like everyone else, I could find nothing in the history section of the library about the War of Liberation," Michael began. "I was becoming very frustrated at the lack of material, so, I started looking through the faculty publications. It was then that I noticed on one of the faculty member's author card that there was a collection of unpublished essays. I found the "author" card for you sir, and it too indicated a collection of unpublished treatises. In this collection, I found your doctoral thesis, and several essays and expositions you had written while a graduate and undergraduate student."

Ivan Draco grinned happily as he turned and strode slowly back to his lectern. When he arrived at his perch, he pulled a small book from his left vest pocket and opened it. He looked back at Michael who had sat down again at his desk. "Number fourteen, what is your name?"

Michael allowed a thin smile to crease his face as he returned to his feet. "Sir, my name is John Michael Sylvan."

Ivan looked at the tall, handsome young man for an instant; then, he marked something in the small book before replacing it in his vest pocket. "Mr. Sylvan, I would like very much to chat with you after classes. Would you be free at 4:00 p.m. this afternoon to see me in my office?"

"Yes sir," Michael answered.

"Good, I'll see you at four o'clock," Draco restated. He smiled, and then he walked away from the lectern and disappeared behind his office door. As the door closed, a loud cheer went up from the class. Michael was stunned by the sudden display of admiration from his classmates and simply smiled. Then, the applause ebbed, and the other students rushed out of the room to go to the library.

Michael walked back to his room with a feeling of pride. He felt as if everyone had heard of his triumph over Ivan Draco and was eager to congratulate him. Indeed, several students did just that. The feeling of euphoria soon faded when a cold wind swept over him. "Michael. Michael," the wind whispered "Michael, the mist will come to the highlands. They await you there."

Michael wanted to scream out at the voices on the wind, but he knew they would not heed him. He trudged steadily toward his room in the hope they would not follow him inside. He slammed the door shut and fell onto his bed as soon as he entered his room. He stared at the ceiling. It was silent. He heard nothing, until Dudley came in a short time later.

"Good work," Dudley offered cheerfully. "It's all over the campus that you earned your name in Draco's class."

"I don't know if it's a victory for sure," Michael cautioned. "Draco asked me to come to his office this afternoon."

Dudley frowned for a moment, then, he shrugged. "I wouldn't worry. You did what he wanted someone to do. The only thing I can see different about you is that you figured it out quicker than anyone else did. What do you say? Let's celebrate with a couple of cold beers!"

"No, I don't think so," Michael smiled. "I want to be cold sober when I talk to Ivan Draco."

The appointed time arrived quicker than Michael thought it would. A thousand questions danced through his mind that he wanted to pose to the professor, but they seemed scrambled and disorganized. Finally, he brought his fist gently down on Draco's office door. The young mentor opened the door with a warm smile.

"Come in Mr. Sylvan, I'm anxious to visit with you."

Michael was taken aback by Draco's warmth and charm, so he warily entered and stood near a chair which faced the professor's desk.

"Sit down," Draco urged happily, as he plopped casually into his own chair. "I want to congratulate you on your research at the library, Michael. Do you mind if I call you Michael?"

"No, everyone does…"

"Good," Draco continued. "As I said, that was good work. You found the right stuff faster than anyone has in my class. What led you to my papers?"

"Actually, I read your papers to see if I could understand you better. I wasn't really looking for the historical rationale that I ended up getting."

"That's the way it is with historical research," Draco sighed. "You plow through a ton of stuff hoping to find the evidence you need to prove a point and you find something you weren't looking for. That has happened to me many times." Draco smiled. "Why were you trying to understand me? I'm not that deep."

The Last Day of the Last Spring

Michael hesitated as he weighed his thoughts then he decided to plow straight ahead. "I was hoping I could find something in your papers that would tell me why you are such a bastard," Michael confessed openly.

Draco laughed heartily for a moment, and then, he quieted himself. "From here on, this conversation must remain confidential," Draco grinned. "Agreed?"

"Yes," Michael said.

"It's simply true," Draco grinned. "My parents had unconventional views about marriage. In short, they didn't believe in it. Subsequently, I am legally a bastard."

Michael flushed with embarrassment. "I didn't mean it that way."

Draco laughed. "No, I know you didn't. I just thought you should know that since I have the title it gives me the license to act like one."

"Are you saying that you like being a bastard toward everyone?" Michael was astounded by Draco's casualness.

"No, I don't like being a bastard," Draco said softly, "I love it."

Michael was shocked by Draco's revelation. "I don't understand."

"Being a bastard has made me socially unacceptable. At the same time, that fact has made me free of social correctness. I can embrace the truth in all its naked unpleasantness, which makes me invulnerable to social snobbery. I can have truth unqualified. I am free from denial to accept life's unpleasant consequences for what they are. How many people do you know who are afraid to state a simple truth? How many people do you know who hide the truth for vanity's sake? Can't you see that our society has embraced delusions because what they want to believe is more pleasant than reality? Can't you see the sickness in that?"

Michael nodded, "but does that give you the right to badger your students?"

"Stop and think Michael. Think of who your classmates are. These are the future leaders of our nation. Do you want them, and yourself, to go through life thinking that everything will be the way mother and father prepared them?"

"What about Dudley Carpenter?"

Ivan smiled. "Dudley didn't have any trouble at all in my class. Do you know why?"

"No," Michael admitted.

"Dudley has been dealing with bastards like me all his life. I was just another bastard in a long list of bastards that kept telling him he wouldn't succeed. He knew the truth about himself though. He knew he had the intelligence and the persistence to reach his goals. Dudley also knew he would have to do it alone. His parents didn't have great wealth or political connections for him to take advantage of."

"Wealth and connections like I can take advantage of," Michael smiled sheepishly.

"Exactly!" Draco hissed.

"Is it still necessary to prove your point with such virulence?" Michael asked.

"Nothing else worked for me, when I was growing up," Ivan stated. "My father was the mining baron, Martin Shiller. I grew up with as large a silver spoon in my mouth as you had in yours."

Michael smiled at his newly acquired insight into the young professor. "It takes one to know one, doesn't it?"

"Exactly," Draco chuckled. "Does that solve the mystery of Professor Draco?"

Michael smiled, "somewhat," he replied.

"I must ask you to keep this information confidential," Draco asserted. "I'll lose credibility with future students if you tip my hand."

"I understand," Michael said.

"Now, I need to understand some things about Michael Sylvan," Draco said. "I know the obvious things about you and your family, but there are things about you which puzzle me. At times, I feel as if you are carrying a great burden."

"What makes you think that?"

"Perhaps, it's the way you stare out the window, as if you are looking for someone. Sometimes, you seem lost in your thoughts, as if you are pondering a puzzle. I must confess, at first, I thought you were simply daydreaming. But, the more I watched you, the less certain I was about you. I'm curious. What's going on with Michael Sylvan?"

Michael sighed, "at times I think I'm going crazy," he said.

"We all feel that way at times," Draco normalized.

"I'm having hallucinations," Michael said flatly. "I'm hearing and seeing things that aren't there."

"What things do you hear?"

"Voices."

"More than one voice?"

"Yes, a chorus of voices."

"What do they say?"

Michael sighed as tears filled up behind his eyelids. "They call my name, mostly. 'Come to the Midlands,' they say. 'Come, they need you to lead them.' Then, sometimes they say, 'Michael, there is a mist on the highlands.' None of it makes since to me."

Draco frowned for a second before he forced himself to smile. "It sounds pretty scary."

Michael paused for a moment. "I went to see the lady in Portston."

"The woman who is seeing the visions of Mary?"

"Yes. I had visions of her for weeks. Then, when I saw a photograph of her, exactly as I had seen her in my mind, I rushed to Portston to see her. She called me by my name before I could introduce myself. She began crying and she said she was sorry that I had to be the one to endure such hardships. Then," Michael paused to remember, "she said, 'the hand that would pull a rose from the garden of victory will prick itself on a gray thorn and the wound will bring death. You must listen to the voices of the past, and if you heed them, the spirits of the dead will rise to protect you. You will suffer great sorrow, as will many others. Do not languish in grief. You will encounter overwhelming odds, but do not despair. Have faith in your judgment and courage in your deeds'. I don't know what the message means."

Draco tugged nervously at his right ear. "Do you read much about Highland Legends?"

"My grandparents live there," Michael said. "I have always found the tales about the wilderness pretty far-fetched in comparison to what my grandfather has taught me about the Midlands."

"Your grandparents live in the Highlands?"

"Yes."

"Where?"

"On Long Ridge."

"Have they always lived there?"

"As far as I know."

"How old are they?"

"Gosh, they're both in the nineties."

"Did they live there during the War of Liberation?"

"No, they built their cabin there after the war."

Draco stared at Michael for a moment, and then he got up from his desk and fingered a collection of books, which stood, on a short shelf behind his desk. He pulled a small, thin edition from the shelf and paged through it. "Listen to this," he said to Michael. "There is a thick, gray mist covering the area they called the Midlands. It's an abnormal fog, unaffected by wind or sun or temperature. The gray is always there, clinging to every branch, hovering about every tree, rising from the very earth. I watch my comrades in arms march into the grayness. I see them breathe the gray air into their lungs and I know it will kill them."

Draco closed the book and placed it back on the shelf. He glanced up at Michael as he re-took his seat. "That was written by the Commanding Officer of the Occupation Forces stationed at Riverview. He wrote that just after he accepted the posting. A day later, he, his command, and Riverview disappeared from the face of the earth as the leading elements of the Liberation Army poured out of the Midlands wilderness." Ivan paused to reflect a moment. "Have your grandparents told you about the Highland Mist?"

"No," Michael smiled, "not the kind of mist you just described. It's always foggy in some areas of the wilderness, though." Michael grinned as his mind recalled a childhood experience.

"What's so funny?" Draco questioned.

"I remember waking up one morning as a child while we were visiting my grandparents. I looked out the window and the entire forest was hidden in fog. I rushed downstairs and announced to my grandfather that the forest was gone. He reassured me that the forest was still there. I insisted that if it were still there, I would be able to see it. He took me by the hand and led me out onto the porch. We went down the short stairway and he pointed toward the fog. He asked me if I remembered the giant oak that stood alone at the edge of the ridge. I said that I did remember it and I pointed in the direction where it used to be. Still holding my hand, grandfather led me further and further into the fog until only the fog was visible around us. Then, slowly, the image of the giant oak began to appear in the mist. It was ghost-like at first; then, as we grew closer it appeared just as I had remembered it. I'll never forget the warm smile on grandfather's face. 'We can't always trust what we see,' he told me. 'Sometimes what we see only covers up the truth'.'" Michael seemed to relax in his reminiscence. "That's strange," he said. "I haven't recalled that day in years."

"Your grandfather sounds like a fine man," Draco said.

"He's special to me," Michael said, "but, truthfully, I don't know why. Maybe it's because he lives in the wilderness."

There was pause in the dialogue for a moment. "There's more to the Midland Mist that just legend," Ivan said. "There are many times in the history of our predecessors when the mist came to the Highlands to save them from disaster. The most recent event was after the surrender seventy years ago."

Draco watched Michael for a moment. "You've been experiencing some pretty strange things recently; the woman in Portston and all the other stuff. If it happens again, I want you to come to me and tell me about it. Will you do that?"

Michael nodded. "Do you think I'm going crazy?"

"No," Draco replied. "You had better go now and prepare for my next class. If you aren't prepared I'll kick your ass," Draco grinned.

Michael smiled; then, his face took a more serious shape. "Thanks for taking the time to talk to me, Professor..."

"Call me Ivan while we're in my office," Draco ordered softly. "Out there, you'll have to call me Professor Draco."

Michael nodded. "Thanks, Ivan. I needed to talk about these things, and I couldn't have talked to my friends about it."

"I understand. Don't hesitate to come here if you need to talk. Maybe we can sort out this mystery. Meanwhile, I wasn't bullshitting you about my class. I expect great things from you, Michael."

"I'll give you my best."

"I'll accept nothing less," Draco beamed.

Michael had gone only a few steps from Draco's office, with his head lowered into a frigid wind, when Dudley, Dianna, and Deanna surrounded him.

"My god, you were in there a long time," Dudley said. "How did it go?"

Michael stammered with uncertainty, for a moment, then he blurted softly. "Draco is a real bastard."

"Yeah, you can say that again," Dudley agreed.

Michael smiled to himself that his ruse worked. "Let's go find a warm place," Michael said.

"I've got a warm spot for you," Deanna taunted provocatively.

"Then, let's run," Michael yelled as he took Deanna's hand and bolted away. Dudley reached for Dianna, and the four laughed loudly as they darted across the frozen campus.

For a long time, Ivan Draco played back the tape recording he had made of his meeting with Michael Sylvan. Finally, he switched off the recorder and sat alone in his office. When his telephone rang it startled him and he jerked the receiver to his ear. "This is Professor Draco's office."

"Ivan," the voice on the phone said, "it's Doctor Henley. How did your meeting go?"

"It went well," Draco said. "Of course it's difficult to reach any conclusions after just one meeting."

"Yes, of course," Henley quickly agreed.

"We are going to meet again," Draco said. "I'm hoping to get him to talk a little more the next time."

"Excellent," Henley congratulated. "Were you able to record any of your conversation?"

"No," Draco lied. "I decided it was too risky to have a tape like that, given the sensitive nature of his family status."

"Yes, I understand. Perhaps discretion is best," Henley agreed. "By the way, Ivan, the President of the University has asked me to thank you for helping with this delicate matter."

"I'm flattered," Draco lied again. "Please express my gratitude to the president."

"I shall," Henley said. "Goodnight Ivan."

"Goodnight Doctor Henley," Draco cooed as he hung up the phone, "you gutless worm."

Barbara awoke suddenly. She listened carefully as a heavy rain pattered on the roof of her houseboat. She got up from her bed and listened more. Finally, she heard something muffled by the sound of the rain. After a moment, Barbara realized that she heard the sobs of a woman.

Instinctively, she burst from her dwelling and rushed toward the sounds. Headlong, she sprinted into the wet darkness, clothed only in a modest, gown. The sounds of the weeping woman grew louder and a small, gray haze glowed at the base of the cliffs. Barbara rushed to the spot, but she was not prepared for what she saw. Her Lady sat upon a stone with her back toward Barbara. The Lady was attired in gray, with a slightly darker gray shawl over her head and shoulders. Stretched across the weeping Lady's lap was her dead son, the crucified Christ. The Lady wept in deep sorrow.

Barbara could not hold back her own tears, and she could not look at the corpse of her Savior. Gently, she placed her hand on the Lady's shoulders. "Oh my Lady," Barbara cried. "Must you endure this pain for all eternity?"

"I weep not only for the death of my Son," the Lady said, "but for the death of all the children whose mothers will weep for them. For seven days, the Highlands will be covered in a heavenly shroud. Tell the women not to despair at the loss of their sons. If they believe in my Son, and pray to Him through me, I will give them comfort."

"I will tell them," Barbara said.

"Do not weep for me, Barbara," the Lady sobbed. "Weep instead for the young man who will take the gray cloak of the Highlands and place it on his own shoulders, for his life will truly be worse than death. Pray for him and ask others to pray for him, for he will offer up himself for their salvation just as my own Son gave himself up for all mankind."

"Oh my Lady, can we not avoid such sorrow?" Barbara implored her Lady.

"We can only endure, what must be. Dedicate your suffering to my Son. I shall leave you now but you will see me again. Trust in my Son, Jesus."

The vision abruptly ended, leaving Barbara uncertain what to do next. She looked about the bluffs, but all was dark. Finally, she sprinted toward the stairway to the road above the bluffs. It was raining harder, but Barbara was determined to get to the bishop. She waved at an approaching car to stop, but it swerved past her. When the next vehicle appeared she stepped out onto the roadway and raised both her arms to signal the driver to stop. Brakes locked and tires squealed on the wet pavement as the car stopped just inches from her.

"You must take me to the cathedral in Portston," Barbara shouted at the frightened driver. Then, she opened the passenger's door and plopped down in the front seat.

Chapter 7

Michael rolled over slowly so as not to disturb Deanna. He carefully reached out with his right hand, then, with thumb and forefinger, he pinched her nose. She instantly slapped his hand away.

"Time to get up," Michael smiled.

"All right," Deanna hissed with disinterest.

Michael sat up and switched on the radio. Gentle music poured from the small box, as he reached for his clothes. Then, the music stopped. The announcer gave the time as 8:00 a.m. and introduced the newscaster.

"For those of you just getting out of bed, we are repeating our lead story about the incredible fog which has settled on the Midland-Highlands wilderness. The Old Road that runs through the Highlands has been closed. Visibility in the area has been described as 'only a few yards'. Things are just as bad above the ground. Aircraft have been diverted from normal landing patterns, as the fog rises several thousands of feet above the region…"

"My god," Michael said hoarsely, "my god."

"What is it, Michael?" Deanna asked with alarm.

Michael didn't answer. He hurriedly began to dress. "I've got to see this for myself," he said. "Get dressed we're going to the Midlands."

A short distance from Deanna's apartment, Professor Draco tried to jump into his trousers, while he spoke to his secretary on the phone. "Cancel my classes today," he said. "Why? Tell them I'm sick." He cursed at himself as he stumbled. "Tell them I have leprosy and I went to my dermatologist," he yelled and hung up the phone. He finished buttoning his trousers as he listened to a newscast about the unnatural fog over the Midlands.

In Portston, Barbara was being admitted to a psychiatric hospital. She couldn't stop crying. No one believed her, even though the mist had come to the Highlands just as she had said it would. They wouldn't let her see the bishop the night before. She begged them, but they wouldn't wake him.

Ann tried to busy herself in the kitchen, but the dim light entering through the window behind her sink was a constant reminder of the thick grayness that clung to the forest. She hurried back and forth from the skillet with the spitting slices of bacon, to the glass-topped coffee-pot. When she heard John close the front door and walk toward her, she couldn't look at him. Not now; with the mist projecting their memories into their minds.

"Coffee?" She asked with a soft voice.

"Yes", John replied.

Ann poured the liquid slowly as if she could prolong the silence between them, but she knew in her heart, she couldn't delay what would have to be said. When both cups were full, she brought them to the table and sat down across from her husband. She looked at him, and smiled. John's face remained grim.

"The mist has returned to the Highlands," John said.

"It's just fog," Ann denied.

"No, it's the mist." John said in a dejected tone of voice. "It's going to happen again. I thought we were the last, but it's here again." John paused to contemplate the grim implications; then, he looked into Ann's eyes. "You knew it was coming, didn't you Ann?"

Reluctantly, Ann nodded. "I didn't know exactly when," she explained.

John stared into his coffee for a moment. "You still have the power, don't you Ann."

The old woman reluctantly nodded. "It has never left me. It's always been there. It taunts me. It confuses me. I never know if the things I see are from the past or the future, so, I have kept it to myself."

"Do you know when it will start? Do you know who the enemy is?"

Ann shook her head. "I never get the whole picture until it's too late."

"What about the children?" John asked. "I don't think that JJ, Joan, or Henry will be able to deal with war. You're right. We should have told them how it was. Our silence could destroy them."

"They aren't the ones who will carry the burden," Ann said.

The Last Day of the Last Spring

John looked into his wife's eyes and in an instant he realized what she knew. "Michael," John said. He shook his head slowly from side to side. "Does it have to be Michael?"

Ann struggled to hold back her tears, but in spite of her calm expression, her eyes filled; then spilled over into the furrows of her face. "I hear his name being carried on the wind," she said.

"Then, this is why I have been able to live all these years," John concluded. "I am the one who must teach Michael. Unless..." John paused thoughtfully for a moment, "unless, this is my last spring."

"How many springs have you seen that you thought would be your last?" Ann asked with a nervous chuckle as she wiped her tears away with her apron. "How many springs blossomed into summers before we started our family?"

"I know," John admitted with a sigh of guilt. "I was certain I would be dead long before now, but here I am."

"You can't forget that day, can you John?"

"I did for a time," John answered. "But, now, I re-live it each spring." John sipped the hot liquid in his cup. "I'm not afraid to die, Ann."

"You never were," the old woman stated with pride.

The old couple sat in silence for several moments while they remembered their youth and the horror of it.

"Do I have enough time to teach Michael a few things?" John asked hopefully.

"I don't know," Ann sighed. "How would you teach him without telling him everything?"

John didn't reply, but the question echoed relentlessly in his mind.

Deanna was unnerved, by Michael's driving. Dudley and Dianna whooped and laughed as they were pressed from side to side in the back seat. Deanna protested at first, but it was apparent that Michael was obsessed with seeing this stupid fog bank on the Midlands. Michael was aware of Deanna's aggravation but he decided to ignore it.

"This road should be packed with curious people," Michael sighed in disappointment. "Don't they understand what this means?" Michael asked Deanna.

"Apparently, you are the only one who places any importance on this fog thing," Deanna said with a huff.

Michael sighed with disbelief, then, he stepped on the accelerator. The two couples fell into an awkward silence for a time then Dudley saw the phenomenon.

"Good lord," Dudley exclaimed. "It looks as if a huge cloud has settled to the earth." Dianna echoed Dudley's awe, and finally, Deanna too realized how strange this occurrence was. Michael kept driving, saying nothing.

The four watched as the earth-bound mass grew larger and larger as they approached closer and closer. It soon seemed as though the entire, southern horizon was shrouded by the dark, gray mist. Michael sped the automobile directly toward the mist. Then, just as they thought they would be able to drive into the cloud, flashing lights on the roadway brought them to a stop. One of the police officers approached the vehicle while Michael rolled down the window.

"Sorry, the road is closed," the officer explained. "You can barely see ten to fifteen feet when you enter that fog bank. You'll have to turn around and go back."

"We drove down here from National University to see this," Michael explained. "Is it all right if I pull off the road and walk the rest of the way?"

The officer shrugged. "As long as you get your vehicle a safe distance off the road," he suggested.

Michael pulled the car well off the road and stopped. "Let's go," he said cheerfully.

"I'm not walking across this muddy field just to stand in a fog," Deanna balked.

"All right, I'll go alone," Michael said.

"Wait, I want to see this," Dudley said.

"Me too," Dianna chimed in.

"Damn it," Deanna complained as she opened her door.

Michael took long steady strides across the field moving steadily southward toward the mist.

"Damn it, slow down, Michael," Deanna protested.

"Sorry," Michael said as he shortened his gait.

Suddenly, they were in the mist, and the forest. The land rose gently at first, then it lowered itself again. The trees appeared one by one as the foursome walked, slowly into the forest.

"We're going to get lost," Deanna pointed out, but no one seemed to hear her.

"Quiet," Michael said. "I hear something." The group froze at Michael's command and watched and waited for him to tell them what to do.

"Over here," he said as he strode into the mist. The others rushed so as not to lose sight of him. A moment later, they too heard something. They heard the sound of rushing water. Then, they saw Michael kneel down beside a small brook that swirled over smooth stones. Vapors seemed to rise from the water and blend in with the fog. Michael slowly slipped his hand into the water, cupping it so as to lift the water from its stream. He watched steam rise from his fingers, as his friends watched him. Michael suddenly turned toward his friends. His face was flat, completely void of expression.

"This is the blood of the earth," he told them.

At Portston Psychiatric Hospital, a young nurse excitedly reported to the doctor on call. She reported that the female patient called "Barbara" had entered a catatonic state while standing in the visitor's room. The psychiatrist followed the nurse to the visitation room, calming her as they walked along the hallway. When they opened the door, they saw Barbara standing in the center of the room. The woman stood straight, with both her arms held straight out away from her sides. Her head was pitched backward and her eyes were opened wide. She stood there motionless.

"How long has she been like this," the doctor asked as he approached for a closer look at the patient.

"Several minutes now," the nurse answered.

Beads of perspiration formed on the woman's forehead as if she had been exercising strenuously, but her breathing seemed slow. Suddenly, the sweat on her brow seemed to change color from sparkling silver to a brilliant crimson. More and more red beads formed on the woman's forehead until they ran together and began flowing in tiny trickles down her face.

"She's bleeding," the doctor said with confusion and surprise.

"Look at her hands," the nurse said. "…her feet."

The doctor took a step back to see the entire woman. When he did, he could see that blood also flowed from open wounds in the palms of her hands and the centers of her feet. Finally, blood seeped through her garment at her left side.

"Behold the power of the Lord!" A voice boomed from behind the doctor and nurse as the two jerked their heads about to see who spoke.

The aged bishop rushed forward then dropped to his knees. He flung his arms around Barbara's legs. "I will punish those who sent you away," the old priest trumpeted. "You will not be rebuked again."

That night, Michael lay awake in his bed. He could only wonder now, what fate held for him. He was certain that his life was about to take a drastic change. He heard the voices calling him with each gust of wind. "The mist, Michael, the mist has come," the wind hissed. Michael tried, but he couldn't ignore the sounds in his head.

In a small corner of the university library, a single light glowed over a collection of books on military strategy. Professor Draco poured carefully over the tomes making notes and then cross checking them with other volumes. Jane Linden stood by Draco's side, waiting to fetch a volume if he asked for one he didn't have before him.

Part Two

Voices of the Past

Chapter 8

After seven days, the heavy mist, which had smothered the Midland-Highlands, simply vanished. The impact of the event also seemed to fade from public interest. At least, people stopped talking about it, but the occurrence was silently shared among everyone. Many people felt that the appearance of the mist was an omen; an omen that forebode struggle and suffering. The students at National University also dropped the topic of the mist and were now waiting for the warmth of spring and the end of the semester.

Michael smiled at his classmates as he strode cheerfully toward Ivan Draco's class. While the drama of the Highland mist was fixed forever in his memory, he had not been bothered by the haunting voices since the mist vanished. Still, he knew his life was taking a far different direction from what he had expected just a few months earlier. He entered the history building with a quick step, and skipped quickly up the short set of stairs that led to Draco's classroom. He entered and took his seat. He didn't bother to watch the minute hand signal the Professor's entrance as he had in the past. There was no need to anticipate his mentor's arrival anymore.

The clock on the wall clunked every sixty seconds, and soon Michael was aware of a murmur around him. He tore himself from his text and looked around the room. Students were whispering to each other and Draco was absent from his lectern. Now, Michael looked up at the clock. To his amazement, Professor Draco was late. The murmurs began to grow louder as the other students began to speculate about the Professor's absence. Then, silence quickly seized the class, as the door to the Professor's office slowly opened and Ivan Draco made his way to the lectern.

The young teacher looked disheveled. It appeared that he had not slept in quite a while. All eyes were fixed on him while he slowly approached the lectern. Draco placed his books on the lectern and looked at the class. His eyes searched each face for a moment, then, passed on to another. There was a continuing, unnerving silence while the professor continued his visual inventory. Finally, he looked at a book on the lectern and opened it. He placed his hands on either side of the book as he slowly looked up at the class. Still, he was silent. He thoughtfully stroked his chin with one hand and then returned it to its resting-place on the lectern. "Class is dismissed," he announced softly.

There was a hesitation, then, students got up from their desks and started for the door. Ivan just stood there, watching them file out of the room. Then, Michael caught his eye. "Mr. Sylvan," Draco called out hoarsely.

"Yes sir," Michael responded.

"I would like to have a word with you in my office." Draco closed his text and started toward the office door. Michael followed the professor and closed the door behind them.

Draco tossed his books onto his cluttered desk while he strode to the window. He stood there staring out on the campus. "Did you go see it?"

"The mist?" Michael clarified.

"Yes," Ivan said.

"Yes, we drove down there the very first day," Michael disclosed.

"So did I," Draco admitted. "What did you think about it?"

"I walked into it," Michael said. "I never saw anything like it. I could only see a few yards. We came to a spring. Steam seemed to rise up from the water, so I stuck my hand into it. It was hot. When I held up my hand, steam rose from my fingers. I couldn't help but recall the tale that Dudley had told me as I watched the steam swirl from my hand."

"Do you recall how you felt when you entered the mist?" Draco continued.

"Yes," Michael said. "I felt relaxed, comfortable. It was as if I was in my room at home. Everything seemed very familiar." Michael waited for Draco to continue the dialogue, but the professor was silent. "What about you, Ivan, did you walk into the mist?"

Ivan turned away from the window and sat on the edge of his desk. "Yes, I did."

"How did you feel?"

"Safe, as if I had entered some sanctuary," Draco smiled. "How far did you walk into the mist, Michael?"

"I'm not sure, maybe a couple of hundred yards," Michael replied.

"Did you walk in a straight line?"

"I don't think it's possible to walk a straight line that far in the wilderness," Michael laughed.

"No," Ivan grinned, "I don't believe it's possible either. So, how did you find your way out?"

Michael thought a moment. "I just turned and walked out," Michael said. "Why?"

"How did you know you were going the right way?" Draco asked.

"I…I just…You know, now that I think about it, I didn't pay any attention to which way I was going when we went into the mist." Michael paused in recollection. "In fact, I didn't really think about which way to go out either. But when we emerged from the mist, we were at the very exact spot where we had entered."

"Same thing happened to me," Ivan said. "I get lost on the campus in broad daylight. So, I went back the next day, to another location at the Highlands and did it again. Same thing happened. I came out exactly where I had started. I went to another location on the third day and had the same results."

"That is peculiar," Michael said.

"Yeah," Ivan sighed, "very, damned peculiar. How about you, Michael, have you noticed any changes?"

"Yes, as a matter of fact, I have," Michael smiled. "When the mist lifted, the voices stopped. I haven't had any 'visions' either."

"Then, everything is back to normal for you," Draco concluded.

"Normal," Michael said wistfully. "No, I don't think my life will be normal again. Fate has something in store for me. All I can do is wait to find out what it is."

Draco nodded in understanding. "Study hard, Michael. You need all the honors marks you can get if you hope to keep your friend Dudley from beating you to the head of the class."

"Thanks," Michael said warmly. "Now, perhaps I can suggest that you ease up on this research your doing. Everyone on the campus knows you've been spending most of your nights at the library."

"You're right," Ivan grinned. "You know how I am. I get obsessed with my work."

Michael smiled and started to leave. When he reached the door, he stopped and looked back at the young teacher. "Ivan, I know how busy you are. Are you certain that you don't mind if we talk from time to time."

"I would consider it an honor," Ivan Draco said. "Now, go and enjoy the warm weather."

"I will," Michael beamed happily. "I'm going to visit my grandparents over spring break."

The old woman stared into the darkness of the bedroom while her husband tossed and turned beside her. She knew the cause of his restlessness. It happened nearly every spring. It was in late winter or spring when he relived a past horror in his sleep. She was frightened this time. This was the seventieth spring since he nearly died, and his reliving of that event. The old woman feared that this would be the last spring, and at the same time she feared that it wouldn't be the end. She wanted an end to the torment of the past, but she knew that would also mean an end to the life of the man she loved. She was torn between these conflicting desires and she wept. Slowly, the tears brimmed over her eyelids and trickled down familiar furrows on her face.

Her husband flinched violently, and she turned onto her side and instinctively reached out with her hand to comfort him. Her touch stopped just short of his shoulder. Her hand was frozen just an inch from him. Then, she withdrew her hand and placed it at her side. She wanted to help him, to comfort him. She wondered if she should enter his mind and share his burden. She could do that; enter his mind as if walking into a motion picture theater. She could see what he saw, feel what he felt, smell what he smelled and hear what he heard. But, no, she had promised him that she wouldn't do that. He trusted her not to use her power, but, her emotions overruled her, and she was there, inside his nightmare. She cringed at the horrible reality that dwelled in his thoughts even though she had lived through it with him at the time. It was seventy years ago and she easily recognized her husband, as he, and another heavily armed man, slowly made their way up a steep slope.

The two men paused in their ascent of the steep ridge. Their breathing was labored, but controlled as much as possible so as not to be heard beyond a very short distance. They said nothing to each other.

The enemy was still nearby, though they had lost count of how many were left. The shorter, stockier of the two men felt the risk to whisper was needed.

"How many do you think are left?" The stocky man whispered slowly.

"Two, maybe three," the taller man hissed softly. "What about you?"

"Two," the other man answered.

"When we get to the top, we'll rest, and then head west to the rocks above the falls," the tall man explained.

"O.K." the other man said in an almost smothered voice.

The two men quietly, slowly began their final climb to the top of the ridge. When they reached the summit they came to a wide trail which meandered along the crest of the ridge. Above them they could see brilliant stars set in a black abyss above the towering trees.

"The mist is gone," the shorter, more muscular man whispered as he stared at the stars.

"All we have to do is follow the starlight through the trees," the other man said. "Let's move carefully. It will be daylight soon, and without the mist we'll be easy to spot."

"If we can hold out until daylight, it won't matter," the companion said cheerfully.

A few moments later, the two men were on their feet. Each, carefully adjusted his heavy pack, and slung his long rifle over his shoulder so that it was held tightly against the pack. Next, they both picked up shorter weapons which were fitted with elongated, curved, ammunition magazines. The tall man also carried a revolver in his belt, while his companion wore a razor sharp dagger and a pistol. They looked ominously at the brightening sky toward the east, and then, clasped each other's hand. When they released their grips, they started along the narrow trail toward the west.

"No, no," the old woman shouted. "Go east, not west." She had forgotten that she was only a visitor in her husband's dream and those words she spoke could not be heard. Then, the pain of the memory struck her. How young the two men looked to her now. Her man looked like her grandson Michael. Though at the time, both were older than she was. The two men continued on, and the old woman sighed. She was now trapped in her husband's nightmare with no ability to change the outcome. All she could do was live through it with him just as she had many years ago. She watched as the two warriors slowly trod along the path that led nowhere.

In spite of the care that the men took with each step, the shorter man's heel caught a stone that caused him to stumble enough to thrust his trailing leg forward. The errant step found a small piece of dead fall beneath the leaves and gave out a loud crack.

Gunfire erupted immediately from the trees just north of the trail, but the fire was instinctively directed toward the sound of the twig snapping and for the most part sprayed bullets indiscriminately into the forest. Unfortunately, one single shot found its mark, and the shorter, stockier of the two men on the trail fell to the ground with a shattered leg. Without thinking, the wounded man crawled into the wood-line and watched for the telltale flicker of flame from the enemy weapons. He spotted it a second later and let go a burst with his automatic weapon. He heard a groan, and then he crawled away again.

It was silent again; dead silent. The two comrades on the trail had been separated from each other and had no way of knowing if the other survived. They also had no way of knowing how many of the enemy troops were near them, though it seemed that there were only two or three. The wounded man suddenly was overwhelmed by the pain of his wound and in his determination not to cry out, he fell into unconsciousness. The tall man, just thirty yards to the west, rested against an ancient oak that had more than enough girth to hide his silhouette from the brightening sky.

Breathing slow, deliberate breaths, the tall man allowed his eyes to dance through the brightening landscape. He was now certain that there were two of the enemy left. He carefully removed a long rifle with a telescopic sight from his shoulder and placed it against the oak tree. Next, he slung the automatic weapon onto his shoulder, and brought the other rifle to a shooting position. The optical sight seemed to increase his ability to see through the predawn light, and after a moment, he spotted one enemy soldier. He could have fired and killed the man outright, but he thought it would be best to locate the second man first before he fired and gave away his position. Several times he raised the long rifle and looked in vain for the second man he was certain was nearby. Finally, with the brightening sky making his own discovery a threat, he raised his weapon toward the only man he could see, and he fired. He saw a piece of the enemy soldier's skull fly upward, then, before he could lower his weapon, a rapid succession of cracking sounds fell all around him. Bark flew from the great oak in all directions, then, he felt himself being slammed into the thick trunk and he fell down the steep slope. He tumbled for what seemed to be a long time, finally coming to rest alongside the rotting hulk of a tremendous oak tree that had recently fallen.

The severely wounded man stared at the blue of the sky and although sunlight had yet to fall where he lay, he knew he had been successful. It was dawn. He had done his job. He had kept the enemy from crossing the huge ridge, and now, he could rest. He coughed, and gagged, as he tasted his own blood in his mouth. He rolled onto his side, and pulled himself with unknown strength to a sitting position against the fallen, wood giant. He coughed again, and waited to die. Suddenly, he heard footsteps in the dry leaves and that part of the brain that keeps all men alive sprung into action. His right hand reached for and found the revolver he kept in his belt. He pulled himself atop the trunk of the dead tree and brought his handgun in front of his view. He could now see that he was on a small flat piece of land that jutted from the steep slope of the ridge. Twenty feet away stood large, limestone boulder, slightly taller than himself. Behind the boulder, he could hear the footsteps. He pulled back the hammer on his revolver, and waited for his target to appear from behind the tombstone-white boulder. His vision began to blur. He could only make out a gold crescent on the rock that was projected by a single beam of sunlight slashing through the trees. His eyes were held on the flickering spot, then, he saw his enemy slowly slide into view. With inhuman strength, he pointed the revolver at his enemy and fired. He saw the man drop his rifle and stumble backward against the boulder as he clutched at his chest. A second shot caused the enemy officer to fall forward, face first into the forest floor.

The nearly dead warrior slumped across the fallen oak again. His revolver slid from his hand and dropped into the leaves. It was quiet, but something made him rise up to gaze upon the body of the man he had just killed. Instead of seeing the corpse, however, he saw only a thick fog that seemed to cling to the earth. A breeze swept the fog into a vertical column that soon turned dark, then black. An image appeared in the dark, misty column. The dying warrior thought he recognized the image and with great pain he asked, "Have you come for me?"

"No," he heard the image reply softly. "I will come for you another day in another spring, and that day will be your last."

The old woman heard the words too, and that allowed her to escape from the depths of her husband's mind. She sighed a sigh of relief that the man she loved so dearly would live another day, and she was grateful.

Just after breakfast, while they were enjoying the last of their morning coffee, the old man took his wife by the hand. "The dreams have begun again," he said flatly.

"Yes," she smiled, "I know."

"I've never been able to keep anything from you, have I Ann?"

"No," Ann answered. "We've been together too long for any secrets."

John sipped slowly at his coffee cup. "One of these mornings, he'll come for me Ann," John said casually.

"And you'll be ready for him," Ann added.

"Yes," John nodded. "I have been ready and waiting for many years."

Michael drove slowly along the treacherous, wilderness, road. He marveled at the simple grandeur of the forest once again. Somehow, he felt as if he was part of it all, though he really didn't understand why he felt that way. So, rather than analyze his feelings, he decided simply to accept them for what they were and not read anything into them. He felt so many things washing over him though that he could not ignore them. Time seemed to have no meaning, no pace. He felt serenity, and a deep sense of comfort. He smiled at his contentment and continued driving the challenging road.

It was well past noon when Michael arrived atop Long Ridge and bounded up the short stairway to the front door of his grandparent's cabin. He received the usual greeting of hugs from the old couple he loved, but he also noticed a strange flicker in his grandmother's eyes. Michael felt as if the old woman was reading his mind, but he quickly brushed off the thought. "It's really good to be here again," he said. "I'm really looking forward to my visit."

"We're always happy to have you," old John said as he wrapped a powerful arm around Michael. "I see your hair is turning white," the old man noticed. "Same damn thing happened to me when I was your age. Did you notice his hair, Ann?"

"Yes," Ann replied softly. "He looks exactly like you when you were young," Ann added with, what Michael saw, as a forced smile. "Bring in your things," Ann quickly commanded, as she was aware of Michael's inquisitive gaze. "You can have your choice of the rooms upstairs."

"All right," Michael beamed as he turned and skipped down the stairs to his car. He quickly gathered his two suitcases, and scampered into the cabin and toward the front, upstairs bedroom. By the time he unpacked, changed clothes and returned downstairs, Ann had prepared sandwiches and soup. The three ate the light meal, and then, Michael left the cabin to walk along the ridge, leaving the old couple alone in the kitchen.

Ann started to busy herself with clean-up, but John caught her by the hand. "That can wait," he said softly. "Sit here with me."

Ann took her chair again, waiting to hear what John wanted to say, but not wanting to hear what he was about to tell her.

"This will be the last spring for me," John said. "I'm certain of it."

"You been saying that every spring for seventy years," Ann smiled.

"Yes, I know, but when I saw Michael today, I became certain," John concluded. "It was almost as if I was seeing myself as I used to be. His hair has already turned completely gray, just as mine did at his age. Will he also inherit a fate similar to mine? Will he have to endure what we had to endure? I saw you staring at him on the porch, Ann. What did you see in him?"

Ann lowered her gaze in embarrassment. John could nearly always tell when her powers were in use. "He has inherited more than your looks," Ann sighed. "He will stand where you stood. He will walk were you have walked. But, he also has the…he can…"

"He has your mind," John interrupted. "He sees the visions."

Ann looked up into John's kind face. "He doesn't know it yet," she said.

John shook his head. "I know I don't have the time to teach him what he will need to know. Even if there were time, I couldn't break my oath. Still, there must be something…" John froze in his thoughts for a second, then, he snapped his fingers. "When I die, there is a trunk, under the stairs in the cellar that you should give to Michael."

89

"Trunk?" Ann feigned surprise. "I thought you destroyed everything from those days."

"I don't know why I kept it," John admitted, "but now, I guess there was a reason for it." John shook his head. "A man should leave his grandson a better life than his own. With your powers, though, he will be able to make good use of his inheritance."

"My powers," Ann scoffed, "it's a curse. You see things and you have to guess at what they mean, or when they're going to happen, or if they have already occurred."

John reached across the table and took Ann by the hand. "It is all we have to give him. Maybe, it will be a help to him."

Michael's walk turned into a hike. He left the ridge for the gentle, downhill slope to the north. He kept easing westward until he arrived at the Old River that dashed though the forest at a swift pace. Here the river was narrow, shallow and quite cold and pure. The young man laid down and sipped at the refreshing liquid, then, he followed the torrent toward the roaring sound of Broken Falls, a short distance to the south. He had to go slowly, for the east bank rose above the river. He climbed patiently and expertly, until he reached the western most point of Long Ridge. The view was amazing, and Michael sat and watched the water thunder though the numerous pathways that had been scoured through the huge stones. It was mystifying to sit and watch the water roar through the rocks, and Michael lost track of time. It was only when the sun shown full onto his face that he realized the lateness of the hour. He smiled at his absorption by nature; then, he jumped to his feet and walked toward the wide trail, which led back to his grandparent's cabin. When he reached the high jutting rocks where he liked to sit and watch the sunrise, he paused for a moment before climbing down to the trail. He took only a few paces eastward, when a procession of people came walking toward him. He stopped and stared; confused by what he saw. Armed men carried litters. The men in the litters were dead or dying. On either side of the litter-bearers marched women and children. Grief was chiseled into their silent faces. Michael froze and watched as the walking horror came directly toward him. Soon, the first litter stopped in front of him. A young girl held the hand of the corpse of a young man, but reached out with her other hand toward Michael. Unsure what to do,

Michael gripped the young woman's hand tenderly. The young woman smiled while tears flowed down her dirty cheeks. "I am very grateful to you," the young woman said. "After I bury my husband, I'll take his place in his brigade."

All Michael could do was nod as he let go of the woman's hand.

"Thank you," she said. "Thank you for all you have done for us."

Another litter moved before Michael. This time a young man, with a hard, flat expression on his face, spoke to him. "I'll be fifteen years old this winter. I'll take my father's place then. I will try to be as brave as he was."

Again, Michael nodded, but said nothing. As the boy walked away beside his dead father, another litter appeared. One by one, litter followed litter; and another; and another. It seemed that the procession would never end, then, suddenly, Michael was alone. He stood quietly; staring at the darkening forest. He wondered about what he had just seen; or thought he had seen. After several moments, he decided that he was uncertain that he had seen anything. He sighed, noting the deepening twilight, and then he darted down the trail. He knew he wouldn't reach the cabin before dark, but he needed to try. He needed to run.

Ann opened the front door of the cabin just as Michael came bounding up the short series of steps. The old woman made eye contact with her grandson for brief moment. Michael seemed held by the old woman's gaze, but he found it comforting; understanding.

"Sorry I'm late," Michael said. "I ... I've been daydreaming, and..."

"I know..." Ann caught herself. "I mean..."

"Yes," Michael interrupted with a puzzled look on his face. "You do know. I can see it in your eyes."

Ann broke her gaze from her grandson's inquisitive eyes. "Supper is on the table, come and eat before it gets cold."

Michael followed Ann to the kitchen and sat across from his grandfather. He smiled at old John; then, he plunged into the sumptuous meal. There was little conversation among the three while they ate, though, Michael felt as if his grandmother could read his thoughts.

Barbara stood naked, with her arms outstretched on both sides. Her head was tilted back and to one side. Her tongue protruded from the corner of her mouth, while beads of blood formed on her forehead. Next, wounds appeared on the tops of her feet, and blood flowed from them. Then, blood began dripping from the centers of both hands. The young priest, and psychiatrist, who had been watching the woman, drew near to her. The doctor clasped one of her outstretched arms and tried to lower it, but the arm wouldn't budge. The priest looked into her face, but her eyes seemed not to notice him.

"Barbara?" The priest said. "Do you hear me?"

The woman remained motionless while the priest waited for a reply. "Barbara," he prodded again. The woman was silent for another moment, then, her eyes snapped onto the priest's gaze with an intensity he had never experienced.

"It begins," she said sharply. "The messenger is returning to lead the gray one into the earth. The last of them will come and pray over him, until the great Angel comes for him. All will be covered in a gray shroud that will rise up from the earth. The air will be heavy and choked with the grayness. The enemies of the young gray one will gasp in the thick air, and they will die." The woman's eyes clouded, and glazed over. She trembled, then, collapsed onto the bloody floor. As the priest picked her up and carried her to her bed, he noticed that the wounds that had been there, where now gone. A nurse joined him in covering Barbara. When the nurse took over, the priest left the room and walked directly to a telephone. His hand trembled as he dialed the bishop's private number.

Two hours later Barbara found herself in a roomy office filled with heavy furniture. She stood at the doorway to the office wondering how she got there. The young priest from the hospital stood beside her and smiled warmly as he gestured to a large man with close-cropped white hair. "Barbara," the young priest smiled, "do you remember Bishop Blane?"

Barbara looked at the bishop. He was old; very old. She knelt before him and kissed his ring. She looked up into the face of the old man. Their eyes met and they locked onto each other's gaze. Barbara smiled as the old priest gently took her hands in his powerful grip and raised her from her knees.

"I can see the image of our Lady in your face. I will not question you further. Would you like to go home now?"

"Yes," Barbara almost giggled.

The Last Day of the Last Spring

The large man looked about the room to locate the young psychiatrist-priest. "Take Barbara home," Blane stated.

The young man was taken by surprise at the quick decision and hesitated for a moment. A stern glance from the Bishop instantly moved the cleric into action, however, and he quickly took the woman by the arm and led her to the door. Soon, they got into a large sedan and began driving toward the river. After a few moments, Barbara looked at the young priest driving the car.

"You think I'm mad, don't you?" She asked pointedly.

"No," the man shook his head. "I thought so when I first arrived at the hospital. But, after I saw you, I was certain you were not insane."

"How can you be so certain," Barbara tested the priest.

"I have worked among insane persons for many years," the priest explained, "and I am never frightened by them. When I saw you, though, I was terrified."

"Terrified? Of me?" Barbara questioned.

"No, it wasn't you," the priest cleared his throat. "It was the power which flowed from you. It was the power of God."

Chapter 9

Once again old John tossed and turned in his sleep as the approaching dawn began to fade the night sky. And again, Ann struggled to stay out of the nightmare that had brought them both such pain for so many years. She heard her grandson stir upstairs which helped distract her from her husband's plight. A few moments later, she heard Michael leave the cabin. She knew where he was going. He would rush up the trail that ran along the top of Long Ridge until he came to his favorite place to watch the sun rise into the heavens. Her thoughts soon returned to John, however. Then he twitched, violently; Ann tried to see him in the dark. She reached out to touch him, but instead she stood watching him cling to his life as he gasped for air. She saw the dead enemy officer at the foot of the large limestone boulder. And, she saw her young man stretched across the fallen tree. There, on that familiar flat which stuck out from the side of the steep hillside, the mist column began to rise and the creature that dwelled within the mist became visible.

"Have you come for me?" She heard her man ask.

The mist-creature paused then Ann heard him speak. "Yes. I have come for you."

Ann snapped up abruptly into a sitting position on the bed. Hot tears burned through her eyes and blistered paths on her cheeks. Beside her, John was still. His breathing was slow and even. Ann forced herself to lie back down, and she placed an arm over John's side. The day she had feared had come, and she tried to come to grips with the grim reality. Even now, the tightly woven fabric of their lives was beginning to unravel. The two hearts, minds, bodies and souls that had been bound together for so long, were beginning to separate; and the process was more painful than Ann had expected. The old woman wept as her emotions took full reign.

As the bedroom turned into gray light, Ann wrestled her emotions under control. She wasn't sure how much more time she had left with

John. Not long, it seemed. She wondered if he would remember the dream. She wondered if he knew this was his last day. Then, she heard Michael rush down the stairs and go out the front door.

Suddenly, John stirred. Ann turned away from him so she could wipe away her tears. She felt John put his arm around her, squeeze her tightly. She instantly knew that John was aware that his life was at an end.

"You're awake awful early," Ann said.

"I thought I'd get up in time to watch the sun rise," John explained.

"Do you have time for coffee?" Ann stumbled.

John smiled. "Sure, there's time for a cup of coffee."

Ann rushed to the kitchen to start the coffee brewing while John dressed. The two of them then sat in the kitchen waiting for the coffee. They didn't say anything to each other. John forced himself to smile, and Ann forced back her tears. Finally, Ann filled two cups with the dark brew and they sat together at the table again. John held her hand. Too soon, the cups were empty.

"I'd better get going if I'm going to catch the sunrise," John smiled.

"Are you going down to the flat on the side of the hill?" Ann asked.

John smiled at Ann's knowledge of his fate. "Yes, Ann. He will come for me there."

Ann couldn't hold back the tears any longer and rushed into a crushing embrace with her husband. "I'll go with you," she sobbed.

"This is one walk, I have to take on my own," John said.

Slowly, they let go of one another. The separation of the one entity they had shared was nearly complete. John walked to the door, opened it, but then turned back to Ann.

"It was wrong not to tell the children about us," John said. "Now, it's too late. When, Bill and Henry get here, tell them to tell our family everything, especially Michael. Michael is the one who will have to deal with the future. Remember the old green trunk beneath the stairs in the cellar. Give the trunk to Michael."

Ann nodded her agreement.

John smiled. "Good-bye Babe," he said; using the old nickname that had been unspoken for decades.

Hearing the unspoken word unleashed a tidal wave of emotion within Ann. "Good-bye Walker," she responded in kind.

John turned and closed the door behind him. Ann made her way to a kitchen chair and was able to sit down before beginning to weep uncontrollably.

Michael sat atop the rocky outcrop watching the gold hue spread into the eastern horizon. There were just a few, thin clouds wafting patiently in the eastern sky, but they added drama to coming event. While he absorbed the beauty above the horizon, his gaze slowly lowered to a point where the treetops met the sky. A tiny, gold crescent burst forth and burned brightly. But suddenly, Michael's view changed. Instead of the horizon, he was looking at the cabin owned by his grandparent's. He knew he was too far from the cabin to able to see it, but the vision held him fast. He saw his grandfather descend the stairway from the porch and walk a short distance up the ridge-top trail. After about fifty paces, old John turned onto a narrow path that dove across the face of the hill. Michael watched his grandfather make the descent to a small plateau that clung to the steep ridge. The image faded away as bright sunlight shone on Michael's face. The sun was nearly half exposed and the treetops were awash with a gold luminescence. Michael had to lower his gaze from the bright sun, and when he did, the vision returned. He saw his grandfather standing near the rotting remnant of a great tree. In the center of the little flat piece of land, a column of mist rose from the rotting leaves. Then, to his horror, he watched the old man fall face-first onto the forest floor.

"No!" Michael yelled as the image disappeared beneath the sun-drenched treetops in the distance. But, Michael knew that this was not just a vision. He was certain in his own mind that the incident he saw, or thought he saw, had actually occurred. He scurried down from his rocky perch, half falling and skidding on the sharp edges of the stones. He ran through the woods, taking no heed of the slashing branches that hacked away at him. When he reached the trail, he broke into a full sprint. He ran and ran. But, he ran more as one in panic than an athlete did. His mouth stayed open; gasping in large hunks of air.

After a few moments, Michael instinctively left the trail and ended up plunging down the steep southern slope of Long Ridge. He fell, tumbled; caught himself on a sapling to regain his footing, then, he fell again. On his fourth fall, he tumbled out onto the flat surface where his grandfather lay. Slowly, reverently, Michael approached the fallen patriarch. Michael already knew the truth, but he hoped he was wrong. When he knelt down and turned old John over and looked into his dead face, the truth could no longer be denied. Michael gently closed his dead grandfather's eyes and mouth, then, brushed away the leaves from his face. He took one of old John's lifeless hands into his own, as tears of grief dripped onto the forest floor. Then, a feeling of déjà vu suddenly overtook Michael. He had seen this scene before; several times. He wondered why he had not accepted the truth before. He knew his grandfather was going to die, and he knew that he would be the one to find him. Why then, he wondered, is the real experience so painful? His mind wrestled with logic, but his emotions were too strong to be overcome by reason.

Somehow, Michael had not noticed Ann approach him until she knelt down beside him and placed one hand on his arm while reaching out to stroke old John's snow-white hair with the other.

Michael tried to blink away his tears and speak to his grandmother, but the words only rattled around in his mind and couldn't find the pathway to his lips. He looked into Ann's tear-filled eyes. At first he thought she had spoken to him, but her lips never moved. He kept his gaze upon her.

"He is at peace now," he heard her say. "After all these years of torment, he's at peace."

Margaret paced nervously back and forth in the foyer of their Capitol City mansion waiting for JJ to exit his limousine and enter the house. The bad news had quickly reached Capitol City, and Margaret had tried to offer her help in setting up a burial in the city. Ann would have nothing to do with the suggestion, which left Margaret in disarray. When JJ finally entered, she took a deep breath and sighed.

"You'll have to talk to your mother," she said. "Ann wants to bury your father up there in the forest."

"What?" He asked in dismay.

"She's insistent," Margaret explained. "I tried to talk her out of it, but she won't hear of anything else. She said that she and Michael have already made all of the arrangements. She wants this to be a private affair with family and a few of their old friends."

"Michael? What's he doing up there? Did he drive down there from the university already?"

"He was already there. He found your father's…" Margaret stopped herself. "I don't know why he was there."

"We'll find out later," JJ concluded. "Did anyone notify Joan and Hank?"

"Michael said he was going to call them after he spoke to me."

"The limousine is waiting to take us to the airport. We'll fly to Riverton and charter a helicopter there," JJ stated.

"I suppose it's all we can do," Margaret sighed. "Perhaps, if we get there quickly, we can convince Ann to have dad buried at Memorial Park."

"Mom can be pretty headstrong," JJ admitted. "But, I guess it won't hurt to try. We'd better go now."

Margaret nodded to the butler who grabbed two suitcases and followed her and JJ to the waiting vehicle.

Ann switched off the short-wave radio, and closed the cabinet doors where the device was kept. "That's everybody," she announced more to herself than to Michael. "Did you contact all the relatives?" She asked Michael.

"Yes, grandma," he answered. "Mom and dad are on a charter flight to Riverton right now. Aunt Joan and Uncle Charles will be here later in the afternoon. Uncle Hank said he and his daughter were coming. I didn't know Uncle Hank had a daughter."

"Oh, yes," Ann recalled. "I nearly forgot about her. Hank sort of took her in when her family tossed her out. It's been good for Hank. He needed some responsibility in his life."

"Anyway, they've all been called," Michael ended.

Ann looked at her grandson. His grief was impossible to conceal. She got up from her chair near the writing table and sat beside him on the couch. "Death is our heritage," Ann said softly. "Don't let this wear too heavily on you."

"You don't understand, grandma," Michael explained. "I knew it was going to happen. I have seen grandpa die several times in the very spot I found him." Michael looked into the old woman's sparkling eyes.

The Last Day of the Last Spring

"I have seen the same thing," Ann confessed. "Every spring, we waited and wondered if this spring was the last."

It suddenly occurred to Michael how little he knew about his grandparents and his ignorance embarrassed and perplexed him. How could he live to be his age and know nothing about his family?

Ann looked at Michael and smiled. "Two very old and very dear friends of ours will be here today," she said. "When they arrive, we'll tell you all about us."

Michael was taken aback by Ann's words. It was as if she could read…He decided to respond with his own thoughts. "I am eager to learn about the past," he said in his mind.

Ann patted her grandson on the hand. "I know you are…" The old woman stopped herself in mid-sentence as she became aware of the curious look on Michael's face. It was too late for her to deny what had happened, but she wasn't ready to explain. "I'm very tired just now. I think I'll lie down for a while."

Michael acquiesced. "Yes, the rest will be good for you."

Ann left for her bedroom, and Michael chose to go out onto the porch. He closed the door behind him and walked to the railing. It was warmer now, and the early mist had dissipated under the bright sunlight. A restless breeze rushed through the trees; uncertain which direction it should take. After several minutes, all was silent. Michael sighed, but it brought him no relief. He relived the harrowing experiences of the morning and wished that he could have gotten to his grandfather to hear his last words so he could have them in his heart. It was meant to be, he finally accepted. There was more in store for him; he felt that his life was about to begin though he wasn't sure why he felt that way.

The wind once again rushed through the trees. "Michael, you will lead them," the wind whispered. "Your pain will become your strength. Listen to the voices of the past."

It was shortly past noon, when a powerful helicopter rushed through the small opening in the trees and swirled the leaves and dust. Michael watched as the machine eased down upon the gravel road, then came to a stop. Next, his mother and father exited the vehicle. His parents came straight to the cabin.

"Michael, you poor dear," Margaret whined. "What a horrible experience to go through," she said as she hugged her son.

"It was a shock," Michael said.

"I'm sure it was," Margaret agreed. "How is Ann doing? I mean, this must be very difficult for her to deal with."

"She's sad, mother," Michael explained, "but she is handling grandpa's death very well."

"Are you sure, dear?" Margaret asked. "I understand she wants to bury John here in the wilderness. Your father and I feel it would be better to bury him at Memorial Park where he could have a proper service."

Michael was suddenly angry with his mother, but quickly found the courage to parry her attempted manipulation. "Grandma has already made all the necessary arrangements for the funeral," he smiled. "Other than family, grandma has invited two of their old friends."

The conversation was broken momentarily by the noise of the helicopter taking off to return to Riverton.

Margaret realized she had been temporarily out-maneuvered by her son, and elected to remain silent. Michael stepped past Margaret to meet his father.

"I am sorry about your loss father," Michael said as he shook his father's hand.

"Thank you, Michael, but, how are you? I understand that you found dad's body."

"Finding grandpa was grim," Michael admitted, "but I'm fine."

"How's mom?"

"She's resting," Michael answered. "She seemed very tired after we notified everyone, and made all the arrangements, so she decided to lie down and rest."

"You said all the arrangements have been made?" JJ asked.

"Yes. Grandma contacted a funeral director in Riverton. They're already here preparing the gravesite. Then, she contacted Hank. I talked to Uncle Charles and Joan. When I finished with that, grandma reached two old friends and invited them."

"I take it the old radio worked," JJ concluded.

"Yes, it did," Michael said. "You seemed surprised about the radio. Has it been in need of repair?"

"No, the radio has always worked," JJ countered. "It's just that sometimes you can't get radio signals to get across the Highlands. It has to do with atmospherics or something. You said they're already preparing the gravesite. Where is it?"

"It's in grandpa's favorite place, just a short distance below the ridge," Michael pointed toward the location.

JJ looked at his son with an expression of utter surprise. "I didn't know dad had a 'favorite place'," JJ admitted.

"I happened to find him there once when I was very young," Michael explained. "He was sitting on an old log. He told me it was his favorite place. He said that every man needed a favorite place to go to just to sit and think. For some reason, the memory of him telling me that stayed with me. But, I felt that it was also grandpa's 'private' place and I never went there again, until today."

"It's a good thing you happened to go there this morning," Margaret said. "It would have been impossible to find him otherwise."

"Margaret is right," JJ said. "What made you go to that place today, Michael?"

Michael struggled to find an answer for just an instant, then, he sighed, "it must have been meant to be."

"Yes, it was meant to be," Ann added as she fully opened the door and stepped out onto the porch.

JJ quickly embraced his mother. "I am sorry about dad," he offered.

Ann patted her son on the back as she held him. "It was time," she said. "It was time."

Michael watched his parents as they comforted his grandmother. He wondered about the sincerity of the sympathy they offered with their ability to always have the right words. He declined to join them in the living room of the cabin, preferring instead, the silence of the forest.

It was little more than an hour later when another helicopter roared toward the cabin. This time, Michael saw his Aunt Joan and Charles Speerman approach him. Along with Joan and Charles was his uncle Hank. Lastly, a young, beautiful woman with long shapely legs and bright, red, hair stepped out of the helicopter and took Hank by the arm. Michael was captivated by the woman's beauty. He couldn't keep his eyes off her for a moment. Then, he realized how inappropriate he was being.

101

Joan broke into tears when she reached the cabin stairs and sobbed loudly. Charles tried to comfort her, but Michael knew the gesture was futile. Joan had always been prone to hysteria. And now, with a proper cause, Joan could collapse into an emotional frenzy that seemed to be her normal state. Michael shook hands with Charles and patted Joan on the shoulder as he ushered them into the cabin and closed the door behind them.

Michael then turned to greet his uncle Hank. "Sorry to have to see you again under such circumstances," Michael said.

"It's all right," Hank smiled. "Damn you look good, Mike. Hair's really gray though. You sure do remind me of dad. His hair was always gray too."

"Grandma says I strongly resemble grandpa when he was my age," Michael said as he cast a nervous glance toward the young woman just rising onto the porch.

Hank recognized the sudden change in direction of Michael's gaze and turned with him. "I'm sorry to be so rude," he apologized. "This is my daughter, Candyce."

Michael couldn't contain his surprise. "I didn't know you were…"

"I'm not married. I adopted Candyce seven years ago," Henry explained. "Candyce, this is my nephew Michael."

The young woman smiled a brief smile. "I'm pleased to meet you Michael. I'm sorry about the loss of your grandfather."

"Thank you," Michael stammered as he allowed himself to be engulfed by the girl's large, emerald eyes.

Hank smiled at the almost instant attraction he observed between the two young people. "Well, I'd rather sit out here and talk to you Michael, but I suppose I'll have to go inside with the others."

"Yes," Michael blushed at his delayed response, then, he opened the cabin door.

The great room of the cabin was mournfully quiet. JJ and Margaret sat in silence on a love seat by the large window that overlooked the porch. Charles and Joan sat on the couch. Joan struggled to smother her sobs in her handkerchief. Michael quickly noticed the angry stare his mother aimed at Hank as he and Candyce approached her.

"Don't start with your fuckin' high society airs, Margaret," Hank threatened calmly. "This is my daughter Candyce." Hank emphasized the word "daughter".

Margaret's face flushed blood-red as her interpretation of Candyce's relationship with Hank proved grossly inaccurate.

"Really, Hank…" JJ began, but Hank cut him off.

"I said, don't start," Hank repeated.

"Hank," Candyce snapped.

"Sorry, Candy!"

Candyce held out a long, slender arm toward Margaret to offer her hand. "I'm Candyce Storer," she said politely. "I'm sorry we couldn't have met under less strenuous circumstances."

"I'm Margaret Woodburne-Sylvan," Margaret said as she politely shook the girl's hand.

"This is my mother," Michael added. "And this is my father JJ." Michael quickly turned Candyce toward his aunt and uncle to continue the introductions and keep the young beauty away from his mother's x-ray scrutiny. As he finished the formalities, Michael saw his grand-mother enter the room. Everyone in the room rose to their feet, behind Michael.

"This is my grandmother," Michael said to Candyce.

"You must be Hank's girl, Candyce," Ann said cheerfully. "He's told me so much about you. You're much more beautiful than he described you though."

"I'm deeply sorry about the death of your husband," Candyce consoled.

Ann took the young woman by both hands and squeezed affection-ately. "Thank you," she smiled.

One by one, each of the relatives extended their sympathies to Ann. Then, Ann announced her intention to prepare coffee and sand-wiches. The women instantly volunteered to perform the task for her, but Ann would only allow their help as she maintained her mastery of her kitchen. While the women rushed into the kitchen, the men huddled in the living room.

Hank went over to an old cabinet and removed a bottle of whisky. He held the bottle up. "Anyone else," he asked

JJ nodded reluctantly, and Charles agreed. Michael went to the kitchen and returned with four glasses. Hank poured about two inches of the liquid into each glass and Michael distributed them in turn. When each man had his glass, Hank lifted his drink high. "To my old man," he said, as he tossed the liquid down his throat. The others followed suit, then, Hank passed among them; filling the glasses again. When he finished, he too sat down.

"You know," Hank began, "on the flight up here, I tried to remember dad. There were a lot of memories, but it suddenly occurred to me, that I really didn't know much about dad himself."

"I know what you mean," JJ agreed. "Dad never talked about himself."

"No, he never did," Hank sipped at his whisky. "I guess we would have known more about him if we hadn't left here at such young ages," Hank concluded.

"There was nothing here," JJ said. "There were no jobs, no opportunities. That's why I left."

"Jobs and opportunities didn't have anything to do with me leaving," Hank disclosed. "I was afraid of the forest. I hated it."

"I can't imagine you being afraid of anything," Michael said to his uncle.

"Every man has a fear," Hank said. "My fear is the Midland-Highlands wilderness. I remember telling dad, when I was about twelve years old, that I was afraid of the forest. I remember seeing ghosts drifting on the wind through the trees. When I told him about the ghosts, he smiled and said, 'those are our friends'." Hank gulped down the rest of his drink. "As we flew toward Long Ridge today, I couldn't look out the window. I was afraid of what I might see."

Michael felt a cold chill roll along his spine as his uncle spoke, but he was not willing to admit that he had seen the ghosts of the wilderness himself. "How old were you when you left Long Ridge?" Michael inquired.

"Fourteen," Hank answered. "Dad got me enrolled in a military school in Portston. I was supposed to be learning how to be a sailor, but I didn't have the discipline to take orders from anyone. I was always in a brawl. Somehow, though, I managed to graduate with high enough marks to go to Western College. When I graduated from there, I went back to Portston. I liked going out to sea where I could see miles in any direction. Later I took a job with a local newspaper and started writing fiction on the side." Hank ended his brief biography by tossing down the remainder of his drink.

"How about you dad?" Michael asked. "When did you leave the wilderness?"

"I was about the same age as, Hank," J.J replied. "I went to a prep school in Capitol City then on to National University. I used to enjoy short visits to see mom and dad, but, to me, the rustic life they led was very boring. I preferred an urban environment."

"Yes," Ann announced the return of the women into the living room, "none of you children were content here." Ann smiled as she passed a platter full of sandwiches to Hank. "John and I knew you weren't cut out to stay here, so we made other arrangements for you."

"I'm very grateful you did, mother," Joan admitted. "It was very lonely here when I was growing up. There was no one to play with."

Ann sighed. "We had very few neighbors, in those days, and even fewer now."

A knock at the door ended the conversation and all eyes were fixed at the portal. Michael and Ann both went for the door and reached it at the same time. "That'll be Mr. Woodson," Ann guessed aloud.

Michael opened the door and the old man that stood on the porch looked stunned as he stared into Michael's face. His mouth was open and his eyes were wide.

"Lord, forgive me!" the old man gasped.

"Mr. Woodson," Ann offered hurriedly, "this is my grandson, Michael."

"Thank God!" Mr. Woodson exclaimed with a gasp. "For a moment, I though old John had been resurrected."

"He bears a strong resemblance to his grandfather," Ann explained with a smile.

The aged Mr. Woodson couldn't take his eyes off of Michael. "He sure does, ma'am. Anyway, we've prepared the gravesite just as you asked. We'll be back in the morning for the services."

"Thank you, Mr. Woodson," Ann said as she squeezed the funeral director's hand.

"It's an honor, Mrs. Sylvan. See you in the morning."

Ann closed the door, looked up at her grandson, and smiled. Michael put his arm around his grandmother and escorted her to her favorite chair beside the fireplace. After Ann was seated, Michael sat on an ottoman beside her.

"We are expecting two old friends of mine to arrive anytime now," Ann announced. "I promised John, before he left the cabin this morning, that I would ask our old friends to tell you about our youth." Ann looked lovingly at her family and smiled brightly. "There is so much you don't know about us. But, today, after my friends get here, you will know what we really were. I can only hope that you do not judge us too harshly."

"How could we ever judge you at all," JJ wondered out loud.

"Really, momma," Joan added, "I can't imagine anything in your past that could change how much we love you."

Ann smiled; then, she cast a knowing wink at Michael. "I need to clean-up and change clothes," she said. "Please excuse me."

The family was silent until Ann closed the door to her room.

Chapter 10

"What is momma talking about?" Joan began. "What could there possibly be in her and daddy's past?"

"Hank and I were talking earlier," JJ said, "and, actually, there is very little we know about mom and dad."

"I know," Joan said, "but momma made it sound like there was something they had to hide."

"Do you know anything about all this, Michael?" JJ asked his son.

Michael didn't hear the question. His eyes were locked on the dark pit of the fireplace as he listened to the sounds of the wind in the flu. "Michael, Michael," the wind called out to him. "Listen, Michael. Listen to the voices of the past."

"Michael?" JJ called out a little louder.

"Oh, uh, sorry dad," Michael stumbled, "did you say something to me? My mind was miles away."

"Yes," JJ said with a little irritation in his voice, "have you been talking to mom and dad about the past?"

"No," Michael replied. "I don't know what grandma meant by all that." Michael made eye contact with Candyce, and for an instant, he felt as though she could look into the depths of his soul. He felt his pulse quicken, and his face flushed. Fortunately, the sound of an arriving helicopter broke Michael from her spell.

"That must be grandmother's friends," Michael guessed as he went to the cabin door.

Ann Sylvan had heard the noise of the air vehicle too, and she rushed forth from her room, quickly excused herself from her family's presence while asking Michael to join her to greet her friends. The rest of the family exited out onto the spacious porch to watch the arrivals, while Ann and Michael approached the airship.

Soon, a very old, white-haired man stepped out of the helicopter. He braced himself on a cane and walked with a horrible limp. JJ recognized the man instantly. "That's Henry Highet," JJ announced with some surprise in his voice.

"The Highet Industries Highet?" Margaret asked.

"Yes," JJ replied.

"I didn't know mom and dad had those kinds of connections," Hank admitted.

"Neither did I," JJ concurred.

Next, another old man exited the helicopter. He was a very large man, about the same age as the other, but dressed all in black.

"That's Bishop Blane of Portston," Candyce identified.

"I'll be damned," Hank said. "It sure is."

The family watched in quiet surprise as each man hugged Ann and shook hands with Michael. The helicopter rose and departed, but the arrival ceremony at the clearing in the woods went on for several minutes. Finally, the ritual ended, and Ann and Michael led the two old men toward the cabin and up the stairs onto the porch. Ann briefly introduced her guests to her family. Each man offered his condolences to each of the family members. Then, Ann asked her family to allow her a few minutes alone with her old friends to discuss an unresolved matter. Of course, the family members quickly agreed with Ann's request. Ann herded the two old friends into the kitchen, and closed the door.

Michael, unwilling to be trapped in a conversation with his mother and father, hastily invited Candyce to see the hot springs just to the north and a little west of the cabin. The men chose to wait outside on the porch where Hank could smoke his cigar. The women elected to wait in the living room for the drama in the kitchen to be disclosed to them.

"Who are these old men?" Joan asked. "How do they know mom and dad?"

"Henry Highet is this nation's wealthiest industrialist," Margaret said. "I haven't seen him since I was a very small child, but I remember my father talking about him. He is a legend in the business world. As for his connection with your family," Margaret paused, "I am as surprised as you, Joan."

"The Bishop of Portston is a surprise to me," Hank offered. "I don't ever remember mom and dad going to church."

"Perhaps they were all childhood friends," Charles Speerman suggested.

"Could be," JJ said. "I'm sure we'll find out pretty soon."

Ann sat her friends down at the kitchen table and wasted no time plunging into the topic. "When John left the cabin this morning, he told me that we should have told the children about us. He said when you two get here to ask you to help me tell them the story."

"I've kept this secret too long," Blane agreed. "It's time to free ourselves from it."

"They won't understand," Highet argued. "They'll look at us like freaks in a side show."

"It's too late for our children," Ann said. "I ask you to tell everything for Michael's sake. He's the one who will need to know."

"We must tell them everything," Blane said. "They have a right to know their parents past. And maybe, just maybe, the younger ones can learn from it all."

Henry Highet looked into Ann's bright eyes. "How do you know that your grandson will need to know?"

Ann broke down under Henry's intense gaze and tears threatened to rush down her cheeks.

"You still have the 'visions', don't you?" Henry asked softly.

Ann could only nod her head up and down.

"Oh, my God!" Blane blurted. "It's all going to happen again, isn't it Ann?"

Again, she answered with a nod. "It's all we can do for them," Ann said. "We must tell them." Ann took each man by one hand.

Blane looked directly into Henry's face, and Henry stared back. "We've been silent too long," the priest said.

Henry protested, but his argument was less strong than it had been just a few seconds earlier.

"We have this woman in Portston," Blane began.

"Barbara," Ann identified.

"Yes. Barbara," the Bishop acknowledged. "She has seen the Blessed Virgin who has warned her of a great horror that will sweep the nation."

"Come on, Bill," Henry chided. "You can't believe that stuff. I know you better than that."

"I know. It sounds incredible," Blane agreed. "I even asked myself if I just wanted to believe her, then, I saw her in the hospital. Had you seen her Henry, you would believe her too."

Henry cast an inquisitive glance toward Ann. "Ann, what do you know about this woman in Portston?"

"I can't see what she sees, nor can I hear what she hears," Ann said. "I have seen her walking along the beach below the bluffs. I have seen her kneeling before the bluffs, weeping. Sometimes I see her talking to someone I can't see. One day, I saw her look up from the beach to the top of the cliffs. There was a small group of people there, but she only stared at one young man. It was Michael, my grandson. Then, I heard Barbara say, 'He is here, Holy Mother. The great angel Michael is with him'."

Henry sighed. "We gave our word that we would be silent," He reminded. "We took an oath. Silence has served us well all these years."

"It was John's last request," Ann said flatly.

"That's all I need," Bill Blane stated.

After several moments of contemplation, Highet nodded his agreement. The three got up from the table. Ann embraced each one to show her gratitude; then, she led her old friends into the spacious living room and asked the men of her family to come in from the porch.

Michael and Candyce obtained additional chairs from the kitchen so everyone could be seated. Hank Sylvan offered a round of drinks, and after the liquor was poured, Ann redid the introductions.

"Everyone, please welcome these two friends of ours," Ann beamed. "This is Henry Highet," she motioned to her left, and "Bill Blane. For the past seventy years, these two men have been the best of friends to John and me. I want you to consider them part of the family." Ann paused to stand near Hank.

"This is our oldest son, Hank," Ann smiled. "We actually named him Henry, but ended up calling him Hank."

"You're the writer, Hank Keel," Henry Highet blurted.

"Yes," Hank acknowledged. "I'm flattered that you've heard of me."

"This is Candyce; Hank's adopted daughter," Ann continued.

"And this is our son JJ," Ann moved on.

"We're very familiar with JJ's political career," Bishop Blane grinned.

"And, his wife, Margaret."

"I believe Mr. Highet was acquainted with my father," Margaret announced. "Do you recall William Woodburne?"

"Yes," Highet beamed, "most certainly. He and I participated in some very profitable business ventures in our youth."

Next, Ann moved toward her only daughter. "Joan is the baby of the family," Ann grinned and this is her husband General Charles Speerman."

"Charles is en route to Capitol City to assume his new post as Chief of Military Operations," JJ disclosed.

"Yes," Charles confirmed. "General Keepstone has decided to retire."

"Congratulations," the two old men offered.

"You met Michael," Ann reminded.

Bill Blane said, "It's difficult for me to look at you and not see your grandfather when he was your age."

"The resemblance is uncanny," Highet added.

Ann ushered her two friends to their chairs. Hank made certain they had glasses of whiskey. When everyone was settled, Ann stood before her family.

"For many, many years," Ann began with a smile; "your father, Henry Highet, Bill Blane, and I have kept silent about our youth. John insisted on the secret being kept until yesterday. Then, he asked me to contact our two old friends so we could tell all of you our story." Ann paused to brush back a tear with the back of her hand. "We have kept this secret among us for more than six decades," Ann explained, "and the remembering of those times and the telling of it will be difficult for us. I can only ask that you listen and try to understand what we experienced." The old woman placed one of her bony hands on Henry Highet's shoulder. "Would you begin, Henry?"

Highet gulped down his drink and handed the glass to Hank Sylvan for a refill. "It was more that seventy years ago," he began. "The country was at war. I had been conscripted into the Engineering Corps right after the war started, but I was soon transferred to an infantry command. I was pretty unsure of myself as a leader of a platoon of light infantry, I can tell you, but the infantry needed officers, and I had a commission.

I learned quickly that I had to follow orders in order to survive and keep my men alive. But, I didn't learn soon enough, and many men died under my command."

"It isn't easy to watch men die," Henry explained, "especially when they're your responsibility. But, they did die, and there was nothing I could do to stop it. The enemy seemed to have better equipment and greater numbers all the time. Their commanders moved them slowly and deliberately with great coordination. All we could do was try to slow them down and hope that our own government could provide new, more effective weapons and better trained replacements. For a time, new equipment did come, and so did the replacements. Still, the enemy pushed and pushed us further into our homeland. Then, the supplies and replacements started slowing down. A mere fourteen months after I had joined my first infantry command just north of Portston, we found ourselves eighty miles south of Riverton, more than a thousand miles from where we had begun."

"We were tired," Henry sighed. "We had ammunition for the small arms, but were running out of mortar rounds. The anti-tank weapons were completely ineffective. Food rations were only trickling through to us, and we had no medicine. We all knew that if the enemy launched a concerted attack, he would destroy us to a man. We began to lose hope. Our own survival didn't matter to us, but the loss of our country and our loved ones was unbearable to us. So, we fought on."

"Suddenly, one fall day, the shooting stopped. We didn't know what was going on at first, then, finally, our commanders told us that the government was discussing surrender terms with the enemy." Henry briefly took a handkerchief to his eyes then returned it to his suit coat pocket. "I cannot tell you how demoralizing it is to realize that you have been defeated in combat. There is nothing more humiliating, or degrading for a man to experience. Hopelessness and despair become deep, bottomless pits. You can think of nothing else. You can't sleep. You can't eat. All you can do is weigh the failure of your efforts and let it crush you. You hope you can die to get away from the indignity, but you don't die. Then, you think of suicide, but your despair has robbed you of the ability to do even that. There is no past to console you with fond memories. The past has been destroyed. There is no future, except slavery and humiliation. There is only the present; and it goes on and on very slowly as though you're roasting over a low fire that refuses to consume you."

Henry visually surveyed the silent faces in the room, before continuing. "Rumors started running through the ranks. Most of them were nonsense, and were easily written off. Other rumors, however, persisted. One of the constant rumors we heard was that a resistance army was forming in the Midland-Highlands. Many men began talking about deserting and making their way to the vast wilderness to the north of us. At first, it was just talk, but the tale seemed to have a life of its own. I feared that my own men would desert and I warned them that the idea of a resistance army was just wishful thinking. I told them it was a fantasy, a myth and they should stay with our unit. At first, they listened to me. But, as the cease-fire went on, men started disappearing from our command and were listed as deserters. Arguments broke out among the men about the rumor of the resistance force forming in the Highlands. In time, those same arguments spread to the officer ranks. More and more men disappeared, and the rumor became enlarged. In the end, I too began listening to the rumors. My curiosity was piqued by the continuing stories about the resistance, and finally, I decided I had to find out for myself."

"Ten days after the cease fire began, I deserted my command." Highet shook his head. "I now became a coward. I waited for darkness; then, I sneaked away like a fox from a hen house. I resigned myself to either finding the resistance, if it existed, or killing myself if it didn't. The resolve seemed to be enough to get me moving northward. I slept during the day, and traveled at night. I was fixed on one thought; find the Resistance."

Highet choked down a lump in his throat and his bright, blue eyes glistened with tears. "This is harder than I thought it would be, Ann. I thought I had forgotten the pain. Now, it's all coming back. I remember the loneliness and the despair. I don't think I can do this."

Ann leapt to her feet and quickly embraced her old friend; pulling his head against her bosom. "The pain will end when you finish," she said. "We have carried this sorrow alone long enough. The time has come for us to let go of it."

As Henry Highet regained his composure, Ann loosened her embrace. Henry seemed to strengthen from Ann's loving comfort, and he continued his tale.

"I wandered for nearly a week," Highet said, "then, just before dawn one morning, I came to within half of a mile of a highway which ran east and west. Enemy vehicles moved in both directions along the roadway. A hundred yards north of the highway was the wilderness, but I knew I couldn't cross in the daylight, so I began looking for a place to hide until dark. I spotted an old barn about a quarter of a mile to the west, and decided that I would make my way to it and stay there until dark. I approached the building slowly, from the south, to keep me out of view of the enemy troops traveling on the highway. I found a door slightly ajar and slipped into the barn."

"Before my eyes could adjust to the darkness inside the barn, I was knocked to the ground and men fell on top of me. 'He's an officer!' One of them shouted and at that moment I relaxed. They pulled me to my feet and I began to knock the dirt from my clothing. I could see in the dim light after a moment, and I was shocked to see so many men crowded into the small building. It struck me how very young their faces were; young and wide-eyed with uncertainty. Then, an old veteran Sergeant approached and introduced himself with a salute. His name was Stone. The Sergeant asked his men to return their posts and to keep watch while he spoke to me privately outside…"

Michael listened intently while Highet went on. To Michael, it seemed as if he was actually standing and watching the old man's story unfold.

"What's your name, Captain?" Sergeant Stone asked with a strong, soft voice.

"Highet."

"When did y' desert?"

"About a week ago," the Captain replied. "How about you and your men?"

"Ten days ago," Stone said.

"How many men do you have?"

"Fifty-three counting me," Stone said.

"Where are you headed?"

Stone sighed as he thrust a thumb over his shoulder pointing toward the wilderness to the north. "Midlands," he said. "Rumor is there's a resistance army forming there."

Captain Highet nodded. "That's what I've heard."

"You believe it?" Stone pressed.

"I don't know. What about you?"

"My men believe it," Stone said. "What I believe, don't matter."

The Captain nodded that he understood.

"We need an officer," Stone blurted.

"Not me," Highet declined.

"My troops are pretty young," Stone continued. "Their morale would be a lot better if they had an officer leading them."

"Not me. I got enough men killed."

"You don't understand, sir," Stone said, as he pushed the muzzle of his pistol into Highet" ribs. "I'm not asking you. I'm telling you my men need an officer and you're it. It's either that, or I kill you right now."

Captain Highet stared into Stone's cold face. He had no doubt that Stone was sincere about his threat. "These men must mean a lot to you," he paused. "All right, I'll take command."

Stone slipped his pistol back into its holster. "I'll tell the men, sir. They'll be pleased."

"Very well," the Captain said. "By the way, Sergeant Stone," Captain Highet grinned, "if you ever pull a gun on me again, I'll shove it up your ass."

Stone allowed a small smile to appear on his blank face. "Yes sir!" He said in a very military manner. "Yes sir, I believe you would." The Sergeant saluted, turned and headed toward the barn. "Captain Highet has taken over the command," Stone announced. The men cheered.

Chapter 11

The family held their gaze on the old man while he took a sip of his drink. "I wasn't happy about commanding this band of deserters. But, when I saw the confidence they had in their faces, there was no way I could refuse. I ordered an inventory of weapons, ammunition and rations. We had plenty of weapons and explosives, but food was in very short supply. After that, I ordered sentries to monitor the enemy traffic on the road. I wanted to make sure we could leave the barn, make our way over the open fields, cross the road, and travel through another open field before reaching the tree line. In all we estimated the open ground to be about twelve hundred yards."

"The sentries watched enemy traffic on the road all day. Finally, that night, we tallied the results. The longest period of time between enemy vehicles was five minutes. The average time between vehicular traffic was three minutes. Sergeant Stone and I quickly agreed that we would need at least fifteen minutes to move everyone safely into the wilderness. The men were tired, malnourished, and laden with weapons and ammunition. To make matters worse, a full moon was expected to rise not long after sunset. We decided to wait until moon set before attempting to cross into the forest. I gave orders to post sentries and everyone else to get as much sleep as possible."

"In the middle of the night, one of the sentries woke me. Sergeant Stone and I both went outside with the sentry and couldn't believe our eyes. It was like God had heard our prayers. A thick, heavy mist was forming on the forest and slowly spilling toward the road. Under the full moon, the fog looked like a living cloud rising, billowing and smothering everything in its path."

Again Michael felt himself drawn into the old man's tale, and again, he was there with the younger version of the speaker. Like his grandmother, he too saw what the old man held in his memory...

"Have you ever seen anything like that?" Sergeant Stone asked in obvious awe.

"No," was all Captain Highet could say.

"I've heard legends about the Highland mist," Stone said. "Now, I think I'm seeing it."

"I don't know much about legends," Captain Highet said, "but I sure do intend to take advantage of it. Let's form up the men and use the mist to cover our movements through this open terrain."

"Yes sir," Stone said as he quickly turned and rushed toward the barn.

A short time later, the blurry-eyed men gaped at the moonlight glowing through the mist before them. It had risen from the forest and slowly flowed over the road and reached out to the men near the barn. The Captain had the men form four ranks of thirteen men each and with Sergeant Stone beside him, led the deserters into the glowing, thick fog. It was a strange, almost religious experience for the men. The bright moonlight defused evenly through the mist to allow the men to walk easily across the stubble of the fields. Just a few minutes after they had begun their journey, they came to the hard surface of the road. Within seconds, they shuffled across the highway, and began making their way up the gradual slope into the forest. When they had ascended the second ridge line, Captain Highet stopped the march. He posted sentries and ordered his men to rest until the dawn.

The next morning, the Captain awoke early. He tried to ignore the eerie light that found its way through the thick mist as he sought out his Sergeant. It didn't take more than a minute, and Highet found his veteran non-com sitting and staring at the mist which seemed to be trapped by the nearly naked branches of the trees. Stone smiled at him.

"Have you ever seen anything like it?" Stone asked cheerfully.

"Like what?" Captain Highet came back.

"The mist," Stone said. "Aren't you familiar with the legends?"

The Captain sat beside his Sergeant. "I'm an engineer, Sergeant. I work with facts, not myths and legends."

"That's too bad," Stone smiled. "What do the facts tell you?"

"They tell me we're nearly out of food," Highet said softly. "We need to find some game."

"We also need to locate the Resistance," Stone added.

"If they exist," Highet countered.

"Oh, they exist all right," Stone hummed softly.

Highet shot an incredulous stare at Sergeant Stone. "Yesterday, you were just as skeptical about the existence of a Resistance as I was. What caused you to change your mind; the mist?"

Stone inhaled deeply. "Maybe it's the look of hope in the faces of these young men. When they saw you take over command, their hope was rekindled. Maybe I'm suffering from combat fatigue. Maybe I believe in fairies. I don't know exactly what it is. All I can tell you is that I had no hope yesterday. Today, I do."

Highet was touched by Stone's words and he looked deep into the soldier's eyes. "Can you generate enough hope for me too?" Highet asked.

"You're goddamn right I can," Stone smiled.

Highet sighed. "Which way do we go; north?"

"North," Stone confirmed.

The Captain pulled his compass from his pocket. He frowned as he watched the needle twitch sporadically. "There must be something wrong with my compass," Highet concluded.

Sergeant Stone glanced at the malfunctioning device in the palm of the Captain's hand, and then reached for his own. He opened the case and glanced down at the instrument. A second later he held his compass out to Captain Highet. "Mine is doing the same thing," Stone said. "I have heard that a compass wouldn't work in the Midlands, but I didn't believe it."

"It looks as though we'll have to believe it now," Highet sighed. "With this fog above us we won't be able to use the sun to navigate by either."

The old soldier looked around. "I'd suggest using the moss on the trees, but there are places in here where the sun never has shined."

Captain Highet removed his pack from his back, placed it on the ground and removed a map. He glanced at the map for just an instant then he tossed it to Sergeant Stone. "That gray blob on the map is the Midlands-Highlands Wilderness. Can you believe that a military map would not have the contour or terrain features marked on it?"

Sergeant Stone studied the map for several moments; then, he folded it up and handed it back to his commander. Finally, Stone pointed at the distance. "That's north," he declared softly.

"I think you're right," Highet grinned. "Let's get the men moving."

Slowly the small band of deserters made their way through the forest. After four hours of walking, mostly up hill, Captain Highet called a halt to rest near a small brook that tumbled noisily across the line of their march. The men quickly descended on the creek and pronounced the water potable. The Captain and his senior NCO also approached the flowing waters to fill their own canteens, but one of their men called out to them to come see something he had found. Highet and Stone returned their empty canteens to their carriers and walked to the excited, young soldier.

"Look at this, sir," the young man pointed down at a small strip of mud.

The Captain and Sergeant instantly saw the footprint and knew that it had not been placed there by one of their heavy-booted troops. Before Highet could give the order, Stone was already calling for security to be posted on all sides. The well-trained men quickly sprung into action. The sentries scurried into position while the remainder took up defensive postures on their stomachs. All eyes searched the woods as far as they could see as a tense silence settled on the scene.

After several minutes, Captain Highet called for all squad leaders to meet. When they were all present, he and Sergeant Stone spelled out the marching orders they would use to navigate the forest. They would move in combat formation from here on. They would stay ready for action to be able to respond quickly to the slightest sign of danger. Then, the order was given, and the small fighting force began its methodical movement northward. Captain Highet ordered his veteran Sergeant to stay by his side during the march.

"It isn't wise for both of us to be together," Stone protested.

"I know," Highet replied, "but I need to know what you think about that footprint. What kind of boot leaves such a smooth imprint on soft soil?"

"Whoever planted their foot there wasn't wearing boots," Stone said. "It almost appeared that they were in their stocking feet."

"I thought so too, for a minute," Highet agreed. "But why would a man walk about in the woods in his stocking feet?"

Stone considered Highet' question for a moment, then, the answer came to him in a flash. "Listen!" He said.

Highet shot a curious look at his sergeant.

"Listen to the men walking through the leaves," Stone continued.

The sound of the leaves loudly crunching under the infantrymen's boots roared in his ears. "I hear it," Highet said with resignation. It was now apparent that the man that left the footprint in the mud was skilled in stealth and could easily find Highet and his men simply by listening to them walk through the forest. He looked up at the trees. The tops of the trees disappeared into the mist. "I'll take the forward position," Highet said to Stone, "you take the rear."

Captain Highet strode quickly forward to catch up with the leading element of his formation. He had the feeling he was being watched. But he didn't know who was watching him and his men, or why?

The feeling of being under surveillance weighed on Highet and his eyes constantly swept left and right looking for a hint of movement. But as the day wore on he saw nothing.

That night, Highet lay awake staring into the darkness. He feared that he had led his men into certain death. They would either starve, or whoever was stalking them would eventually attack and kill them. He struggled to come up with an alternative plan, but nothing he thought of seemed to have any value. They were trapped. They would continue this fruitless search for a non-existent resistance army until they all died. That was it. Then, the footfall of an approaching soldier caught the officer's attention. It was Sergeant Stone.

"You should be asleep, Captain," Stone said.

"Yes, I know. What about you?"

"Ever since we found that footprint, I feel as though someone is watching me," Stone confessed. "I'm starting to see things."

"Seeing things?" Highet questioned. "Like what?"

"Bushes moving from tree to tree; a clump of leaves rolling over a ridge line; things like that," Stone explained. "I just get a glimpse of movement out of the corner of my eye; nothing real positive."

"I thought I was hallucinating. Thanks for telling me." Highet said. "How many do you think there are?"

"I'm not sure," Stone admitted. "It could be only two or three. It could be more."

"Well, they aren't enemy troops, or they would have opened fire on us," Highet conjectured.

"Maybe," Stone said. "But, if they're only a small force, they may be waiting for more help to arrive. One thing for sure, if they were friendly they would have introduced themselves by now."

"I'm afraid you're right about that," Highet confirmed. "They've had all day to look us over and figure out who we are."

"Try to get some rest, Captain," Stone suggested softly.

"You too!" Highet countered.

"Oh, by the way," Stone added, "we ran out of rations this morning. We'll have to forage for food as we go."

"Right," Highet acknowledged, then, he heard Stone walk away.

It was still dark when the men were awakened the next morning. Nothing was said about the lack of rations, but Highet could hear empty stomachs growling. The march was organized and when it was barely light enough to see the trees, the march was resumed. The men walked slowly, warily, though the trees and progress was very slow. The terrain seemed to rise and fall more sharply than it had the day before and the ever-present mist clung to the tree tops blotting out the sky. Still, the forest brightened under the diffused light and at times it even appeared that the sun might penetrate the fog but it never did.

At mid-morning, as the infantry group was making their way up the side of a hill, a single shot rang out and echoed through the forest. Instantly, the troops fell into the leaves and waited. Highet moved quickly up the hill to his point men some fifty yards ahead of the main body.

"That shot wasn't directed at us," one trooper announced to Highet.

"No," Highet agreed, "but it wasn't far away. Any idea which direction that shot came from?"

"I think it came from just the other side of the hill, sir," the other scout declared.

The Captain instructed one man to go back to Sergeant Stone and tell him to move the men to an on-line position just below the crest of the ridge. Then, he turned to the second man. "You come with me," he smiled.

Highet began making his way up the hill in a crouched position. The man following him walked the same way. As they approached the ridge, Highet began crawling slowly until the other side of the hill came slowly into view. The hill gently fell away from him to display the open woods.

121

About a hundred yards away, a small creek ran from left to right across his line of sight. He placed his field glasses to his eyes and scanned further. Just fifty yards beyond the creek, the image of a man removing the entrails from a deer popped into Highet lenses. The hunter seemed completely unaware of Highet's presence and busied himself with the dead animal. Highet was amazed at the hunter's camouflage clothing. Had he not been moving, Highet realized that he would not have seen him at all. The coloring of the deer slayer's clothing was nearly the same as the leaves on the ground. Then, Highet noticed the man's rifle propped against a nearby tree. He had never seen a rifle with such a long, thick barrel or such an elaborate telescopic sight. Highet put down his field glasses and turned to his scout. "Tell Sergeant Stone to move up to the ridge. I'm going to go talk to that hunter. If anything happens to me, Stone is in charge. Get going."

Highet watched his scout scurry down the hill; then, he stood up and began walking the other way toward the hunter. He walked at a normal pace, carrying his rifle in his right hand with his finger on the trigger and the barrel resting on his shoulder. He kept his eyes moving from side to side as he approached the busy hunter. Highet crossed the creek before the hunter looked up at him. To Highet's surprise, the man kept on working on the deer, so the Captain kept walking until he was only ten paces away.

"You have a cook in your outfit?" The hunter asked with a smile as he wiped a bloody knife on the leaves before placing it in its sheath.

"Outfit?" Highet feigned. "I'm alone."

"Don't bullshit me, Highet," the hunter beamed.

"How do you know my name?"

The hunter pointed toward the nametag above the Captain's uniform pocket.

Highet felt himself blush with embarrassment.

"The venison is for you and your men," the hunter said.

"We have plenty of rations," Highet countered.

"Sure you do," the hunter chuckled. "That's why all your men have belts that are six inches too long. Give me a break Highet! You can hear their stomachs growling from here."

Highet scrutinized the hunter. This time he noticed the animal hide boots the hunter was wearing.

"Are you the one who's been stalking us the last couple of days?" Highet asked.

"Wasn't really stalking you," the hunter denied. "I just wanted to know who was moving into my forest."

Highet paused as he looked into the hunter's gray eyes. "I won't bring my men out into the open until you do the same," Highet said.

Now the hunter paused as he studied Captain Highet. "Fair enough," the hunter said. Then, he gave out a whistle that strongly resembled the cry of one of the local birds. Highet slung his rifle over his left shoulder and held his right hand aloft moving it in a circle. He and the hunter kept their eyes locked on one another while they heard the leaves being trampled around them. Within a few moments three other men appeared behind the hunter. They too were attired in the same clothing as the hunter. All three carried the long, telescopic rifles over their shoulders and a shorter automatic weapon in their hands.

"We've come here looking for the resistance army that we heard was being formed here," Highet said. "Are you part of the resistance?"

"We're, sort of, forest rangers," the hunter said. "We try to keep people from getting lost and stuff."

Sergeant Stone arrived at his Captain's side. "You're carrying a lot of firepower for forest rangers," Stone observed.

"You never know what you're going to run into in the forest these days," the hunter smiled.

"Do you guys have names?" Highet asked.

"Yeah, let me introduce you to my fellow rangers," the hunter said. "The big guy with the beard is 'Blackie'. The little wiry fellow we call 'Spider'. And, the tall one here is 'Hornet'. We've left some equipment nearby for you. Blackie will show you and your sergeant where it is. I'd like you to stay here until we can get back to you sometime tomorrow. Is that all right?"

Highet nodded. "You forgot to give us your name."

"Oh, they call me 'Walker'," the deer killer grinned.

The family waited while the old man telling the tale broke down and cried. It took a stiff drink and the comfort of Ann and the old bishop to quiet him. After a time, Henry Highet was able to continue.

"That was the first time I met your father," Highet rasped, "although it would be several years before I found out his real name. Even after that, I couldn't help but call him 'Walker'."

"The one they called 'Blackie' showed Sergeant Stone, and me, the 'equipment' Walker had mentioned. It was three enemy machine guns. It became obvious by the way the guns were situated that our small band would have been shot to pieces had we barged over that ridge and opened fire."

"Was grandpa, and the other men you met that day, part of the resistance?" Michael asked.

"From that very first day," Highet replied, "we all believed that those four men were organizers of the resistance. During the winter that followed, we saw them in action against the enemy. They were all killing machines. No standard military training was sufficient for survival against them. They in turn taught us their tactics and techniques and we became nearly as proficient at warfare as they."

"Did the surrender occur just after you entered the wilderness," Charles Speerman asked.

"Yes," Highet replied. "Blackie told Sergeant Stone that the country had surrendered the very next day after we first crossed the highway and entered the forest. Sergeant Stone went on and on about the Highlands mist. He said he should have known when the mist formed over the Midlands that the end had come and a new beginning was at hand."

"Mister Highet," Charles Speerman began…

"Henry," the old man corrected.

"Henry," Charles continued, "I'm most curious about your assumption that dad and his comrades were the organizers of the resistance. There is no evidence in military annals of anything but a grass roots uprising after the surrender, but you give me the impression that dad's group was somehow put in place deliberately."

Henry paused briefly. "I think they were trained by the government and put in place long before the surrender," Henry concluded. "What do you think, Bill?"

The old priest nodded. "There's no doubt in my mind," the bishop said.

"Ann?" Henry inquired.

The Last Day of the Last Spring

She too, nodded her agreement. "They knew too much. They were too professional. We were full of hatred. They were calculating, and seemed to be free of the emotion the rest of us carried."

Michael watched the faces of the others in the room. Charles frowned with consternation. JJ, Margaret, and Joan appeared stunned, almost in shock. And, Candyce sat there silently with tears streaming down her fair face. Hank seemed calm, as if he really wasn't surprised at all.

Aware of the growing stress on her family, Ann asked Bishop Blane to continue with his own story. The big man smiled as he rested his huge arms on his girth.

"I was a newly ordained priest," Bishop Blane began. "I was assigned to St. Michael the Archangel parish in a small town called Riverview just before the war began. Riverview is gone now, but it was a beautiful place nestled on the banks of the Old River in the heart of the Midlands. There were only a few thousand people living there at the outset of the war, but the population swelled as families fled the approaching invasion forces. By the time of the surrender, most of the young people had fled into the countryside with dreams of becoming partisans. That left the town with mostly old people, children and occupation troops."

"The enemy had learned of the rumors about the resistance force being formed in the Highlands and they flooded into Riverview by the hundreds since it was accessible by river and the northern most point they could access and re-supply. Here they believed they could easily launch forays into the Midlands and easily dispose of the fledgling resistance. All winter long, I watched the enemy send troops into the wilderness. It was easy to guess what the occupation force was up to, since our church was on the eastern outskirts of the town and at the edge of the forest. The occupation troops had to pass by us most of the time."

"Sometimes they would send three or four companies of troops into the forest. Other times they would send only groups of thirty or forty. The large units would usually return seven to ten days later without seeing any resistance fighters. The smaller groups never returned at all."

"Then the resistance was operational immediately after the surrender," Charles concluded.

"Yes," Bishop Blane answered with his deep melodious voice. "At the time, I felt the resistance fighters were stupid. I made up my mind that if I came in contact with them, I would tell them so. Then, just

125

before Christmas, something happened that changed my thinking and me forever. I was preparing for the daily 8 o'clock mass. A young cat I had adopted kept jumping in my lap while I tried to prepare my sermon. I had a deep affection for that silly, little cat…"

Chapter 12

"You have to get down now," the young priest said as he swept up the cat with his powerful hand and gently placed the animal on the floor. The tabby whined his discontent then rubbed himself on the priest's leg, causing the large, muscular man to chuckle. "I'm just about finished," he smiled as he spoke to the animal.

A few minutes later the priest had finished his sermon and pushed his chair back from the desk. Instantly, the cat pounced into his lap. The priest laughed, as he cradled the cat in his arms while he left the rectory and started for the church. When he reached the side door of the church, he affectionately petted the cat and set it on the ground. "It's very warm for this time of year," he said to the cat. "So, I think it would be best for you to play outside."

The cat mewed as if it understood, and bounded away after an invisible prey. The priest laughed at his pet's antics, then opened the door and entered the church. He peeked at the early arrivals in the front pews; then, he glanced at his watch and decided he had better hurry. He quickly donned his vestments, took one more look at his sermon, and proceeded to the altar. He would have to celebrate mass alone today, none, of the young men in the town had volunteered to serve for him. He smiled at his faithful as he approached the altar to begin mass. But, the sudden opening of the door at the rear of the church caused him to freeze in his tracks. Two occupation soldiers, their rifles held at the ready, rapidly strode down the center aisle and approached the surprised priest. Two other soldiers, each with an automatic rifle took up positions at each corner of the back of the church. Finally, an officer, with his pistol drawn, came forward and ordered everyone out of the building. The frightened old people and children huddled together as they withdrew from the building. The officer made them line up in ranks facing an open truck with a machine gun mounted just behind the cab. Another young soldier manned the horrible weapon and pointed it at the already frightened worshippers. The two sentries, with automatic rifles, who had been at the rear of the church, now took up new positions at a 45-degree angle at each corner of the ranks of civilians. One soldier held the priest on the front porch, while another stood beside the officer.

"What is this all about…" Father Blane blurted, but the butt of the soldier's rifle driving into his mid-section stopped his complaint and left him gasping for air. He doubled over from the blow and struggled to regain his breathing.

"You people are hiding and aiding the cutthroats hiding in the forest," the officer shouted at the old people and children. The officer strode arrogantly along the front rank brandishing his pistol. "Today, your resistance to occupation will end. You will tell us where this vermin is hiding, or you will be punished."

Suddenly, a young girl of about ten years of age bolted from the ranks and started to run. To his utter horror, Father Blane saw the man behind the machine gun in the back of the truck swivel the weapon toward the running girl. Before Blane could call out, the soldier fired a burst of bullets into the girl. The child was tossed, twisted in mid-air then slammed onto the pavement. As rage filled Blane's heart, he was bewildered as he saw the machine gunner's helmet fly straight up into the air. He hadn't heard the shot that struck the gunner. Pandemonium reigned. People screamed and began running every-which-way. There was a second shot, and the soldier standing near the officer fell to the ground. The two other soldiers with the automatic rifles began firing short bursts into the woods just across the road as they ran toward the truck for cover. The soldier with Blane also swung his weapon toward the woods, but the priest's powerful hands closed tightly on his neck. The officer darted to the truck as well, but a bullet struck him as he climbed the sideboards. The officer's right foot slipped through the wooden slats and he hung upside down on the side of the truck. Blane didn't see the other two soldiers die. He was too intent on the wriggling man in his grasp, and fell down on top of him without losing his grip. After some time, Blane thought her heard someone talking to him.

"You can let go now," a voice said to the priest as a hand touched his shoulder.

The Last Day of the Last Spring

Blane's arms trembled from the force he was exerting. Then, he realized that the man in his hands was dead. So strong had been the priest's lock on his enemy that his hands refused to obey.

"Relax," the voice said. "Let go. We have to get out of here."

Finally, Father Blane was able to pull his hands away, but the reality of his actions was overwhelming. His hands trembled.

"I killed him," he said, for the first time looking at the man who had been talking to him. The man was dressed in camouflage colors, exactly like the forest. He held a long rifle with a telescopic sight mounted on it.

"Yes, you did," the man said calmly. "We can't stay here. We have to go."

"Wait," Blane said, "I can't leave without my cat."

"Your cat will be fine here. We can't take the time to find him now," the man explained.

"Yes, you're right," Blane said as he got up from his knees.

"Get in the truck," the man with the long rifle said.

Blane obeyed, and got in on the passenger side. The other man got behind the wheel and the truck lunged forward, straight into the woods. They drove for about twenty minutes, before the driver stopped the vehicle.

"Are you all right?" The rifleman asked.

"They killed Anna," Blane said.

"Was that the name of the little girl?" the man asked.

"Yes," the priest answered. "Anna would come to visit me in the afternoon and we would play with my cat," Blane explained. "She was a good girl," he was able to say before he broke down and wept.

The fighter from the forest comforted the priest until he was able to gain his composure. "What kind of cat did you have?" He asked.

"It was just a little tabby," Blane said. "I really loved it though. He was my companion."

"I know some people who could use a priest," the driver said.

Blane considered the man's statement, then, he looked at his hands. "I can't pray to a god that will allow innocent children to die," Blane said. "I have killed a man. Now, I must follow that path. Can you teach me how to fight; how to use weapons?"

"Sure, if that's what you really want," the man replied.

Blane stepped out of the truck, hastily removed his vestments, and tossed them into the brush. He never looked back as he got back into the truck. "Teach me all you can," he said.

The other man responded by putting the truck into gear and driving off through the trees. A short time later, he stopped the vehicle again. "Some of my friends are waiting here for me," the man driving explained before getting out of the truck.

Blane also got out of the vehicle on the other side. He saw three other men approaching the vehicle. They too were dressed like the man who had killed the soldiers at the church.

"This is Spider," the rifleman introduced the first man to approach. "This is Blackie, and Hornet."

Blane shook each man's hand as they came near. "I'm pleased to be with you," he said.

"This is my new friend from Riverview," the other man said. "I call him Tabby."

Blane smiled at his new friend. "I like that name," he grinned.

"Tabby!" Blackie cried in disbelief. "Look at the size of this guy. He's too big for a name like Tabby."

"He's quick as cat," the other man countered.

"All right," Blackie laughed. "Tabby it is."

"Wait," Tabby said to the man who had taken him from the church. "You didn't tell me your name."

"Walker," the man replied with a smile.

The old priest sighed audibly. "I lost my faith in God that day," he admitted. "I had never experienced hatred before, and it consumed me. For many months, all I wanted to do was kill the enemy soldiers who had invaded our land. And, I did just that for nearly five years."

Bishop Blane put a hand on Highet's shoulder. "The next day, I met the Hawk."

"Spider gave me that name," Highet said. "When I asked him if he called me 'Hawk' because of my keen eyesight, he said no. He said that my nose was shaped more like a hawk's beak than a nose."

Blane and Ann chuckled at Highet's disclosure. The rest of the family was uncomfortable with the levity of the moment, except for Michael. He was curious.

"Did the Highland Mist last through the winter?" Michael asked.

"It lasted longer than that," Highet replied. "The mist was there for years. Sometimes it would rise to the very height of the trees. Other times it would settle onto the ground, but it was always there."

"When it clung close to the ground, it was nearly impossible to see, except for a few feet," Blane explained. "It affected the weather in the Midlands too. Those were very mild winters in the Midlands, while everywhere else, people suffered in very frigid conditions." The bishop crossed himself. "It was the strangest phenomena I have ever experienced. It was more than just a mist. I believe now, that it was the breath of God; warming us, protecting us."

The complete sincerity in Blane's voice added a religious mystique to the emotions of the family, and everyone weighed the priest's words in silence for a moment.

Then, General Speerman, his eyebrows knitted together in curiosity, finally spoke.

"How many men did you have after Father Blane joined you?" Charles asked.

"Fifty-five," Highet answered.

"But you had been engaging the enemy for nearly two months, how were you able to do that with such a small force; how did you get the supplies; the ammunition?" Charles continued.

Highet raised his eyebrows. "When Walker told me we were going into action, I asked the same question," Highet said.

"Walker told me, that it was simple. The enemy would bring equipment and supplies to us. I told him that I thought he was crazy. He laughed; then, he told me he would prove it to me. The next day we set up an ambush on the highway we crossed to enter the Midlands. We waited for a small convoy to come by. Finally, about six trucks were moving slowly along the road because of the fog. When we opened fire, I couldn't believe it. The soldiers stopped the trucks and abandoned them. We sent a few men after the soldiers to keep them running away, while others got into the vehicles and drove them into the wilderness. We left two trucks, which had been carrying troops, on the highway. We set them afire. Two of the other trucks were loaded with ammunition and weapons. There were two, three-inch mortars, and four, heavy machine guns. The other two trucks we took were filled with rations."

Highet chuckled. "I never questioned Walker again after that first action. By Christmas, we had enough equipment to engage larger convoys. We began to plan more actions against enemy troop movements in the spring."

"Why do you think you were able to be so successful?" Charles asked.

"Hornet told us that we would succeed," Highet responded, "because the enemy thought the war was over and they had already won. He said that 'victory' would keep them stupid for a long time, and by the time they figured out that there was an organized resistance, it would be too late for them to be able to stop it. He was right. That's exactly what happened."

"It didn't seem quite that certain that first spring," Blane interjected.

"No," Highet hissed, "it sure didn't. Why don't you take over, Ann?"

"Yes, this is where I enter the story anyway," Ann beamed. She glanced at each of her family. "I was raised in Riverton," she started. "Shortly before the end of the war, my parents sent me to Riverview to live with my grandparents. They were my father's parents. I liked being in Riverview. I felt safe there. It was sad though. I never saw my parents again after I left them in Riverton. When the war ended with our surrender, I was in shock. I couldn't believe it. Then, when the first occupation troops arrived in Riverview, I had to accept it. I was terrified of the soldiers. They were very loud and would get drunk frequently. So, I stayed close to my grandparents' small cottage, just north of the town."

"At first," Ann continued, "there were only two hundred soldiers in Riverview. By that Christmas, after the surrender, there were close to a thousand occupation troops in the town. With the exception of the incident at St. Michael the Archangel Church, there was never a shot heard in Riverview. There were rumors of course, and the increase in occupation troops seemed to verify the rumors of a resistance movement operating out of the Highlands. The soldiers changed too. At first, the enemy soldiers were veteran combat troops. After Christmas, however, most of the older men had been moved out and replaced by younger, Special Police units."

"As spring drew near, we started seeing casualties among the new Special Police. It seemed they were no match for the clandestine resistance fighters and could easily be drawn into ambush. They became frustrated and took out their frustration on the town's people. By the first of May, no one ventured into town unless absolutely necessary to obtain the small rations the soldiers gave out. My grandparents insisted that I not go into town for any reason, and I obeyed. Finally, they too felt that staying in Riverview was too dangerous, and decided we would all be better off hiding in the Highlands to the north. On May 2nd, my sixteenth birthday, we started toward the wilderness…"

The old couple and their granddaughter strode as quickly as they could from their farmhouse to the dirt road that disappeared into the forest. At first, it seemed they would be able to walk away from the area without being noticed, but when they reached the end of their property, they stopped in their tracks. Three Special Policemen leered at them suspiciously as they quickly encircled the family. The girl, Ann, quickly recognized the smell of alcohol on the breath of the young soldiers.

"Where are you going?" One of the men shouted at the old man. "You're going to join the resistance, aren't you?" He shouted angrily.

"No," the old man replied with a trembling voice.

The soldier started beating the old man with a pistol. "Don't lie to me you old bastard!" The soldier screamed as he forced the old man onto his knees and shoved the barrel of his pistol into his mouth.

The old woman rushed to the defense of her husband, but she was met with a rifle butt that crushed the side of her skull. As Ann fell to the ground to help her grandmother, she heard a "pop". She looked up in time to see her grandfather slowly fall onto his side with a hole in his head. She screamed at the horror she had seen. The young men looked at her for a second, then, they began to laugh. The one who had shot her grandfather pointed his pistol at her grandmother as he grinned at her. When the soldier holstered his weapon, Ann thought her grandmother would be saved, but then, she realized that the blow the old woman had taken had killed her. The other two soldiers placed their rifles on the ground. When Ann realized what was about to happen, it was too late. The two riflemen grabbed her and began tearing at her clothes. She struggled. But, when the third man joined the others she couldn't withstand them. Slowly, deliberately, they ripped her clothes off until she was completely naked. The young men stood around her in a tight triangle, leering and laughing at her for a time. Then, they pounced upon her. One held her from behind with his arms crossed over her breasts, while the other two held her legs apart.

Ann struggled, but to no avail. She went limp. Then she felt the erect penis of one of the men holding her legs. His organ sporadically made contact with her thighs, then, her crotch. She was able to muster a final burst of energy to prevent penetration, but her struggle ended as they all collapsed onto the grass. Ann heard them laugh again. She wanted to kick and flail, but her body wouldn't respond. She filled with hatred as she glared at the young soldier kneeling between her legs. Then, all of the sudden, the left side of the soldier's head exploded and he fell across her right leg. She instinctively began kicking at the corpse to get it off her legs, when she heard the second shot and saw the other man, who had been holding her legs apart, collapse also. Now, she sprung free of the man holding her from behind and pulled herself to her feet. Her legs buckled at first, then, she steadied herself and looked down at the man who was still on his knees. To her surprise he began to cry. An instant later, Ann heard someone walk up behind her. She didn't turn at first as she tried to understand why the enemy soldier was crying.

"Are you all right?" A voice asked Ann.

Without taking her eyes off the weeping soldier, Ann said, "Give me a gun."

A second later, a camouflage-gloved hand appeared in front of her with a revolver. Ann grasped the weapon in her hands.

"Do you know how to use it?" The voice asked.

Ann cocked the hammer back on the weapon. "Yes," she said softly as she pointed the handgun at the crying soldier. She looked at him for a moment. The terrified soldier urinated in his pants just before the girl fired a single shot pointblank into his face. Ann stood over the dead man for a moment; then, she turned toward the voice and handed him his pistol.

The man was donned in forest greens and browns. Even his face was colored the same. He pushed the revolver into his belt then began pulling the clothes off one of the dead men. "Put these on," he said

Ann complied with the forest-man's order. She pulled up the trousers, but had to tie the belt around her to keep them up. She buttoned the shirt she was given, and then she paid her last respects to her grandparents.

"I'll find the resistance," she told them. "I will kill as many of them as I can."

Her rescuer handed her a pair of boots. "These will have to do for now," he said.

Ann sat on the ground and laced the oversized boots as tightly as she could. Occasionally she would look up at the man that had come to her aid. He was tall and carried a long, telescopic-rifle in his hands. Hung over his shoulders was a heavy pack and an automatic rifle. When her boots were finished, she got to her feet. "My name is…"

"Babe!" The man said. "We don't use our real names. I'll call you Babe, for Babe in the woods."

"I'm not a child," Babe said.

"No," the warrior said. "You're a woman. I just like the name Babe."

Babe stared at the camouflage-clad warrior for a moment. Then, without warning, her emotions overflowed. "Thanks," she said. "You saved my life."

"Glad I happened to be here," the man said as he placed an arm around the girl to comfort her.

Babe struggled to regain her composure. "Are you a partisan?"

"We're trying to be partisans," he smiled.

"I don't even know your name," Babe said with a crack in her voice.

"Call me Walker," the man said.

Joan rushed toward her mother and flung her arms about her. "Oh, mom! I had no idea that you went through such a terrible time."

Ann accepted Joan's comfort with a smile, but as she looked at the stunned faces of her family, her smile faded. "Those were very difficult days," Ann understated. "Somehow we got through it all."

"We got through it because we had to," Henry Highet stated.

"Yes, Henry you're right," Bishop Blane agreed. "We had to survive or die, and we chose to survive."

Ann watched as JJ shifted his weight nervously on his chair. "Do you have a question, JJ?"

JJ blushed at his inability to hide his curiosity. "In truth I have many questions," he said sheepishly, "but I don't believe this is the time to ask them."

"There may not be another time," Ann counseled her son.

The old woman's encouragement allowed JJ to continue. "After you joined the others, how many fighters were there."

"Fifty-nine," Ann answered, "Hawk and his fifty-three men, plus Walker, Blackie, Spider, Hornet, and me."

"You mean that you had suffered no casualties through the winter?" JJ gasped. "I find that amazing."

"We fought on our terms," Highet explained. "If we could not overpower the enemy, we let him walk by. As the larger units entered deeper into the forest, we would set up traps and snares to injure them. We made certain they never saw us. Sometimes we would snipe at them. Usually after a few days of frustration, the larger forces would turn back to Riverview. That is when we really started to hit them. We found we could quickly conceal explosives in their line of travel. Slowly their casualties mounted, until finally, their fighting force was greatly reduced because they had to carry and care for their wounded. When they became vulnerable, we finished them off."

"You make it sound very simple," General Speerman observed.

"It was easier than you think," Ann replied. "They were especially vulnerable at night. They would post sentries, and we would sneak up on them and slit their throats. After a while, those assigned sentry duty realized they had been given a death sentence."

"But there was only sixty of you," JJ said.

"Yes," Blane echoed, "only sixty. But each of us had a job and each of us carried it out. By that first summer, we would routinely engage units of 200 men."

"But where was the rest of the army?" JJ asked with a hint of impatience.

"Throughout the winter and that first spring, we thought we were the resistance army," Highet grinned.

"I'm still not sure how you were able to keep yourselves supplied," Charles Speerman said.

"Initially, Walker and the others brought us everything," Highet explained. "They had uniforms, rations, ammunition, telephone equipment, you name it. It was only toward the end of the war that we found out where it had come from. After the initial supply, we learned to capture or steal what we needed from the occupation forces."

"How is it you were so successful against the much larger numbers of enemy troops?" Charles posed.

"They were young and inexperienced," Highet answered. "The veteran forces were all put on leave, or even sent back to their homeland and discharged. The replacements were easy prey."

"But didn't their commanders report their casualties and losses?" Charles pressed.

"They lied about their early casualties," Blane interjected. "I didn't realize that fact until just now, but I don't believe they thought the resistance was serious at first. Also, they probably didn't want the people in the homeland to be alarmed about a 'few pockets' of resistance. I think that's what I remember them reporting that first year after the surrender."

"Yes," Charles said, "I think you are right about that. I'm sure that they didn't want to stir up any political unrest at home by overstating the problem of occupation to their countrymen."

"At least not at first," Blane said. "In time though, they had to increase the numbers of the occupation force. Apparently, though, they kept the build-up a secret. There is no reliable historical information to prove it though." Blane smiled at the General.

Ann continued. "We didn't realize just how large the resistance was until near the end of that first summer. I'll never forget the morning Walker called us all together with Hornet, Blackie and Spider…"

Chapter 13

Walker smiled as Hawk, Tabby, and Babe sat on the ground with him and his comrades. Blackie and Spider welcomed the trio with warm handshakes. Hornet just sat there, demonstrating his usual disinterest in meetings.

"You three have been asking a lot of questions," Walker began. "Today, we decided to give you some answers. Are you ready for a hike?"

"Where to?" Hawk asked.

"North," Blackie said.

"It'll take about three days to get there," Spider added.

"Unless you can keep up with Walker," Hornet clarified. "He can do it in two days."

Hawk, Tabby, and Babe exchanged glances with each other to see if there was a consensus to go. Hawk decided to probe some more. "Is that where the Resistance Army is located?" Hawk asked.

"You'll see what's there when you get there," Walker offered lightheartedly.

"Then, I guess we'll just have to go," Babe said.

Hornet rose to his feet and swung his pack into position on his back. "Let's get going," he said. "I'm tired of talking about it."

Within just a few minutes, the small band fell into a single file behind Walker and started the long journey north. As they proceeded, they noticed that the ground became steeper and their pace slowed. They also noticed that Walker seemed to show no signs of fatigue as he kept a strong pace and had to stop and wait from time to time while the others tried to catch up. In fact, they marched the entire day and didn't stop until it was totally dark. Exhausted, the group fell asleep quickly.

The next day the group continued the march. The ever-present mist protected them from the heat of the day, but it was still warm, almost cozy in the deep woods. Several times each experienced an almost mechanical response as their legs kept moving while their minds wandered. The forest at times added to the loss of concentration, with the mist both filling the valleys and floating in the treetops as they strode through the center of it. Something they all experienced, however, was the comfort the quiet woodlands offered. Combat seemed far away, even though they knew it was all around them.

On the morning of the third day of the northward hike, the seven fighters ascended the steep, southern slope of Long Ridge. Twice they had to stop the ascent to catch their breath, but finally, just before mid-day they stepped onto the peak of the ridge. Walker encouraged them all by telling them that they were very near the end of their journey. His words were welcome news to the now tired hikers, as they proceeded on through more forgiving terrain. They passed several hot springs that steamed in the warm air, then, they came upon other branches whose waters were very cold. At the cold, sparkling branches they stopped to fill their canteens, and enjoy the cold freshness in their mouths. But, they rested only a minute or so before Walker had them moving forward again.

Two hours after leaving the peak of Long Ridge, Walker called them all together.

"Stay close together, now," he ordered with a soft voice. "We are very near to our destination today." He motioned the group forward along a narrow path though the trees. Babe took the lead. Hornet was next, then, Walker, Tabby and the others. They had only proceeded for a few minutes when Babe suddenly stopped them. On the path in front of them was a small boy, about five years of age. He stared at them with large curious eyes for a moment. Then, he turned and darted down the path.

"Mom, mom," the boy called out as he ran. "It's the rangers! The rangers are here!"

Babe smiled at the small boy and hurried after him with a smile on her face. The others followed closely behind her. The trail turned down a small bank an opened onto a sight Babe, nor Tabby and Hawk, had expected to see as the small boy rushed to a woman nearby. "It's the rangers, mom!"

Babe was taken aback a moment as she looked at the open woods with its tall, majestic trees and hundreds of people living in makeshift shelters all about them.

"Smile," Walker said to his group. "Don't accept any food from them," he added. Then, he walked toward a small group of men who approached him.

Babe, Hawk, and Tabby stayed together while they wandered among the forest dwellers. The others they had arrived with split up and each went in their own direction.

Babe soon encountered a young girl clothed in tattered rags. "How old are you? The girl asked with a rough voice.

"Sixteen," Babe answered.

"I'll be sixteen in two more summers," the girl announced proudly, "then I'll be able to fight."

"Maybe we'll be able to fight together," Babe grinned.

"Yeah," the girl smiled.

A short distance from the girl, and old woman approached them. Tears flowed down her gaunt, bony face. "God bless you," the old woman gasped, "God bless you."

Tabby took the old woman and embraced her with his powerful arms. "Thank you," he said.

Now a group of young boys clustered around the three warriors. Each of them wanted to shake hands, and none of them were disappointed.

The "rangers" stayed only an hour or so with this group of refugees and Walker led them back in the forest. Once again, they walked north. The group was silent as they concentrated on keeping pace with their leader. After another hour of forced march, the group entered another camp. This camp was much like the first they encountered but it was much more crowded. Again the fighters were welcomed with warmth and enthusiasm, and again, they responded. They each mingled with the happy, under-nourished people. They would sit and talk with one group of people, only to leave that chat session and go onto another. It was nearly dark when Walker reassembled his force, but Hornet was missing.

"Has anyone seen Hornet?" Walker asked.

The group was silent for lack of an answer.

"We can't leave without him," Walker said.

Just then Babe spotted Hornet. "There he is!"

The others turned in the direction Babe was facing, and they saw their comrade approaching them. Hornet walked slowly with a procession

140

formed behind him. In his arms was the body of a very old, skeletal man. When Hornet was face to face with his comrades he stopped. The followers behind him stopped too.

"Help me bury him," Hornet said. "He would like to be buried up on the hillside overlooking the stream."

Walker dropped his pack and removed a folding shovel. The others followed Walker's lead and followed behind Hornet and his dreadful burden. When he reached a point just beneath the crest of the hill, Hornet stopped. He turned and looked down at the small stream below. "Here," he said.

Without hesitation, the other warriors put their shovels to the task, while Hornet stood with the corpse in his arms and waited. Babe occasionally would glance up at Hornet, but his eyes were locked on some distant image in the darkening valley.

In a short time, a shallow grave was opened and Hornet stopped the work. Tabby helped him place the corpse in the grave, then, they both stood at either end of the opened earth.

"He killed himself," Hornet explained. "He couldn't work. He didn't want to be a burden on the others." Hornet sighed, but the expression on his face never changed. "He deserves a proper burial. I'm not good at praying, and neither are the rest of us. What about you, Tabby? Or, you, Babe?"

Tabby glanced anxiously at Walker, who quickly looked away. Babe shook her head to indicate she wasn't the one either. "I'll try," Tabby surrendered.

The large man turned to the small group of refugees; then, he lifted his gaze to the darkening mist above the trees. His voice boomed and echoed through the forest. "St. Michael, Great Archangel, Conqueror of Lucifer, Warrior of the Heavenly Host, hear our prayer. This day this man has willingly given up his life for a cause he believed was right. We ask you to carry his soul to the Lord God our Father and in the name of Jesus Christ, his only son, implore Him to absolve our fallen comrade of his sins and grant him eternal rest in paradise. Amen." Tabby flushed with embarrassment as he finished the prayer, but no one noticed.

An old woman came forward with a blanket and draped it over the body in the grave. Hornet knelt down and began covering the body with earth with his bare hands. "That was a good prayer, Tabby," Hornet said without hesitating in his task.

Ann sighed as she prepared to bring the tale of the refugee camps to a close. "That night we camped a short distance from the grave site. It had been an emotional day for us. We were tired. Finally, Walker, your father, called us together. He asked us if we had been able to answer some of our questions. We just sat there, staring into a small campfire, and said nothing."

"That was the only day I saw Hornet display any emotion," the aged Bishop added. "When he told me that I had offered a good prayer, I noticed a single tear slide onto his cheek. It stopped there; halfway down his face, as if he had willed it to stop."

"Really?" Highet's question was uttered with a high pitched squeak of disbelief. "I never saw Hornet show any sign of humanity, other than carrying a comrade to his grave. I always felt that he had the feelings of a meat grinder."

"He was an intensely sincere man," Ann added. "He was quite bright. And, although he never expressed it, I always felt that he considered us his family."

"He was certainly loyal," Highet agreed.

"Anyway," Ann returned to the subject, "our first look at the refugee camps was our first look at the Liberation Army. It was apparent that it was only an embryo of an army and that it would take time for it to become a mature and effective fighting force. Our job was clear. It was up to us to provide the army the time it needed to grow."

"How many of these camps were there?" Charles Speerman asked.

The three old people glanced at each other, before Highet replied. "We never knew how many there were. If there was a count, no one would want to know it for fear of divulging it if they were captured. We do know that there were many camps and the farther north, the more numerous they were. In fact, that was the night we all took an oath of silence. We swore never to divulge our activities or anything else about the war."

"Did the three of you participate in the training of the freedom fighters?" Speerman continued.

"We were always rotating new fighters through our unit," Highet added. "In fact, as units expanded, Spider took over the western region and Blackie was in charge of the areas east of the Old Road."

"Didn't the enemy step up their efforts to engage and destroy your units?" Speerman asked coldly.

The question echoed in the quiet room as the three elderly people struggled with bitter memories. Bishop Blane spoke first. "Unfortunately, as we learned, so did the enemy. They were slow for a couple of years, but then, they began to improve. They would send small units out to try to draw us into areas where larger forces waited in ambush. Of course, we adjusted our tactics to make it look as though they had succeeded. We would willingly walk toward one of their traps then try to get them to pursue us. We always managed to stay one step ahead of them, but sometimes, just barely."

"How was it that you were able to out-maneuver them?" The General asked

Highet and Blane both glanced at Ann to see if it was all right to continue.

Ann smiled at her old friends and saved them from their fears to disclose something that might offend her. "We had a secret weapon," Ann said softly, as a pink hue spread over her white cheeks.

"Secret weapon?" Charles asked with a skeptical tone.

"I'll explain," Ann continued. "During that first winter after joining the Rangers, I began having…" she paused with nervousness, "…visions."

"Visions?" Margaret chimed. "Do you mean psychic visions?"

"I don't know," Ann said with a bowed head. "These things would just appear in my mind; like a dream, but while I was awake. I tried to keep it a secret, at first, but the visions became stronger and stronger. Then, Tabby noticed that something was wrong. I was afraid I was losing my mind, so I told him about my experiences." Ann paused as Michael twisted nervously in his chair. "It is a terrible experience," Ann continued with her eyes locked on her grandson. "There were times I wasn't certain if I were seeing events yet to come or things which had already happened. I would share my 'visions' with the others and we would discuss them. Sometimes I could describe a place, and we would go there."

Bishop Blane felt compelled to interrupt Ann and spare her the pain of self-disclosure to any larger extent. "Babe was always right about what she 'saw'," he stated. "None of us understood what was happening to her, but we were grateful for her abilities. I saw it as a gift from God. I suppose the enemy would have seen it as a curse from hell. She led us to the enemy with her insights, and we nearly always destroyed them."

"There was another aspect to her talent," Henry Highet joined in. "She could always locate Walker. She seemed able to read his mind, whether he was with us, or not."

Ann broke into tears. "That was the horrible part, being so knowing about his thoughts and feelings. I felt as if I was stealing from him; violating his privacy. I felt terrible about it all, but I couldn't stop it. It just happened."

"Bishop Blane," Speerman addressed the cleric, "you said that Ann's abilities enabled you to nearly always destroy the enemy. I take it that you were not always successful, even with Ann's prior knowledge."

"No," Blane answered, "we always defeated them, up until the very end."

Speerman's face suggested that he was confused.

"Toward the end, they came up with their Insurgent Combat Force," Highet disclosed. "These troops were hand-picked veterans. They were highly trained and highly motivated. They would enter the Midlands and operate independently for several weeks at time. In time, they became our greatest fear; especially during the final days when the Army of Liberation was about to break out of the Highlands."

"Thank God, they didn't develop those combat teams sooner," Ann added. "All might have been lost."

"It damn near was anyway," Highet sighed.

"How large were these combat units?" Charles asked.

"There were fifteen men in a team," Highet answered. "We were able to destroy them when they worked independently. But, even then, we took more casualties than we had before. You had to kill all of them. If there was just one of them left alive, he would continue the mission."

"And what was their mission," Charles questioned.

"To find the Liberation Army they knew was being built in the wilderness," Ann answered. "Our job was to stop them until the Army was ready to make a sustained attack."

"Mister Highet," Charles began, "you said you were able to destroy these teams when they worked independently."

"Yes, we were," Highet grimaced, "but then, they got smart…"

The Last Day of the Last Spring

Walker wore an anxious expression on his face when he addressed his comrades. He waited until the five of them had sat down; then, he unfurled a slip of paper. "This is a message from the commanding general of the Liberation Army, General Wood," he began. "Spider reported engaging an enemy unit three days ago. There has been no contact with his group since then. General Wood asked me to re-establish contact with Spider and make certain the enemy unit is destroyed. Babe, is there anything you can tell us?"

The others were aware of Babe's "intuitive" talents, and all eyes focused on her.

Babe was silent for a moment. "No," she replied softly.

Walker smiled at the unhappy young woman. "Let us know if you come up with anything. Meanwhile, we'll cross the Old River and move toward Spider's last known location. There'll be just the five of us and we'll be moving fast. Any questions?" Walker smiled at the silent response. "Let's go!"

The small band was instantly on its feet. Walker took the lead. After watching and counting out ten paces, Tabby went next. Hawk, Babe and Hornet followed the same procedure, and the trek was begun. The group stayed at the required distance all day long, and closed into a tighter formation at dusk. They didn't stop until they heard the sound of water gushing and splashing nearby.

"The noise is coming from Broken Falls a short distance to our north," Walker explained. "We'll cross the river here. The water is shallow, but very swift. The bottom is solid rock and slippery in places. Take your time crossing. Take one step at a time and make sure your feet are well planted. The water is going to be cold, so let's get across quickly. We'll camp a short distance into the woods on the other side. All right let's go."

The group stayed as close to one another as possible, but not so close as to pull a comrade down if one of them fell into the cold waters. Within a few minutes, the group forded the river and climbed a low hill that would serve as their camp for the night. Hornet quickly scouted the area while the others removed wet trousers and boots and replaced them with dry ones. Babe was asked to take the first watch and await Hornet's return. Halfway through Babe's watch, Hornet returned but had nothing to report. Babe suggested he get some sleep, which Hornet immediately agreed to do.

Just before daylight, Tabby woke the small band of warriors. They didn't tarry with breakfast, as they were all eager to locate their comrade, Spider. Quickly, almost recklessly, Walker pushed his comrades in a westward direction through the open woodlands. They stopped only once to rest, near midday, then, they ate only a little, before taking up the search again. At mid-afternoon, the sound of distant small arms fire caused them to halt.

The search party dispersed among the trees and waited. Everything was quiet for a few minutes; then, there was another burst of gunfire. This time the shots seemed to be closer, and Walker gestured to his group to take up an ambush formation. Within seconds, the highly trained fighters took up concealed positions and waited for targets to appear. The moments slowly passed with periods of quiet followed by sounds of gunfire coming ever closer. Then, a long period of quiet ensued. The five lay prone on the forest floor in a sweeping arc, while their eyes danced over every shadow, and their ears analyzed every sound.

Hornet, who had taken a position on the far left, fired a single shot. The distinctive sound of his long barreled weapon echoed through the forest. Babe shouldered her shorter, automatic rifle, and pointed it to the right of Hornet's position. Out of the corner of her eye, she saw Hawk slither forward to a spot fifty yards on her right. An instant later, two men sprinted directly toward Hawk. Spider's spindly frame was instantly recognized as he dashed from tree to tree. Then, the horrible happened. A burst of automatic rifle fire crashed out of the silence. Spider lurched and twisted as the deadly missiles ripped through his flesh and then, he fell. Spider's comrade went to his aid, but a single shot struck him in the side of the head and he collapsed at Spider's feet. Now the five stared into the forest with unblinking eyes. This was not a time for grief, but a moment for vengeance and death; and the five waited to deliver the final blow. They did not have to wait long. They could hear the footsteps of the enemy in the crisp leaves coming closer to them. One of them called out to announce their triumph. Another answered. Soon, the three enemy soldiers came into view. Five seconds later, all three soldiers were dead.

The Last Day of the Last Spring

Walker was the first to reach Spider, but the others were only a split second behind him. Spider struggled to speak. "We underestimated them," he gasped weakly.

"Don't try to talk," Walker counseled as he removed Spider's pack.

"Don't make the same mistake," Spider hissed. "They killed Blackie, too. We didn't know what we were dealing with."

"Don't talk Spider!" Tabby scolded as he worked on the little man's wounds.

"There were three left," Spider gagged.

"We got 'em all," Hornet advised.

Spider smiled as he nodded that he understood. "Pistol…" he said with wide eyes focused on Walker.

Walker sighed, but pulled Spider's pistol from its holster and placed it in the dying man's hand.

Spider forced himself to smile, but it faded into a wince. "There's at least one more group like this one northwest of here," Spider advised. "Don't let them cross the Old River."

Walker nodded, and then patted his comrade on the hand. Then, he got up and walked away a short distance. One by one, the others bade Spider farewell, until they all stood with Walker. The leader pointed in a northwesterly direction then started the march.

Chapter 14

"We had only walked for a minute or so," the old bishop said, "when we heard a muffled "pop" behind us. We didn't stop, or look back. Our job was in front of us and we had to leave our sorrow behind."

"My God! How awful!" Joan wailed. "How can you speak about all this horror?" She burst into hysterical weeping.

"I am sorry," Ann apologized. "I know how difficult it must be for you all to hear such terrible reflections. But, try to understand. We have carried these memories for all these many years and have not been able to talk about them. The pain of the past was always with us, every hour of every day. It is time we free ourselves of it now."

"Could I ask a question?" Michael intervened.

"Sure," Ann replied with a smile.

"These new enemy units, and the death of your friend Spider, did they both occur in the spring when the War of Liberation began?"

"Yes," Ann answered, "it was that spring. For us, it would be the last spring we would fight together. And, for a time, we wondered if it wasn't going to be our last days alive. That was also the last time that the mist covered the Midland-Highlands."

"Those last days must have been filled with anxiety," Charles surmised.

Bishop Blane slowly nodded his head. "Yes, there was great anxiety," the priest said, "and fear, and terror, and hatred, and every other emotion a person could experience."

"What happened?" Michael asked.

"The enemy had dispatched more special warfare teams into the Midlands," Highet answered. "Each team was made up of fifteen men. At first, based on what Spider told us, we thought there were only two teams. When we found out about the third group, we nearly all got killed. At dark, the night before the Liberation Army was poised to move south, we encountered the third unit. Somehow we were able to survive a brief, but intense, exchange of gunfire and lead the northernmost group south toward the survivors of the other two teams which had combined into one. We broke off contact from the northern team and retreated hastily southward. Knowing we were trapped between the two units on the north and south and the Old River on the east, we drew up a hasty strategy. We would split up into two groups. Walker and I would engage the enemy unit to the north, while Tabby, Hornet, and Babe would make contact with the unit to the south. The plan was to draw the two units toward each other and hopefully create a situation where they would open fire on each other. While they were shooting at each other, we would slip across the river and head due east along the base of Long Ridge. If they pursued, we would go north, up the steep face of Long Ridge and try to slow them down until the entire Liberation Army reached the ridge at first light."

"Did your strategy work?" Charles asked the obvious.

"Yeah, somewhat," Highet answered. "We were able to get the two units to close and open fire on each other, but shortly after we began racing for the river, they figured out what had happened and quickly picked up our trail again. We battled our way to the shallow spot just below Broken Falls, south of the spot where Walker had led us across the river to look for Spider. For some reason, Hornet stayed behind the rest of us. We heard him open fire at the pursuing enemy, but we never saw him after that. The rest of us took up positions on the eastern side of the river and waited for the enemy to attempt the crossing. We shot a couple more of them as they tried to follow us across the river, but we were not certain how many had survived. Then, Walker made the final plan. Babe and Tabby would go north and try to make contact with General Wood to get help. Walker and I would continue to draw the enemy along the base of Long Ridge. After a couple of hours, he and I would turn north and try to climb up to the center of the ridge."

"That's where the nightmare always begins," Ann said with soft sadness as tears fell from her face.

"Nightmare?" Hank asked.

Ann wiped the tears from her face with the flat of her hand. "I'll explain later," Ann sobbed. "Tell them what happened that night, Henry."

Henry cleared a lump from his throat, and began. "After we split up, Walker, I mean, John and I opened fire on the pursuing enemy soldiers, then, darted away a few meters and took up new positions. It was difficult fighting in the pitch dark. We had to rely on muzzle flashes from the enemies' rifles to try to figure out how many there were. When we fired, we had to wait for a grunt or groan or the sound of a man falling into the leaves to know whether or not our bullets had struck the target. Then, after firing a shot, we would crawl away a few yards then run a few yards and fall to the ground again to listen for the approaching enemy. I think we did that for nearly two hours, then, we started up the southern slope of Long Ridge."

"About half way up," Henry went on, "we stopped to rest. We could hear our pursuers making their way up the slope below us. We were both exhausted, but we had put enough distance from them and us that we decided to rest. We both took off our packs and I laid down staring up at the night sky. Then, I nearly panicked. I could see stars in the night sky. The mist that had smothered the Highlands for all those years was gone. I whispered my observation to John. 'What does it mean?' I asked him. 'It means General Wood will be victorious,' he whispered cheerfully. His words reassured me and I lay there wondering how long it had really been since I had seen stars in the sky. The crack of a piece of dead wood below us though, made us both sit straight up. We decided that there were only two, or three following us and that we would finish them off before continuing the climb to the top of the ridge. We opened fire with our automatic rifles and when the enemy soldiers returned fire, we rolled grenades down the hill. It was quiet after that, and we continued our climb to the top of the ridge at a leisurely pace."

Henry glanced at Ann for encouragement and after she nodded, he continued his story. "We stopped just below the top of the ridge, and crawled to the summit. It was still pretty dark in the woods, but the night sky, which was visible above a trail running along the crest of the ridge, had turned from black to a dark blue. We rose to our feet slowly, each of us sort of crawling up a tree until we reached our full height. The woods were quiet, but my instincts told me there was danger lurking in the trees on either side of the trail. I reached out and took John by the sleeve to warn him of my fears. He gently patted my hand and I understood that he was feeling the same thing I was feeling. It was too quiet."

"John stepped very slowly from behind his tree and stepped on the trail. I waited a minute, then, I slowly, quietly, moved to the right side of the trail facing west. The sky was turning brighter and the forest was a dark gray. John took a step, then another, before he stopped. I followed his lead and drew parallel to him again. We kept up this snail's pace for several minutes following the star path above the trees. Then, I stepped forward and my heel landed on a loose stone. I slipped and was forced to catch my balance on my other foot. I didn't have time to place the errant step though, and I heard a loud crack beneath me. The sound of the breaking branch was followed almost immediately by automatic weapon fire. We both ran, but I was struck in the leg and knocked down. It didn't hurt right away and I was able to shoot at the muzzle flashes from the woods on our right. As I fired, I could hear John continuing down the trail and I was glad he had escaped without injury. I fired a second time, and I could hear John open fire a short distance in front of me. I heard one of the enemy cry out in pain, then, it was quiet. Suddenly, my leg exploded with pain. I clenched my teeth to keep from screaming, then, I passed out." Henry shook his head to try to check his tears, but he failed. "When my friend needed me the most, I let him down," Henry sobbed.

"It's all right, Henry," Ann comforted her old friend. "There's nothing you could have done."

Ann waited for Henry to compose himself; then, she took up the remainder of the story. "Tabby and I rushed north after separating from Hawk and Walker. The climb up broken falls slowed us considerably, but after that, we moved much faster. When we encountered the advance units of the Liberation Army Assault Force, they quickly put us in touch with General Wood. At our request, General Wood allowed his central command to push forward, ahead of the time schedule in hope of saving Hawk and Walker. While we rushed toward Long Ridge, I went into one of my visionary states. I could see Hawk and Walker making their way up the steep slope of the ridge as if I was hovering above them. Not only could I see them, I could hear them and all the other sounds of the forest. I could also see the enemy soldier lying in wait near the trail that followed the crest of the ridge. I urged everyone to hurry and broke into a run myself. Tabby was right behind me. Then, my vision showed me the enemy troops firing at Walker and Hawk. I could hear the shots. I could also hear the same shots coming from afar, as we bolted through the forest. I was near panic, when I saw Hawk fall. Finally, there was another burst of gunfire, and my heart sank with dread. Pieces of bark and shards of timber exploded from the tree Walker had chosen for concealment. But, the shots came from the west and Walker was looking eastward. The bullets were striking the tree and passing through him. A second later, he began tumbling down the southern slope of the ridge. As I ran, I saw him come to rest on a small flat that extended outward from the face of the hill. He forced himself to his feet and managed to stagger a short distance before crumpling beside the trunk of a fallen tree. He managed to sit with his back against the tree, and then he heard the footsteps of the enemy coming from behind him, on the West Side of the flat. He reached for a weapon, but he had lost both his rifles during his fall down the slope. At last he reached for his revolver, which he kept inside his belt. With great effort, he turned and half lying against the tree trunk, brought his revolver forward and rested his arm on the tree. The sun was rising, and in spite of the fact that we had not seen a sunrise in years, I could only see Walker dying. We were very near the top of the ridge, when the enemy soldier that pursued Walker approached a large, limestone boulder perched on the west edge of the flat, only twenty paces from were Walker lay. He approached warily, and slowly peeked out from behind the rock. The sun had risen high enough now to flood the boulder with sunlight, which shone directly into the enemy soldier's eyes. Although Walker lay just a short distance from him, he couldn't see him. When he stepped from behind the huge stone, Walker fired his revolver, and the enemy fell dead beside the stone. Walker slumped over the tree trunk. We had just reached the top of the ridge, and exhaustion overtook me. I collapsed. When one of our soldiers stopped to help me, I ordered them down the slope to find Walker."

"As I sat there, gasping for air. I could still see Walker stretched across the fallen oak. Then, a mist began to rise from the forest floor and a cool breeze sprang up from the east. I was transfixed on the mist. It swirled in a slow whirlwind for a moment; then, it grew darker and darker. I was surprised to see Walker lift up his head and speak to the mist. 'Have you come for me?' He asked." Ann began struggling to hold back her tears. "Then, I heard a voice, the likes of which I had never heard before. It came from the mist. 'No,' the voice said. 'I will come for you another day in another spring.' I rushed down the slope, falling several times. When I reached Walker, the medical corpsmen were already caring for him. The column of mist was gone."

Ann surveyed her family as they sat in silent astonishment. "For more than sixty springs, Walker, your father, would re-live that morning in his nightmares. And, I would re-live it with him. Each spring he would wait to die. He would walk down the hillside to that small flat and sit on the fallen tree waiting for death to come for him."

"That was grandpa's special place," Michael said softly. "It's the same place where I found his body."

Ann smiled at her grandson and nodded her head. "Yes, it was his special place, and that is where he will rest."

"Ann?" Bishop Blane asked. "I know this is painful for you, but I have to know. This morning…"

Ann smiled in anticipation. "He had the same nightmare this morning," Ann said. "And, when it came to the part where he asks, 'Have you come for me?' the mist answered, 'Yes. Today is the last spring; the last day." Ann began to weep. "He got up and we had coffee together. He was ready to meet the darkness in the mist and there was nothing I could do to make him tarry. When he opened the front door to leave the cabin, he stopped. It was then he told me to contact Hawk and Tabby to tell the rest of the family about us."

Silent grief collapsed on the Sylvan Family. The old people comforted each other with great tenderness and understanding. The younger members of the family struggled to accept the death of their father along with the discovery that they had known nothing about him. Michael watched with uncertainty. He was unsure how he should act, or what, if anything he should say. He fought back tears, but then, Candy embraced him sensing his need. Michael wept in the safety and comfort of Candy's arms.

Unexpectedly, Hank began to laugh. He wiped his tears from his face and gulped down another drink. "I'm proud of you mom. I'm proud of dad and your friends. You were forced to live a lifetime of regret. I can't imagine how much courage that took. I certainly don't have the guts to do what you did."

"Thanks, Hank," Ann smiled. "You've made me feel less ashamed of the terrible things we had to do during the war." Ann looked at the blank faces on J.J., Margaret and Joan. "We should rest the remainder of the day so we can give John a proper burial."

It had been a long day for the Sylvan family, and a troubling one. For decades each had thought they knew who they were, where they had come from, and where they were going. Now, they learned that they never knew their parents and they somehow felt both rewarded and, they also felt separated. Too much had happened today for them to deal with. It would take time for them to come to understand, but what they didn't know, is that they would have no time.

Henry Highet offered a helicopter ride to anyone wishing to spend the night at a hotel in Riverton. Charles and Joan accepted the offer. The helicopter departed in the fading afternoon sun and Michael, his parents, Ann, Hank and Candyce waved them away before returning to the cabin. Margaret tried to take charge of the kitchen again, but again, Ann would not hear of it. The men were left to sit and wait for the women to announce dinner.

"This goddamn forest is haunted," Hank sneered. "I knew it when I was a kid. It scared the shit out of me living out here."

"You're talking nonsense," J.J complained.

"Go ahead and scoff," Hank countered. "I'm telling you the goddamn place is haunted." Hank poured himself another shot of whiskey. "What do think, Mike? You know about the Midland-Highlands. Do you agree with me?"

"I agree that there are a lot of strange things that happen here," Michael dodged with a weak grin.

"There are scientific explanations for the things that occur here," JJ offered with a hint of impatience in his voice.

"Yeah, right," Hank sarcastically stated. "I'm telling you God created this wilderness as a special place for special people, and I know I'm not one of them." Hank re-filled his glass. "You could live here, couldn't you Mike? Don't answer," Hank quickly advised his nephew, "it'll just piss-off your old man."

"I resent that, Hank," JJ protested. "Michael's opinions are as valid to me as anyone's."

"Don't bullshit me, JJ!" Hank snapped. "I know you and Margaret. It's my bet that you have Mike measured for a debutante wife, with the proper financial connections, and a double breasted desk job at Woodburne Industries right after graduation."

JJ looked perplexed. "We have planned for Michael's future, and part of that is starting work at Woodburne…"

"That's not a bad future," Michael interrupted.

"I don't know for sure what your future holds, Mike," Hank smiled, "but I think you're meant to do more than hang around your mom's company waiting to be a social dandy."

"The future's unpredictable," Michael blurted before his father could express his obvious anger at his brother.

"Sometimes it's very predictable," Hank countered. "I have a gut feeling that you already know what yours will be."

"It's starting to take shape," Michael smiled. "I think I'll step out on the porch for a while," he concluded.

"Mike, do me a favor, will you?" Hank's request sounded as if he were almost pleading. "Take Candy with you. She doesn't get to meet any young men like you. She needs to know there are intelligent young men with higher aspirations than just getting into her pants."

Michael considered the request only briefly before going to the kitchen and emerging a moment later with the beautiful young lady on his arm. He ignored the stares of his mother as he led the attractive girl to the door and finally onto the porch.

Candy blushed. "I heard what Hank told you," she said. "I am really embarrassed by him sometimes."

"He's always been like that," Michael smiled, "we have learned to expect him to say the embarrassing thing."

"He was right, though," Candy acquiesced. "I have never met a man quite like you."

"I would have thought you would have met many men my equal or better," Michael responded.

"No," Candy denied. "You're very different from others I have known. There's something deep inside you that I don't understand, but I can feel it when I'm near you."

"It must be grief for my grandfather," Michael offered.

"Yes, I thought that at first," the young woman agreed, "but now, I sense something else."

A cold breeze erupted from the growing darkness causing a chill to strike the young couple. They glanced at each other in surprise. Then, as the wind faded into the trees, Michael heard its familiar chorus. "Michael. Michael," the wind called out. "The mist will come to the Highlands. You will rise from the mist and take your place."

"I...I'm afraid!" Candy blurted suddenly.

"It's only the wind," Michael said softly.

"Yes," Candy quickly agreed, "only the wind," she echoed nervously.

"My grandmother and her old friends must have frightened you with their stories," Michael suggested.

"It must have been horrible for them," Candy said. "Their youth was lost in the terror of a war, and they had to bear their pain silently for so many years. Their story is very sad."

"Have you wondered, while you listened to them, how we would act if we were in the same situation?" Michael looked deeply into Candy's eyes and she accepted his stare.

"I fear I would not have the courage to survive as they did," Candy admitted.

"I wonder if courage is something that some always have, or if it is something which is gained by living through strife," Michael pondered.

"Let's not talk about it anymore," Candy pleaded as she huddled against him for security.

Michael was instantly stimulated by her closeness. It was as if an uncontrollable force transmitted itself from Candy directly into Michael's flesh. He quickly brought up another topic. "How did Hank come to adopt you?"

"Long story," Candy blushed.

"I have time to listen," Michael smiled.

"My parents threw me out of the house when I was fourteen," Candy began. "My parents were very religious. One afternoon, my father came home early and found me and my boyfriend on the sofa. My father went into a rage. He began beating both of us with the belt he pulled off his trousers. The boy ran grabbed his clothes and ran away. I had no place to run. He finally got tired of beating and cursing me. He tossed my blouse and blue jeans to me and told me to get dressed. When I finished, he grabbed me by the hair and threw me out the front door. He said he wouldn't have a whore living in his house." Candy started to cry.

"I didn't know what to do or where to go. I just started wandering. I wound up on the piers that evening. I watched the street walkers for a while, and then I realized that I was most likely to be one of them. I sat down in a small hallway and cried. Suddenly, a man was kneeling near me asking me if he could help. It was your uncle."

"No one would believe that Hank is that compassionate," Michael said.

"I know," Candy agreed. "He can really be gruff sometimes. That first night he asked a woman friend of his to take care of me. She saw the welts on me from my father's belt and told Hank. He wanted to beat the shit out of my father, but I wouldn't give him the address."

"Now that's more like my uncle Hank," Michael grinned.

"He's really a very good man," Candy said, "when he's sober. When he's drunk he's a different man. It's strange though, he always treats me like royalty; sober or not."

Michael gave Candy a hug. She seemed to melt into his arms. He quickly remembered the necessity for propriety. "Let's go back inside," he said. "Tomorrow will be a trying day."

As Michael and Candyce returned to the living room, JJ stepped passed them in a huff. Michael started to ask his father what was wrong, but Hank beat him to the punch.

"I pissed JJ off," Hank explained. "He would rather go outside and cool off than punch me in the nose." The front door slammed shut. "I would have had more respect for him if he had punched me," Hank admitted as he poured himself another drink.

"Hank," Candyce said sternly.

"I know, I know, I'm an asshole." Hank grabbed another glass, poured some whiskey into it and handed it to Michael. "Here, Mike, have a seat and talk to me."

Michael and Candyce took chairs on either side of Hank. Michael sipped at his drink, while Candyce kept a nervous gaze on her stepfather.

"Mike when you found dad did he say anything?" Hank asked.

"By the time I reached him, he was already gone," Michael said softly.

"What did you think of the stories we heard from these old voices from the past," Hank queried.

Michael felt a charge of energy strike him when he heard the expression "voices of the past". Candyce noticed the sudden brightening of Michael's facial expression. "I am going to try to learn from them," Michael said. "I will listen to the voices of the past."

Hank felt that Michael's response was strange, but before he could follow-up on his hunch, Margaret appeared in the room to announce Dinner.

The meal unfolded in a strained environment. JJ was obviously angry with Hank. Margaret was angry with both of them. Michael let his memory replay everything he had heard earlier in the day. While Candyce fought the yearning she was developing for Michael. Only Ann felt relaxed. She had unburdened herself and she felt good about it. She smiled as she reached for the salt shaker. Michael had anticipated her need and held the shaker in his hand to offer it to her.

"He has the power too", Ann said to herself.

Michael spent most of the night sitting on the edge of his bed staring out a window into the darkness. "Michael! Michael!" The voices chorused on the wind. "They will come to you to lead them. The mist will fall upon the Highlands." The young man was exhausted and wanted very much to go to sleep, but he had no way to silence the whispers that flowed through the night air.

It was only a short time after sunrise, before the family and friends re-united outside the cabin. Ann asked her grandson to take her arm; then, they led everyone down a path cut into the side of the hill. It was a gradual descent and, after only a few moments, everyone could see a small piece of flatland sticking outward from the steep ridge. On one side of the flat, a casket rested on its bier just beside the rotting hulk of a fallen tree. On the other side, stood a huge chunk of limestone with a small white cross at its base. The gravediggers huddled near the boulder, while the funeral director waited at the casket.

The family and friends lined up in a single file facing the casket, and the director opened the lid so they could have their last view of John Sylvan. JJ, Hank, and Joan were the first to pay their final tributes. Joan broke down into uncontrollable weeping. Charles and Candyce followed. Finally, Ann led her old friends and Michael to the casket. Michael stared at the likeness of his grandfather. He realized that the man he had known, no longer existed within the empty likeness in the box. When the last good-bye was said, everyone rejoined the single line. Ann nodded to the funeral director. Taking his cue, the man stepped up and sealed the casket shut. Joan wailed even louder as the man screwed down the lid.

Ann broke the rank, and stood facing her family. "Tabby," she said to the old priest, "please recite the old prayer and send Walker on his way." She walked back to her grandson as the old bishop stood in her place. Tears fell freely from the old priest's face as he stretched out his arms and looked up into the treetops. His voice boomed and resounded throughout the forest.

"St. Michael, Great Archangel, Conqueror of Lucifer, Warrior of the Heavenly Host, hear our prayer. This day, this man has willingly given up his life for a cause he believed was right. We ask you to carry his soul to the Lord God our Father, and, in the name of Jesus Christ, His only Son, implore Him to absolve our fallen comrade of his sins and grant him eternal rest in paradise. Amen."

Ann announced the end of the proceedings and asked everyone to return to the cabin. Charles and Joan went first. Hank and Candyce went next and were followed by JJ and Margaret. The old people and Michael went last. The group moved slowly up the path as they kept glancing back at the burial site. The gravediggers were already lowering the coffin into the grave. Then, something happened which caused everyone to pause on the trail. There was a noise in the distance. It was only a distant, hum, at first, coming out of the west. The noise grew louder and louder. The trees began to sway back and forth as a strong wind roared through the forest. The leaves on the burial site began to rise into a swirling whirlwind that formed a funnel at its base which danced over the gravesite, then, hovered over the grave itself. The climbers on the path had to hold onto one another to maintain their footing in the swirling leaves.

The wind stopped. Leaves that had been brought aloft by the blast of air, now, fell lazily back to earth. For a moment, no one was sure what had happened. Then, Ann cried out tearfully. "He came for him, Tabby. He came and took my John."

The old priest fell to his knees with his hands tightly woven together in prayer. "Our Father, which art in Heaven, hallowed be thy name…" the old priest prayed and the others, still shaken by what they had seen, joined the prayer with him.

Chapter 15

It had remained quiet in the cabin throughout breakfast. Now, the dishes had been washed and people began talking of leaving Long Ridge to return to their other worlds. "I have just one more thing to do," Ann said to everyone. "Please stay just a while longer. Michael, there is an old trunk behind the stairs in the cellar. Would you bring it up to me?"

"Sure," Michael replied as he instantly bounded down the cellar stairs. Ann led the family into the living room. She took a chair in front of the fireplace, while the others took seats on either side of her. A minute later, Michael returned and lowered an old, green trunk to his grandmother's feet.

"This is all that John left as an inheritance," Ann began, "and he specifically told me to give it to Michael. Go ahead," Ann urged her grandson, "open it."

Michael pulled a wooden peg from the hasp and lifted the lid. The odor of mildew and oil stung his nostrils. He looked at the contents with surprise. Carefully mounted in the lid were two rifles. Each rifle had been broken down into its two main components. One rifle was made with a bolt action receiver and a long, thick barrel with a very long telescopic sight. The other rifle was shorter, and was obviously one of an automatic design. In a shallow tray, just atop the lower part of the trunk, there was a long barreled revolver and several clips for the automatic rifle. Michael lifted out the tray and placed it on the floor. The rest of the trunk was filled with camouflage clothing. On top of the clothing was a leather bound book with a hasp and a single photograph. Michael removed the book and photograph. He placed the book on the floor, while he studied the black and white picture. He was astonished to see himself in the photo, then, he realized that it was not he, but his grandfather. Michael smiled with understanding as he recalled the strange stares he had received by the old men. He looked up at Henry Highet. "I do look a great deal like my grandfather," he said as he handed the photo to the aged industrialist.

Highet smiled at the glimpse into the past. He pointed a bony finger at one of the camouflaged men in the picture. "That's Hornet," Highet said.

Michael handed the photo to others to look at; then, he turned his attention toward the weapons held inside the deep lid of the chest. He studied the long barrel and receiver of the bolt action rifle, then, he pulled it free and joined it to its stock. He fondled the weapon for a moment, and the cool smoothness of the piece was pleasant to his touch. It was as if the rifle had always been his. He tried it against his shoulder. The fit was perfect. Now, he passed the long rifle on to others to examine and he reached for the revolver. The handgun too, fit perfectly in his hand, as if tailored to his grip. He ignored the look of disdain on his mother's face and continued his inventory of the trunk. He assembled the automatic weapon, then, handed it to his father. Margaret marveled silently and fearfully at her son's knowledge of the weapons.

"Really, Ann," Margaret whined, "why do you think John would leave these things to Michael?"

Ann, as well as her two old friends, locked their gaze on Margaret, then, Ann replied. "It's Michael's inheritance," she said.

"I don't understand," Margaret said impatiently. "What will he do with these things?"

The three old people stared at Margaret in silence. Then, JJ broke into a chuckle.

"Oh! Come now," JJ beamed. "You don't think we are going to war again?" JJ waited for a reply, but he heard only silence.

Michael looked into his grandmother's sparkling eyes and, as he did, he heard her say, "Tell them the answer, Michael," but he quickly realized that he was the only one who had heard her voice. He stood above the trunk and turned to look at his family and friends, then, Michael turned back to his grandmother. "I will tell them," he said to Ann.

Ann smiled at her grandson. "Please do," she encouraged.

Michael paused for a moment, trying to find a place to start, then, he spoke. "I went to visit the woman in Portston who claimed she was seeing the Virgin Mary. When I spoke to her, she told me that she had met a man who had brought her a message telling her she would be visited by the Blessed Virgin, Mary." Michael took a deep breath. "The woman told me that the Archangel Michael stood beside me, and that our Lady had told her about me. She started to cry when she told me that I would have to endure a great tribulation, but that I would be successful." Michael cast an anxious glance at his mother, who stared at him with an open mouth. Michael felt uncomfortable with his mother's skepticism, but somehow he pressed onward. "Now, I understand it," Michael announced cheerfully. "The voices, yes, it all makes sense to me now."

"Stop it Michael!" Margaret blurted anxiously. "You're frightening me."

"I'm sorry, mother," Michael said with great sincerity. "I don't mean to frighten you. I believe we have already seen a sample of the mist this winter, haven't we grandma."

"Yes," Ann nodded, "that is the Midland Mist you saw, and you will see it again."

"This is nonsense!" JJ snapped angrily. "All this talk about legends, and visions, and now my son saying he is hearing voices. There is no indication of any hostile action being directed at our country."

"I fear I must agree with JJ" Charles Speerman added. "I've been the head of military intelligence for the past several years, and I have no indication of any military threat to the country."

"You didn't see the mist, did you, General Speerman?" Michael asked the general, as he handed him the leather bound book.

"No," Charles replied, "I didn't."

"If you had stepped into the mist, as we did, I believe you would find our opinions more viable," Michael concluded. "There is nothing normal about the mist we experienced."

"Really, Michael," JJ countered with obvious irritation, "the mist is just an atmospheric event."

"I think you're all trying to be too rationale about this," Hank Sylvan boomed. "You all saw what happened, just a short while ago, at Dad's grave site."

"That was the wind," JJ barked angrily.

"Perhaps it was just the wind," Hank said. "But, you must ask yourself the questions; why that wind, in that place, at that time?"

"Coincidence!" JJ shouted. "You're letting your imagination rule you Hank. That's always been your problem. You're always imagining instead of thinking."

An embarrassed, unexpected silence followed JJ's verbal assault on his brother. Hank, uncharacteristically, paused before responding. He began his argument by nodding his head.

"You're right about me, JJ I always submitted to my daydreams. But the wind that swept over Dad's grave was not a figment of my imagination. It happened, and I believe I saw a divine event."

"It was a miracle," Bill Blane clarified. "There's no doubt in my mind that St. Michael himself caused that swirling force as he carried your father's soul to heaven." The old cleric rose and placed a hand on Michael's shoulder. "Barbara told me about you. But, until this moment, I didn't know it was you that she referred to in her story. Use what your grandfather has left you to the best of your abilities. The Lord has sent His champion to stand by your side."

The group fell into confused silence, as they wondered if they believed in miracles, or if respect for the old priest was more important than protest. The look of conviction on the old people's face seemed to be enough to convince Michael, but JJ couldn't accept it. Charles Speerman watched while each person searched his soul for faith.

"Let's suppose," Charles began, "that all we have learned these past two days is a warning to us that we should prepare for war. Perhaps we should warn our countrymen and start building a stronger military."

"Even if I believed that was true," JJ began, "who would believe me? Who would believe any of us? Who believes that poor woman in Portston?"

"You're right of course," Bishop Blane agreed with JJ. "Our countrymen are too optimistic to look for trouble."

Hank stared at his mother. Ann shifted nervously under her son's gaze, which reassured Hank that his thoughts were accurate. "It's too late for us, isn't it, mom?" Hank asked his mother. "That's why Michael inherited the trunk. He's the only one of us who will be able to do anything with it."

Ann lowered her eyes downward. The truth of Hank's assertion was too much for her to bear. Soon, the two old men interpreted her silence as an affirmation of Hank's speculation and they, too, lowered their heads in sadness.

"There you have it, JJ," Hank chuckled. "It doesn't matter who believes anything. We're all going to be dead meat."

"Stop it! Stop it!" Joan blurted tearfully. "I don't want to hear anymore talk about wars, death and dying."

Hank reached for a bottle of whiskey. "I'm fixing drinks, if anyone wants one," he offered.

"I'll have one," Charles said as he began paging through the old leather bound book that Michael had taken from the old trunk. There was a chorus of other acceptances for drinks and the topic of a coming war, and all its horror, vanished from the conversation momentarily.

Michael started re-examining the weapons from the trunk with renewed interest. Charles Speerman studied the strange notations in the old diary that John Sylvan had kept in his youth. JJ and Hank tried to smooth each other's feelings, while Margaret tried to comfort the hysterical Joan. Ann huddled with her old friends and Candyce, Candy for short, locked her bright green eyes on the handsome young man with the gray hair and wondered about his approaching destiny. She wanted to reach out to him, embrace him, cry for him, but she did nothing but stare at him.

"What do you make of the entries in this book, Mr. Highet?" Charles asked as he handed the book to Henry Highet.

The old man studied the book for a moment, quickly thumbing through its pages. "It appears to be a critique of another publication," Highet answered.

"Yes," Charles agreed. "Unfortunately, without the source book, most of these comments have little or no meaning."

"You're right," Henry said. "The entries all begin with a number or sets of numbers separated by decimals which must be specific paragraphs in a manual or something. Does the military write its procedures that way?"

"No," Charles replied. "The only publications I have ever seen constructed with that type of numbering system are procurement specifications. Our procedures are always in an alpha-numeric system." Charles closed the book and handed it to Michael. "Keep this safe," he said to his nephew. "It might be important."

Michael smiled and carefully latched the book closed and placed it back into the trunk. Suddenly, he was aware of Candy's gaze. "I guess you think this is all pretty weird?" Michael said softly to Candy.

"No," she said as she lowered her eyes, "I think it's all very sad." Large tears emerged from her eyes and ran down her fair face.

The remainder of the morning passed in relative quiet. Joan finally brought her weeping under control, and the controversial trunk was sealed and carried out of view. No one talked about the War of Liberation and no one talked about the future. In their minds, however, the horror of what might be flashed in their thoughts.

After a sumptuous lunch, Henry Highet's helicopter carried everyone off Long Ridge except Ann and Michael. Henry insisted before they left, that he and Bill Blane would be back the next day to get Ann. The old woman and her grandson waved as the helicopter churned up the leaves and disappeared down the south slope of the ridge, then, they stood there waiting for the silence to return to the forest. After a moment, Michael turned to this grandmother.

"I have many questions, grandma," he announced. "There are times I think I hear you talking to me, but your lips aren't moving."

"I know," Ann sighed. "We'll talk later. I am very tired just now."

"I understand," Michael said. "This has been a very tiring day for all of us."

Ann excused herself from Michael's presence and went to her bedroom. Michael returned to the great room and re-examined the items in the trunk. When he grew weary of trying to understand the writings in the diary, he decided to go for a walk. He meandered down the narrow trail and returned to the gravesite. It seemed different now. Only a low mound of earth marked the place where his grandfather's remains were placed. He scanned the small flat. Then, suddenly a small white object at the base of the large limestone boulder caught his eye. He approached the huge stone, and then knelt at its base. He reached into the brush that had grown up and his hand fell upon a small wooden cross. The graying, chipped, white paint carried part of an inscription that read "Enemy Officer. Killed…" The date was obliterated. Michael placed the cross in an upright position propped against the stone; then, he climbed back toward the cabin. He listened to the wind rush through the trees, then, as he reached the top, he heard the voices, hissing his name in the wind. "Michael, Michael," the voices hummed. "You must lead them, Michael. You have heard the voices of the past. Lead them from the depths, and they will bring you victory."

Michael tried to block the sounds from his ears, but there was no use. He hurried across the trail and ascended the stairs to the porch. The voices had faded away, but now another sound came to him. It was the sound of footsteps coming along the trail. He looked both directions and saw nothing at first. Then, from the east, he saw the first of them. They were warriors from every time in history. Some were naked, with their bodies painted green and brown. The naked ones carried bows and spears. There were others in leather, still more in mail and armor. Some came in more modern attire; then, others came marching from the west. The marchers were torn with horrible wounds, and Michael knew they couldn't be alive, but the macabre parade gripped him. He watched as the two groups converged on the trail only to turn and march right up to the cabin. As they marched they chanted his name, over and over again. "Michael. Michael. Michael." The voices chorused as they crowded against the porch. Michael stared at them in wonder and awe, when suddenly he was aware of his grandmother standing beside him.

"Do you hear them, grandma? Do you see them?" He asked her.

"Yes," the old woman said.

"Who are they?"

"These are the mist dwellers. The ones who survived in the grayness in times past," Ann answered.

"What do they want, grandma?" Michael asked with an anxious voice.

"They want you to be their leader," Ann answered. "Go to them."

Michael hesitated for a moment as he glanced at the legion of corpses then back to his grandmother. Finally, he slowly made his way along the porch while the macabre mass chanted his name. He turned, descended the stairs and reached out to take the hands that were offered to him. A great cheer went up from the dead warriors as their champion answered their call.

Immediately after their return to Portston, Hank headed for one of his favorite bars near the waterfront. Afraid he would get into trouble,

Candy went with him. It was a warm, humid night, and Hank preferred to sit on the great verandah of the saloon and stare across the wide river toward the limestone bluffs on the West bank of the river. He said nothing for a long time, but he drank quickly, and soon, he was very drunk. Candy sat diligently beside him, sipping soft drinks. She knew better than disrupt Hank when he got into one of his moods, and he was in one of them now. He would glance at her every now and then, to reassure himself she was there. Finally, he began to release the pent-up anxiety that boiled within him. He patted Candy on the hand, then, he pointed into the darkness across the river.

"Right there!" He said, before gulping another drink.

"Where?" Candy asked softly.

"On the other side of the river, on the bluffs," Hank slurred.

"I don't see anything, Hank," Candy said apologetically.

"That's where she was, but she's gone now."

"Who's was there, Hank?" Candy asked.

"The Blessed Virgin was there. That woman, Barbara, saw her, and my nephew, Michael was there. A miracle happened there, and I missed it." Hank laughed, a drunken, hysterical laugh, then, quickly became somber again. "I'll be there when the end comes, though. I'll fuckin' be there."

JJ sat on the edge of the bed, absently staring at the wall.

"Are you all right?" Margaret asked her husband.

"Yeah, I'm fine; just tired. It's been a very long day." JJ slipped under the light blanket, and Margaret switched off the light, before sliding into bed beside him.

JJ lay there staring into the darkness as he recounted the events of the day. He could only wonder about the tales he had heard about the past and he was afraid to think about the portents for the future.

JJ wasn't the only one to spend a sleepless night that night. Professor Draco paced back and forth over the small rug in front of his desk while he smoked cigarettes in rapid succession.

General Speerman watched his brandy swirl in a glass, just as the leaves had done at his father-in-law's funeral, but his mind was on his job and the defense of the nation.

The next morning, the two old men returned on the helicopter. Ann packed a few things, but wouldn't take anything that would prevent her from returning. Reluctantly, her old friends agreed that they would bring her back to the cabin when she wanted.

Michael was happy to see his grandmother leave the cabin. There was too much there that would connect her to her memories, and now, she needed respite from being reminded. Henry and Bill obviously had great affection for Ann and would look after her needs. He embraced Ann just before the threesome was ready to fly back to Riverton.

"I'm going to miss you, Michael," the old woman smiled.

"You'll be in my thoughts," Michael smiled.

"I wish it didn't have to be you," Ann sighed softly.

Michael appeared very sure of himself. "I have learned from the voices of the past," he said. "Now, I must learn the rest."

Both the old men embraced him in turn. Neither man said anything to him. There was no need for words. There were no words that could be appropriate. All that needed to be communicated among those men was done with the embrace. After the hugs, the old warriors disappeared into the helicopter. Michael stepped away as the rotors began to spin. He waved, and the aircraft slowly rose then was swept away by the wind.

"Good morning, General Speerman," a young woman in a naval uniform greeted with a musical voice.

"Good morning," Charles echoed unenthusiastically.

"The staff is waiting with General Keepstone in the conference room," the young woman smiled as she nodded toward a closed door.

Charles nodded and followed the officer into the room. High-ranking military personnel from all branches of the services filled the room along with an appropriate number of political types. Charles instinctively took an open chair near the head of the table. He forced himself to smile as the change of command ceremony swung into full gear. Three hours later it was over. The doors to the conference room swung open and a cascade of fresh air entered the stuffy room. Charles continued to shake hands with his subordinates until the room emptied. General Keepstone was the only one left.

"General Keepstone," Charles sighed, "could I speak with you privately, before you leave the command center?"

"Sure," Keepstone grinned with his usual confident air.

The two generals walked a short distance to Speerman's office. Keepstone directed his replacement to the large, overstuffed swivel chair behind the ostentatious desk, while he pulled a comfortable chair up to the front of the desk.

"I believe you'll find a particular kind of brandy in the bottom left compartment of that desk," Keepstone beamed knowingly.

Charles bent over and rose up with the bottle of brandy and two glasses in his hands. He placed the glasses on the desk while he opened the bottle. After he filled the glasses, he reached into his valise and removed a packet of cigars that he handed to Keepstone.

The retiring general smiled at the generosity of his replacement. "What's on your mind, General Speerman?"

Charles looked Keepstone directly in the eye. "Why did you pick me for your replacement? I'm not one of the Military Institute boys. I thought I had been blackballed from any higher rank. Did I get this job because of my brother-in-law's political ascent?"

Keepstone smiled at Speerman's directness. "I've been in the military for forty years," he said. "Forty years." The elder general clipped the end of a cigar and placed it in his mouth. "Do you remember those unconventional warfare pieces you wrote a few years ago?"

"Yes sir," Speerman answered. "It was right after those publications that I heard about being blackballed from a higher rank."

"You're right," Keepstone grinned. "You were blackballed right after that. I'm the one who did it. No one from the Military Institute would write the things you did."

"So that means I'm here because of my brother-in-law's political clout," Speerman concluded.

General Keepstone nodded as he smiled broadly. "That's what I want everyone to think." Keepstone lit his cigar while he studied the confused expression on Speerman's face. "You might be the smartest thing I've done in forty years," Keepstone said softly.

"I'm confused General," Charles admitted. "First you blackball me from promotion, then, you select me to be your replacement."

"It's brilliant, Speerman," Keepstone chuckled. "It's fuckin' brilliant."

Charles was unable to hide his exasperation from Keepstone, and finally the old general got up and walked to a vault near the desk. "Do you mind?"

Charles nodded his assent. Keepstone opened the door to the vault and removed a thick publication that he had to carry with both hands. As the volume was placed before him, Charles read the cover page. "Army in Concealment: Organization, Operations, Recruitment,"

"A little more than three years ago, I found this buried in our archives," Keepstone explained. "That publication was written more than seventy years ago."

Charles paged through the massive volume and his heart began to race. "This is incredible," he exclaimed.

"When you have time to read it all, you'll realize just how incredible it is," Keepstone concluded. "One thing you'll notice right away is that book wasn't written by a graduate from the Military Institute. They aren't trained that way and they don't think that way."

"Then you believe this publication has credibility?" Charles asked.

Keepstone puffed on his cigar, then, looked directly into Charles' eyes. "I believe that document was the blueprint for the Liberation Army more than seventy years ago."

"General Keepstone, are you telling me that this program was written by someone other than a military strategist and that it was put into operation by our high command?"

Keepstone grinned confidently. "You know," he paused, "it took me nearly forty years of military service before I learned that the military doesn't have all the answers." The aging general leaned over to tap the ash free from his cigar, then, he continued.

"After I found this tome in the vault, I went back and read your papers. It was then, that I had my breakthrough. You're right. Our high-tech mentality is wrong. Your metaphor about a man with a six-gun trying to hold off six men with knives still haunts me." Keepstone puffed on his cigar. "One of those bastards is going to cut you."

General Keepstone rose to his feet. His face was stone hard. "I'm leaving you a bucket of trouble, Speerman. But I can't think of anyone else who may be able to devise a plan for our national survival." Keepstone offered Speerman his hand.

The Last Day of the Last Spring

The two men shook hands; then, General Keepstone turned and walked out the door. Charles Speerman collapsed into his overstuffed swivel chair and grabbed his glass of brandy. He took a large drink then leaned back in his chair and stared at the ceiling.

Chapter 16

Professor Draco hurriedly pulled a piece of paper from his jacket and handed it to the librarian. "I need these right away," he said hastily.

Jane Linden quickly looked over the list. "I believe most of these are in the archives. Why don't you have a seat…?"

"No, I don't have time," Draco snapped. "Have someone bring the books to my apartment."

"Sure Professor," Jane replied. "I'll see to it personally."

Draco turned and rushed out of the library. Jane watched him leave, then, with the list in hand she started searching the card files.

When he returned to his apartment, Draco found Michael Sylvan seated on an old green trunk just outside his door. "Sorry to hear about your grandfather, Michael. Have you been waiting long?" Draco asked.

"Thanks," Michael said. "No, I've only been here a few minutes. I was wondering if I could leave this trunk with you. The administration will go berserk if they find it in my room."

"Why?" Draco asked.

Michael got off the trunk and opened the lid.

"Wow! You're right about that," Draco grinned. "A military assault rifle and sniper's weapon are not considered collegiate accessories." The professor opened the door to his apartment and helped Michael carry the old trunk inside.

Michael closed the door, then, helped lower the trunk to the floor in the foyer. "Do you have time to talk, Ivan?"

"Sure," Draco smiled. "Let's go in the office." Michael opened the trunk and grabbed the leather-bound book before following his host to the other room.

"I'm doomed, Ivan," Michael declared softly. "Maybe we're all doomed. There's going to be a war."

"I agree with you about the war," Draco said. "I studied too much about the past, however, to try to make predictions about the future. The dread you feel may not be an accurate predictor of the actual outcome."

"What can we do, Ivan?" Michael implored.

"Prepare," Draco snapped with friendly smile. "We have an insight into the future which only a few men ever have. We are obligated to prepare for what is coming."

Michael nodded his head while a weak smile crept slowly across his face. "You're right, Ivan. And, I guess I've been trying to do that by reading my grandfather's book. Trouble is I can't make any sense out of it."

"What book?" Draco asked.

Michael tossed the diary to the teacher.

Draco opened the clasp and began thumbing through the pages. "It looks like a critique of another document," Draco said. "Without the other documents or books or whatever, it will be nearly impossible to understand it. Do you have any other books with you?"

"No," Michael replied.

Just then, the 5x7, black and white photograph of the old freedom fighters fell from the pages. Draco picked up the picture and studied it. One by one he searched each of the young, grim visages which stared back at him from the photograph.

"You know," Draco paused, "this fellow here reminds me of..." Draco's jaw fell open. "Oh my god!"

Draco jumped from his chair and attacked the bookshelf behind him. Volumes cascaded to the floor as the professor went into a rage. Michael was taken aback for a moment by Draco's swift assault on the books, but he relaxed when Draco seemed to find the text he was looking for and began paging through it.

"There!" Draco shouted as his forefinger landed like a dart on one page. He pushed the book in front of Michael's face. "This is the same man," Draco said with great enthusiasm.

Michael looked at the picture in the book and shook his head. "I'm not so sure," he said stoically.

Draco thrust the old photograph onto the open book so Michael could make a better comparison. "There does seem to be a resemblance,"

Michael finally concluded. "This guy was called Hornet, according to my grandmother and her friends. Who is this other man?"

"Professor Richard Woodman," Draco said softly, "my teacher. My mentor," Draco added with an angry laugh. "The old son-of-a-bitch let me squirm and search and study, when the whole time, he had the answers." Draco broke into laughter. "Now, I'm going to have the last laugh, Woodman."

"I don't understand," Michael said.

"For years I was curious about the War of Liberation," Draco began. "My history professor was Richard Woodman. He pushed me to dig and research the war. But, I would always come up empty. I could never find the link I needed to prove the Liberation Army was created before the war and was waiting to rise and strike at the right moment. Now, with your grandfather's diary and this old photograph I have half of what I need. We're going to see Woodman to get the other half."

"Is he still alive?" Michael asked.

"Yes, I saw him over the semester break. He lives in a home for the elderly just thirty miles from here." Draco grinned. "He knew all the time. He just wanted to see how long it would take me to find out."

"If Professor Woodman is this man," Michael said, "his silence wasn't meant to test you. He made the same promise my grandmother and her old friends talked about."

Draco stared at Michael. "What promise?"

Michael related all that he had heard from his grandmother and her old friends. Draco listened intently, absorbing everything Michael told him. When the tale ended, Draco smacked himself on the forehead.

"That's it!" Draco celebrated. "He couldn't tell me, so he hoped I would find out on my own so he didn't break his word."

"If we confront him he'll just deny it," Michael stated.

Draco nodded his head slowly. "Right again. I need to think about this some more. I'm sure Richard Woodman is Hornet."

"Well, I'm going to leave my trunk and things here. I need to get back to my studies," Michael concluded.

"Yes," Draco answered somewhat absently. "I'll let you know when I come up with a plan to present our findings to Woodman."

Michael yawned. "I'll talk to you later, Ivan."

The Last Day of the Last Spring

Draco was lost in thought and didn't respond. Michael let himself out of the apartment and headed toward his room. He didn't notice Jane Linden approaching from the library with her arms full of books.

Resigned to his fate, Michael returned to his studies with intense vigor. His love making with Deanna Bartlett took on an almost firestorm character. Deanna was pleased with Michael's renewed passion, but she often wondered if she had as much influence on his heart as she did on his body. Deanna decided to accept Michael's attentions regardless of the motivation. She could not imagine having a life without him.

Dudley was happy to see Michael acting more like his old self, but he also noticed something different about his friend. Michael seemed determined to experience everything he could. He acted as if there wasn't enough time to do all he wanted to do. He slept little, ate little and worked and played with tremendous intensity. Even Doctor Henley noticed the elevated activity, but agreed that Michael's current behavior was an improvement.

Nearly a week passed, since General Speerman took his new post, and he finally was able to sit down and start reading the ancient manual he kept locked in his private vault. He went through a lengthy introduction of several pages before reaching the index to the volume. Then, it struck him. He had seen the peculiar numbering system for each segment of the manual before. He wondered about it a moment, then, he recalled the "diary" his father-in-law had left in the trunk that was given to his nephew. Finally, he slammed the book closed and hurriedly locked it inside the safe. Next, he snatched his telephone receiver from its cradle.

"Get my brother-in-law, JJ on the line," he ordered. "I'll wait."

Only a few seconds passed before JJ answered the call. "Hello Charles. Is there something urgent?"

"Well, yes," Charles replied. "It concerns Michael. I need to speak to him right away. I just wanted to reassure you that this is more about your father than your son. Can you keep this confidential, JJ?"

"Absolutely Charles; I just hope that Michael can be of service to you."

"I'm certain he will," Charles concluded.

175

"I'm not sure this is a good idea," Michael protested to Ivan Draco as the two men walked through the corridor of the rest home toward Richard Woodman's room.

"Trust me on this, Michael," Draco insisted. "I'm sure it will work." They stopped and Draco knocked on a door.

"Who is it?" A strong voice challenged from the other side of the door.

"Ivan Draco and one of my students," Draco announced.

"It's open!" The voice said curtly.

Draco smiled at Michael; then, he opened the door and went into the apartment. Michael followed.

Michael watched as Draco and the old man bent over in a wheel-chair, greeted each other warmly. After a minute, Draco stepped aside to allow Richard Woodman to have a full view of Michael while he introduced him. Woodman's reaction, however, surprised even Draco.

Woodman hurriedly slapped his glasses onto his face as he wheeled toward the tall young man standing before him. Woodman's stare was intense, and at that moment, Michael knew that Woodman was the man called Hornet by his grandparents.

"Who the hell are you?" Woodman challenged angrily.

"I'm the grandson of a man you fought with during the war years," Michael said. "You called him Walker."

"Never heard of him," Woodman snapped.

Michael pulled the old photograph from the leather bound book and handed it to the old invalid. Michael pointed to one of the young men in the picture. "This is you, Hornet."

Woodman's gruff exterior melted away as a single tear moved slowly down his cheek. Michael pointed to another person in the photo. "This is Babe, my grandmother, and this is…"

"Tabby," Woodman interrupted softly, "and Hawk." The old man looked up at Ivan Draco. "You did it, Ivan. I knew you would."

"Richard," Draco sighed, "we have one hell of a lot of questions."

"Yes, Ivan," the old man said, "you always have a lot of questions." He started to spin his wheel chair, but stopped himself to look up at Michael. "When I first saw you, I thought I was seeing a ghost," he said to Michael. "What's your name?"

"John Michael Sylvan."

"What was your grandfather's name?"

"John Sylvan," Michael answered.

"John Sylvan," the old man repeated. "I never knew his real name. It was not permitted for us to use our real names. After a time, we forgot we had names." The old man glanced down at the photograph. "What are the names of the others?"

"Babe, my grandmother, is Ann Sylvan. I don't know her maiden name," Michael confessed. "The stocky one, Tabby, is Bishop William Blane."

"A bishop?" Woodman couldn't contain his surprise.

"Yes," Michael affirmed. "The other one is Henry Highet."

"Highet," Woodman repeated, "his name is familiar."

"He's a very wealthy, reclusive industrialist," Ivan explained.

"Hawk is Henry Highet," Woodman shook his head, "I never would have guessed. I thought they were all dead."

"My grandfather was just buried," Michael disclosed. "The others are still alive. They thought you were killed the night before the Liberation Army broke out of the Highlands."

Woodman stared at Michael. "Damn, you look like your grandfather. You say he passed away."

"Yes," Michael confirmed, "just a couple of weeks ago. Before he died, he asked my grandmother to get Hawk and Tabby together with the family to tell them about the war. He left me an old trunk. In the trunk was this book." Michael handed the book to Woodman. "Professor Draco and I were hoping you could tell us more about it."

Woodman paged through the small volume, stopping from time to time, but then he snapped it closed and handed it back to Michael. "I can't help you," the old man snapped. "We gave our word that we would never divulge what we did or what we knew about our activities during the war. I have kept this oath all my life. I will not break it now."

"You are to be complemented on your loyalty," another voice boomed authoritatively.

"Uncle Charles!" Michael was astonished to see his uncle and three other men and one woman. All were attired in civilian dress, but their military postures were unmistakable.

"Who the hell do you think you are, coming into my room like this," Woodman challenged angrily.

"I'm General Charles Speerman, Chief of Military Planning and Operations," Charles stated formally. "From what I heard before we came in, I suppose you were the Commando named 'Hornet' during the war of liberation. Your actual name is Richard Woodman?"

"Yes sir," the old man replied in a military manner.

The woman in the entourage opened a small briefcase to remove some papers that she handed to General Speerman. The general handed the paper to the old man in the wheelchair. "Mr. Woodman, you have just been conscripted into the army. You will retain the rank of Colonel and report immediately to Military Planning and Operations Headquarters in Capitol City. You will be assigned to a top secret staff to work on a top secret project."

"And what if I refuse, General?" Woodman asked angrily.

"Then I will order one of these men to drug you and we will take you anyway," Speerman answered coldly.

"How do I know you are who you say you are," Woodman challenged.

Speerman quickly provided a photo I.D. while Michael added the comment; "He's my uncle."

Woodman studied the identification before allowing a thin smile to break across his hard face. "I'm an old man, but I am willing to do what I can for you," Woodman said.

"Thank you Colonel," Speerman said softly, "I am in your debt. Please gather your things. These men will help you."

Woodman spun his wheelchair around and began ordering the young men accompanying the general to the task. The woman retrieved more papers.

Speerman turned his attention to Michael. "Here are your enlistment papers. You will report for active duty exactly two weeks following your graduation. Your enlistment will be voluntary of course." Speerman paused. "I believe this is your destiny," Speerman said to his nephew as he reached for the book. "We need this," he explained. "I am afraid we won't be able to return it to you."

"Is it that important, Uncle Charles?" Michael asked sadly.

Speerman nodded. "Yes, it is," the General answered.

Michael nodded his agreement, and then Speerman turned to Ivan Draco. "I don't know what to do with you, Professor. You are smart enough to surmise…"

"You have the book this diary critiques, don't you?" Draco asked point blank.

"As I said," Speerman continued, "you present some special problems for me."

Speerman turned to the young female officer. "Give me the special agent contract, Lieutenant Ash."

Lieutenant Ash quickly complied by handing the General what he requested.

Speerman handed the paperwork to Draco. "This contract will make you an undercover operative of my staff. The bottom line is that if you keep quiet about the diary, our visit here today, and our contract, I won't have to have you killed."

Ivan Draco froze at the implications. What had begun as a historical investigation had now thrust him into a real-time issue, which he frankly had not considered a possibility. The look on General Speerman's face though was proof enough, however, of the gravity of the situation that he had entered. For the first time in his life, Ivan Draco was speechless. All he could do was nod that he understood.

"We're ready, sir," a young man announced to Speerman as he pushed Woodman's wheelchair.

"Do you know what to tell the staff here at the home?" Speerman questioned the old man.

"Yes sir," Woodman acknowledged. "These are long lost family members who have been searching for me for decades."

Speerman smiled. "Good job, Colonel. Have a nice trip."

The three young men left with Woodman, and the young woman pulled another document from her valise. Charles took the document, looked it over, and then he handed it to Draco. Without hesitation, Draco signed the document and returned it to Charles Speerman.

"We'll stay in touch," Speerman said. "I'll be contacting you soon. Sorry, for the disruption."

"We understand, sir," Michael smiled.

"Yes, we do," Ivan agreed.

"Thank you," Charles grinned. "You made a distasteful job easy for me. I am grateful to you both. I must leave now."

"We'll go out with you," Michael volunteered.

Woodman and his three "relatives" were already seated in a large limousine. One of the passenger doors was left ajar for General Speerman and the young woman. After a quick good-bye, Charles and the young woman entered the vehicle. As soon as the door closed, the car sped away.

General Speerman looked back at his nephew and the professor through the rear window, and then he turned to his female aide. "Do we have someone to keep an eye on Professor Draco?"

The young woman quickly removed a small booklet from her suit pocket and scanned a couple of pages. "Yes sir as a matter of fact we do."

"I want Draco under surveillance right away," Charles ordered. Then, after a moment of reflection, the General addressed the young officer again. "Put General Keepstone under surveillance as well," Speerman ordered. "I want a list of everyone the General has come in contact with since his retirement."

The woman picked up a wireless telephone that was mounted in the back of the seat in front of her. "Yes sir," she replied as she dialed the phone.

Michael and Ivan watched the limousine disappear before they began their drive back to National University. They hardly spoke for a time as they allowed their minds to absorb what they had experienced. Finally, Ivan broke the silence.

"This is difficult for me, Michael," Draco disclosed. "I have always studied history; now, I'm being swept up in it."

"Now, you know how I feel," Michael said.

"Yes, I do," Draco admitted. "I'm scared to death."

"That's the feeling," Michael smiled weakly.

Part Three

Acceptance and Preparation

Chapter 17

For the remainder of the semester, Ivan Draco pushed himself to the brink of his endurance as he read everything he could find on military strategy and tactics. He was such a frequent visitor to the campus library that he even begun a casual relationship with Jane Linden. He was flattered that she showed so much interest in his "research" on military history and warfare. At times, Jane would even recommend other books that Ivan Draco had not discovered. Jane seemed to have more than a casual interest in military things but she brushed it off as idle curiosity when Draco commented upon her expertise in certain areas.

The coming end of the school year was also a busy one for Dudley Carpenter and Michael Sylvan. The Bartlett twins were abandoned as the two young men began the final phase of study to receive their degrees. Somehow though, the scholastic enterprise seemed less challenging than other events Michael expected to occur in the future. Dudley too, came to accept the momentary delays in conversations with Michael. When his friend was slow to respond, Dudley would simply ask, "voices?" Michael would usually nod and the two would go on as if nothing serious had happened. Still, Dudley was unaware of the pain Michael bore.

Then, it finally ended. The last exam booklet was turned in and the students at National University waited for the grades to be posted. There was great speculation among the graduating students who would take the top academic rating, but there were only two choices. It would either be Dudley Carpenter or Michael Sylvan. What the other classmates didn't know is that it no longer mattered to the two contenders who would be number one in their class. They both had other things to think about.

Dudley watched his friend stare out the window of their room. "Michael, are you sure about this military thing?"

"Positive," Michael replied. "I have already received orders to report to Officer Candidate Training." Michael smiled, "what about you, Dudley?"

Carpenter grinned proudly. "I just received a letter from Highet Industries."

"Really? That's great!" Michael congratulated his friend.

"Well, I'm not on the payroll, yet," Dudley cautioned, "but at least they want to talk to me."

"You will be on their payroll," Michael reassured his friend.

Suddenly a noticeable ruckus could be heard in the hallway outside their room. Michael opened the door to see what the noise was all about.

"Grades are posted!" A young man shouted at Michael's blank stare. Michael closed the door and looked at Dudley. "Did you hear that?"

"A deaf man would have heard him," Dudley quipped weakly.

The two friends looked at each other in silence as they realized their lives together were coming to an end. In a few more days, they would follow their own paths into a future that was filled with uncertainty. "Do you want to check the postings?" Michael asked.

"No," Dudley said as he stepped past Michael and opened the bottom drawer of his desk. He removed a large magnum of champagne and two glasses. "I'm afraid it's warm," Dudley apologized.

Michael quickly glanced at the label of the bottle. "Excellent choice, Mister Carpenter," Michael smiled.

"Only the best is good enough for my friends," Dudley explained. There was a soft "pop" as the bottle was uncorked. Soon, Dudley offered a glass of the bubbling liquid to Michael while he held another.

"I would like to offer a toast to John Michael Sylvan," Dudley announced loudly, "who accepted me as his friend."

Michael smiled, then, gulped down his drink along with Dudley. The glasses were refilled and Michael held his glass aloft. "May we stay friends," he said softly.

Ivan Draco stood at his window for a moment to watch the students rush across the campus to get their grades, but he had little interest in the event. He went to his refrigerator where he found a cold can of beer, then, he returned to a book on his desk. The hardbound book was a deep green, with gold lettering. The title blared, "Insurgent Tactics versus Conventional Forces: Volume One - Urban Areas of Operation." Ivan sat down and opened the book. He switched on his tape recorder to make comments as he read.

The Last Day of the Last Spring

Charles Speerman adjusted the lamp on his desk so he could read the hand written text in the diary he had taken from his nephew. Across from him was the aged warrior once called "Hornet". "Let me see if I understand this now," Speerman repeated. "These numbers here, in the diary, correspond to these paragraphs in the manual. Is that correct?"

"Yes sir," Woodman replied, "that's correct."

"Can you recall what happened this day to cause Walker to make this entry?"

Woodman only had to glance at the entry. "Yes sir, I recall that day very clearly. We encountered a group of deserters. According to the manual, deserters were considered to be friendly and easy for us to recruit. The book didn't tell us that deserters might also be thieves and murderers."

"So what happened?" Speerman asked.

"We killed them," Woodman replied.

Speerman nodded as he entered notes into a journal.

Margaret entered JJ's office with a dramatic flair. "Really, dear, we have an important luncheon date…"

"It will have to wait, Margaret. You'll have to reschedule it," JJ said distantly as he studied a budget report.

"But, JJ, this luncheon…"

JJ slammed his report down on his desk. "Reschedule it Margaret!"

"Really, JJ, you have really become moody since your father…"

JJ had already picked up the report and began studying it again. Margaret could see that she was not going to break JJ away from his task, so she left the room in a huff. JJ smiled to himself over Margaret's anger. Then, he picked-up his phone.

"Charles, this is JJ," he said. "I think I found a place in the budget to suit your needs. Don't you think the army would be best suited to update the geological survey of the country?"

Ann walked along the narrow trail atop Long Ridge. Her grief weighed heavily upon her at the loss of her husband. Her pain was made more severe by the mournful sounds carried by the wind that beckoned to her grandson. She could hear the voices of the past just as Michael did.

"Michael, Michael" the wind moaned softly. "We wait for you in the Highlands. Come Michael. Your time is near."

Ann wanted to shout back at the ghosts of the forest, but she knew the futility of such an act. All she could do was wonder why it was her family that had to carry the awful burden.

Dudley emptied the bottle of Champagne into Michael's glass; then, he leaned back in his chair. "What are we going to do, Michael? Everything seemed so certain last summer, but, now."

"Now, we deal with life as it unfolds," Michael said. "All we can do is try to prepare for whatever fate delivers to us. The only certain thing in life is uncertainty. The only constant in the universe is change."

A knock at the door interrupted the two friends. Michael answered. Deanna and Dianna Bartlett, improperly, but enticingly attired in summer casual wear, grinned brightly.

"You two had better check the grade postings," Deanna taunted.

"The whole campus is buzzing," Dianna added.

"Let's go see what all the excitement is about," Dudley prodded.

In a flash the two couples were marching toward the library. As other students saw them, they joined in with the foursome.

"We're drawing a crowd," Dianna announced to the others.

"We are not drawing a crowd," Dudley countered. "You and Deanna are drawing a crowd. They're waiting to see if your tits pop out of those tops you're wearing."

"No, they've seen tits before," Deanna argued.

"Not like yours and Di's," Michael suggested.

The four broke into laughter all the way to the library, where a crowd had gathered at the billboard where the grades were listed.

As Dudley and Michael approached, the students parted. They all wore a silly grin on their faces which Dudley found annoying, especially because of the comments which he overheard.

Soon, Dudley and Michael stood in front of the board. In the center was a single sheet of paper that was entitled, "Class Standings, With the Highest Honors". At the top of the list was the name "Dudley Carpenter".

"Congratulations, Dudley," Michael blurted enthusiastically as he hugged his friend.

The Last Day of the Last Spring

"Wait a minute," Dudley said softly. "Look at the grade-point averages."

Michael studied the document a second time. His and Dudley's grade-point averages were identical, to within three decimal places.

The two young men stared at each other in confusion for a moment, then, they both broke into hysterical laughter. The other students joined in the festive atmosphere, and when the two top students were able to control their joy, the other students passed by to congratulate them. When they had shaken everyone's hand, they speculated as to how it happened that they could have both ended up with identical grades. Finally, the realization struck them both at the same time. They turned toward each other and jointly announced their conclusion. "Draco!" They chorused.

"Ivan! Open the door immediately," Doctor Henley shouted angrily. The door to Ivan Draco's apartment opened and Henley stormed inside. "You did this on purpose Ivan."

"Did what on purpose?" Draco asked calmly. "What are you talking about?"

"You deliberately gave Sylvan a grade that you knew would cause him to end up with the exact same grade point as Carpenter," Henley accused.

"Doctor Henley," Draco sighed, "how could I do that? I had no idea what Carpenter was doing in his classes. I didn't even know what he was studying this last term."

Henley plopped down in a chair. "I wish I could believe you Ivan, but I can't."

"You could begin by telling me what happened," Draco suggested.

"All right, I'll play your game," Henley hissed, "Carpenter and Sylvan finished their degree programs with identical grade point averages. That has never happened before in the history of National University, and you know it."

"You give me too much credit," Draco scoffed. "I must admit though, now that you mention it, I would have done it, had I thought of it. They are both excellent students."

"This is a disaster, Ivan," Henley asserted. "Don't toy with me."

"You say this has never happened before at National?"

"No, never," Henley repeated.

"Then, it's just a statistical anomaly," Draco said. "I don't have the time to plan such nonsense. I am busy doing research in my spare time."

"What am I going to do, Ivan? It is my responsibility to name the top student in the graduating class. Now, there is no graceful way for me to award the position to Sylvan. He comes from such an important family."

"I see your problem," Draco empathized. "Giving the top honors to a commoner like Carpenter is pretty distasteful, but his grade point is the same as Sylvan's."

"Yes," Henley whined.

"Well, if you ask me, there is only one way out of this," Draco said.

"What's that?" Henley asked with a desperate gasp.

"They'll simply have to share the honor," Draco said. "You can open the ceremonies by saying how wise and understanding the honors committee was in reaching such a just conclusion."

Henley considered the proposition. "It would show a certain flare for problem solving by the University," he mused.

"Yes," Draco said, "I believe you've hit upon the solution. You could let them speak in alphabetical order at the commencement and note that this was the only way the University could distinguish between these two excellent students."

"Yes, that will work," Henley sighed. "It will dispel some of the myth about National University being only for the affluent members of our society."

"Exactly!" Draco lauded. "That's just the kind of publicity the University needs."

Doctor Henley got out of the chair and rose to his feet. "We'll turn this to our advantage," he said. "I must start preparing my speech." He started for the door, which Draco rushed to open.

Henley paused at the open door. "I am sorry for accusing you of mischief," he said.

"Think nothing of it," Draco said. "You had a stressful situation to deal with. I understand what you must have gone through."

"Thank you Ivan," Henley smiled. "I am very grateful."

"We members of the faculty must rely on one another," Draco said softly.

"Yes," Henley agreed. "I'll consider you a friend from now on."

"I am truly honored," Draco said.

The Last Day of the Last Spring

Henley left the apartment and joyfully strode back toward the administration building. Draco watched him for a moment, before he broke into loud, boisterous laughter.

The graduation was set out of doors in a small area in front of the Administration building, heavily shaded by a grove of tall Walnut trees. The ceremonies went very much to schedule and the speakers were brief and to the point. Finally, the new graduates were able to mingle with family and friends. Michael had a large and distinguished entourage of guests. He hugged his mother and father first. After that, he turned to his grandmother and her two friends, Henry Highet and Bishop Blane. Next, he shook hands with his Uncle Charles and Uncle Hank before rushing into the arms of his Aunt Joan. When he left his aunt's embrace he found himself staring into the bright green eyes of Candyce Storer. Time seemed to stop as he looked at the tall young woman and he felt his chest tighten to make his breathing difficult. Candy was only able to offer her congratulations, when Margaret seized her son by the arm.

"You said you wanted to make an announcement to the family," Margaret reminded her son. "I can hardly wait to hear it."

"Well," Michael hesitated as he searched for Candy. He became anxious when she didn't immediately come into view. Finally, he saw her standing next to Hank.

"Don't hold us in suspense," Margaret prodded.

"I've decided to join the army," Michael announced. "Uncle Charles was good enough to use his influence, and I will join the Officer Candidate Training School in two weeks."

More kudos rained down on Michael, but he was well aware of the pain in Margaret's face. Everyone else seemed very supportive, and Candy broke into a bright, contagious smile. Margaret composed herself and hugged her son.

"You have made a choice I wouldn't have made for you," she said.

"I know mother," Michael agreed.

"The army is gaining a fine young officer," Margaret stated cheerfully. "I hope you appreciate him, Charles."

Charles smiled at Margaret, but he said nothing, as the other relatives and friends gathered around to congratulate Michael again on his career decision. The warmest wishes came from Ann and her friends, and Michael could feel the emotion of their words of encouragement. It took the arrival of the Carpenter family to break up the Sylvan group, and Michael was glad to remove himself from his mother's dismay.

The Carpenters, of course, were very supportive of Michael's military option, and they heaped congratulations on him. "You're an inspiration," Mr. Carpenter said. "It's unusual for men with your background to volunteer for the military these days. I am sure proud that Dudley is your friend."

"You're very kind, Mr. Carpenter. This army thing though is just something I felt I had to do."

"The military is an excellent thing to have on your resume," Mrs. Carpenter added. "It will certainly not harm you if you decide to enter the political arena later on."

Michael smiled at the small talk that was directed toward him, but his interests were focused on the three old people who stood patiently nearby. "Excuse me Mrs. Carpenter," Michael said. "I would like you to meet my grandmother."

"That would be very nice," Mrs. Carpenter responded.

Michael waved to get Ann Sylvan's attention. "Grandma," Michael called out. "Over here!"

Ann instantly came toward her grandson. Her old friends, Bill and Henry stayed at her side.

Michael made the introductions to the Carpenters. Mrs. Carpenter expressed her sympathy to Ann on the loss of her husband. Mr. Carpenter and Dudley echoed the sentiment.

"Thank you," Ann said. "You're very gracious."

Henry Highet seized the moment to usher Dudley and his family off to the side for a private conversation. Bill stayed behind with Ann.

"Are you doing all right, grandma," Michael asked.

"I'm fine," Ann answered cheerfully. "Congratulations on your graduation."

"Thanks," Michael beamed.

Ann sighed. "I wish it wasn't you, Michael."

"I know," Michael smiled. "At least I can share my thoughts with you, grandma. That is a great comfort to me. Otherwise, I fear I would go insane."

The Last Day of the Last Spring

"You will be immersed in madness, but you don't have to surrender to it," Ann advised. "Keep your goals in sight at all times. Do not be diverted from your task."

Michael smiled at the reassurance his grandmother so easily provided him.

"You will not be alone, Michael," Bishop Blane emphasized with a firm grip on the graduate's shoulder. "The Great Archangel, your namesake, will be near you. Call upon him when you are in need."

"There will be others helping you as well," Ann added. "Henry will see to it that much will be done ahead of time. You will not lack equipment, or supplies."

"I am worried," Michael admitted. "I am full of doubt about myself."

Ann and Bill smiled at the young man. "Your fears and doubts are signs of wisdom," Bill Blane grinned. "Only a fool would feel otherwise."

Michael suddenly was aware of the hubbub behind him as Henry Highet approached with the Carpenters. Henry thanked the Carpenter's for visiting with him, then he rejoined Ann and Bill. Dudley and his parents were very excited.

"You won't believe this, Michael," Dudley gasped. "Mr. Highet has personally invited me to come to his world headquarters for a job. This is fantastic."

Michael smiled broadly as he shared in his friend's happiness. "I knew you'd do it."

"I don't know what to say," Dudley gulped. "I have just realized my dream, and I'm surprised by it."

"Highet is getting one of the top graduates in the nation," Michael reminded his friend. "That might have something to do with the long term success he's had."

While Dudley and Michael chatted, Hank and Candy joined in to congratulate Dudley. Candy took advantage of her closeness, to steer Michael toward a nearby elm. "Are you sure about the Army?" She asked.

"You were there, at my grandfather's funeral," Michael reminded. "The army goes with my inheritance."

Candy nodded, and her face took on a serious expression. "Somehow, I believe my fate is wrapped up in yours," she said. "I'm not sure how."

"I hope not," Michael said. "I see only suffering in my future."

Candy's face brightened as she smiled. "Next year, it's my graduation. Will you come?"

Michael couldn't resist the girl's brightness. "If the army will agree, I'll come to your graduation."

"I'd like that," Candy answered.

Hank interrupted the couple's conversation and hugged his nephew. "I always knew you had balls, Mike," Hank smiled. "You'll make one hell of a soldier. I know it."

"Thanks, Hank," Michael grinned.

"We won't be able to come to Capitol City for your party," Hank said. "I have a chance for a book deal and I have to meet with this guy. I expect to see you next year in Portston for Candy's graduation though."

"I'll be there," Michael promised with a firm slap on Hank's shoulder.

The hubbub of the graduation finally ebbed, and Michael and his parents were soon riding in silence toward Capitol City. The Carpenter's on the other hand were raucously celebrating Dudley's degree and the fact that Henry Highet had personally given Dudley a job with Highet Industries. Hank slept on the flight back to Portston, while Candy wistfully stared out of the window of the plane. Ann agreed to stay the night in the University Hotel, where Bill Blane and Henry Highet would try to talk her out of returning alone to the Highlands.

A few days later, Dudley struggled to keep his heart rate at an acceptable level as he waited outside the executive offices at Highet Industries. For years he had dreamed of this day, but now that it was here, he was near panic. He shuddered as the great mahogany doors swung open. An elderly, refined woman approached him.

"Mr. Carpenter, Mr. Highet will see you now."

Dudley leapt to his feet, choked down the knot which had formed in his throat, and followed the woman into the chief executive's office. Highet was already hobbling toward him on his cane.

"Dudley. Good to see you," Highet greeted. "Please, come in, and make yourself comfortable."

Dudley groped uncertainly for a chair that was placed beside another in front of the executive's desk. The elderly woman took the other seat, while Henry Highet limped behind the desk. "This is Mrs. Waterson," Henry smiled.

Dudley turned, and this time he looked at the woman. He was immediately reminded of Ann Sylvan, and his gaze locked on the woman.

"How are you?" Dudley greeted.

"Fine, thank you," Mrs. Waterson replied. "Have we met before, Mr. Carpenter?"

Dudley blushed as his stare was obviously noticed. "No," he answered. "However, you bear a strong resemblance to a relative of a friend of mine."

"Ann Waterson has been with me for many, many years," Highet smiled. "She will help you fill out all the necessary paperwork after she has introduced you to the rest of the staff. I have a special project for you Dudley. I assure you, that your work will be both challenging and rewarding."

"I am anxious to begin," Dudley admitted

"Good," Highet beamed. "I like enthusiasm."

Michael stood at rigid attention, with his shoulder blades locked together. He kept his eyes focused forward, purposefully avoiding making eye contact with the lanky sergeant that stood before the forty officer candidates. They had been standing there in the hot sun for several minutes, waiting for the sergeant to say something, other than the word "attention" which he had uttered a long time ago. Now, they just stood there, waiting for something.

"My name is Sergeant Sims," the non-commissioned officer blurted unexpectedly, as he glared angrily at the young men before him. "The Army has assigned me the task of making you men, not just soldiers, but officers." Sims moved forward a couple of steps. "After studying you men for a short time, I think the Army has lost its fuckin' mind. Two thirds of our Candidates don't receive a commission. I'm bettin' that none of you make it." Sims turned and returned to his original place and glared back at his charges.

"Sixteen years, I've been in the Army," Sims said, shaking his head, "sixteen years." Sims paused to take a deep breath. "In those sixteen years, I have never seen a group of shit-heads like you." The sergeant shook his head slowly and let his eyes lower to stare at the ground.

He sighed audibly; then, as he jerked his gaze toward the sky he fell onto his knees. With an agonized expression on his face and his arms spread outward, he bellowed, "Why me, God? Why me?"

Michael asked himself the same question.

Eight weeks later, Michael was allowed a weekend pass. He had dreamed about having some time away from the constant badgering of Sergeant Sims, but now, that he could leave the training camp, Michael felt as if he had no place to go. He put on his dress uniform, thinking he would go into the town near the Army post, but instead he ended up just lounging on his bunk and staring at the ceiling. He enjoyed the silence of the empty barracks for several minutes. Then, he heard the door open at one end. He turned to see Sergeant Sims enter the building and that caused him to leap from his bunk and stand at attention.

"Relax," Sims quickly shouted. "What the hell are you doing here anyway, Sylvan? It's been eight weeks since you've been out of here. You should be in town having a good time."

"Yes sir," Michael answered. "I just don't have anywhere to go."

"Bullshit!" Sims sneered. "Look, there are three things I know a lot about; drinkin', fightin', and fuckin'. This little town outside the post offers all of that. Come on. I'll drive you there. You can catch the post bus if you can't find something to do."

"I'll accept the ride, sir," Michael smiled.

"That's the spirit," Sims said. "Get drunk! Get laid! It'll do you good."

Chapter 18

A short time later, Michael was wandering aimlessly along the "strip" which ran through the center of the small town. Bars bragging about the "best looking strippers in town" lined both sides of the street. Michael strode slowly along the street. He was both uncertain and uninterested in the available entertainment, but with no other choices, he finally entered one of the saloons. He barely got past the door, when he turned and walked out.

Michael took a deep breath as he searched the bright signs looking for a place that he might enjoy. Nothing seemed to stand out. Finally a flashing red sign caught his eye; "Ice Cream" flashed just a few doors away. He entered the shop and a small bell signaled his arrival. A young girl popped up from behind a tall counter. "Help you?"

Michael glanced at the menu high on the wall behind the girl. "I'll have a large, chocolate sundae, please."

The girl immediately took to the task, and in just few moments, the order was filled. Michael paid the girl and sat at a small table against the wall across from the counter. He looked through the glass window watching people pass by as he slowly consumed the ice cream. The tinkle of the bell turned his eyes toward the door. A very old woman and young boy entered the store. The old woman looked at Michael and froze.

"C'mon Grammy," the boy whined.

The woman looked down at the boy and guided him to the counter. She placed the order with the young girl, but turned to stare at Michael while she waited. The young boy quickly noticed his "Grammy's" concentration on the young man with the Gray hair. "Do you know that soldier, Grammy?"

The old woman hesitated. "No," she answered curtly and turned the boy to face the counter. Soon the girl appeared with the ice cream cones and the old woman searched her purse for the exact change. Suddenly, she saw a uniformed arm reach out and place money on the counter.

"My treat," Michael smiled.

The old woman burst into tears. "I saw you…years ago…in the Highlands," she sobbed. "You were one of the rangers."

"That was my grandfather," Michael smiled.

"I should have known," the old woman smiled nervously. "I'm getting stupid in my old age. But you look so much like him. And, you are just as kind. I'll never forget him."

"Enjoy the ice cream," Michael said as he squeezed the hand of the old woman and walked away.

Back out on the street, Michael surveyed the area for his next stop. He walked to the end of the "strip" and entered a small tavern. He soon realized that he had entered a bar that was frequented by the local townsfolk. He was also surprised to see Sergeant Sims. The veteran soldier saw Michael in the mirror and asked him to join him at the bar. Michael quickly pulled up a stool next to the sergeant and ordered more drinks.

"Thanks," Sims slurred.

The Sergeant tossed down his drink then sipped at the chaser. "I don't get you, Sylvan," Sims confessed. "Why are you in the fuckin' army? You're the biggest silver spoon I ever met," Sims said loud enough to get a caution from the bartender.

Michael appeased the bartender by buying the bottle and moving to a table in the rear of the tavern.

"Sorry," Sims slurred. "I get loud when I drink."

"You're loud when you don't drink," Michael smiled.

Sims laughed out loud. "You're all right Sylvan, but I still don't get it; why the army?"

"It's the only way I can get my inheritance," Michael said.

Sims considered the reply for a moment before rejecting it. "Families like yours don't impose that kind of thing on their heirs," he scoffed.

"No, they don't," Michael agreed. "I accepted the inheritance voluntarily."

"That makes more sense to me," Sims said. "I can't see you doing anything that you don't want to do."

Michael smiled and let the discussion end there. There was no point in telling Sims that his inheritance was dictated by fate. He would never believe it.

The Last Day of the Last Spring

Ivan Draco poured frantically over the books he had ordered on military strategy. He had been studying the art and history of combat for weeks, but he felt that he had learned little.

"Professor?" A woman's voice penetrated Draco's thoughts.

"Yes," he replied before looking up to the young librarian smiling at him.

"I have to close the library," Jane Linden grinned.

"Good god!" Draco sighed. "Is it that late?"

"Yes sir," the woman answered. "Actually, I should have closed an hour ago, but you were so involved that I didn't want to disturb you."

"I'm sorry Miss Linden," Ivan stumbled as he gathered his texts.

"Professor?"

"Yes."

"Some of the students have formed a new organization on the campus, and they were wondering if you would have time to visit with them," Miss Linden announced.

"New organization; I wasn't aware of any new student organizations being approved by the administration this summer," Draco said.

"This group hasn't petitioned for recognition," Miss Linden grinned confidently. "They prefer to remain anonymous."

Draco stared at the young woman for a moment, but his curiosity had been piqued. "What is this group's main interest?"

"I believe both you and this organization have common interests," Miss Linden grinned. "You both read the same books."

Draco was really curious now. "Indeed," he smiled, "then I must meet these 'anonymous' people."

"I'll drive you," the librarian said as she took Draco by the hand.

Draco sat quietly in the passenger seat as the young woman drove into an old part of town to an old factory site. Jane Linden smiled to reassure Draco, as she pulled inside the building and brought the car to a stop. The professor followed the woman down two flights of stairs and into a well lit room. There were two long tables placed end to end with more than two dozen young people seated around them. Draco instantly recognized all the faces as students at National University. In fact, they were among the brightest of the students at the university. Jane Linden took a seat at the end of the tables and motioned Ivan to an empty chair beside her. Draco complied and exchanged glances with the others in the room.

Jane opened the meeting. "You all know our guest," she said. "There is no need to speak his name. Before we begin, I want to take a moment to explain to our guest why we have formed this group." Miss Linden turned to the professor. "The mist has come to the Highlands," she said. "This group knows what that means and has decided to assemble in hope of developing a strategy to deal with the inevitable strife that will follow. As I told you earlier this evening, you are all reading the same books."

Ivan started to object, but the librarian cut him off. "We have rules. First, no one may refer to anyone by name. Second, the business of this group is only to be discussed here, nowhere else. Do you agree to our rules?"

"I have questions before I can agree to anything," Draco said softly.

"Fair enough," Miss Linden smiled. "Our goal is to survive the coming conflict and create an army of resistance. This group is made up of botanists, chemists, pharmacists, physicists, sociologists, and psychologists. We are still recruiting for physical therapists, dietitians, and geologists and a host of skilled construction and manufacturing people and medical staff. We believe that most of the latter jobs will be filled by refugees flooding into the Midlands for safety." Miss Linden paused, "we are also looking for a leader."

Draco took a deep breath. "I see," he dodged. "I am curious about the nature of the work the botanists are doing."

The young woman nodded toward a young man on her left, who instantly began talking. "We have found a small yellow berry that grows on a scrubby bush in the Midlands. When properly processed, the berry can produce a chemical that is a powerful hallucinogen. It isn't toxic, but it will certainly distract a person from their ability to function normally. The warfare implications for this berry are obvious."

"Chemist?" Draco asked.

A young woman at the other end of the table spoke up. "We've been working on sanitation problems," she began. "If we see a large influx of people into the Highlands, we need to have a good waste disposal system that the enemy can't detect."

The Last Day of the Last Spring

The meeting went on for two hours with each person reporting on his specialty. When the meeting reached its end, all eyes turned to Draco.

"We have much in common," the professor said. "I would like to attend your next meeting. There is much we have to discuss."

All the young faces around the room broke into broad grins.

General Speerman removed a book from his safe and placed it on his desk before sitting down and resuming his discussion with the soldier seated nearby.

"All right," Speerman said, "tell me about Sylvan."

"I spoke to his training sergeant, a Sergeant Sims. Sims tells me that Sylvan is progressing very well. His words were, 'that kid is smart as hell'."

"Any problems noted by Sims?" Speerman continued.

"He doesn't think that Sylvan has much of a social life," the soldier continued. "Sims says he doesn't get drunk, and is too choosy about women."

Speerman stared into space thoughtfully for a time. "When does he complete the Officers Training Program?"

"The end of September."

"That's only another month away," Speerman mused, and again fell into thoughtfulness. "When he receives his commission, I want him to go to the chemical warfare school in Portston."

"Sir, it might be wise to let Sylvan have some time off for social activities of his own liking," the soldier suggested.

"He'll enjoy Portston," Speerman smiled. "He has an uncle and a young woman friend that live there. Now, tell me about Ivan Draco."

The officer sighed. "Professor Draco has joined a group of students that are preparing for the next war."

Charles Speerman's bright visage faded into a dark mass. "What has Draco told this group of students?"

"Draco hasn't told them anything that would compromise your agreement with him," the officer replied.

"What is this student group up to?" Charles couldn't hide his anxiety.

"They have one hell of a plan to build a guerrilla force from the expected influx of refugees into the Midland-Highlands."

"I'm not comfortable with a bunch of academics playing at war," Speerman scoffed.

"General," the officer began, "I have good information on their plans. This isn't just a bunch of bookworms playing games. This is a collection of some of the best students in the nation."

"Are you telling me we should support this effort?" Speerman snapped.

"My recommendation is to leave them alone," the officer volunteered. "Draco's group is ahead of the Military Institute in the way they're thinking. The boys at the Institute think the war rumors that grew out of the mist which covered the Highlands this winter is just a bunch of nonsense."

General Speerman got up from behind his desk and began pacing around the room. After a few minutes he stopped, and sat on the front edge of his desk. He looked directly into the face of the junior officer that had been briefing him. "Have Ivan Draco get in touch with me. I want to talk to him about this group he's involved with."

Ann rocked slowly back and forth in her rocking chair on the front porch of her cabin. The leaves had started to turn then fall onto the forest floor to dry and wither under the relentless winter that promised itself on each breeze. Ann ignored the cold autumn wind as her mind recounted her life with her husband. She had been lost in her thoughts and had forgotten about the time. A stiff breeze pushed the old woman's fine, white, hair eschew. Then, she heard the whispers. "Michael, Michael," the wind called out. And, suddenly, the young man was there, walking from a car.

"Hello grandma," the young man called out.

Ann's heart nearly exploded with joy at the sight of her grandson. "Michael! What a surprise!" The old woman blurted cheerfully. "Come sit by me."

Michael dropped his duffel bag onto the porch, and then he pulled a chair up to his grandmother.

"You're such a fine looking officer," Ann gushed like a schoolgirl.

"Thank you grandma," Michael responded.

"What brings you here?" Ann quizzed.

"I'm on my way to a school in Portston," Michael explained. "They gave me four days to get there, so I thought I would spend a couple of them here with you."

"I'm glad to see you, Michael," Ann smiled.

"I'm glad to be here," Michael said as he took the old woman by the hand.

They sat there together; grandmother and grandson holding hands. They had little to say. Their hearts seemed to say everything for them.

The wind pushed through the trees. "Michael. Michael," the wind called out, "the mist will return to the Highlands. The Virgin Mother dwells on the cliffs of the river. They will climb up from the earth to join you. You will lead them."

Michael smiled at his grandmother, but she could see the pain in his eyes.

"I'm sorry," the old woman said. "I knew you would be chosen, but I didn't know why until the mist appeared in the Midlands. I wish it didn't have to be you, but I am so very proud that it is. Can you forgive me?"

"There is nothing to forgive," Michael smiled. "I have accepted my fate. I have learned from the voices of the past and I will do what needs to be done."

"Do you hear the voices on the wind? Do they ever leave you?"

"Yes," Michael said, "I hear the voices, but I didn't know that you heard them as well."

"I heard them the first time a year ago in late summer," Ann said. "I tried not to hear them, but it was no use. I kept hoping that it wasn't your name they called out, but I was just hoping against hope. Do the voices frighten you?"

"No," Michael smiled, "I have grown accustomed to them."

"Do not trust them," Ann cautioned. "They never tell all that you need to hear."

"Most of the time, I don't understand what they mean at all," Michael confessed.

"It's just as well," the old woman sighed. "Have you learned much from John's old diary?"

"No, I didn't grandma," Michael admitted. "There is more information in that small volume than you would suspect, though. I gave it to Uncle Charles. He seemed to have a greater need for it."

"Good," Ann grinned. "Then John was right about telling about the war."

"Yes, grandma, he was right."

Michael looked into his grandmother's eyes. "Grandma, it's time you leave the Highlands. I know that Henry Highet has offered to move you to an apartment in Capitol City, and I think you should accept his offer."

Ann smiled at Michael's concern. "You're right," she sighed. "I'm too old to stay here alone. I know that."

"Then, you'll accept Henry's offer?"

"Yes," Ann said. "He said he would be here next week. He doesn't want me to spend the winter here. When he comes, I'll tell him that I'll go."

Michael was pleased with Ann's response and he smiled at her acceptance. Then, he asked the other question he needed to answer.

"Grandma, there are times that I feel I can read your thoughts. Sometimes, I feel as though you can read mine. Is that possible?"

Ann turned and placed her hands on either side of Michael's face. They sat there for several moments; then, tears flowed down Ann's face. Michael softly took her hands from his face and held them tight.

"My god, grandma," can we always do that?"

"No," she said. "That's the curse of it. Sometimes we will be able to think to each other. Other times, no matter how desperately we try, we won't be able to communicate at all."

"Will I be able to do that with other people?"

"I don't know," Ann admitted. "I was only able to do it with John, then, only recently, with you."

"Don't trust in this ability you have," Ann cautioned. "You can't rely on it."

"Are the voices and the visions all part of this?" Michael asked.

"I think so. Somehow, it all seems to be connected," Ann smiled.

Michael released the old matriarch's hands. "I'll make some coffee," he grinned.

Ivan Draco nervously held the telephone receiver to his ear while he waited for General Speerman. His heart skipped a beat when he heard the General's voice.

"Ivan Draco here," he stammered.

"Oh yes. Thanks for calling Professor Draco. Tell me about this "unofficial" student group you're working with."

Draco reviewed all that had happened to bring the group into existence and a summary of their activities to date. When he finished there was a long pause from the other end. Draco was on the verge of panic. "Should we continue," Draco asked.

"Yes," Speerman answered. "It is imperative, however, that no one outside the group learns of your plans."

"I can assure you we are taking every precaution," Draco said.

"I am grateful for your assurance, Professor, but I'll be watching you and your group's progress."

"I understand sir," Draco sighed.

The call ended and Draco relaxed for a moment. He stared at the photograph of Richard Woodman and wondered what he had gotten himself into.

Hank and Candy met Michael at the airport. Hank was grim, but cordial. Candy seemed to have trouble looking Michael in the eye. Hank drove directly to his home which sat upon a hill that overlooked the city. Taking advantage of the warm humid weather, they sat on the large back porch and stared out at the city.

"So, how's mom?" Hank asked.

"She's well," Michael reported. "She's going to move to Capitol City pretty soon."

"Really," Hank exclaimed with surprise. "Gosh. I didn't think she would ever leave Long Ridge."

"It's too much for her," Michael explained. "There are too many memories for her to deal with alone in the wilderness. Besides, in Capitol City she'll be close to mom and dad and her old friend, Henry."

"I think it's great that she won't be alone," Candy interjected.

"Yeah," Hank said. "I know about being alone. Fortunately, I have Candy."

The young woman blushed, so Hank changed the topic.

"How long will you be in town, Mike?" Hank asked softly.

"Four to six weeks," Michael replied.

"That's not very long," Candy lamented. "I mean, I was hoping you would be able to stay longer," she blushed again.

Hank smiled at Candy's awkwardness, but didn't embarrass her. "Yeah, that isn't much time," Hank agreed. "We'll have to make the most of it, won't we Candy?"

The girl nodded, but her shyness held her speechless.

Hank poured drinks and passed them to Michael and Candy. The last one he held aloft. "To the future," Hank toasted.

"The future," Michael echoed, then, he finished the drink with a single draught.

"It's truly amazing," Hank said. "We sit here looking out upon a city at peace, all the while knowing that the horror of war will soon rip everything apart."

"Maybe it won't happen," Candy offered hopefully.

"That would be all right with me," Michael smiled.

"Do we have any idea how much time we have left, Mike?" Hank asked softly.

"No," Michael sighed.

"I've been wondering what we could be doing to prepare," Hank disclosed, "but I can't really think of anything."

"Perhaps you're looking for something too big," Candy suggested. "Maybe there are small things we could do."

Hank slapped his leg with the palm of his hand. "Damn it, Candy, you're right. I have been thinking on a grandiose scale. I'll take a new approach to my guess work."

"Will you share it with us when you discover it?" Michael asked.

"Absolutely," Hank grinned. "In fact, I'm going down to 'Pier 13' and get started on it right now."

"What's pier 13?" Michael asked.

"Saloon," Candy smiled. "It's Hank's favorite watering hole."

"It's more than just a bar," Hank countered. "I have had some of my best ideas there."

"We'll go with you," Candy said protectively.

"No way," Hank said sternly. "You two can find something else to do besides bother me when I'm working."

Hank jumped up and went inside, leaving Michael and Candy alone on the large porch. "Should we try to stop him?" Michael wondered out loud.

The Last Day of the Last Spring

"No," Candy said. "It wouldn't do any good." The long legged woman got up and picked up Hank's empty glass. "I'll make something to eat," she said.

"We could go out to dinner," Michael suggested.

"I'd rather stay here," Candy smiled. "Just the two of us," she added.

"That sounds great," Michael reassured her.

An hour later, Michael and Candy were both carrying dirty dishes into the kitchen. "I'll get those," Candy said.

"You don't understand, Candy," Michael said. "The government has spent a fortune training me to be a good housekeeper. I must stay in practice."

Michael took the dishes from Candy, and briefly, their hands touched. Michael felt a surge of energy flow through his hand, electrifying his entire body. He looked into Candy's green eyes. He felt captivated by her, drawn to her. As his chest constricted and his breathing became erratic, he wondered if Candy had felt what he had experienced. He couldn't find the courage to ask. He turned and set the dishes near the sink and turned on the water. "I'll wash," he volunteered.

Candy caught Michael's hand on the tap and shut the water off. She looked into his eyes. "I haven't been able to get you off my mind since I first met you," she announced softly. "I can't help myself, now," she sighed as she embraced Michael and kissed him. Michael met her frankness with his own passion, and for a while, time stood still for them as they fell headlong into their desire for each other.

Chapter 19

Dudley glanced at his wristwatch. It was 10:30 p.m. He closed the books he had been working with and locked them in the vault hidden behind his bookcase.

"You're working too late," a voice resounded from the office door.

Dudley instantly recognized his mentor, Henry Highet. "I don't know how much time I have," Dudley replied.

Highet entered the office and with some difficulty, he lowered his frame into a chair. "We never know how much time we have," the old man grinned, "but we must take time to rest."

"You're right," Dudley smiled. "Anyway, I've finished the plans. All I need to do now is accumulate the raw materials, machinery and people I can trust."

"I anticipated your staffing needs," Highet smirked as he removed a folded piece of paper from a breast pocket. He handed the paper to Dudley, who instantly opened it. "Those people are all retired now, but each is a master craftsman."

"Do you think they would be willing to go back to work?" Dudley asked.

Highet chuckled. "I've already talked to them," he said. "They're waiting for you to call."

Dudley shook his head. "You're an amazing man Mr. Highet."

"No, there's nothing amazing about me," Highet denied. "But, my friends, they are really something." Highet smiled cheerfully, then, he rose to his feet assisted by his cane. He slapped Dudley on the shoulder. "Come on, now. Go home. Tomorrow, I'll call my customer and tell him we've finished the first phase."

"And we're beginning phase two," Dudley added emphatically.

It was the night of December 6th. A cold, north wind swept down the Old River and assaulted the city of Portston. Just before sunset, Barbara found herself standing before the bluffs, staring at the rocky clefts. Finally, what she had been waiting for came into view. Barbara walked toward the sheer, wall of stone and reached up slightly at the glowing light. When the vision came into full view, Barbara knelt on the rocks and lowered her gaze.

"Oh Holy Mother, how can I serve you?" Barbara said.

"Look up, Barbara. See how I appear to you, and listen to my words."

Barbara slowly tilted her head back. The Virgin Mother stood upon the rocks. She was clad all in gray. Her face was soft and peaceful.

"Go to the Bishop. Tell him what you saw. Tell the bishop that the gray one has heard the voices of the past and has taken their council. Tell the bishop that his sins have been forgiven and he should not despair. He will suffer no more."

Bishop Blane quickly welcomed Barbara into his office. He could see by her manner that she had experienced another visit from the Blessed Virgin. Barbara seemed to glow with her own brightness.

Barbara obediently delivered the message that she was commanded to state, then, Bill Blane, Bishop of Portston embraced her with a powerful arm. "Stay with me a moment," he asked softly. He led Barbara to a comfortable chair; then, he went to his desk and clicked on the intercom. "Ask Father Moss to come in here," Blane said into the intercom. "Tell him to be prepared to hear a confession."

Moments later a very young priest entered the office. He glanced nervously at the Bishop, then at Barbara. Blane motioned to him to sit beside him.

"I need you to hear my confession," Blane said to the priest. "Barbara must hear it also, so she may tell our Holy Mother that I received her message."

The priest kissed his scapular and placed it hurriedly around his neck. Barbara stared at the floor.

"During the war I lost my faith," Blane began. "I threw off my vestments and took up weapons to slay other men. I killed many men during the war. I don't even know how many. I was filled with hate and there was no room in my heart for anything else."

"When the war ended, I returned to the church as a priest. I never divulged my sins. Then, to add to my guilt I was elevated to monsignor, and finally bishop. All these years I lived the lie that I was the dutiful priest. All these years I have despaired that I had lost my soul. It took the death of my friend for me to realize my error. And now, I must denounce my sinful pride. I ask the forgiveness of the Lord through the grace of our Holy Mother. Amen"

While the stunned priest administered absolution to the Bishop, the old cleric turned to Barbara and smiled. "When you see Our Gray Lady next, tell her how grateful I am for the return of my faith."

"I will," Barbara said.

"Father Moss will take you home now," Blane ordered.

The next morning, just before Father Moss was preparing for the early mass at the basilica, he found the Bishop's body at a small side altar before a statue of the Virgin Mary.

For the next three days, the nation mourned the passing of the old priest. Thousands upon thousands of people passed by the casket displayed at the cathedral to pay their last respects. At the gravesite an old woman, and an old man that hobbled on a cane, placed a placard at the foot of the Bishop's casket. On the placard was a simple prayer that read: "St. Michael, Great Archangel, Conqueror of Lucifer, Warrior of the Heavenly Host, hear our prayer. This day, this man has willingly given up his life for a cause he believed was right. We ask you to carry his soul to the Lord God our Father and in the name of Jesus Christ, his only Son, implore Him to absolve our fallen comrade of his sins and grant him eternal rest in paradise. Amen."

Ann Sylvan and Henry Highet were allowed to linger at the casket of their old friend before he was carried to his final resting place, beneath the massive altar. The two old people were solemn, but accepting of their friend's death, as they walked hand in hand from the cathedral. It was a cool, sunlit day, as the heavens seemed to rejoice at the arrival of the old priest.

Michael waited at the door of Highet's limousine as the ancient pair approached.

"I understand you're going to Capitol City," Highet said to Michael. "Would you like to travel with us?"

"No sir," Michael declined softly. "There is someone I must see before I leave Portston."

Ann smiled at her grandson. "I understand," she said. "Come see us when you return home."

"I will grandma," Michael said. He opened the door and assisted the elder pair into the back seat. When they were both comfortably settled, he closed the door, and the chauffeur drove away. Michael stepped beyond the police lines that had been set up to control traffic and walked one block before he hailed a cab.

"Where to?" The cab driver asked.

"West bank," Michael answered.

A short time later, Michael asked the driver to stop. He paid the fare, and then stepped out of the cab. He took a few steps toward the edge of the cliff and looked down upon Barbara, who knelt before a glowing light in the limestone. The kneeling woman looked up, as if she had been waiting for him. Michael looked at the woman, and suddenly, unexpectedly, he saw what she could see and heard what she could hear.

Barbara instantly knew of his power. "He is here Holy Mother," Barbara said to the apparition on the rocks.

"Yes", the Gray Lady smiled.

"He can see…and…and he can hear…" Barbara stumbled.

"Yes," was the reply from the cliff, "he sees and hears the truth."

"I can sense his sadness," Barbara said. "Must he suffer so much?"

"His suffering and the suffering of all your people will not be in vain."

Barbara began to pray and she bowed her head. When she looked up again, the young man was gone.

"This is preposterous," JJ said to his aide as he glanced up from a report. "We have not violated our trade agreement with their country."

The young man shrugged. "Perhaps they're just trying to get us to renegotiate the treaty," the young man suggested. "I don't know why you're letting this upset you."

JJ checked his emotions and smiled. "You're right, of course. It's strictly politics," he sighed. JJ plopped the report on his desk. "Tell the ambassador that we are pleased to receive his report and that we will begin an immediate investigation."

"Yes sir," the young man smiled and left the office.

JJ immediately picked up the phone and called General Speerman's office. After a couple of transfers, Speerman finally answered. "Charles, this is JJ"

"Yes Mr. Sylvan, how can I help you?"

Charles' very formal response cued JJ that he wasn't comfortable speaking. "It's your turn to buy lunch," JJ said. "Shall I pick you up at 11:30?"

"That would be perfect," Speerman replied. "See you at 11:30."

It was exactly 11:30 when General Speerman entered JJ's limousine and sat beside his brother-in-law. "Sorry JJ," Charles said, "I wasn't free to speak with you when you called earlier."

"I gathered as much," JJ smiled as the limousine pulled into traffic.

"I'm glad you were able to understand," Charles sighed. "What can I do for you?"

"Our old enemy has accused us of a trade violation," JJ said as he handed a document to Charles.

The general glanced over the document and handed it back. "This is the excuse they're going to use to get their people in the right frame of mind," Charles stated coldly. "They've done it before."

"I would have thought they would have learned their lesson the last time," JJ said hopefully.

"You would have thought we would have learned too," Charles added solemnly.

"What do you mean by that?" JJ asked curtly.

"If they want to go to war with us right now, they'll win," Charles admitted. "Their navy is already twice as large as ours, and our intelligence reports tell us they are adding another fleet."

"Surely we have time to prepare our defenses," JJ suggested.

"Even if we had the time, the government will never appropriate the money," Charles observed. "We're a nation of merchants, not warriors. Our people believe we can negotiate our way out of any tough situation."

"You're right," JJ reluctantly agreed. "We would never be able to convince the country that there is a threat now. And, by the time they realize there is a threat, it'll be too late."

"That's the way I see it," Charles concluded.

"Surely you have a plan," JJ pleaded.

The Last Day of the Last Spring

General Speerman just looked at his brother-in-law and smiled. "At least we know for sure who the enemy is," Charles beamed. "That gives us a lot of information to work with."

It was raining when JJ's driver stopped in front of the Military High Command Offices. Charles waved good-bye to JJ before dashing from the car to main entrance. The infantryman at the door brought his rifle to a saluting position. Charles returned the salute and went directly to his office.

"Major Wilder is here to see you General," a young officer announced. "I took the liberty of allowing him to wait for you in your office."

"Well done," the general complimented the officer, as he turned and opened the door to his office. Major Wilder rose from his chair and saluted. The general returned the salute and asked his old friend to take a seat and be comfortable. He could see that the infantry commander was shaken.

"What's on your mind Frank," Speerman asked cordially.

"General may I speak openly," Wilder stammered.

"Frank, what's this general stuff. We're old friends. Tell me what's bothering you."

"Charlie," Wilder sighed, "I met your nephew last night."

"Really; where?"

"Mountainview Federal Penitentiary," Frank Wilder replied.

"What the hell were you doing up there?" Speerman asked cheerfully.

"I had an invitation from Willie Barber. He's in charge of the military prison up there. Anyway, when I arrived there yesterday afternoon, he told me that there was an execution scheduled, but that it was also a top-secret military thing. He wasn't very pleased with the arrangement, I could tell. He asked me to take his place as witness to the execution. I agreed, and Willie was visibly happy that I had accepted."

"When the time came," Frank continued, "I went to the death chamber. When I got there, one of your Military Intelligence guys was getting ready to do the briefing. He said his name was Colonel Tipton and that this execution was a training exercise for one of their trainees. He explained that the prisoner that was scheduled for execution had agreed to the terms, but that the trainee would not be told until just prior to the event. The deal was that the room would be empty except for a very sharp knife on the floor in the center of the room. The prisoner would be in one corner, the military trainee would be in the other, and when a signal was given they would fight to the death. If the prisoner killed the trainee, his sentence would be commuted to life and he would live very comfortably. On the other hand if the trainee killed him, then the sentence had been carried out as it should have been." Frank's voice cracked

"Would you like a drink Frank?" Speerman offered.

"Whiskey, if you have it," Frank said softly.

Speerman opened a desk drawer that was equipped for such occasions and poured his friend a glass of whiskey. Frank took half the liquid in one draft.

"After both men were put into the room, the observers were moved to a viewing room with a one way mirror. A couple of minutes later, the signal was given. The prisoner dove for the knife and grabbed it. But, no sooner did his hands close on the weapon than the trainee kicked him in the head. The first kick seemed to stun the prisoner, but the soldier followed up with two more kicks to the head in rapid succession. Then, the young man plunged his right knee into the middle of the prisoners back while grasping his skull at the same time. He gave a quick pull and twist and broke the man's neck." Wilder gulped down another glass of whiskey. "The whole thing only took five or six seconds."

"Come on Frank," Speerman encouraged his friend, "you've been through this sort of thing before."

"Yes, I have," Wilder agreed. "After it was over, Lieutenant Sylvan exited the death chamber. Colonel Tipton slapped him on the shoulder; then, he and the other observers left the room. Sylvan approached me. He asked if I was all right. I told him I was o.k. We began to talk; just he and I. He acted as if nothing had happened. It was as if he had swatted a fly instead of killing a human being." Wilder stared at his empty glass, and then looked up at Speerman. "I was afraid of him, Charlie."

Speerman filled Wilder's glass again then took a glass for himself. "What you saw didn't happen," Speerman said.

"If you're willing to make your own nephew into something like this, we must really be in trouble," Wilder concluded.

"You've been in the Infantry too long," Speerman said. "I need a good tactician on one of my teams. You're one of the best. I want you to take the job."

"I'll take it for two reasons," Wilder said. "First, I have to know what the hell is going on. Second, I feel that I've seen something I shouldn't have seen and my life may be in jeopardy."

"You'll be a good addition to our group," Speerman concluded.

Deanna Bartlett glanced repeatedly at the door to the bistro as she slowly sipped her drink. She knew it was too early for Michael to be there, but she couldn't help herself.

"Relax Dee," her sister Diana demanded softly, "he'll be here soon."

"It's been a long time," Deanna smiled sheepishly. "I really miss him. I didn't think I would ever feel that way about a man."

"Wow," Dudley exclaimed. "I never thought I'd hear a Bartlett woman admit how she felt."

"We're not unfeeling people," Dianna corrected Dudley with a stern look on her face. "We just have a sense of propriety."

Dudley glanced at the more than subtle exposure of Dianna's cleavage. "Right," he smiled.

"There he is," Deanna announced.

They all watched as Michael stood near the door, scanning the room for them. He was in uniform, and Deanna found him quite desirable. She stood up and waved. Michael spotted her; removed his black beret, and started toward them. It had been months since they had seen Michael, and as he approached, they wondered if he was the same man they had known. He seemed taller with his erect posture. When he reached his friend, Deanna crushed herself against him.

"Damn it Michael, why didn't you write?" Deanna scolded.

"Not much to write about," Michael said.

"It's good to see you," Dudley smiled as he slapped Michael on the shoulder.

"It's good to see all of you," Michael beamed.

The four young people sat down at the table. A waiter instantly appeared and they ordered drinks. Michael paused at first, but then he changed his mind. "Whiskey will be fine for me," he said. The waiter turned and vanished into the crowd.

"So tell us about the Army," Dudley began. "I see you received your commission."

"Not much to tell about the army," Michael said. "I'm still a trainee. I haven't seen the real army yet."

"What are they training you for?" Dianna asked.

"Killing," Michael answered soberly.

The expressionless face of Michael took them off guard for a moment, but they all silently seemed to know that there was no point in pursuing the issue any further.

"Why did you join the Commandos?" Dudley asked.

"It's all part of the plan I put together," Michael said. "The Commandos are supposed to be the elite of our nation's combat units. I guess I wanted to be one of the best."

The waiter returned and handed out the drinks. Michael emptied his glass with one gulp and handed it to the surprised waiter. "We'll have another round," he said. The waiter disappeared without a word.

"Don't overdo the alcohol," Deanna cautioned. "I need you to be alert and responsive," she hissed in her sexiest voice.

Michael smiled. "I'm just priming my pump," he countered.

Dudley grinned, but he knew that the Michael he had known in college was not the same man seated across from him now.

The evening went on. After several rounds of drinks, Dudley was beginning to feel woozy. Dianna and Deanna were obviously beyond their limit. Only Michael seemed to be impervious to the liquor. Finally, Deanna suggested they leave.

"I don't want to seem rude," Deanna said, "but I want to be alone with Michael tonight. You two can come by for breakfast in the morning."

"Fair enough," Dudley laughed, and the foursome began making their way to the door. Suddenly, a man bumped into Michael.

"Excuse me," Michael said.

"Oh no, excuse me," the man said loudly. "I should have stepped aside for a Commando."

"Thanks," Michael smiled.

"Wait a minute," the man shouted as he grabbed Michael by the arm, "I'm talking to you." Michael was aware of two other men taking up positions just behind the loud man that held his arm.

In a flash, Michael grabbed the hand that held his arm and with his thumb he crushed the man's own thumb into his own hand. The man yelled, but then, Michael stomped the man's right knee, before twisting the man's arm in an outstretched position. Michael's left fist came down on the man's elbow and the sound of breaking bones was unmistakable. A second man rushed from Michael's left. Michael met the man with a kick to his knee and a quick punch to the nose. With the first two men on the floor, the third man pulled a knife.

Michael smiled at the man. "I killed the last man that tried to use a knife on me," he said, while he kept his eyes locked on his would be attacker. The man hesitated, then, slowly backed away and went out the door. Michael turned to his stunned friends and ushered them to the door. "Just a couple of barroom brawlers," he reassured them. "They just had too much to drink." The two couples went out the door just as the man who had pulled the knife began running down the street.

"I've never seen anything like that," Dudley said. "The army has obviously taught you how to fight."

"They weren't prepared for me to attack," Michael said. "That's why it worked. If they had been ready for it, they would've kicked my ass."

"I don't think so," Dianna said.

"Me neither," Deanna added wide-eyed.

"I was lucky. That's all," Michael concluded.

"You're luck has just begun," Deanna smiled as she cuddled against Michael provocatively.

"Jesus Dee," Diana scolded. "Are you going to have sex with him in public?"

"Hmmm," Deanna hummed.

"No," Michael said. "There are some things even Commandos don't do in public."

The next morning Michael and Deanna awoke in each other's arms. Michael stared at the beautiful woman next to him. He wondered how she felt about him. He wondered how he felt about her. Then he thought about Candy. He felt attracted to her as well but it was different than the attraction he had for Deanna. He also felt that Candy had deep affection for him. Yet, here he was with Deanna. Michael felt confused. He smiled at Deanna. "What do I mean to you?" He asked.

Deanna smiled. "What do you mean?"

"I'm trying to find out if I mean anything to you," Michael asked.

"You're my lover," Deanna answered. "You've always been my lover."

"Is that all we'll ever be, is lovers?" Michael inquired.

"If we try to be anything else, our lives will be completely fucked up by our families," Deanna predicted.

Somehow, Deanna's response didn't seem to be what he wanted to hear. Then, he really wasn't sure what he wanted to hear. He concluded he may not live long enough to commit to Candy or Deanna. Michael nodded his head in agreement. "You're right. It would take accountants several years to sort out who owned what."

"Exactly," Deanna grinned. "This way, we can help each other escape from all that."

Michael smiled. "I am really happy that we can escape together. I need that, especially now. There is little I can do to plan for the future." If there was to be a future, he wondered if Candy would be part of it. Don't think about a future, he reminded himself.

"You can expect me to be here for you," Deanna sighed. "I'll be here for you to take and do whatever you want." She wrapped her arms around Michael's neck and kissed him to rekindle their lust.

After breakfast with Dudley and Diana, Dudley dropped off the two women and drove Michael to his parents' house. The drive gave Dudley an opportunity to talk to his friend alone.

"Michael I checked up on those two fellows at the bar last night. They're both in the hospital," Dudley disclosed.

Michael nodded his head as if he expected that result, but said nothing.

"Good God, Michael. Don't you understand? You broke the one guy's thumb and arm and shattered his kneecap. The other guy had a broken leg and nose," Dudley admonished.

Michael was silent for a second then he responded coldly. "You don't understand, Dudley. That was what I was trying to do."

Dudley did a double take on his friend then continued. "Well at least your bluff with the guy with the knife kept anyone else from getting hurt."

"Bluff?" Michael asked.

"Yeah, don't you remember? When the guy pulled out a knife you told him that you killed the last man that tried that," Dudley reminded.

The Last Day of the Last Spring

Michael looked out the window of the car for a moment; then, he turned to face his friend. "That wasn't a bluff," he said. "I don't bluff."

Dudley looked into his friends' eyes long enough to see the simple truth Michael was telling him. He felt a cold chill run through his body. "The army has changed you, Michael. Are you being what you want to be?"

"You're right about the army," Michael agreed. "It has changed me. As for being what I want, I am being what I must be."

Finally, the drive ended. Dudley left Michael off at the front door to the urban mansion, and drove off.

Chapter 20

The next day, Dudley sat at his desk and stared thoughtfully out his window. He was so immersed in his thoughts, that he didn't hear Henry Highet enter the room. The old tycoon quickly sensed his young executive's state of mind.

"How was your visit with Michael?" Highet questioned.

Dudley smiled at his mentor's perceptive abilities. "I don't know," he answered. "Michael has changed a lot since he went into the army. Some guys tried to start fight with him last night, and he put two of them in the hospital." Dudley paused. "A third man pulled a knife. Michael just stared at the man for a moment; then, he told him that he had killed the last man that attacked him with a knife. The man backed off, then, he ran away. I thought Michael was bluffing. Now, I know that Michael would have killed him. The man with the knife was smarter than I was. He could tell by the look on Michael's face that he was no match for Michael even with his knife." Dudley shook his head. "My friend has become a killer, Mr. Highet. I'm trying to decide how I feel about that."

Highet stroked his chin with one hand. "Don't rush to judgment, Dudley," the old man advised. "Few men are able to realize their dreams and aspirations. Many are forced to react to life circumstances they have no control over. In order to deal with life's twists and turns, men have to change. Sometimes the changes men have to make are quite severe. Instead of being able to choose what they want to do, they are forced to do what they must."

"That's exactly what Michael told me," Dudley said. "He said he was doing what he must do."

Highet pulled a chair up beside Dudley and sat down. He placed both hands on his cane and rested his brow on top of his hands. After a moment he looked into Dudley's face. "There is something I must tell you about this secret project I gave you. And more important, I must tell you about your friend's grandparents. You must swear to me, that you will tell no one about this."

Draco poured over the maps spread out on the table before him before finally thumping the table with his fist. "Damn it!" Ivan fumed. "There must be maps of the Midland-Highlands that are more detailed than this."

Jane Linden tried to comfort the professor by offering him a cup of coffee. Draco took the coffee.

"I'm going to Capitol City tomorrow," she announced. "I'll stop by the geological survey office and see what they have."

Draco sipped the hot coffee. "How long will you be away, Jane?"

"Just a few days," the young woman replied. "My mother asked me to look in on her sister, my aunt. She's getting up in years."

"It would be nice if we could get more detailed maps," Draco said. "We'll never be able to navigate the Midlands without accurate maps."

"I'll see what I can find," Jane reassured Draco.

"Hurry back, Jane," Draco said with an unfamiliar sense of urgency in his voice. The young woman looked at the dark-haired man for a moment, uncertain what to say. "I'll miss you," Draco confessed.

"If my aunt is in good health, I'll return right away," Jane promised with a smile. "Meanwhile, why don't you inventory our map library to make certain we aren't overlooking anything."

"Good idea, Jane," Ivan nodded as he buried himself in the task. Jane smiled at the obsessed professor, then, she left him to his work.

General Speerman noticed a small flashing, red light on his telephone. The light pulsed to indicate he had a call on his top-secret extension. He picked up the receiver. "Hello?" He said.

"Falling Leaf needs to speak to you," a robot like voice said.

"Tell Falling Leaf to take a cab to the National Museum," Speerman replied, then, he abruptly hung up. In a flash, the military man was up from his chair to open a secret closet. He selected a pair of denim trousers, tennis shoes, and a sweatshirt. Quickly, Charles changed into the clothes he had taken from the closet, while carefully hanging up his uniform. Lastly, he grabbed a leather jacket, a knit cap, and a pair of sunglasses. He touched another concealed place on the wall, and an elevator door opened. Charles entered and took the elevator to its only destination. When he emerged, the cap and sunglasses were on his head. He walked directly to a taxi. The keys were in the ignition.

Just a few minutes later, Charles stopped in front of Barrett House to pick up a young woman. Jane Linden entered the back seat of the cab.

"National Museum," Jane said to the driver.

"Not much to see there in the fall," Charles informed.

"The new exhibits start each spring," Jane replied.

Charles glanced into the rearview mirror to watch Jane's face when she heard the code words.

"Start each spring".

"I'm Falling Leaf," Jane disclosed.

"Stale Cake," Charles replied.

"I thought we were going to meet at the museum," Jane smiled.

"That's what I wanted the enemy to think," Charles explained. "I always assume they have access to my communication system."

"Do you really think they have penetrated your communications?"

"I don't know that they have, but if I assume they have, it won't matter. How is the campus club doing?"

"They're as ready as they can be from a planning standpoint," Jane said.

"How about Draco," Stale Cake queried.

"He's a natural leader. Everyone respects him because he empowers them to do what they do best." Charles carefully watched the woman while she spoke.

"Security," He asked.

"I have to admit that I am really surprised about the secrecy the group has maintained. Outside of the participants, no one else on the campus knows the group exists. The whole group meets at a place and time Draco selects. No one is told anything until the very last moment. Usually, the subcommittees meet with Draco individually and most frequently. The number of large meetings has been greatly reduced."

"Sounds good," Charles said. "You must guard against complacency though."

Stale Cake drove up to the main entrance of the National Museum and stopped. "Is there anything you need?"

"We need topographical maps of the Highlands?" Jane said as she started to exit the vehicle. "What do I owe you?" Jane asked as a young couple approached the taxi.

"Eight-twenty five", Charles read from the meter.

Jane opened her purse and removed a ten-dollar bill. "Keep the change," she smiled.

"Thank you very much, Miss," Charles beamed.

Jane closed the door to the vehicle, and Charles drove off.

Minutes later, Charles was back in his uniform striding toward the Special Operations Group he had created under Colonel Richard Woodman. Everyone rose to his or her feet as Charles walked through the door. "As you were," Charles quickly commanded. "Have they finished their brain surgery on you Colonel Woodman?" The General asked with a smile.

"They've picked everything out of my brain four times," Woodman answered cheerfully.

Charles smacked Woodman on the shoulder. "We appreciate what you're doing Richard. I hope all this isn't too hard on you."

"This? Hard?" Woodman grinned knowingly. "No, this is enjoyable. What I went through seventy years ago; that was hard."

Charles smiled with admiration of the old man. "Richard, have you and your team discussed topographical maps of the Midlands?"

"Sure, several times."

"Then, they do exist," Charles declared.

"Not exactly," Richard said. "I'll explain. When I was first dispatched to the wilderness with our team, there were only topo maps for the areas where the Old Road was constructed, and where the barge companies could navigate the Old River. Of course there were good topographical records for Long Ridge. When we put them together, it gave us an "H" shape. Most of the areas left and right of the "H" were missing."

"We have a computer simulation," a staff officer volunteered.

"Yes, Major Short, please go ahead," Woodman said. "I forget about computers," Woodman acknowledged sheepishly.

"It's up," Major Short announced.

Richard and Charles moved toward an available terminal and looked at the large screen. "That's what we had to start with," Woodman explained. "Bring up the latest one," Woodman ordered.

A second later, another map appeared that contained many times more detail except in the northwestern quadrant. "That's incredible," Charles stated.

"It's not as incredible as it seems," Woodman cautioned. "Zoom in for us, Major."

Charles watched carefully, as more detailed maps appeared on the monitor. But, as the detail increased, the number and size of undefined areas became more numerous. "I see what you mean," Charles hissed. "By the time we get to a map ratio that an infantry commander could use, there are going to be as many open holes as there would be contour lines."

"Exactly," Woodman confirmed.

"It gets worse, general," Major Short added. "We've tried satellite photos, radar imaging and microwave imaging. The photographs are the best of the lot, until we try to get to a high resolution. The more we zoom in, the more distortions there are. We finally sent an aircraft over the area with passive sensors on board. We found random radiation levels, all in the lower frequency ranges, along with changing heat readings from the surface. Each pass we made over the wilderness, we got different readings."

"What's your conclusion Major?" Charles asked.

"It would literally take an army of surveyor's years to complete a topographical survey of the Midland-Highlands." The Major shook his head. "It's almost like the goddamn place is alive."

"Maybe it is," Charles suggested with a thin smile. "I want you to make one copy of the maps we have."

"Even with all the holes in them," Major Short asked with surprise.

"Yes," the General acknowledged. "Take heart Major. The problems we're encountering are nothing compared to what our enemy is going to go through."

Michael was stationed at the Secret Special Warfare School just north of Portston. Everyone knew the military base was there, but none knew that is was to be the training grounds for Michael's insurgent force. Even the post commanders were excluded from knowing about Michael's activities.

The first phase of Michael's job was to select a team of ten men. Michael was given special access to all combat trained personnel, but he concentrated mostly on commandos that had already been screened by the military's processes. He selected two hundred men to interview and sent a request to the proper channels to bring the men to the base at Portston. Waiting for his potential comrades at arms to arrive, gave him time to attend Candy's graduation.

Unlike the cuddly ceremony at National University, Candy's graduation was being held in a sports arena that was large enough to accommodate the two thousand plus graduates and their families. The contrast between his own graduation and Candy's was not lost on Michael. Still Michael found the event to be fun. It was much more raucous and celebratory than his own graduation and he found the liveliness very much to his liking.

Candy's brilliant red hair easily distinguished her from the other grads and Michael lost track of time as he continually watched her. Finally, she approached the stage and received her Bachelor of Science in Physics. She graduated Summa Cum Laude. Michael was almost as proud of her as Hank.

After the official ceremony was ended, Hank took the new graduate and his nephew to Pier 13 where a lavish meal and party awaited. Again Michael noted the contrast in life styles. His parents and the Bartlett family seemed to be overly proper, where here there was only unbridled joy.

Hanks friends were truly amazing. He had surrounded himself with artists, writers, poets, musicians and other people from nearly every walk of life. Michael thoroughly enjoyed talking with these free spirits who had a common thread that united them. They had no expectations for each other. They accepted people as they were.

Candy was the star of the moment, and all of Hank's friends had to dance with her; men and women alike. Candy was obviously embarrassed by all of the attention, but she knew it would be impolite to refuse it.

"Isn't she the most beautiful creature you ever saw," a woman said to Michael.

Michael turned to reply to the tall, buxom brunette. "Yes she is," he agreed.

"You must be Michael," the woman correctly assumed. "I'm Margo."

"Yes, I'm Michael, hi Margo."

"Hi," Margo smiled. "God you're good looking Michael; almost good looking enough for me to go straight."

Michael laughed out loud.

A shorter blonde approached Margo and put an arm around her. "This is my partner Edie," Margo introduced.

"Hi Edie, I'm Michael."

"Yeah, I know," Edie smiled. "Candy is always talking about you."

"I was telling Michael that he's almost good looking enough for me to go straight," Margo disclosed to her partner.

Edie laughed. "Go for it, but you'll have to get past Candy first."

Margo smiled. "I guess I don't want to break up a good friendship," she concluded.

Suddenly, Candy grabbed Michael. "I'd better rescue you from these two beauties," she smiled. "Besides, you haven't danced with me."

Michael silently acquiesced as the band began playing a soft dreamy melody. Candy melted into his embrace and molded to his form. They moved in unison in their own world while the revelers cheered their approval. Michael relaxed in Candy's arms and never thought about Deanna.

It was the second winter after Dudley had graduated from National University when they found Henry Highet dead in his bed. Ann Sylvan was there with him at the end. It was a very large and elaborate funeral with a procession of vehicles that choked city traffic for three hours. Now, the formal mourners had gone, and only three remained at the grave. Ann, Dudley, and Michael stared into the hole where the casket had been lowered. Finally, Dudley took Ann and Michael by the arm, and led them to the waiting limousine.

The trio said little at first, but Dudley found the silence too much to bear. "I hear you've finished your training, Michael?" Dudley said.

"Yes, finally," Michael answered. "I'm looking forward to a regular duty assignment."

It became silent again, and again Dudley tried to get a conversation going. "Henry, Mr. Highet, told me all about your grandparents, and Bishop Blane, and himself," he disclosed. "It explains a lot about your behavior, Michael. I'm sorry I wasn't smart enough to figure it out on my own."

"If it hadn't been for my grandparents, especially grandma here, I would have thought I was going insane," Michael admitted. "I'm glad Highet told you, Dudley."

"I wish I knew what lies ahead," Dudley said.

"No. No, you really don't want to know that," Ann stated firmly. "You will learn everything you need to learn as you live through the future. Concentrate on your strengths and stay focused on your tasks. The outcome is not determined. You will have control of the situation. Success and failure are both possible. You will have to earn your success, or live with your failure."

"I don't believe I could live with failure," Dudley sighed.

"Nor do I," Michael added.

Ann smiled at the two young men. She was reassured by the calm, firmness in their voices. It was not a statement made in braggadocio. It was a statement of determined young men; determined young warriors. She was proud of them both.

JJ collapsed into an overstuffed recliner and stared at the ceiling. Margaret approached with a glass of whiskey over ice. JJ pushed himself upright and took the glass. In one draught the glass was empty.

"I brought the bottle," Margaret smiled as she brought the container into view and refilled the glass. "I take it things aren't going well with the trade negotiations."

"We are now officially enemies," JJ said. He sipped at his drink. They walked out of the negotiations and sent a letter terminating their diplomatic mission here."

"What's the next step?" Margaret asked hopefully.

"We wait for them to attack," JJ hissed.

"Surely, they won't take military action over a trade dispute," Margaret countered.

"This isn't about trade," JJ corrected his wife. "It's about revenge and domination."

"Revenge; over losing a war more than nearly seventy years ago... That doesn't make sense," Margaret scoffed as she sat on the arm of the easy chair.

JJ patted Margaret on the thigh and smiled at her. "We are a nation that takes pride in our ability to reason and strive for understanding. We are dealing with a country that measures their pride by their ability to impact the rest of the world. There is nothing reason will provide them. They must win. They must remove the blemish of defeat from their souls."

"You sound just like the old men at your father's funeral," Margaret accused.

JJ nodded thoughtfully. "Yes," he agreed, "you're right. I do sound like mom and dad's old friends. But, it is only because I have come to realize that they were right."

"You can't believe this is going to end up in a war," Margaret hissed in disbelief.

"No, I don't believe they'll go to war with us," JJ said. "I am certain of it."

"That's enough," Margaret said sternly. "I won't have any talk of war while Michael is home on leave."

"Why not, mom," Michael asked as he and Deanna Bartlett entered the room. "That's what I've been training for all these months."

Margaret grew stone silent. Deanna wore a confused expression on her face while she waited for someone to explain what was going on.

"War," Deanna asked as if the word was unknown to her. "Who is going to war?"

"You and your sister," Michael smiled. "We're already late for Dianna's dinner party."

"Oh my," Deanna sighed as she looked at her watch. "We do need to be going, Mrs. Sylvan. I'm sorry to rush off."

"That's all right, dear," Margaret beamed with all her social polish. "You two go have a good time."

"Later, folks," Michael waved. "We'll talk if you're still up when I come home dad."

"Sure," JJ smiled until the young pair left the room. He sipped at his drink and glanced up at Margaret.

"What will we do?" Margaret asked. "…if there is a war?" She added.

"You and I have only two choices," JJ began. "We can die, or become slaves."

Margaret paused thoughtfully. "You know JJ," she began, "I have never considered a life of servitude."

JJ chuckled and placed an arm around Margaret's waist. "No, my dear Margaret, I don't see servitude in our future at all."

Margaret clutched JJ close to her breast and allowed her head to rest against his. JJ let his other arm circle his wife and they stayed locked together for several minutes until the front doorbell rang.

"That'll be Charles and Joan," JJ explained. "I invited them over so Charles and I could talk. Would you mind entertaining Joan while he and I talk politics?"

"No," Margaret smiled and then kissed JJ and went toward the front door. She arrived just as the butler opened the door to the spacious foyer.

The two couples exchanged pleasantries for a moment, then, Charles and JJ slipped into the den, while Margaret and Joan relaxed in the library.

Charles nervously swirled the glass of brandy that JJ handed him, as he waited for his host to fill his own snifter.

"You heard about them walking out of the negotiations," JJ guessed out loud.

"Yeah," Charles answered.

"We'll have to inform the public about our diplomatic failure fairly soon," JJ advised.

Charles sipped the heady liquor. "I need more time," Charles said. "I need all the time you can give us."

JJ considered the urgency in Charles' voice. "We might be able to grant them more trade concessions just to make it look as though they're being unreasonable" JJ offered unenthusiastically.

"I know they're doing everything they can to sabotage the negotiations," Charles acknowledged. "I just want to screw up their timetable so we can give them as many casualties as possible before they overwhelm us."

JJ had long ago learned the futility of questioning his brother-in-law about details, so he decided to take a different approach. "I'll try to convince the committee that we offer them nearly everything they are asking for," JJ said. "If nothing else, world opinion may delay them for a while."

Charles smiled, but said nothing, other than to pat JJ on the shoulder.

"We're all but dead aren't we Charles?"

"When it starts, head for the Highlands or the Eastern Mountains," Charles suggested.

JJ shook his head. "Margaret and I have already made our decision," he smiled. "We won't be traveling then."

Charles looked at his politician brother-in-law with new respect in his eyes. "Perhaps, when the end comes, we'll have enough time for one more glass of this excellent brandy," he said softly.

Ivan looked upon the bright young faces in the dim light of the room. "Are there any questions or issues you want to bring up?" Draco asked.

"Just one," a thin young woman stated. "How much time do we have before we become fully operational?"

"I've been thinking about that very thing myself," Draco disclosed. "I believe the latest invitation to our enemy by JJ Sylvan's negotiating team is nothing more than a ploy to stall for time. Therefore, if my assumption is correct, I believe the Highland Dragons should become operational immediately." The professor looked around the room and as he made eye contact with each of the students; he saw only smiles on their faces.

"Is there no dissent?" Draco asked nervously. "Is there no one who would talk us out of this madness?" The room was silent. Still, Draco searched for that one person who would balk at what they were planning. In the end, there was no opposition made. "Very well," Ivan concluded, "how shall we begin?"

Instantly the group sprang into action. Ideas flowed freely as each young brain poured forth all it could offer. Draco felt that he had just activated a gigantic machine and he was certain that once it began to work it would have a life of its own. No one man would be able to control it. The professor felt proud, but he also felt that he would break into tears.

When he entered the house, Michael noticed the den was still well lit. He stuck his head in the doorway and saw his father staring into a glowing fireplace.

"Dad?"

"Michael, you're home early," JJ observed.

"I'm not in a party mood tonight," Michael disclosed as he sat down on the end of the leather couch near his father's recliner.

The two sat there staring into the fire for several minutes. Then, JJ turned toward his son.

"Michael, is there anything I can do for you?"

The young commando smiled. "I have everything I need, dad."

"For the first time in my life, I feel completely helpless," JJ admitted.

"Maybe everyone is helpless and just doesn't know it," Michael suggested.

"Could be," JJ acknowledged. "We grow up being told we are masters of our own lives depending on the choices we make. No one tells about the outside forces all around us that can take choices away from us."

Michael smiled. "Your parents didn't seem to have many choices. Maybe our success is measured more by how we deal with the unexpected."

"Can we prepare for the unexpected, Michael?"

"I think so dad. I try to expect everything and at the same time expect nothing. That way I'm not surprised by either."

"Did the army teach you that?"

"No, dad, grandpa did."

JJ looked at his son with some jealousy. "You knew my father better than I did."

Chapter 21

Two hundred men answered the army's call for volunteers for a top secret mission. When they arrived at the Portston Army Post, they were met by a young captain with gray hair and cold gray eyes. The officer studied the men in the ranks. They came from all different parts of the country. Some were enlisted men; others were non-commissioned officers and junior officers. All seemed to be very athletic.

"Welcome," the young officer greeted the men. "The first thing I want you to do is to remove your name tags from your uniforms. Do it now." The command was followed by the sound of tearing threads as name tags were removed.

"I need ten of you," the young officer said. "I will keep only those of you who can keep up with me." There were some smiles among the young men in response to the challenge. The officer in charge ignored the cocky grins. "Follow me," he ordered and began running down the road. The two hundred men followed.

After running for more than an hour around the post the men returned to their starting point. They formed up behind weapons and heavy packs.

"When I give the command, strap on your gear and follow me," the officer said.

"Now!" Michael shouted as he swung the eighty pound pack onto his back and quickly cinched the straps. Next, he grabbed his rifle and started running. The men hurried to don their equipment and catch up to their mentor.

The men were led down the main road of the post then to a smaller road that became gravel. The gravel road became a track and the track soon became a path. Finally, they were in the open woods. Two and a half hours later, the leader stopped.

"Take up defensive positions near the top of the ridge," the leader ordered. The men who had kept up sprung into action, while the training officer rounded up the stragglers. When the last of the stragglers arrived, the officer instructed them to return to the post adjutant to be returned to their original units.

The hearse arrived at an open grave in the National Military Cemetery in pouring down rain. The flag team stood in two rows of three men and efficiently removed the casket from the vehicle. With crack military precision, the six men carried the casket to the waiting bier and placed the shining, black box into position. Next, they extended the national flag over the casket and held it taught.

There were only two mourners at the grave. One was General Charles Speerman and the other was Captain John Michael Sylvan. The two officers stood in silence for a moment. None of the men seemed to take notice of the drenching rain. Finally, the General nodded and the Captain stepped forward to the head of the casket then, he looked up into the falling rain.

"St. Michael, Great Archangel, Conqueror of Lucifer, Warrior of the Heavenly Host, hear our prayer." The Captain paused and lowered his gaze. "This day, this man, Colonel Richard Woodman, has given up his life for a cause he believed was right. We ask you to carry his soul to the Lord God our Father and in the name of Jesus Christ, His only son, implore Him to absolve our fallen comrade of his sins and grant him eternal rest in paradise. Amen."

Michael stepped back from the casket, and the military pallbearers folded the wet flag. Michael accepted the flag. Seven rifles fired three volleys in unison. As the echo of the shots faded a bugler sounded a sad lament. Finally, Michael and Charles walked a short distance to a waiting car. Charles got in the car first, then, Michael. As soon as the passenger door closed, the driver put the vehicle into motion. The two men in the back seat were quiet for a moment, and then Michael looked into his uncle's face.

"Grandma is the last of them, now." Michael stated.

Charles nodded, but said nothing.

"When she dies, they'll come," Michael predicted.

"They could attack us at anytime," Charles clarified. "Your father has done a great job delaying them with his political genius."

"Yes sir," Michael agreed. "Dad is a skillful negotiator."

Charles opened a small compartment in front of him and removed two glasses and a crystal flask. "Whiskey," He asked.

"Yes sir," Michael replied.

General Speerman half filled each glass then handed one to Michael. "To Hornet," he said as he raised his glass.

"Hornet," Michael echoed as he tapped Charles' glass with his own. The glasses were emptied in a single draught.

"Are you ready for the future?" Charles asked.

"Yes sir," Michael smiled.

"What about your team?"

"They are ready, sir."

"Have you decided on a name for your group?"

"Yes sir, we are now the Midland Grays," Michael announced proudly.

Charles smiled. "I like the name. It has a certain kind of flair."

"Thank you, sir."

The summer was hot and unusually dry. The leaves on the trees began to fall in late August, even though the change in their colors was weeks away. Michael and his team trained throughout the summer, and he pushed them to their physical and emotional limits. But, they met his every challenge, and Michael considered himself fortunate to have ten men that were as dedicated and driven in their work as he was. So, satisfied, when he had completed their training tasks, Michael requested leave for himself and his men.

When he returned to Capitol City, he was surprised to find the front door ajar. When he entered, he saw his mother and father locked in a tight embrace. His father was weeping.

"Mom, dad," Michael stumbled.

"They've taken mom to the hospital," JJ said as he struggled to regain his composure. "We are going to…" Once again, JJ emotions overwhelmed him.

"Were going to the hospital," Margaret said. "Help me get JJ to the car."

Michael wrapped a powerful arm around his father, and started toward the door.

"I hope she's alive when we get there," JJ sobbed.

Michael said nothing and stayed at his task. Slowly, he guided his father into the limousine then got in beside him. Margaret entered from the other door. The trip was brief and silent. Before they knew it, the car stopped at the main entrance of the hospital.

Michael opened the door and helped his father out of the car. Margaret rushed from the other side to join them. A small group of photographers exploded flashes in their faces as they made their way into the hospital. Two men met them in the entry and immediately ushered them to a waiting elevator. Seconds later, JJ and Michael stood on either side of Ann's bed. Each man gently held one of Ann's time withered hands. Margaret stood at the foot of the bed.

Ann's doctor talked to Margaret. "She has had a very severe stroke," the doctor said.

"Will she be able to recover?" Margaret asked.

The doctor hesitated for a moment. "Mrs. Sylvan, I'm not sure why she is alive right now. I don't believe she will recover."

Although JJ never looked away from his mother's face, the doctor's words cut into his heart. Tears streamed freely down his cheeks.

"Can she hear us," JJ asked.

"I don't know," the doctor answered.

Michael looked at his grandmother's face. She wore an expression he had seen many times before when she was concentrating on something. He decided he would try to talk to her with his thoughts. "We're here grandma," he said in his mind, "JJ, Margaret and me. We're all here."

Michael watched the gnarled face. He noticed her eyes showed movement even though they remained closed. "Yes, Michael. I know you're all here," Michael heard in his mind.

"We're worried that we're going to lose you," Michael thought.

"It's time for me," he heard Ann reply. "John. John is here waiting for me. I told him I couldn't go until I warned you, Michael."

"Warned me?" Michael returned.

"Yes. They are coming with the first snow, Michael. Be ready for them; the first snow."

"I'm ready grandma," Michael replied with his thoughts.

"Tell JJ and Margaret not to grieve. John is here with me. We must go, Michael."

Michael stared silently as the expression on Ann's face relaxed into a peaceful expression, and then her eyes opened and rolled back in her head.

"She's gone, dad" Michael said aloud.

The doctor rushed forward and Michael relinquished his place at the bed. He paused a moment to embrace his mother, then, he went out into the hallway in tears. A short time later, JJ and Margaret joined their son, and the three left the hospital knowing that the woman they had known and loved no longer dwelled with them.

Barbara rushed along the riverbank to the special place on the cliff. She pressed herself against the limestone wall and looked up into a bright light. The image she had come to expect appeared in the brightness. The Blessed Virgin smiled with kindness. "You have done well," the image said to Barbara.

"I have done so little," Barbara confessed.

"It is the little that shall tip the balance." The Virgin Mary said. "The small shall become great. The meek shall become courageous. Keep faith. Tell the people to pray to my son and he will hear them."

"I will," Barbara vowed.

"I will visit you once more. Afterward, the tribulation will begin. Do not lose faith. Pray for those who will die, so they may not walk in eternal darkness."

As the image faded away, Barbara felt unusually at ease. She smiled as she walked back toward her houseboat.

Dudley, Dianna, Michael and Deanna sat at a small table near one end of the large swimming pool. The two couples were unaware of Margaret's analytical gaze.

"Give the young people their privacy", JJ suggested softly.

"I'm not spying on them," Margaret denied. "I'm worried," she huffed as she walked away from the window.

"About what," JJ asked.

"About two young men more interested in their conversation than two, nearly naked beauties just inches away from them," Margaret sighed. "It isn't natural. Michael lost his youth and all the pleasures that go with it."

JJ walked casually past the window to glance outside. Then, he returned to his favorite chair. "I think you're worrying about nothing," he argued. "You underestimate the power of those meager bikinis."

Margaret turned with an angry flash in her eyes, but her memories rushed back to her, making her smile. "Did my bikini overpower you when we were dating?"

JJ shook his head, no. Margaret countered by throwing a pillow at him.

JJ laughed, and Margaret plopped on his lap.

"I haven't heard you laugh since Ann died," Margaret observed.

"No, but it's time. We've been burdened with death and gloom and there is nothing we can do to change it. It's time we start enjoying the rest of our lives."

"There may be little time left," Margaret cautioned.

"Then, we'll have to enjoy all the time that's left," JJ concluded. "Why don't you and I get our evening clothes on and go over to the country club. There won't be many more warm nights like this to dance under the stars."

"I have the perfect outfit," Margaret said as she jumped to her feet. "That black silk sheath has been hanging in the closet too long."

"I'll race you," JJ challenged.

Margaret giggled and darted for the stairway. JJ was in close pursuit.

"All right you two," Deanna said to Dudley and Michael, "knock off the serious stuff. You have two willing women here to talk to."

Michael smiled. "Thanks for bringing me back to reality."

"I'll bring you back to reality," Deanna offered suggestively as she clutched Michael's thigh.

"Oh, hello, Mrs. Sylvan, Mr. Sylvan," Dianna cooed. "Wow! What a great dress!"

"Thank you," Margaret grinned.

Michael was surprised to see his mother in the clinging, revealing garment that draped seductively over her trim frame. "You look terrific, mom," he understated.

"Thanks," Margaret said. "JJ and I decided to go over to the country club for a late dinner and dancing. The place is all yours."

"And don't wait up for us," JJ beamed as he took Margaret by the arm and led her away.

The young people watched as the elder pair happily walked toward the garage.

"That is really neat," Dianna whispered. "I never thought of my parents as lovers, until now."

"Me neither," Michael admitted. "I've never seen such an outward display of affection from them."

"Can you picture me in that dress, Michael?" Deanna wondered aloud.

"Not while you're wearing that bikini," Michael teased.

Deanna giggled as she darted toward the pool. Michael gave instant chase and nearly caught her. As they both dived into the water, Michael managed to grab her by the ankle.

Dianna smiled at the antics of her sister and Michael. Then, she turned to Dudley. "We could join them," she said.

"Come here," Dudley invited as he patted his thighs with his hands. Dianna complied and sat on her man's lap. "Life will never be better than it is right now," Dudley sighed.

The society crowd at the country club was astonished by the overtly romantic aura that glowed about Margaret and JJ. As the evening wore on, the ambiance created by the couple seemed to transmit to everyone who saw them. JJ and Margaret, however, were totally immersed in each other and barely knew anyone else was around. Memories of their youth flooded back from the past and filled them both with intensity for each other that had been shelved and forgotten for too long. But now, each touch rekindled their lapsed passions and they wallowed in the warmth of it.

The next morning, the Sylvans awoke in a luxury suite at the Barrett House Hotel. Outside of their door was a newspaper. The couple was pictured on the front page and the caption stated; "Politician Caught Romancing His Wife". Below that article another headline declared, "Trade Agreement Being Considered – Tensions Ebb"

The Last Day of the Last Spring

Ivan Draco smiled as he glanced at the front page of the paper, but when he saw the lower headline, his smile faded. Voraciously his eyes absorbed the newsprint about the lessening international tensions and the new trade agreement. When he finished the article, he could feel his pulse pounding in his temples and his blood racing through his veins. He hurriedly grabbed his telephone and dialed Jane Linden's number.

"Hello?"

"Jane, its Ivan Draco. Have you seen the paper this morning?"

"Yes, how about that, JJ Sylvan scored twice."

"Could we meet for breakfast; my treat?"

"A librarian can't pass that up," Jane quipped. "Is the "Cafeind" all right?"

"Sure. Thirty minutes?"

"Twenty."

"Good see you in twenty minutes."

After they both hung up, Draco folded the newspaper under his arm and started across the campus. The Cafeind Coffee Shop had become an integral part of campus life over the past several years and offered a respectable meeting place for faculty and students. No one would expect anything other than an academic discussion at the Coffee Shop. It was as secure a place, as Draco could think of for a private talk with someone about national security issues.

When Ivan reached the diner, Jane was waiting for him. They went inside and selected a small booth in the corner where no one could approach them without being seen. The two made small talk until they had placed an order and dismissed the waitress. Then Draco placed the newspaper on the table.

"What are your thoughts on this "peaceful solution" they're writing about?" Ivan asked

"It's all bullshit," Jane smiled.

"That's exactly what I think," Ivan agreed. "We need to get everyone together."

"No problem," Jane responded. "It'll take a couple of days though. Where do you want to meet?"

Draco considered the question for a moment. "I can get the Faculty Education Room in the Administration building."

"That's a very public place," Jane cautioned.

Draco considered the issue for several seconds. "We can call it an invitational forum on current events. Of course, only our people will be invited. When the administration sees the list of some of our best students, they'll go along."

"It's a bold plan," Jane grinned, "but I like it," she concluded with a squeeze of Draco's hand.

The touch of their hands sent a lightning bolt of discovery through them both. They paused and looked at each other in utter surprise. Finally, the spell was broken when the waitress interrupted them with the food they had ordered. Slowly, reluctantly they allowed their hand-holds to loosen and fall away.

The man and woman stumbled clumsily through small talk during their breakfast. Somehow they managed to talk about things for which they had little interest. They were unable to find the courage to talk about the feelings they were having for each other. Both were grateful when breakfast ended and they could step outside into the cool fall air. But, their feelings still nagged them. Draco became frustrated at his cowardice.

"Jane," he started.

"Yes," she replied hopefully.

"I just became aware," Ivan hesitated then concluded he would deal with the pain of rejection later. "I just realized that I have these feelings…"

"What kind of feelings?" Jane asked as she stepped close to the professor.

"Romantic feelings."

"Tell me about them," Jane encouraged as her arm wrapped around Draco's waist under his overcoat. "When you're finished, I'll tell you about my feelings," she concluded as she pressed herself against him.

Draco held her tight. "This isn't the time or place."

Jane pulled back slightly and smiled. "My apartment is a good place," she said. "As for the time, if not now, when? Besides, we're both going to end up dead anyway."

Ivan acknowledged Jane's reasoning with a smile, before they began walking toward the woman's apartment.

Charles and JJ laughed as they discussed the newspaper article about JJ and Margaret. "So how much did you pay this guy to write this article?" Charles teased.

"Had I known he was going to do such a great job, I would have made him my campaign manager in the next election," JJ quipped. But his frivolity soon turned somber. "If there is a next election," he added softly. "What do you think, Charles? Will there be another election?"

"I don't know," Charles admitted, "but I doubt it."

"Do you think they'll attack this winter?"

"Michael said he believes they'll come this winter," Charles disclosed. "My Military Academy geniuses think next spring would be more advantageous for them."

"What do you think, Charles?" JJ prodded nervously.

Charles ran his fingers through his hair as if the gesture would organize his thoughts. "My brain tells me it will be spring. My gut tells me the winter. There was something about the way Michael gave his opinion that makes me believe that he knows he's right."

"What are you trying to say about Michael?" JJ queried. "Do you think he's psychic?"

"Your mother told us she had 'visions'. Do you remember?"

"Yes, yes I do," JJ agreed.

"Maybe Michael has the same ability," Charles wondered aloud.

"Where is Michael now?" JJ asked.

"I have him doing some coordinating work. I promised him he would be able to come home for Christmas," Charles stated casually.

Chapter 22

It was raining, but Michael paid little attention to it. He stood in the forest, just off the old road, waiting for his contact to arrive. He tucked his arms under his poncho and found his flashlight. He held the light over his wristwatch then switched it on. He was careful not to let the light shine so it could be detected. After a couple of seconds, he switched off the light and returned it to his belt. Then he removed the arm with the watch from under the poncho and easily read the luminous dial. His contact was due.

The unmistakable sound of a small truck could be heard just to the north and coming closer. A moment later the slit headlights of the vehicle were illuminating the rain. The vehicle stopped just a few feet south of Michael's position in the wood line.

"I'm Falling Leaf," a woman's voice announced.

Michael walked onto the road. "I'm Gray Thorn," he announced.

"Get in," the woman commanded.

Michael walked in front of the vehicle and entered on the passenger side. He glanced at the driver, but it was too dark for him to see any features of the person.

The driver quickly maneuvered the vehicle in the narrow road and turned back to the way she had come. Neither spoke.

A short distance later, the vehicle slowed then turned into the forest. Both driver and passenger bounced from side to side for several minutes, before the vehicle turned again into what appeared to be a cave. The small truck moved even slower now, before coming to a stop. The driver switched off the lights.

"We get out here," she said. Michael obeyed and the two stood in the darkness.

The driver made a signal with a flashlight. Another light flashed a short distance away. "Who goes there?" A voice asked from the darkness.

The Last Day of the Last Spring

"Falling Leaf and Gray Thorn," the woman answered. "Who are you?"

"Miner and Dragon," a voice replied. Lights went on everywhere and the four people looked at each other in astonishment. Michael instantly recognized his old friend Dudley, Professor Draco, and Jane Linden. There were hugs and handshakes and looks of surprise.

"We must remember not to use our real names," Jane reminded. "We are operational now." No one objected to Falling Leaf's reminder.

"I didn't know these caves existed," Gray Thorn admitted.

"Neither did anyone else," Miner explained, "Henry Highet told me about them when he assigned me to work on a special project."

"Where is the power source?" Gray Thorn continued.

"Steam powered generators," Miner answered.

"How do you generate the steam?" Falling Leaf inquired.

"We don't. The earth does. We're using geothermal energy." Miner smiled at his old friends. "But, there is a lot more. Come with me."

The others filed behind Miner as he led them a short distance to a wide, metal door. Miner pressed some buttons on a box mounted into the rock, and the door opened. "Come on," he invited.

The others followed Miner into a small square place they recognized as an elevator. Miner operated the control panel and the box quickly began descending. "I am going to skip the lowest level," he explained. "That's where the generators are, and it's too damn hot to go down there." The elevator began to slow. "We're going to the second level." Miner said.

The elevator stopped with a jerk then the door opened. The foursome stepped out into a large, open area. There were seemingly uncountable rows of computer stations and five, large, digital displays were fixed on one wall.

"This is Headquarters," Gray Thorn said. "It's exactly the way they described it to me."

"This is incredible," The Dragon finally spoke. "How did all this equipment get here?"

"This is the special project Henry Highet assigned to me," Miner answered.

Gray Thorn slowly inspected the entire area, while the others stared with awe. "What else do you have buried here, Miner?" Gray Thorn asked.

"Above us are machine shops and assembly areas for manufacturing small arms and munitions. There are also large stores of raw materials, chemicals, dried foods; you name it. We even have the capability to put together a hospital. We have stocks of medicines, bandages, all those types of things."

"Did Henry Highet plan all this?" Falling Leaf asked with wonderment in her voice.

"No," Miner said. "All this was planned and built more than 70 years ago. The caverns are all natural formations but were connected by Shiller Mining Company. All we did was to update everything with new technology and restock it."

"Shiller Mining Company!" Dragon exclaimed in surprise. "My family is the majority stockholder in Shiller Mining," he disclosed with a smile. "I guess my grandfather was part of your family's vow of silence, Gray Thorn."

"I'm not surprised," Gray Thorn shrugged.

"How many people can live in here?" The Dragon asked.

"I don't know," Miner admitted. "I can tell you this though. There are 10,000 workstations throughout the entire complex of caves and tunnels. There are machine shops; electrical shops; carpenter shops; just about everything."

"All we need are the people to man those stations," Gray Thorn suggested.

"Yes," Dragon sighed. "When the time comes, they will be here. Can I tell the rest of the Highland Dragons about this?"

"No," Miner answered flatly. "Gray Thorn will be the only one who can authorize any additional disclosures about this place. Those are my orders," Miner concluded.

"It all makes sense to me now," the Dragon hissed. "This is how they did it. This is how they won the War of Liberation."

"It had a lot to do with it," Miner smiled.

"Who will fill me in on when I can tell others about this place?" Gray Thorn asked.

"I was told to tell you that you will receive your final instructions from a person who will identify himself to you as Stale Cake. That's all I know," Miner said.

The Last Day of the Last Spring

Falling Leaf remained silent when she heard the code name for Charles Speerman. She knew that her silence would be expected.

"That's the end of the tour," Miner said happily. "When you meet here again, it will be under very ghastly circumstances. Good luck to you all."

Gray Thorn embraced his friend, then Falling Leaf, and finally the Dragon. With that emotional exchange, the four re-entered the elevator to ascend to ground level and go back into the darkness of the forest. Once the cave entrance was sealed, the four people stood silently in the darkness. With the exception of steady dripping sounds from the rain, the forest was completely silent. There was a lingering attitude among the group; an unspoken reluctance to break away from each other. Gray Thorn felt compelled to speak.

"There will come a time when we will not have to slink away in the darkness," he said. "Then, we will openly speak each other's names and we will do it with great pride."

"To that day," the Dragon echoed as he placed one arm on Gray Thorn's shoulder and his other on Falling Leaf. Miner locked his arms on Gray Thorn and Falling Leaf to complete the circle. They just stood there in the rain with their arms locked and interwoven while their souls forged together into a terrible commitment.

Barbara had visited the bluff every day, for the past two weeks, certain that the Blessed Virgin would appear to her. But the vision never came. Barbara was beginning to become restless. The steady feeling that the vision would come had never been wrong before, but now she could only wonder. She walked along the gravel bar below the cliffs again around midday; still there was no apparition. Reluctantly, she returned to her houseboat and prepared a modest meal. After she ate, she sat outside, where she could keep an eye on the spot on the bluffs.

Barbara lost track of time, until a cold, north wind brought her back to awareness. The sky had grown overcast and gray, and the wind seemed to pierce her light garments. She got up to go inside and get a warmer wrap, when she saw a familiar flicker of light in the bluffs. Urgently, she bolted toward the light; running recklessly over the stony beach. She lost her shoes, but not her pace, as she arrived at the spot and fell on her knees. She gasped, breathlessly, as the image emerged from the light, and she could see the Holy Mother. The Virgin was attired in gray with a black shawl draped from her crown. Her face was sorrowful, but she shed no tears.

"Hail Mary, Mother of God," Barbara greeted. "Why are you wearing these colors?"

"These are the colors of mourning," the Virgin Mother replied. "I will show you why we should attire in such clothes as these."

The image of Mary blurred, as the light burned bright. Barbara wondered if she would be able to keep her eyes open. But, then, the light faded.

"Turn and see," the Holy Mother's voice called.

Barbara rose and turned and from where she stood, as far as she could see, dead men, and parts of men were piled high on the bank to the water's edge. The city was aflame and in ruin. Ships and parts of ships were also ablaze. Bodies and debris of every description flowed downstream. Barbara buried her face in her hands as her heart filled with horror. "I cannot watch anymore, Holy Mother," Barbara said.

"What I have shown you will come to be," Mary said. "Those who have sought this end will find it. The small shall be great. They will rise up from the earth and bring horrible destruction. When the gray mist comes to Portston, all will perish who resist him. Go now. Pray for those who will suffer this day. What you have seen is for you alone. None will believe you if you tell them what you have seen. Farewell Barbara."

Just as quickly as it had begun at the tavern it now ended. When she rose to her feet and turned, she was aware of the large crowd that had gathered. She smiled at the solemn faces. "It is over," she said. "The Holy Mother will not come here again. Go home," she encouraged the crowd, as she began walking back to her houseboat.

Across the river, Hank watched Barbara tread the rocky beach through a telescope. He let go of the telescope and looked into Candy's worried face.

"Did you see her?" Candy asked.

"No. I only saw a light," Hank answered. He plopped down on a chair and took a drink from his glass. "She was there, though. I don't think she's coming back. It won't be long now, Candy."

The Last Day of the Last Spring

Candy couldn't hold back her tears. She missed Michael and had no idea where he was. She was afraid of the future, but couldn't find a way to avoid it. All she could do was to wait; wait for the future to become the present.

Margaret spared no expense in preparing for the Christmas holiday. She had planned a lavish and abundant meal. The house had been decorated in the finest lighting and accouterments. No detail had been left to chance. She was determined to make this the very best Christmas ever.

The guest list was short: Charles and Joan, Dudley Carpenter, the Bartlett twins, Michael and of course her and JJ. A squad of servants bustled about for the entire dinner hour, then, after desert, Margaret dismissed the help with a very generous amount of cash, and well wishes for the holidays. When she returned to the upper living room of the mansion after letting the servants out the door, she stopped and let her eyes and ears absorb the joy spread before her. Everything was perfect. There was no talk of war or politics. Joan giggled in conversation with the Bartlett girls. JJ and Dudley were sampling cigars. Charles and Michael were enjoying brandy. Margaret felt tears fill her eyelids but she elegantly blinked them away. When she was certain she had her emotions under control she joined in the bawdy conversation with Joan and the twins.

"So Dudley proposed?" Joan asked in surprise.

"Well…" Dianna hesitated.

"Propositioned," Deanna sniped. The women broke into laughter.

"Well…" Dianna drawled with an electric smile as she held out her left hand, "he did give me this…"

The women roared when they saw the diamond ring.

JJ turned to see what the ruckus was all about.

"I think someone just disclosed a secret," Dudley grinned.

"Everyone! Everyone!" Margaret blurted happily. "Dianna and Dudley have an announcement to make."

Soon everyone was crowded around the couple.

"This is the worst kept secret," Dudley blushed.

"I couldn't help it," Dianna pouted.

"I have asked, and Dianna has accepted my proposal of marriage," Dudley beamed innocently.

"Congratulations!" Michael blurted as he embraced them both. Others quickly joined in the celebration. Then, the usual comments from the "old" married men began to ease into the conversation.

"You know Dudley, marriage can completely change a relationship," JJ began.

"Just ignore what you're about to hear," Margaret challenged cheerfully. "I'll get the champagne so we can have a toast."

Margaret rushed to the dining room and found an unopened magnum of the elegant champagne then she collected a tray of glasses. While she busied herself, she watched her son laugh and smile at the awful advice JJ and Charles were giving Dudley. Then, she realized just how long it had been since she had seen Michael legitimately enjoy himself. She raised the full champagne bottle in the air. "Let's toast the lucky couple," she shouted.

Several times the glasses were filled and several times toasts were offered. Soon everyone was feeling the effects of the alcohol. Joan took Deanna by the arm and asked her to help her out onto the balcony so she could get some fresh air. Deanna opened the double doors and a swirl of cool air rushed through the room.

"Oh, that feels heavenly," Margaret cooed and she joined Joan and Deanna on the balcony.

Michael glanced at the women on the balcony then returned to the banter with his father and uncle and the hapless lovers. He turned toward the balcony again when he heard his name called.

"Michael! Michael!" Deanna called to him. "Look! It's snowing. It's beautiful."

Michael froze in his tracks while the huge white flakes fell furiously to the ground. "NO!" he shouted. "NO!"

The bombs had been dropped in a ripple of six. The first two exploded a short distance from the house. The third bomb struck directly beneath the balcony. The fourth and fifth explosives collapsed Woodburne Mansion into ruins, while the six destroyed the garden.

Huge explosions followed as Michael pushed the rubble off himself. Strange smells burnt his nostrils and lungs as he struggled to his feet. He could only see for brief moments when other explosions flashed. It was during one such brilliant flare that he saw the upper half of his mother's torso nearby. Her face was locked with her eyes wide open and her mouth agape. Michael turned his head away. His pulse quickened to an exhausting rate.

"Margaret?" Michael heard his father call out. "Margaret?" Michael found JJ and helped him to his feet. "Margaret?" JJ asked.

"She's gone dad," Michael explained sorrowfully. "Come on. Let me help you out of here."

There were more flashes. This time fires provided the illumination. Michael saw Dudley and Dianna crawling toward him. "Come with me," Michael said to his friends. "Try to make it to the garage."

The young couple quietly obeyed. Then, Charles joined the group as well. Soon, the survivors were inside the garage. Michael found a lantern and lit it. "Is everyone all right?" Michael asked.

"What the hell happened," Dudley wanted to know.

"Air raid," Michael replied as he held the lantern over his father. JJ was bleeding from the nose and ears, and his right arm was broken. "Dad, you have a broken arm. Do you feel any other pains?"

"I…I'm having…difficulty breathing," JJ gasped. Michael held the lantern closer and noticed blood oozing from the left side of JJ's chest.

"I think you have a punctured lung, dad. We'll have to try to get you to the hospital." Michael shifted the lantern toward Dudley and Dianna. "How about you two?"

"I'm not sure," Dianna trembled. "I don't think I'm bleeding or anything."

Michael looked at his uncle. Charles had a nasty gash on the side of his head that bled freely.

"Dudley, I want you to help me with dad. Dianna, I want you to help Charles," Michael ordered softly.

"What about Deanna?" Dianna asked.

"And Joan," Charles added.

"They're both gone," Michael said. "I don't think we'll ever find them."

Dianna broke into tears.

"Come on, Dianna," Michael urged gently, "I need you to help Charles. Dudley, you ready?"

"Yes," Dudley and Michael locked their arms to carry JJ. Dianna allowed Charles to place his weight on her shoulders as she guided him along.

Slowly, the survivors moved toward the street, which was strewn with debris and pieces of the wounded and the dead. "Keep moving," Michael exhorted his charges. "Keep looking ahead." They ignored the falling snow.

Everywhere fires erupted. Explosions seemed to occur at will. The cries of pain and panic filled the cold night air. Michael kept talking to his small band until they had gone one city block then he stopped to rest. In the midst of the chaos, an armored military vehicle lurched to a stop beside them. An officer leapt from the vehicle and approached them.

"General Speerman?" The Major asked.

"Yes," Charles answered. "We must get this man to the hospital. Dianna you go with him. I want to talk to Michael and Dudley."

The Major motioned toward the vehicle and in an instant two soldiers grabbed hold of JJ and placed him in the back of the armored car. Dianna was helped inside to take a seat beside him.

Charles grabbed both young men by a shoulder. "I am Stale Cake. You will proceed to your duty stations in the Midlands. The Highland Dragons will have their advance party in place. Miner, you must open the mine. Gray Thorn, the Midland Grays will be heading to the wilderness right away. You both know what you have to do. Good luck to you both." Charles started toward the vehicle, then, stopped. "Gray Thorn?"

"Yes sir?"

"Kill them! Kill all of them if you can," Charles ordered with tears in his eyes.

"I'll do my best sir."

Charles turned and entered the vehicle. The doors slammed and the vehicle sped away.

Suddenly people needing help surrounded the two young men. "Come with us," Michael said. "We'll help you to the hospital."

"My baby! Take my baby!" A mangled woman cried out. Dudley took the child from her and held it tightly to his chest. Michael grabbed the woman and swung her off her feet into his strong arms. They both moved as quickly as they could without dropping their precious cargo. A few minutes later they arrived at the hospital.

Hundreds of people hovered at the entrance to the hospital. All were in desperate need of care. Dudley pushed forward through the mob, and Michael followed. Dudley spotted a nurse and a nun and struggled toward them. "I need help for this baby," Dudley shouted. The nurse looked at the infant, then at Dudley.

"The baby is dead," she said, "put the body over there."

"This is the baby's mother," Michael added.

The nurse inspected the woman in Michael's arms. "Follow him," she said as she glanced toward Dudley.

Silently, the two men moved toward the place the nurse had pointed out to them. It was a pile of lifeless humanity. Michael and Dudley gently, reluctantly let go of the corpses in their arms and placed them on the pile. They stood there in horror; uncertain what they should do next.

"Come on you two," a woman challenged. "We need all the help we can get."

Mechanically, Dudley and Michael followed the nurse.

Throughout the night Dudley and Michael worked at the hospital. They did whatever was asked of them and returned to fulfill yet another request when they had finished the previous job. Neither man spoke. They just kept working. It seemed as though it would never end.

It was well after daybreak when Michael and Dudley, realized that there were no more people to help. They were unsure what to do next, when an old nun approached them with an urn of hot coffee. Both men accepted the drinks and thanked the ancient woman for serving them. She smiled and turned toward other volunteers who had collapsed nearby.

"My god, what happened?" Dudley asked. "Tell me this is a nightmare and I will wake up and everything will be normal again."

"We may never see 'normal' again," Michael whispered.

Dudley considered the possibility Michael had proposed. "I'm sorry about your mother," Dudley said. "...and Deanna...and your Aunt Joan...and..." Dudley broke into tears.

Michael put his arm around his old friend until Dudley regained control over his grief. Then, he stepped toward the door and looked out at the snow.

"It's amazing," Michael declared, "how a few inches of snow can make ugliness appear to be beauty; as if we could forget the ugliness beneath it."

Dudley looked into his friend's face and he saw a face void of feeling. There was no expression of love, hate, fear or any other emotion visible on Michael's visage. It was the cold mask of death.

The old nun returned with the hot coffee again. She smiled brightly at Michael as he extended his cup toward her.

"You must be a great warrior," the old woman said.

"What makes you think I'm a warrior?" Michael asked.

"Because Michael, the Great Archangel, stands beside you," the nun replied. "You're the gray one the Blessed Virgin promised would come."

Michael was taken aback by the old nun's perceptions about him. He turned toward Dudley for help reassuring the woman that he was only a man. But Dudley just stood there staring at him as if he was in shock. The two men finally broke their gaze.

"I have to go," Michael said.

Dudley nodded that he understood. He threw his right arm around his friend's shoulders. "Good bye, Gray Thorn," he sobbed.

Michael's face was expressionless as he turned his head to reply. "Good bye, Miner."

The two men embraced briefly then they separated and each headed toward his own destiny.

Part Four

An Oak in the Mist

Chapter 23

Heavy snow blanketed the Highlands. Deep drifts choked the narrow valleys. Gray Thorn peered through the slit in the hood of his white and light blue combat uniform as he watched a small group of men struggle through the snow. He smiled as the men cursed the snow and the war that had sent them into this vast wilderness. So intent were they with their complaints that they walked right up on Gray Thorn without seeing him until the last second.

"I could have killed all of you," Gray Thorn announced to the group.

The men instantly recognized their leader, and felt embarrassed that he was able to surprise them so easily. They stared into their leader's gray eyes waiting for a torrent of rebuke, but Gray Thorn smiled instead. "If you can fight as well as you can bitch, the enemy is in for pure hell," he quipped. "Come with me. There is a cave nearby that has all the comforts of home." Silently, the men fell into a single line behind Gray Thorn and followed him to a sheer limestone wall a short distance away. When all were close together, Gray Thorn removed a plastic card from a pocket and inserted it into an almost invisible slit in the rock. Magically, part of the rock twisted to expose an opening. The men rushed inside, then, the door sealed shut behind them. As the door closed, lights went on and the men could hardly believe what they saw.

Eleven military bunks were against the far wall. At the foot of each bunk, was a large locker. At the other end of the bunks, against the limestone, were double-wide lockers, six feet tall. On each locker was each warrior's name. Death Bird, War Eagle, Mad Dog, Hard Bark, Catnip, Snake Man, Boots, Water Boy, Foghorn, Blue Boy, and Gray Thorn. To either side were openings to other rooms.

"Weapons, ammunition, uniforms, and equipment are to the right," Gray Thorn instructed. "To the left are our food rations." He held up the card that he had used to unlock the opening in the cliff. "There is one of these for each of you. We'll re-program the entry code each time we leave." Gray Thorn smiled. "No one; I mean no one is to know about this cave outside the eleven of us." He looked each of his comrades in the eye to see if they had any comments or questions, then he motioned them to the room on their right.

The group passed through the large armory and entered another room. On the wall facing them as they entered was a large, gray banner. In the center of the flag was the silhouette of an ancient, gnarled oak in full foliage, but shaded gray in color. On the top of the banner was the word "Midland" and on the bottom the word "Grays".

"This is our battle flag," Gray Thorn announced with pride.

"An oak in the mist," Mad Dog grinned. "I like it."

In the center of the room there was a large, wooden table surrounded by ten chairs. Gray Thorn opened a cabinet behind him that contained scores of maps rolled into tight scrolls. He pulled one of the maps out and unfurled it on the table.

"This is our meeting room," Gray Thorn explained as others helped hold the map down flat on the table. "Our first job is to fill in these blank spots on these maps," he announced. "Until the war ends and we become combat operational we are map makers." He looked up at his team members. "You are the very best our country could find to staff this team," he explained. "We will prevail in the long term. Now, sit down and let's plan a strategy to do this map work," Gray Thorn invited.

Draco listened carefully to the radio in his apartment. "Enemy forces appear to be establishing two beachheads east and west of Portston. Two divisions of paratroops were deployed by the enemy early today just north of the city and are advancing southward virtually unopposed. It is apparent that Portston is the primary objective..." The phone rang and Draco turned down the volume on his radio to answer it.

"Hello, yes, yes, I've been listening. Yes, I heard about the para-troops," Draco paused to listen for a moment. "Yes, I would like to get out of the apartment for a while, dinner sounds like a good idea. Sure, I can be ready. I'll see you in twenty minutes." He hung up the telephone and returned to the radio.

"There are reports of heavy fighting and casualties in an area thirty miles east of Portston where the enemy invasion force first landed.

National Defense units are reported to be holding the enemy at bay. West of the city, however, the news is less encouraging. Enemy troops are just 12 miles outside the city and threaten to break through at any moment." Draco switched off the radio and began pacing nervously back and forth. Suddenly, a car pulled up in front of his apartment. He grabbed a heavy jacket and went out the door.

Jane Linden reached across the vehicle to open the passenger door and Ivan hopped inside. An instant later the car lurched forward. There was little for the two people to say at first, and they drove in silence. Hours later, Jane swung the vehicle off a narrow, rural road onto an even narrower track that meandered west toward the Highlands.

"What are you worrying about?" Jane asked.

"Paratroops," Draco answered.

The Dragon and Falling Leaf weren't the only ones in the Midlands who were concerned about the enemy's bold use of paratroops. The Midland Grays were also discussing the latest enemy strategy.

"It's going to work Snake Man," prophesied. "No one was expecting the airborne troops. Portston will fall soon."

"It was a brilliant strategy," Catnip said. "Once our defenses were deployed, they put their real plan into action. The defenders at Portston will be split in two."

"You give up too quickly," War Eagle challenged. "They haven't taken Portston yet."

"What will we do if they decide to use paratroops to take the Highlands early on?" Mad Dog asked.

"That's a good question," Death Bird observed.

"Yes it is," Gray Thorn agreed. "They no doubt remember what happened in the last war and will try to remedy that mistake right away. In other words, if they can take away the Midlands, they can take away a rallying point for a resistance to form."

"If they take the wilderness early on, that would devastate our people's morale," Death Bird stated.

"Let's assume Death Bird, is right," Gray Thorn said. "The enemy will establish his beachheads, take Portston, consolidate the Portston area as a stronghold, then strike at the heart of the country in the Highlands." Maps were quickly spread on the table as Gray Thorn spoke.

Charles Speerman carefully studied his own troop dispositions again, even though he had considered numerous scenarios countless times. Now, he had made up his mind. He picked up the telephone and contacted his field commanders directly. On the 19th of January, the plan was put into action. Those units defending the western approaches to Portston moved northeast to join an attack formation with the defenders inside the city that moved directly north. The units deployed to the east of the harbor town also moved due north, but swung suddenly to the west to prevent the two enemy divisions of paratroopers from crossing the Old River. The enemy paratroopers were caught moving southward and had no time to prepare a defense. The effect on the two enemy divisions was devastating. On the other hand, Portston was lost and the enemy was firmly entrenched in Speerman's homeland.

Candyce and Hank stealthily moved through the smoldering rubble. Hank had been wounded by shrapnel, which punctured his left lung, so he was able only to move short distances before having to rest. Candyce struggled to help him all she could, but her frame was too light to handle the stocky writer. Finally, they both collapsed to the ground gasping for air in the smoke choked atmosphere.

"Fuck it! I'm not going to make it!" Hank blurted.

Tired and frightened, Candy began to cry. "Yes you will, Hank. Let's try to get inside that bombed out church over there."

"No Candy. I just can't do it." Hank rolled onto his left side and removed a plastic cylinder from his shoulder. He handed the cylinder to Candy. "Keep this safe," Hank gasped.

"What is it?" Candy sobbed.

"The key to the city of Portston," Hank gasped. "When the country is ready to retake Portston, give it to someone in charge of the army." Hank coughed and wheezed. "Promise me Candy."

"I promise," the young woman sobbed.

"Now, get going. Head north. Try to get out of the city. Get to the Midlands if you can."

"I can't leave you like this, Hank," Candy pleaded, "you'll die if you don't get help."

Hank smiled through a cough then pulled a pistol from his coat pocket. "It's time for me to die," he smiled. "Get going if you don't want to watch me do this."

The Last Day of the Last Spring

Candy could see the resolve in Hank's eyes. She had seen that look many times before and she knew she would never be able to talk him out of his plan. Somehow, Hank's determined visage helped her ebb her sorrow. "I love you, Hank."

"You were the best daughter a man could have," Hank smiled. "I was lucky to have you with me."

"You were a terrific old man," Candy forced herself to smile. "I know you don't like to hear this word, but I love you dad."

Hank offered no protest. "Love you, Candy. Get going. Don't look back."

Candy picked up the plastic cylinder then rose to her feet. She could see Hank smiling in the darkness then she turned and started making her way through the destruction that had once been a city. She listened for the single shot she expected to hear, but she never heard it. There was simply too much noise. She made her way to the destroyed church and slithered into the debris.

Candy watched from a concealed place in a cellar as men and women on the streets were being rounded up by enemy military police. The civilians were handled roughly by the troops as they were forced onto trucks and taken away. The young woman was horrified by what she saw, but she could not pull herself away from her vantage point for fear of being discovered herself. Finally, the horror on the streets ended and the trucks moved away. Candy turned from her peephole and sat down on a wooden crate. She was hungry again. She would have to find food, somewhere, but where? She surveyed the dingy darkness around her for a possible idea, but there was no stimulus in the dreary cellar. She got up from the crate and looked outside again. It was quiet. She decided to wait until dark then try to move north again in search of an escape route from the city. She had little hope of finding a way out, she knew that, but something drove her to try anyway.

Throughout the winter, enemy forces secured Portston. The severity of the winter was both a hindrance and a help to the defenders. Both sides were only able to use limited air power, and the defenses on the ground were able to provide greater resistance. On the other hand, the nation under siege could do little to dislodge the invaders. So, the war quickly became a ground battle, of armored vehicles, artillery and infantry. Still, the invaders were better equipped, and had greater numbers. Slowly, the enemy pushed the gallant defenders from their path.

Right after the first air raids, people began to flow from the major cities to the Eastern Mountains, the Western Ranges and the Midland/Highlands wilderness. With clearing weather, enemy aircraft frequently attacked the long columns of refugees, hoping to demoralize them. But the attacks had the opposite effect. The helpless refugees were infuriated and outraged by the tactic and filled their hearts with hatred too terrible to describe.

In early April, the enemy launched a bold offensive sending huge numbers from the stronghold that was once Portston. Intelligence reports of the enemy activity were rushed to General Speerman.

Charles took the communiqué from the messenger and quickly read it. After a moment he looked up at the messenger and simply said, "Thank you. That'll be all."

The messenger was flabbergasted. "But sir, the enemy is launching a major offensive…"

"Yes," Charles acknowledged quietly. "Would you be so kind as to ask General Wilder to see me?"

"Yes sir," the aid replied then he spun on a heel and walked off.

A few seconds later an angry General Wilder reported to Speerman with a salute that looked more like a threatening gesture that a show of respect. "God damn it, Charlie, when are you going to let me get into this fuckin' war?" Wilder was fuming.

"Sit down, Frank," Charles said. Wilder plopped into a folding chair and glared back at his superior.

"You don't like me very much do you, Frank?" Charles smiled.

"No sir," Frank answered.

"Why is that, Frank?"

"You're a politician's general, not a soldiers general. I should have had your job, Charlie. The only reason I don't is because of your fuckin' politician brother-in-law."

Charles hesitated for a moment. "You have some good points, Frank. Now, let me tell you why I haven't given you a command," Charles began calmly. "First, you don't think. You're impulsive, Frank. The fuse to your temper is shorter than your dick. Until you learn how to think, I'm not going to let you get a lot of our people killed. Second, the enemy expects me to commit you to battle, and I'm not going to do what they expect me to do."

"God damn it Charlie, give me a command and let me die with honor. You know we're going to lose this war," Wilder protested.

"You're not paying attention, Frank," Charles hissed angrily. "I'm going to put you somewhere where I know you'll be alive, until I need you."

Wilder started up from his chair.

"Sit down, General," Speerman commanded through clenched teeth. Wilder was frozen by the intensity of Speerman's glare, and slowly re-took his place. "I'm sending you for some training. Are you familiar with University City?"

"Yes sir," Wilder snapped.

"At exactly 8 p.m. tomorrow you will arrive at a coffee shop called the 'Cafeind'."

"What kind of training is this?"

"Shut up and listen, Frank. Once inside the coffee shop a person who will call themselves 'Falling Leaf', will contact you. You will do exactly what this person tells you to do. You will do it without protest. Do you understand?"

"Yes sir, is there anything else?"

"Yes, you will travel without any military identification in civilian clothes. That is all General Wilder."

Wilder shot up from his chair saluted and stomped off. Immediately, one of Speerman's aides approached him.

"How did things go with General Wilder," the officer sneered.

"Quite well," Charles replied, "quite well, indeed."

It was precisely 8 p.m. when Frank Wilder entered the coffeehouse. The few customers in the establishment glanced up at him nervously before returning to their business. Wilder took a seat near the window, as an elderly woman approached to take his order. "I'll just have a regular coffee, black." Wilder said.

"Make that two," a woman said as she approached Wilder's booth. The smiling woman slid into the booth next to him. "I'm Falling Leaf," the woman smiled. "We'll have to take our coffee with us."

"Where..." Wilder caught himself. "That's fine," he said.

Falling Leaf smiled, paid for the coffee and escorted her charge to a waiting automobile. She ushered the general into the passenger seat, then walked to the driver's side. Wilder found himself staring into the cold faces of two young muscular men in the back seat, as Falling Leaf slid behind the wheel.

"This is Mad Dog, and Boots," Falling Leaf said. "They're your body guards."

Wilder looked at the two men, who gazed back at him with blank stares. He was unsure if the two men were protectors or assassins. They were obviously very physically fit, and very sure of themselves.

After driving a short distance out of town, Falling Leaf stopped the car beside an off-road vehicle. "Have a nice trip, General," she smiled. "Mad Dog and Boots will take you to your final destination."

Wilder exited the sedan to find his two "escorts" on either side of him. The one called Mad Dog motioned him to the passenger seat in the front, while Boots took the driver's side. Falling Leaf pulled away, as Mad Dog took a seat behind the general. Then, Boots handed the general a black hood.

"You'll have to put this on," Boots said.

Wilder wanted to protest, but instead he snatched the hood from Boots, and placed it over his head.

"You'll need to have your seat belt fastened," Boots explained as he leaned over and fastened the nylon belts to secure his passenger. The vehicle roared into motion, and the final leg of the journey began.

For the first couple of hours, the drive was smooth and restful. Wilder could sense they were moving at a high rate of speed. Then, the vehicle turned and the trip became tedious. The vehicle moved slowly, but surely, through turn after turn, tossing the general from side to side. After what seemed to be endless hours, to General Wilder, the vehicle slowed and turned again. Now, the ride really became unbearable as the vehicle was obviously being driven across country. The engine roared, tires slipped, as the vehicle groaned and loped along. Wilder braced himself to keep from being injured by the violent bumps and jerks. Finally, they stopped.

When the hood was removed from General Wilder's head, he saw that he was in the middle of a vast wilderness, surrounded by several young men. He only recognized Mad Dog and Boots. The rest of the men were strangers to him.

"Who are you guys?" Wilder challenged.

"We are your trainers," a voice called out from behind a tree. Wilder turned his eyes toward the young man with the gray hair who approached him with an aggressive gait.

"Yeah, and who are you?" Wilder asked sarcastically.

The young man walked directly up to the general and placed his face within inches of the other man's. "I am Gray Thorn."

Wilder's anger seized him when he recognized Speerman's nephew and he thrust both hands into the chest of Gray Thorn to shove him away. But, as soon as his hands made contact, Gray Thorn brought both of his hands on top of the general's and bent forward at the waist, causing Wilder to fall to his knees and wonder if both arms were broken.

Gray Thorn took a stance over the man on his knees. "We have been ordered to train you," he said. "From now on, you will not speak, unless one of us asks you a question. We have very little time to accomplish this task. If we decide you cannot complete the training, you will be killed. Do you understand?"

Wilder was in too much pain to speak, so he just nodded his head.

The transition from general to trainee was difficult for Wilder, who the "trainers" named "Slug". He had gone from a position of power and prestige, to a position of vulnerability and nothingness. Still he had to admit that these men were much better at hand-to-hand combat than he was and he had the bruises to prove it. His complacency was gone. His ego had been reigned in, and he had learned the virtue of silence and the pain of talking out of turn. He had run until unconscious, while his trainers barely puffed. He had been left in the outdoors tied to a tree during a flood. He had gone without food or water for 48 hours at a time. He had been forced to live outside in the wilderness. He had encountered a loneliness that he had never known before. But, he also realized that he was becoming tough. He was going to be a tough as his "trainers".

At the end of the fourth week, Slug was snuggled in a small indentation in a limestone bluff, when Gray Thorn and the other men approached him. He jumped to his feet ready to fight. Gray Thorn stopped a few feet away from the wild animal against the bluff.

"We have decided that you have earned the right go to the next level," Gray Thorn announced. "The vote was ten to one. I was the one that voted against you. Anyway, congratulations." Gray Thorn extended his hand to Slug, who looked at the open hand warily, then slowly reached out. The two men clasped hands strongly for a moment, then separated. "You may speak now," Gray Thorn empowered his charge then he stepped away.

To his shock, Slug saw the other ten men lined up to shake his hand. They were all smiling at him. Boots reached out with a firm grip with his right hand then embraced Slug with his left arm. "Welcome brother," Boots said proudly as he stepped aside. Next Gray Eagle approached and then each man in turn. All shook Slug's hand and embraced him and called him brother. When the last man had offered his congratulation, Slug could no longer hold back the tears that rushed down his face.

Gray Thorn smiled a quick smile and tried to turn away before anyone saw his glee. Mad Dog, however, was too observant. "You're proud of him, aren't you?" he asked his leader.

"He took every rotten thing we gave him. He's tough," Gray Thorn concluded.

"What's the next level?" Mad Dog asked.

"At this point we have his ass," Gray Thorn smiled. "In the next level I want to have his heart."

"What about his mind?" Mad Dog pushed.

"If we can get the first two, the third will follow." Gray Thorn grinned. "What I just told you is confidential. Don't you tell him anything I just said."

"I won't," Mad Dog agreed.

"Come on, let's take Slug to Gray Havens," Gray Thorn urged.

Gray Havens was the name the Midland Grays gave to their cave, which they had left for the past month to "train" Slug. When Slug watched the limestone shift to expose an opening, his eyes opened wide in surprise. The other men smiled, having experienced the same feeling when they saw the cave for the first time. Gray Thorn led them all into the darkness, and when the outer door closed the lights came on. Once again Slug was awed by what he saw. He was particularly moved when he saw the name "Slug" on one of the sets of lockers.

"Is that my bunk?" Slug asked softly.

"All yours," Snake Man replied cheerfully.

Slug inspected the bunk and the lockers. Suddenly he realized that his trainers had spent the last four weeks away from this comfort. He turned suddenly to the group. "Do you mean to tell me that you guys left this place for an entire month just to kick my ass?" He asked.

There was a brief ripple of laughter. Even Gray Thorn smiled. "We don't bring a brother into our team that hasn't lived through what we have lived through," he explained. "Mad Dog, give Slug the tour and finish up in the briefing area."

A short time later, Slug entered the briefing area. Gray Thorn was seated at one end of a large, wooden table. Mad Dog explained about the room, then, turned Slug over to Gray Thorn.

"Sit down, Slug," Gray Thorn said. "We're about to begin the next phase of your training. This phase will be one on one with me." Gray Thorn looked into the older man's face and saw the same flicker of defiance, but he also saw the constraint. "This phase is called 'questions and answers'. You ask the questions and I'll try to give you answers. Some questions I may not be able to answer until phase three." Gray Thorn turned his seat to allow him to face Slug. "You may begin."

Slug's mind was sent spinning as a flood of questions splashed into this head. "Who are you guys," he stammered.

Gray Thorn told Slug that the Midland Grays were an unconventional warfare unit that would be activated upon the surrender of the Nation. Then, they would begin a guerrilla action while training a liberation force to overthrow the occupation forces. Slug asked another question. Gray Thorn answered. And so it went for several hours. Finally, Slug rubbed his eyes as fatigue over took him.

"Get some rest," Gray Thorn said. "Tomorrow I'll take you to another place in the wilderness so you can get a better idea of what we're trying to do."

Slug nodded wearily then left for his bunk.

JJ Sylvan seemed distant to Charles, as if his mind was somewhere else. He just sat and stared into his cup of coffee with little interest. "We all have a lot on our minds," Charles said to his brother-in-law.

"Yes," JJ replied without looking up. "When will we end this, Charles? I mean, what is the point in getting anymore of our young men and women killed?"

"I don't believe we will be able to resist through the coming winter," Charles stated simply. "By next spring at the latest, we will be an occupied nation."

JJ was silent. He just sat still, staring into his cold cup of coffee. Charles patted JJ on the shoulder and left him to his thoughts.

The summer months proved very successful for the enemy assault troops. Their Armored units quickly swarmed over the plains and prairies to isolate the Western Mountains from the rest of the country. A three-pronged attack from Portston to the north and east was also well executed. The eastern most columns would block off the Eastern Mountains. The center column was progressing toward Capitol City. The Western most columns were driving to cut off the flow of refugees into the Highlands. It seemed that nothing would stop the enemy from overwhelming the country with sheer numbers alone.

Speerman sat in his office with his brother-in-law JJ reading a report from Gray Thorn. He didn't disclose the message to JJ. "Care for a drink JJ?" The General asked.

"No, thanks Charles," JJ replied softly.

Speerman filled his own glass and slouched in his chair.

"How could we have been so wrong Charles? We had technically superior weapon systems compared to them."

"We didn't have enough of them," Speerman concluded. "The enemy knew our capabilities, but we didn't know theirs."

"Is it that simple, Charles? Is war just a numbers game?"

"Sometimes it's numbers, but not always. The enemy also had a good strategy and good execution of their plans."

JJ nodded that he understood, but the reality of it was still depressing to him. "Do you miss Joan?" JJ changed the topic.

Charles sighed. "Sometimes I think I see her. Yesterday, I thought I saw her just sitting there in that chair." Charles stopped himself from plunging into self pity.

"I really miss Margaret," JJ sighed.

The Last Day of the Last Spring

A flashing light on a telephone on Speerman's desk interrupted the conversation. He picked up the phone. "General Speerman," he answered. "When?" He paused. "No, I'm glad you informed me," he said. "Thanks," he ended the call and hung up the phone.

"Good news?" JJ asked hopefully.

"Maybe," Charles replied. "Mist is rising from the Highlands."

"Then, this is the end," JJ concluded.

Chapter 24

Michael stood in the mist. He was relaxed and comfortable with the gray moistness. He felt calm.

"Is this the legendary Highland mist?" Slug asked.

"Yeah," Gray Thorn smiled.

"You sure?" Slug challenged.

"Yes, I'm sure," Gray Thorn replied. "The trees will hold their leaves. There will be no fall or winter season in the Highlands after this."

Slug could sense the utter sincerity of Gray Thorn's demeanor, but he couldn't understand it. Still, he did find the thick mist fascinating.

"It's time for the last phase of your training," Gray Thorn announced.

"Will it be as bad as the first two phases?" Slug asked with a sarcastic grin.

"It will be worse," Gray Thorn acknowledged with an expressionless face. "Follow me."

Slug fell in behind the young mentor as Gray Thorn strode briskly into the thick fog. At first, Slug thought they were only going a short distance, but as darkness fell, he realized that they were on a journey. He had many questions he wanted to ask, but the first two training sessions at the hands of the Midland Grays had taught him that he would be told information only when he needed to know it. He contented himself to stay silent. In the end he would learn everything he would need to know.

The two men walked all night, then, as daylight tried to pierce the thick mist; they approached a wall of limestone. Slug watched as Gray Thorn approached the solid rock, and was amazed when the rock opened. He followed Gray Thorn inside, as the rock sealed behind them. A light appeared above them, and steel doors closed. The metal box they were in began to descend. The elevator moved slowly at first then faster and faster. Finally, the box slowed and came to a stop. The other end of

266

the elevator opened, and Slug and his teacher stepped out into a wide hallway. There were three other people there to greet them.

Slug recognized Falling Leaf, but not the other two men.

"This is Dragon; commander of the Highland Dragons," Gray Thorn introduced. "And this is Miner, and I believe you will recall meeting Falling Leaf."

Slug tried to contain his curiosity as he exchanged greetings with the strangers.

"This way please," Falling Leaf commanded.

The group proceeded along the hallway a short distance then followed Falling Leaf through a doorway. They were in a small room with a utilitarian desk and chair. On the desk was a stack of thick volumes centered between two smaller tomes. Falling Leaf pulled a large brown envelope from the desktop and handed it to Slug.

"If you need anything, you may call us by using the intercom on the desk. Once we leave this room, you will be the only person to be able to access it again. No one will be allowed in this room without you."

The group started to file out of the room but Slug stopped them. "Wait," he said. "What's in here?" He asked as he held the brown envelope aloft.

"We don't know," Falling Leaf smiled. "You are the only one authorized to open it and read the contents."

A moment later, Slug was alone in the room. He stared at the envelope for a moment then tore it open. The first document was a letter from General Speerman.

The winter was unusually cold and harsh and the battlefield fell into a malaise. The snow and ice rendered the enemy army's progress to a crawl, but there was little cause for hope in the hapless nation. By spring, the enemy would quickly regain the initiative and the end would be near.

In mid-February, Charles Speerman and his brother-in-law considered the bleak future in General Speerman's command bunker 5000 feet beneath a mountain in the Eastern Ranges.

A messenger approached the two men and handed Charles a communiqué. Speerman read the one page document quickly, then handed it to JJ. "They are telling us to surrender," Charles informed.

"Hmmph!" JJ grunted as he placed the unread piece of paper on the table. "I'll offer them a ninety day cease fire to consider the offer," JJ grinned devilishly.

Charles chuckled. "You're a politician to the end."

"That's all I know," JJ said.

"I'll send the message," Charles said as he motioned the messenger toward him.

Quickly, Charles scrawled out a message and handed it to the waiting officer. "Send this one hour before midnight tomorrow," he ordered. The officer took the message and walked off.

"Surrender is not a viable alternative for me," Charles revealed to JJ.

"Nor for me," JJ agreed. "So I've been wondering what the enemy would do if there was no surrender. With the exception of me, nearly all the other government leaders have either been killed or have run away. So what happens if we don't surrender?"

"Good question," Charles grinned. "I'll have to think about it."

General Wilder stared into space as his mind tried to digest what he had read. Finally, he pressed a button on the intercom.

"I want to see Falling Leaf, Miner, Dragon, and Gray Thorn," Wilder said.

Just a few moments passed before the four people stood before General Wilder. "I am to inform you that I accept the position," Wilder stated.

Dragon opened a closet and pulled out a neatly tailored uniform that bore the rank of General of the Army. "You'll need this, sir," Dragon smiled.

Wilder examined the bright stars on the shoulder boards and shook his head. "General of the Army," he sighed.

"General of the Liberation Army," Gray Thorn corrected.

"Yes," Wilder snapped enthusiastically while removing his shirt.

"You can change in here," Miner suggested.

Wilder ducked into the closet and emerged just a minute later. When he appeared, all four saluted while wearing broad grins. Wilder returned the salute. "Thank you," he said softly. "I will do anything and every-thing I can to earn your faith in me."

No one commented.

The Last Day of the Last Spring

"Let's get started," Wilder said. "Dragon, Miner, I have read your report summaries. If this facility Miner built and Dragon staffed is half of what they claim, we are about to become a very serious pain in the ass to our enemy."

"Are you ready to begin the tour, sir?" Miner asked.

"You bet I am," Wilder smiled confidently.

Dianna dropped her sheer gown to expose the nearly perfect beauty of her body. The enemy officers cheered at her while they ogled her nakedness. She forced herself to smile while they groped her flesh. Then, she brought her own hand down on a Captain's crotch and squeezed his erect penis. "O my," she smiled, "I do hope you won't be too impatient."

The other men broke into laughter as the room was suddenly filled with other women, who were also very attractive, nearly naked, and apparently very eager to satisfy their guests. The gathering quickly exploded into a night of unrestricted sexual pleasure.

For months Candy had avoided detection by the enemy troops, but she had little confidence she would be able to succeed much longer. She still clung to the plastic tube that Hank had given her. It was the only property of Hank's she had and she protected it as if it were her most valuable possession.

The sound of an approaching vehicle made her look frantically for an escape route. She was only a block away from the river and she hoped that she could at least hide there and perhaps make her way north along the riverbank to the Midland-Highlands wilderness. It was just a hope; her last hope and she anxiously broke into a sprint and hurled her body into the darkness. The river drew nearer and nearer, then, suddenly she fell off the steep bank. She was stunned. The combination of running, fear, the lack of food and sleep had caught up with her and she fell unconscious.

It was the first of March, when JJ and Charles met with the invading army's high command the second time. The meeting lasted only an hour, and JJ and Charles left the meeting in silence. The enemy had been very clear about not extending the cease-fire beyond the 15th of the month. JJ and Charles agreed to return to the meeting place before noon of that day.

Once the two brothers-in-law were safely resting at Speerman's command post, they felt comfortable to speak.

"Good work, JJ", Charles complimented. "I'll put the next two weeks to good use."

"I don't want to surrender," JJ said softly.

Charles poured two drinks and handed one to JJ. "Maybe we won't," he offered timidly. "Let me run some ideas past you. I need your opinion."

Dragon and Falling Leaf strolled through the Highland Mist and entered Camp Alpha. Groups of young men and women marched by in columns of four.

"It's amazing that this many have made it through the enemy lines," Draco sighed.

"It will be even more amazing to the enemy when they find out," Falling Leaf laughed.

Draco was absorbed by Falling Leaf's dark eyes, which seemed to beckon to him. He placed a hand on her shoulder. "If we survive... I mean...now isn't the time...but if sometime in the future..." he stumbled.

"I am here for you now," Falling Leaf said softly. "There is no need for words between us."

Draco smiled as he squeezed the young woman's shoulder. Falling Leaf brushed a tear from her face, then, they continued their inspection of the camp.

Many of the students that had been part of the "campus club" greeted the two as they made their rounds. "Hello Dragon! Hurrah for the Dragon! And other salutations were offered as cheers by the grateful survivors. Ivan the Dragon was buoyed by the positive spirit that flowed among the refugees. Hope was as abundant as the mist that clung to the trees.

Each of the students Ivan had collaborated with was anxious to explain how they were able to provide sanitation and food. The use of the land was maximized for sanitation while the plant life, protected by the mist, provided high protein food stuffs.

So far, things were going as planned. But, there would be more and more refugees as time went on and they would need weapons and ammunition.

Dragon called the leaders of Alpha Camp to a meeting. Once everyone was assembled, he asked them to find skilled machinists, electricians, carpenters, masons and any other craftsmen they could find. Without disclosing the existence of the underground factories, he advised his leaders that the people selected would have to leave Alpha Camp for another area of the wilderness. The leaders had already identified some skillful people in their community and agreed to make a list but argued against sharing all of them. Ivan smiled as he agreed that he would take only those who might be excess to the needs of Alpha Camp.

On the morning of the 15th of March, General Wilder addressed the personnel in his underground headquarters. "I have just received word from General Speerman that the enemy is expecting our country to surrender at noon today. Officially, we are to bring the headquarters here in the Midlands to operational status and await a final communiqué from General Speerman at approximately noon today."

The large room was silent as the reality of surrender began to sink in. On the other hand, Wilder could sense a strong feeling of commitment. "Miner, take command and bring us into operational mode."

Miner placed a headset into position and began giving orders. His men sat at their computer terminals and began powering up their systems. The five, huge electronic displays at the front of the room began to flicker. Maps appeared on four of the screens that showed enemy positions throughout the country. The largest screen in the center remained ominously dark.

General Speerman and the National Leader, John Sylvan Junior sat quietly in the back of Speerman's limousine. Charles closed the privacy screen between the driver's seat and the passenger section. "We have to make a decision, JJ", Charles said.

"About what? It's over," JJ sulked.

"Do you recall asking me what would happen if we didn't surrender?" Charles prodded.

"Yes," JJ replied.

"Well, I thought about that for quite a while, but I couldn't be certain how it would impact the enemy occupation. Then, I decided that it wasn't my problem to deal with, it was theirs."

"So what are we going to do?" JJ asked

Charles leaned forward and produced a bottle of fine whiskey and two glasses. He filled the glasses and gave one to JJ; then he removed a small box from the liquor cabinet. He opened it and pulled out a small capsule. "These little things can kill a man in a matter of seconds. It induces drowsiness, unconsciousness, coma, and finally death."

"Do you have more than one of those," JJ asked.

"There are four," Charles answered, "but you don't have to do this, I do. I can't fall into their hands."

"If we surrender you won't have any secrets…" JJ paused as his mind came to a new understanding. "My god, I just remembered Dad's funeral; the diary. You figured out what it meant. You've set up something Charles."

"JJ I can't…" Charles began to protest.

"Please, Charles, let me go to my death with just a spark of hope for the future. Don't deny me that."

Charles smiled, "I was hoping that you would make that choice." Next, Charles told JJ what he had organized.

At 1150 hours, the limousine came to a stop at the enemy headquarters. As the sentry opened the rear door, he unknowingly activated a transmitter. When no one exited the vehicle, he looked inside. There were two dead men in the back.

Deep beneath the tossing terrain of the Midland-Highlands wilderness, all eyes in the Liberation Army Headquarters were locked on the huge center screen as General Speerman's last message scrolled across the device in huge letters. The message was brief.

"John Sylvan Junior," the message began, "the leader of our nation, and I, could not insult the honor of our country by surrender. We chose instead to die. Let those who have brought chaos to our land reap their reward. Let chaos reign."

Everyone instantly felt the impact of the words "Let chaos reign." This was the command many had waited for and many had dreaded. The four other screens began lighting up with other indicators.

"What are those markers?" Miner asked aloud.

"Those are the teams Speerman created in anticipation of this day," General Wilder smiled. "There are two thousand of them."

"My god," Miner hissed. "Two thousand teams like the Midland Grays. Over twenty thousand men like Gray Thorn."

Gray Thorn could not hold back his tears. The death of his father and uncle came as a shock to him. Then, he heard the voices on the wind. "Michael. Michael. The mist has come to the Highlands. They will rise up from the earth. You will lead them. They will kill those that stand before them. Remember the voices of the past."

Spring faded into summer, and the enemy combat troops began returning to their homeland. Their replacements were wary at first, but soon they relaxed under the summer sun. Their victory appeared to be overwhelming to their captives, crushing their spirit. The new troops became complacent. Even the tight security units that ringed the Midland-Highlands wilderness began to complain about duty so far from the cities that held willing women and an abundance of alcohol.

Soon summer ended. The fall colors came and leaves fell. It was then that General Wilder began his work.

"Miner," Wilder said. "Activate the concealed teams in these large cities." Wilder handed him the list.

"Yes sir," Miner replied. "He sat down at a computer terminal and entered the communication codes for the selected teams.

When the large screens began lighting up, Wilder's headquarters staff realized that the liberation of their country was beginning. A spontaneous cheer chorused throughout the cavern.

Wilder nodded, to acknowledge the enthusiasm of his charges. Then he handed another written order to Miner. "Send this to Gray Thorn," he said.

Gray Thorn assembled his team in their underground barracks. He spread a map on the table and smiled at his team. "The Grays have been ordered to engage the enemy troops positioned to the northwest of the Highlands near the place we call the Labyrinth. We are to become very violent with the enemy occupation troops. We are to create mayhem and take no prisoners. The plan is to get them to chase us back into the Labyrinth region where the Highland Dragons Alpha and Delta Camps will be positioned in ambush along these areas." Gray Thorn traced the areas on the map with his finger. "We are ordered to select our own target and commence at our own schedule. The Dragons will be waiting."

"Let's get this war going," Mad Dog blurted. "I'm tired of calisthenics and weight lifting."

"Let's do it!" Gray Thorn grinned.

The War of Resistance began without fanfare. For the first few months, battles were confined to small actions and assassinations in the occupied cities. The forays from the Midland-Highlands were kept small to give the enemy the belief that the refugees who had fled into the mist were not much of a tactical threat.

In fact, the factories in the caverns were turning out large quantities of small arms and explosive devices that were distributed throughout the Midlands.

Medical facilities also sprang up in the camps. And the medicines that had been stockpiled in hidden caches were readily available to the training freedom fighters.

Of course, the nearly constant 58 to 64 degree temperatures in the Midlands kept many of the normal seasonal illnesses under control. Even the elderly seemed to prosper and were eager to help with camp chores.

Gray Thorn's unit became so efficient at harrying the occupation forces near the northwest edge of the area called the "Labyrinth" that the enemy would break off contact with the Midland Grays rather than fall victim to the Highland Dragons that waited in ambush.

In the second year of the occupation, General Wilder only slightly increased his guerilla war. Some were frustrated by his decision, but Wilder wanted to make certain that adequate time was available for his fighters to gain experience.

The complaints waned when the occupation forces were redistributed to reinforce the men surrounding the Western Mountains and Eastern ranges. Wilder's strategy caused the enemy to keep a much smaller number of enemy troops near the Midland-Highlands, which was exactly what he wanted.

The Last Day of the Last Spring

As the third year of the occupation began, Gray Thorn's thoughts turned more and more toward the visions that came to him in bits and pieces. Often, he wished that his grandmother was with him to explain the happenings in his mind, but he recalled her warning that he should exercise care in trusting the apparitions.

Between actions, while resting in the Midlands mist, Gray Thorn would think of Candy Storer. He desperately tried to have visions of her but was unsuccessful. Still, he hoped she was alive and well. He wondered if he would ever see her again. He hoped he would.

Jane longed for Ivan's company, but the Dragon was too absorbed by the needs of the camps and the war. She knew he loved her. But, she also knew he would not forego his priority of helping the refugees and building an army to satisfy himself. She wondered if that was why she loved him.

Ivan was always aware of Jane's feelings for him. He was both thrilled to have her heart, but fearful he would be killed and cause her sorrow. Reluctantly, he held his romantic impulses in check by seeing her only when other people were around. He kept telling himself that if they both survived the war, he would spend the rest of his days doting over her. He would not allow himself to talk to her about his feeling for her for fear he would lose control of himself.

Miner became General Wilder's right hand man. Dudley's organizational skills were amazing. He always seemed to know who should do what and how. Miner accepted Wilder's every wish because it kept him too busy to think about what might have happened to Dianna or what would happen in the future. The future Miner hoped for could easily end in a flash and he couldn't forget that.

In the third year, the occupation forces learned the impotence of high tech weapons in an unconventional war. They never knew who was simply a citizen or an insurgent. They never knew if they were in a safe location. Their morale began to plummet. Seeing the ebb in enemy morale, Wilder once again stepped up insurgent activities in the major cities while relaxing action from the mountainous regions and the Highlands. He watched enemy reactions carefully and developed a sense of how they thought.

More than once, Gray Thorn's "anticipation" of enemy movements proved to be right. His men openly asked him if he was psychic. "I'm just lucky," Gray Thorn would smile. His team would accept that answer without comment, but among themselves they would argue that his tactical skills were more than mere good fortune.

As the fourth year of the occupation began, General Wilder called Dragon and Gray Thorn to his headquarters buried deep underground. Proceedings began as a re-union and there were many hugs to go around among Miner, Gray Thorn, Dragon, Falling Leaf and Slug. Soon, however, the pleasantries faded and all thoughts returned to the war.

"What's on your mind, Slug," Gray Thorn began. "You didn't ask us here just because you were lonely."

"No," Slug chuckled, "but I wanted to; many times. No, I asked you here to run a plan by you. How many troops can you put into the field, Dragon?"

"Four full divisions of light infantry; four battalions of mechanized infantry; both with artillery support," Dragon answered.

Surprise was evident on Slug's face. "Wow you have been busy. Are they all trained?"

"Not only trained, but combat tested," Dragon announced.

Slug paused for a moment. "I think I know how the enemy thinks," he disclosed. I want to prove my theories this year. If I'm right, we'll launch our liberation forces next year."

Smiles broke out on the other faces. Dragon sighed. "It seems like I have been waiting to hear you say that all my life," Dragon confessed.

"Could it be that we can re-take our homeland?" Jane asked openly.

"I need to prove my theories," Slug repeated, "but I think we can do it."

Gray Thorn stared into space. He saw himself lying in the ruble of a collapsed building covered in blood. Miner recognized the blank stare.

"What do you think, Gray Thorn?" Miner asked.

There was a slight delay before Gray Thorn responded. All he could do was nod his head.

"That's all I have for now," Slug said almost apologetically. "It was good to see you all well. When I call you back here, it will be to initiate a final strategy."

The meeting ended as it had begun; with a round of hugs. There were no words of good-bye, just anticipation that within one more year they would seek to end the misery that had befallen their country.

The Last Day of the Last Spring

The next twelve months proved to be pure hell for Gray Thorn and Dragon. Anticipation drove their every waking moment and time seemed to slow down. More anxiety was brought on by the lack of action the two men craved.

General Wilder continued his pace of trial and observation. Miner would comment time after time that the General's anticipation of the enemy seemed to be flawless, but Wilder would always say, "We've got to be certain".

Finally, as the fifth year of occupation began, Slug ordered the group back to his headquarters.

"I know you think I'm holding you back," General Wilder began, "and you're right, I am. Today, however, I am going to tell you why I have held you so tightly here in the wilderness." Slug pushed a button on his control console. "Look at the center screen," Dragon and Gray Thorn locked their gaze on the largest screen and an image of their nation popped into view.

Wilder went on to explain his plan. "I want to begin with breakout assaults from the Western Ranges and Eastern Mountains," Wilder disclosed. "The idea is to draw most of the enemy troops away from the Midland-Highlands and stretch their supplies lines from Portston east and west." Wilder paused, "in addition, guerilla actions will be started in our major western and eastern cities at the same time. I want to cause as much confusion and chaos as I can."

"When do we get into the war?" Gray Thorn asked dejectedly.

Wilder looked into Gray Thorn's eyes, then Ivan's. "When I have their strength spread out from Portston to the east and west, The Highland Dragons will attack directly south; take the city of Portston and hold it."

"So when does the Liberation begin?" Gray Thorn asked.

Slug smiled, "At zero-zero-zero-one hours April 1st."

"April Fool's Day," Dragon beamed.

"The Highland Dragons will take up final assault positions in the southern Midlands beginning on that day," Wilder continued. "You will have to insure that your deployment is kept secret. After that, you'll have to wait for my command."

"Yes," Jane, Ivan and Gray Thorn chorused together.

Chapter 25

At first, Dragon, Falling Leaf, and Gray Thorn were busy with the assemblage of the Highland Dragons in the southern Midlands. After eight weeks, the Army was poised like a coiled snake; ready to reach out, strike and kill. But the order to attack didn't come.

Gray Thorn and Draco had to constantly exercise their troops to keep them busy, but neither man was happy. The summer began to wane and the first hints of fall began to show outside of the Midland-Highlands. Still there was no word from Slug.

General Wilder had been carefully studying the enemy placements to decide his next moves. When he ended his contemplation, he sent for Gray Thorn. He met the young commando commander alone in the General's private quarters.

"I'll come right to the point," Wilder began. "Unless we neutralize the enemy fortifications in and around Portston, the enemy will be able to keep fresh troops and supplies flowing to his occupation force."

"I agree," Gray Thorn said.

"We cannot take Portston with what we have," Wilder continued. "Their fortifications are too strong for a ground assault. We need someone to get inside and figure out a way to open a door or two."

"You want the Grays to go to Portston and open those doors," Gray Thorn concluded.

"I can't bring myself to order you to do this," Wilder confessed. "I may be asking you all to go to the grave. But, all the enemy supplies are there. If we can take out their supplies and clog the harbor, we have a chance to take Portston. If Portston falls, they lose. It's that simple."

"I'll talk to my men," Gray Thorn said. "I'm certain they'll want to take on the mission."

Wilder could find no more words. He patted Gray Thorn on the shoulder then led the young man back to the elevator that would carry him to the surface.

The Last Day of the Last Spring

An hour later, a messenger handed a note to General Wilder. It read, "Slug. We accept; working out the details. GT."

For two weeks, the Midland Grays developed their plan to infiltrate the enemy lines, travel hundreds of miles without being detected, and finally, enter the enemy fortress constructed at Portston. Wilder read and re-read the plan several times before meeting the Grays above his underground command post.

The commando team came to attention and saluted as the General appeared. "At ease you guys, it's only me, Slug."

The men laughed at their leader's humility, but hugged and greeted him heartily. Finally, Slug spoke to them again.

"I've been over your plan a dozen times trying to find a reason not to do it," he disclosed. "In the end, I had to conclude, that this is a pretty good strategy. I'm confident in everything except the very last part about penetrating the security areas around the city. That will be the most dangerous part." Wilder paused and lowered his head. "There is no other team I would consider for this job, because I believe you are the very best I have." He paused again. "If you succeed and enter the enemy fortifications without being discovered..." Wilder stopped. "When you are ready to go into action, send this message. "The mist has come to Portston."

"When we receive that message we will assume that your action will begin 96 hours later." Wilder concluded, "Any question?"

His answer was smiling, silent faces.

Three days later Gray Thorn watched the sun slide beneath the horizon. "We'll be leaving as soon as it's dark," he said to the infantry commander.

"I'll give you our latest password," the commander offered.

"That won't be necessary," Gray Thorn said. "We won't be coming back."

A short time later, the eleven men proceeded toward the enemy positions just three hundred yards away.

The Highland Dragons stayed in their positions in the southern portion of the wilderness and awaited orders. General Wilder kept his focus on the continuing success from the Western Ranges as the open heaths, prairies and soft, loamy soil made maneuvering difficult for the enemy's heavy armor and artillery.

Dragon paced nervously back and forth in his canvas command post. Falling Leaf sighed. "Relax," she said. "We'll be put into action any day now."

"We've been sitting here for weeks," Dragon lamented.

"There's probably a good reason," Falling Leaf suggested.

"I wish the hell someone would tell me what it is," Dragon blurted.

General Wilder motioned Miner to sit next to him. "Any word," he asked.

"No," Miner replied. "They should have reached Portston yesterday."

"Let me know the minute you hear anything," Wilder ordered.

"Yes sir," Miner answered.

Gray Thorn felt strong arms dragging him out of the water. "What happened?" He asked.

"Ambush," he heard a voice reply. "Are you all right?"

Gray Thorn considered the question for a moment. He couldn't feel any pain. "Yeah, I think so. How bad was it?"

"We got our asses kicked," Mad Dog said.

"We're the only ones left," Catnip added.

"What about the enemy…" Gray Thorn was cut off.

"Dead," Mad Dog interrupted.

"What happened to me?" Gray Thorn asked.

"Concussion, judging from the blood coming from your ears and nose," Catnip observed in the darkness. "Sounds like you can hear o.k. though."

"Do you see anywhere we can take cover for the rest of the night?" Gray Thorn asked.

"I caught a glimpse of something a little farther downstream," Catnip said. "It looked like some kind of concrete structure."

"Let's try to get to it," Gray Thorn said, as he struggled to his feet.

"This way," Mad Dog said.

Slowly, the three men moved along the riverbank. Soon, they could make out the opening Catnip had described.

"I'll check it out," Mad Dog volunteered then he hurled himself into the darkness. Gray Thorn and Catnip waited, and just moments later Mad Dog was back.

"It's some kind of huge storm drain," Mad Dog explained.

"Let's move in," Catnip suggested. "I don't want to be out here in the daylight."

The three men moved into the large culvert and proceeded until they came to an opening where three other culverts converged.

"It's mostly dry," Catnip observed.

"Let's get some rest," Mad Dog suggested. "I'm exhausted."

General Wilder crumpled the note the messenger handed him and let it fall to the floor. Miner was instantly aware of the pain etched on the General's face.

"Bad news, sir," Miner asked softly.

All Wilder could do was nod his head. Miner picked up the note. "Do you mind if I read this, sir?" Miner requested.

"No, go ahead. Read it," Wilder replied.

Miner felt his heart sink when he read the brief report. He sighed, then, he read the report again. "Maybe some of them got through," he said.

"Yeah, maybe," Wilder echoed unenthusiastically. "I'm going to leave headquarters for a while," Wilder announced. "I want to deliver this message to Dragon myself."

"Yes sir, Miner" acknowledged as he handed the slip of paper back to the General.

Catnip woke up when he felt a cold, metal object press against the skin behind his ear. He couldn't see well in the darkness of the culvert, but he assumed he was feeling the muzzle of a rifle against his skull.

"If you make any sudden moves, I'll blow your head off," someone said. Then, a cloth bag was placed over his head and his hands were expertly bound behind his back and through his belt.

Mad Dog slowly moved his hand toward the place he last remembered placing his weapons, but a boot pressed down on his searching hand. An instant later he felt a knife at his throat, then, a cloth was bound about his head.

Gray Thorn underwent the same procedure.

"On your feet," a voice ordered. The three captives had little choice but to obey.

Next, the captives were tethered together then they were moved through the concrete tunnel toward an unknown fate. The pace was slow, but steady. After an hour or so, the captives were halted. The tether that had held the three men together was cut.

"Sit," the voice ordered. The commandos obeyed.

It was silent for several moments before the blindfolded men heard footsteps all around them.

"Remove their hoods," a woman's voice commanded.

Gray Thorn struggled to adapt his eyes to the bright light. It took several seconds, but finally, he recognized Candyce Storer staring at him with an expression of utter shock on her face. Around her were heavily armed, very young boys and girls. Their faces bore hard expressions.

The weeks passed. Fall was quickly turning to winter. The Liberation Army's advance slowed to a crawl on all fronts, and General Wilder could feel momentum slipping away from him and his combat units.

Then, early in the morning in the first week of November, General Wilder dozed at his duty station deep beneath the wilderness. Suddenly, a cheer erupted through his staff. He sat up, startled by the unexpected uproar. Then, his eyes saw the message scrolling across the center screen. "Slug, the mist has come to Portston. GT. 0230." kept scrolling across the screen.

Wilder grabbed a telephone hand set and shouted into the mouth-piece. "Get Dragon immediately," the General bellowed into the phone. "Wake him goddamnit!!"

Dragon used a broomstick to point to the large map. "In exactly three hours, we will attack and breach the enemy lines at this point." The broomstick tapped a spot on the map: "From here, we will move east-southeast as fast as we can. We will not stop to engage enemy units. I repeat we will not stop our advance to engage any enemy units." Dragon paused to emphasize his admonition. "Ten hours after we begin, we will link up with two other divisions moving west from the Eastern Ranges. The plan is to make the enemy believe we are going to assault Capitol City from the south. We will deploy as though that is our intent. Eight hours after the link up, we will actually move south, in the same battle formation." Dragon waited until the next map was in place. He pointed with his broomstick. "We are going to attack Portston," he shouted. His officers cheered in response.

"It is imperative that we approached the outer ring of the enemy fortifications no later than 0630 hours the fourth day. Are there any questions?" Dragon paused but no one responded.

"I would like to make one of those speeches that commanders make when they lead their forces into a maelstrom of combat knowing that the action they are about to start will be a turning point in the war. Unfortunately, we don't have time for that shit. Let's take back Portston!"

There was a brief cheer, but Dragon cut it short. "We'll celebrate in Portston!" His voice boomed.

"I want to go with the Dragons," Miner announced to General Wilder.

"You haven't been trained in combat," Wilder argued. "You'll get killed."

"Probably," Miner smiled. "I want to die with my friends."

Wilder sighed. In his mind he knew how important Miner was to his technical staff, but his heart pulled him in another direction. He looked into the clear, determined face of Miner, and saw a reflection of himself. Miner was asking for Wilder's own heartfelt desire to enter the battle. He couldn't refuse.

"Tell Dragon I am assigning you to his staff as my communications officer," Wilder said as though he didn't care.

Miner saluted the General. "Thank you, sir," he said softly.

"Go on! Get out of here," Wilder barked. "You'll have to hurry to catch up with them."

Miner turned and hurried to the elevator that would carry him to the surface of the Highlands. He didn't see the sadness on Wilder's face.

Gray Thorn, Mad Dog, Catnip and Candy carefully reviewed their attack plan for the umpteenth time. Candy was beginning to get annoyed with the endless repetition Gray Thorn insisted upon.

"Why don't you just come out and admit that you don't have any confidence in the kids?" She challenged the three warriors.

The three men looked at each other to see who had the courage to disagree with Candy. Neither of them wanted to speak. The silence irked Candy even more.

"These kids are good fighters," she stated. "They have been fighting with nearly nothing for five years. They'll die to win if they have to."

Catnip finally admitted how he felt. "They're kids!" Catnip blurted. "The average age is twelve years old. Their commander, Waters, how old is he? Sixteen?"

"Fifteen," a voice answered.

The adults turned to see the young man smiling at them. "What's the matter; you guys lose your nerve?" Waters chided.

"It's not a matter of nerve," Mad Dog corrected. "It's a matter of sending an army of children into combat to die."

"Who else do you have to send?" Waters shouted angrily. "We have watched our families be murdered or put into slave labor. We have been fighting the enemy with sticks and stones for years. Now, we have weapons, training, explosives and a good plan. We are ready to put that plan into action. We'll do it alone if we have to."

"You're just kids," Catnip sighed.

"We are the spirits of the dead," Waters countered.

Gray Thorn placed a hand on the boy's shoulder and looked directly into his eyes. "Can you handle the outer perimeter defenses east of the city?"

"Yeah," the young fighter answered.

"How long will it take you to put everyone into position?" Gray Thorn continued.

"They are in position now," Waters disclosed.

"The plan is operational," Gray Thorn said. "Everything is on schedule. You may inform your command, Major Waters."

The young man saluted and walked off to brief his fighters.

"Any questions," Gray Thorn inquired. His fellow Grays remained silent. "Very well, get with your commanders and make final preparations."

Mad Dog and Catnip obeyed without comment and left Gray Thorn and Candy alone.

"Thanks," Candy said. "You have given the kids hope, which is something they haven't had in years."

"Hope is something none of us has had in years," Gray Thorn sighed. "Now tell me how you got the schematics of the drainage system under Portston."

"Hank gave them to me," Candy said. "I don't know how he came by them."

"These maps are the key to taking Portston," Gray Thorn acknowledged. "Hank obviously thought about the possibility of hiding an army in the sewers and drains under the city."

"So did the occupation forces," Candy said. "They've sealed the access points in many locations."

"Yeah," Gray Thorn smiled. "They think they've taken care of everything."

Their eyes met and locked onto each other. For a moment, there was only the two of them. There was no war, just them. Slowly, their arms encircled one another. Their spirits forged together before their bodies and they only thought of each other and the times they had stolen together to demonstrate their love. This was another one of those times. And, like the other times, it could easily be their last.

The Highland Dragons were now moving south at a rapid pace. The enemy misinterpreted the movement as recognition of the defenses they had put up south of Capitol City. That night, when the real attack on the city came from the north, they realized their error.

Wilder's multiple attack strategy at Capitol City, along the east bank of the Old River and the western plains was complicated by covert disruptions throughout the country. The result was that the Highland Dragons, re-enforced by the divisions from the Eastern Ranges, were dashing toward Portston, unopposed and unnoticed.

Candy looked at the man who called himself Gray Thorn. His white hair, cold gray eyes and expressionless face made him appear more animal-like than human. But in her heart, she saw Michael; the man she loved. She wondered if her love was strong enough to melt the cold, killing machine called Gray Thorn into the affectionate Michael she longed for. "You had better rest now," she said to Gray Thorn as she motioned him beside her in her sleeping bag.

Gray Thorn placed his weapons in an accessible position beside the sleeping bag. He removed his boots then slid next to Candy. He felt her warm embrace. Images of their time together in Portston flashed through his mind. Then, he saw the explosions that collapsed his family's mansion and mutilated his mother. He saw himself open the green trunk that his grandfather left him and the apparitions of Henry Highet and Bishop Blane wafted out of the box. He heard Barbara weeping on the rocky beach beneath the cliffs. Dudley, Draco, Jane, where are you, he asked himself. "Yes grandmother," he said in his sleep. He sighed, then relaxed in Candy's loving embrace. "Michael, Michael," the familiar voices echoed in his mind. "They will rise up from the earth to fight. Kill the enemy! Kill them! Kill them!"

General Wilder was approached by one of his aids. "General something is happening?"

"What?" Wilder asked in an alarmed manner.

"The mist, sir.

"What about it?"

"It's gone, sir."

The General jumped into his boots then hurried to the elevator with the aide. A few moments later he stood on the forest floor. He looked up into the star-filled sky, as a cold breeze washed over his face.

"What does it mean, General?" The aide asked nervously.

"Victory," Wilder replied. "We no longer need the mist. We will prevail."

Gray Thorn spread out his maps for the last time. "Are the enemy ships still where they were?" He asked.

"Yes," a wiry boy answered.

"Has any change occurred in the enemy routine?"

"No," a girl replied.

"Let's review the plan one last time," Gray Thorn began. "Patricia's demolition teams will detonate charges beneath the enemy barracks and headquarters at 0230 hours. The explosions will be the signal for the rest of us to attack our objectives. I'll attack the core defenses with the naval guns on the east of the harbor. Mad Dog will do likewise on the west. Waters will attack the second perimeter artillery positions in the east; Catnip will do the same in the West. Waters and Catnip will sweep though the second-tier positions and attack the outer perimeter positions from the rear. Any questions?"

"Do you have any final thoughts, sir," Waters asked.

"Only one," Gray Thorn offered. "Kill them. Kill as many as you can as fast as you can. Do not leave any wounded alive. Don't take prisoners. Kill them! Take your objectives."

Everyone was silent for a moment. Then Waters stepped forward.

"Let's get started," he smiled brightly. The final meeting ended and the fighters set out to their final attack points.

At 0100 hours, a thick fog descended on Portston. An hour later, a person could see only a few feet. The lack of visibility meant nothing to the more than six thousand boys and girls that scurried beneath the city through the drains and sewers. They had rehearsed this act a hundred times. They could carry out their appointed tasks blindfolded.

At 0230 hours, chaos erupted from beneath the city. Shock and confusion overwhelmed the occupation forces. The infantry assigned to defend the large naval guns that had been placed in an arc along the inner core defense, rushed from their posts to help their ill fated comrades in burning barracks. Patricia's demolition teams cut the unorganized reaction to pieces with automatic weapon and machine gun fire. After quickly neutralizing the knee-jerk enemy reaction, Patricia trained her teams on the rows of troop transports moored along the piers. Small arms fire fell like rain upon the ships along with three-inch mortar rounds. Within minutes one ship was ablaze. The ships commanders tried to get their vessels unmoored and underway, but Patricia's force poured devastating fire into them.

Gray Thorn, Candy at his side, quickly led successful assaults on the first three gun emplacements. The gun crews were dispatched with ease, and the young warriors began manipulating the deadly hardware for their own use. Two enemy aircraft carriers came under fire from their own radar controlled, land mounted naval guns at shortly after 0300 hours.

Mad Dog marveled at the discipline and effectiveness of his young charges. One by one, each of the nine huge guns fell into their hands. By daylight, all the guns west of the river were in "rebel" hands.

Catnip and Waters' reinforced battalion, easily brushed aside the artillery crews in the second tier, then they engaged the veteran infantry in the outer perimeter.

Wilder watched his information screens with wide-eyed enthusiasm. Reports flowed quickly from Portston and Wilder's intelligence teams translated the messages into visual images on the large screens.

"General Wilder," an officer blurted. "We have just intercepted an enemy message ordering all its occupation forces to converge on Portston."

"Relay that message to all commanders," Wilder responded. "Tell all units to maintain contact with enemy and retard their movement to Portston at all costs. Order all concealment teams to do the same. All rail and air transportation facilities are to be disabled. Interfere with all electronic transmissions."

The officer left as quickly as he had arrived to follow the general's instructions.

Chapter 26

At 0730 hours Ivan the Dragon looked at the city of Portston shrouded in fog. The continuous flashes of light beneath the mist indicated the fierceness of the battle that was raging in the city. "Hurry," he said to his driver.

It would be another 90 minutes before Draco led his Highland Dragons toward the enemy's outer defenses. They approached quickly, almost recklessly. To Draco's surprise, there was no resistance. Then, he saw two young boys and a young girl waving a short distance from his vehicle. Draco ordered the driver to approach the heavily armed trio in camouflage combat uniforms. The vehicle stopped and Draco jumped to the ground.

"Greetings Dragon. I'm Major Waters. This is Captain Finn," the young boy saluted as he was introduced. "And this is Captain Green," the young girl also saluted.

Draco saluted, but he was unnerved by the battle hardened faces on the young people before him.

"My orders are to relinquish command of this area to you, sir," Waters said. "We expect the enemy to counter-attack at the earliest opportunity."

"Where did the enemy go?" Draco asked.

"Most of them ran away," Waters replied. "The rest died."

"Which way did they run?" Draco continued.

"North," Waters pointed. "I have orders to allow you to relieve me," Waters repeated.

"And may I ask who gave you your orders, Major?" Draco asked.

"Gray Thorn," Waters answered.

"Then, he's alive," Draco observed.

"He was eight or nine hours ago," Waters clarified. "I don't know about now. Are you ready to assume command of this area?"

"Yes," Draco said.

"Good," Waters said. "I'll be moving my unit back toward the piers to help my comrades. Would you mind burying our dead? We didn't have the time."

"I would be honored," Draco said, as he fended off his emotions.

"Then, we'll be on our way. Thanks Dragon," Waters saluted.

Draco returned the salute and watched the young officers begin walking back toward the city center. Other child warriors appeared from behind the captured defenses and fell in behind their officers.

A loud cheer exploded in Wilder's Headquarters as news of the Highland Dragons arrival east of Portston was displayed on the screens. Wilder allowed the celebration to continue, but he knew that the end was not yet in sight.

By the end of the day, Gray Thorn and his force had secured six of the massive guns. The enemy had destroyed the other three to prevent their capture.

The final battle for the piers of Portston was underway, and Gray Thorn moved the rest of his force to the river. When he arrived, he quickly encountered Patricia who was preparing another assault on the rows of troop carriers.

"What's your plan?" Gray Thorn asked the young girl.

"I'm going to finish them off with mortar fire," she replied.

"How?"

"I'm positioning a third of the mortars close enough to fire point blank with anti-tank ammunition," the girl answered.

"That should do it," Gray Thorn agreed.

"How come they didn't try to get away down the river?" Gray Thorn asked.

"They did," the girl replied. "We captured a freighter and sunk it in the channel to trap them where they are."

"Good work," Gray Thorn complimented. "Let me know when you're ready. We can supply supporting fire until you get your guns into position."

"Can you get your troops on those roof tops?" Patricia asked.

"Sure," Gray Thorn answered. He turned and ordered his unit onto the rooftops. Then, he noticed Candy standing nearby.

"How long have you been with me?"

"All day," she answered.

Gray Thorn looked into Candy's caring green eyes. "Thanks," he said then he turned to lead his young fighters into battle. Candy was one step behind him.

When Gray Thorn reached the area near the piers, he and his unit came under intense small arms fire. The enemy troops aboard the troop carriers had left their ships and elected to fight for control of the high buildings overlooking the wide river. The young boys and girls had been well trained, however, and they immediately went into action.

The enemy occupation forces had re-enforced the old buildings making them more than a fortress. Whoever controlled this group of buildings would win the battle.

General Wilder watched anxiously as reports of enemy troop movements were displayed on the large electronic screens. The enemy had given up its grip all along the Eastern Ranges and Capitol City as they pushed toward Portston for a counter-attack. The Highland Dragons had been warned and were quickly turning the captured defensive structures to their own use.

"Do we have communications with the Midland Grays," Wilder barked.

"I have a young girl called Patricia that says she's a Major…"

"Put her on the speaker," Wilder boomed.

"This is Patricia," the young girl yelled. The sounds of combat were making it impossible for her to hear.

"This is General Wilder of the Liberation Army. What's your location?"

"We're engaging the enemy soldiers on and near the troop ships," the girl yelled. "I can't talk now. I have to re-deploy my guns."

Only a loud hissing sound came out of the speakers. "We lost her sir," a voice acknowledged. "Shall I try to re-establish contact?"

"No," Wilder said softly.

Patricia finally got four of her eight, three-inch mortars where she wanted them. The guns went into action right away and began lobbing death into the overcrowded enemy positions along the pier.

Gray Thorn immediately took advantage of Patricia's gunners' marksmanship and moved his unit into the buildings. They fought from floor to floor, room to room and captured the two northern most of the row of buildings. By noon, Gray Thorn was on the rooftop firing at the enemy on the adjacent structures.

The view from the rooftop was both informative and dangerous. The entire harbor was aflame and smoke filled. Three of the troop ships were ablaze and taking on water. The two other ships were enduring repetitive explosions as the three-inch shells continued to fall upon them. Enemy dead were everywhere Gray Thorn looked. Bodies were stacked up near the ships. Countless bodies bobbed in the quiet waters of the river. Then, through the smoke, he could see hundreds more huddling on the west bank beneath the bluffs. Gray Thorn hurriedly established rows of machine guns to discourage the enemy from launching a rooftop to rooftop assault.

On the east perimeter, Dragon waited for the coming counter-attack. He could hear the battle raging in the center of the city. He wanted to send help to the Grays, but he had been ordered to hold the east perimeter. As night fell, all the Highland Dragons watched the flames and explosions from the city center. Then, suddenly, chaos fell upon them.

For the next two days, the battle raged. Attack after attack, was repelled by the Dragons and the enemy regrouped. There was a quiet period for twenty-four hours; then, the enemy renewed their attempt to retake the city that was their lifeline. This time they put everything on the west bank of the river and attacked in a southerly direction right along the riverbank. They met heavy resistance, but slowly they pushed forward. Dragon decided to send a fourth of his command north of the city center to engage the determined enemy across the river.

Wilder studied the large screens for the last time. "Order everyone we have to push toward Portston," he said. "Anyone who can fire a weapon is to be sent to Portston." He got up from his command point and donned a weapons belt and helmet. "Let's go!" He shouted. "We'll set-up a mobile command post until we get to Portston."

The personnel in headquarters hesitated for a moment, then, there was a scramble for weapons and ammunition.

The weakening attacks on his area caused Dragon to grow bold. He called his commanders together and explained his plan. The Highland

The Last Day of the Last Spring

Dragons would attack along a line from their positions on the east-bank of the Old River, North of Portston and swing like a gate. Dragon hoped they would be able to force the enemy to the south and east then trap them along the southern coast. No one objected and Dragon notified General Wilder of the plan.

Gray Thorn and his determined fighters had taken a third building in the so-called "wall" that overlooked the harbor and docks. They had been fortunate so far. The enemy attacked with an almost hysterical frenzy in the beginning. Now, they were more composed and organized. In fact, they greatly outnumbered the child army, but they were contained in a crowded and confined area with little room to maneuver. By now, Gray Thorn concluded that the troop ships were empty, as the men aboard them had long left them due to Patricia's deadly mortar bombardment. The shells still rained down upon the enemy positions within the wall, but the structure seemed to withstand the constant battering.

Throughout the entire battle to this point, the Highland mist hovered over the city. Enemy aircraft were forced to stay on the ground or on one of the remaining aircraft carriers that had escaped the shelling from the captured guns in the city. The enemy air effort was generally ineffective, and the would-be liberators took little notice of the aircraft.

On December 4th, just after dawn, Dragon waited for an enemy contingency under a white flag to approach. He was surprised to see such high-ranking officers, but he was in no mood for niceties. Falling Leaf stood on Dragon's left. Both wore expressionless faces, as the enemy leaders filed before them.

"We are here to discuss terms," the highest-ranking Field Marshall said.

Dragon looked at the officer with hatred searing inside him. "Terms," Draco sneered. "You invade our country, destroy our cities, foul our streams and contaminate our fields, and now that you're low on supplies you want to save your filthy asses?"

"I wish to save the lives of as many of my men as I can," the officer replied.

"Frankly, I'm not interested in saving any of your men," Draco roared. "I'm in a position to kill all of you bastards and there is nothing you can do about it."

"We realize the impossible position we are in," the Commander admitted, "or I wouldn't be willing to surrender."

Draco glared at the man for several moments. "I'll talk to my staff," Draco said. He turned a walked away from the enemy officers. Falling Leaf walked beside him.

"You're not going to kill them are you?" Falling Leaf asked.

"No," Draco hissed, "but I sure do want to."

Draco watched as the naked enemy soldiers marched to the holding area setup for them. Then, he left another officer in charge of the prisoners and turned his assault troops toward the center of Portston. They entered the city in late afternoon and immediately came in contact with the enemy.

Upon seeing the oncoming Highland Dragons the enemy frantically pushed toward the river. They boarded anything that would float and tried to escape across the river. Draco urged his men forward but the intensity of small arms fire gave them pause. Draco was astonished at the large number of enemy infantry, but he quickly realized that they were green troops that had panicked in the face of defeat or death.

"Welcome Dragons," a young girl called out. "I'm Patricia. Welcome to Portston."

Draco returned the girls smart salute. "Patricia, do you know where Gray Thorn is?"

The girl pointed to a row of buildings that had been connected together. "I think he's in the fifth building from the left," she said. "I'm re-deploying my guns again to fire point blank into the buildings on the south. There are still a lot of enemy troops in there."

Draco directed the young girl to one of his officers for additional support and a battery of howitzers, then, pressed on toward the "wall". Falling Leaf trailed Draco with a squad of infantry and they entered one of the buildings held by friendly forces. The young warriors manning the building were firing their weapons as fast as they could. Other, very young boys and girls ran from point to point with ammunition.

"We're looking for Gray Thorn," Draco shouted to one child.

A little girl immediately pointed upward. "Roof!" She shouted back.

Draco led his team up several flights of stairs. When they reached the rooftop, which had been re-enforced with concrete and connected to the other rooftops, they were immediately part of the battle. Small arms fire pinged and whizzed all around them. Finally, Draco spotted Gray Thorn and moved forward. He made it to the third building when an artillery shell thundered into the building collapsing the roof. Draco fell through to the next floor and lie crumpled and bleeding upon the rubble.

Gray Thorn and Candy rallied their young fighters together as the enemy made one more desperate attempt to retake the rooftops. They rushed toward the Grays in a swarm. Bodies fell upon bodies. Parts of men flew in all directions, but the enemy kept moving forward. Then the liberators and conquerors were locked together in an orgy of death. They fought with bare hands, rocks and anything else that could be used as a weapon.

Candy saw Gray Thorn fall, and she fired her handgun point blank into enemy faces as she ran to reach her lover. She fell over a corpse and got up again just in time to see an enemy soldier rushing her with a bayoneted rifle. She fired her pistol. The soldier staggered then slashed at her causing a long wound to open on the right side of her face. She fell on her back from the force of the blow. Then she saw Gray Thorn grappling with another soldier just a few feet away. She leapt to her feet just as Patricia's howitzers began delivering devastating fire into the southern row of buildings. Now, she was in the grasp of another soldier who had placed a wire around her neck. She was about to fall unconscious, when she saw Gray Thorn spring upon her attacker. All three fell onto the bodies strewn upon the rooftop. Candy loosened the noose from her neck. When she next saw Gray Thorn, he had opened his mouth and plunged his teeth into the man's throat. Blood spurted from the man's severed jugular vein, but Gray Thorn held his bite. Then, the entire roof exploded.

What was left of the enemy forces now decided to push toward the river and make for the west bank. Their swim was to end in death as the large number of men on the narrow beach and the base of the cliff had no protection. Mad Dog quickly moved his force onto the southern end of the beach, but before he could organize an attack he was shot in the chest. He knew he was dying as he lay on the rocky beach. He saw a young face appear above him and he grabbed the boy's jacket in a clenched fist. "Kill them," he gasped, "kill them."

"We will," the boy answered as Mad Dog's hand loosened its grip then fell.

Just before sunrise General Wilder searched the rubble of the "wall" looking for his comrades. The battle, indeed, the war was nearly over. Portston was liberated. Now was the time to find comrades, bury the dead, care for the wounded and guard prisoners. Oddly, it was not a time of joy.

The smell of burnt flesh was mingled with the smell of burnt gunpowder. Blood ran down the gutters of the streets. Wilder was beginning to think the worst.

"We'll find them," Miner said.

"Yes," Wilder agreed weakly. "But, will they be alive?"

"Look, there's Falling Leaf!" Miner blurted then dashed forward. Wilder broke into a run behind him. A short distance later both men stopped. Falling Leaf was tending to a badly wounded man. It was the Dragon himself.

"Ivan's going to make it," Falling Leaf smiled.

"She means that most of me will make it," Draco said. "My left arm is useless and I was told I lost my left eye."

"I'll take it," Falling Leaf smiled as she embraced Draco.

"It looks like these two want to be alone," Wilder said to Miner.

"Have you seen Gray Thorn?" Miner asked hopefully.

"The last time we saw him, he was on top of the wall," Falling Leaf answered.

"Wall?" Miner asked.

Falling leaf pointed to a long pile of bricks and concrete. "It used to be over there," she said.

Miner's heart sank as he looked at the destruction.

"Let's go look for him," Wilder said.

The two men approached the debris with little hope. Most of the people they saw were dead. Some of the bodies had been hit so many times it was not possible to identify them as friend or foe except for the children. The child warriors' small frames were easily distinguished.

"Who are you looking for?" A voice asked.

Miner and Wilder turned to see a young boy on crutches with one leg missing. "We're looking for Gray Thorn," Miner replied.

"He pulled me out of the ruble last night," the boy answered. "I was lucky."

"Do you know where he is now?" Wilder questioned.

"No. He and Candy were fighting together while pulling wounded out of the buildings. Candy took me to a medic then went back to the wall. A little later she came back and asked me if I had seen Gray Thorn. I think she went looking for him."

"Who is Candy?" Miner asked.

"The woman who kept all of us kids alive during the occupation," the boy stated proudly. "It turned out she was Gray Thorn's girl friend."

Miner and General Wilder exchanged quizzical glances.

"I hope you find him," the boy continued. "He had been hit. I could tell."

"Thanks," Miner said. "We'll find him."

"General Wilder?" a man called out.

"Yes, what is it?"

"I just came from the west bank. There are enemy bodies piled up six feet high over there as far as you can see."

"No survivors?" Wilder asked.

"No sir, they made sure of that."

"They?"

"He means 'us'," a young girl announced defiantly.

Wilder looked into the cold stare of the skinny girl. He felt a chill run down his spine as he realized how the children of Portston had become cold blooded warriors determined to exterminate their enemies. He saluted the young girl wearing captain's rank. "Carry on, Captain. I'm sure you want to check on your troops."

"My company is intact, sir," the girl replied. "We ask permission to join the Eastern Rangers in the battle west of the city. The war is going to end soon and we want to kill as many as we can."

Wilder looked at his aide. "Notify the Eastern Rangers to expect another company of light infantry."

"Excuse me, General," the girl interrupted. "We are not infantry, we are Midland Grays." She pulled the patch sewn to her left shoulder into view. Both Miner and Wilder recognized the "Oak in the Mist" image on the patch.

"My apologies, Captain." Wilder saluted then turned to the aide again. "Notify the Eastern Rangers that the Midland Grays will be re-enforcing them."

"Yes sir," the aide saluted smartly then turned and walked away.

"Thank you, sir," the young Captain said. "Sorry about the mess we left here." She saluted and ran to catch up with Wilder's aide.

Miner and General Wilder watched in shocked silence as the girl rushed toward battle.

Dianna Bartlett sat naked in the middle of a cold, barren room. Her head had been shaved and her arms were tied behind her. She had been accused of "collaborating with the enemy" by providing them "comfort" and "entertainment". She knew she would be found guilty and executed. She had no defense. At least she had no defense anyone would accept.

The door to the room opened and a man and a woman approached her. They said nothing as they helped her to her feet and led her out of the room to a platform outside. She could not mistake the hatred in the eyes of the people looking at her. Just below her place on the platform was an open truck containing several, naked bodies. She couldn't take her eyes off the corpses.

"Dianna Bartlett, you have been found guilty of treason and are sentenced to death. Your sentence will be carried out immediately. The woman behind her placed a pistol to the back of her head.

"Hold on there!" A man's voice boomed nearby.

Dianna was stunned and unsure what to do.

"We have had enough of our countrymen killed by the enemy," the man's voice said loudly, "there is no need for us to kill each other."

"This woman is a collaborator," someone protested.

"Then, I'll place her under arrest," the man said.

Dianna felt a poncho being pulled over her naked body. She allowed the poncho to be put in place but she couldn't look up into the faces of those around her.

Candy searched frantically for Gray Thorn. She knew he had been wounded and needed medical attention, but she couldn't find him. Driven by pure instinct and ignoring the hideous wound to her face, Candy moved north along the east bank of the Old River. The sounds of battle were still going on, but the noise seemed to be far away. Everyone she met she asked the same question. Have you seen Gray Thorn? Finally, she met a woman who recognized the description of the man.

"Yes," the woman said. "His hair was very gray as well as his eyes. I tried to get him to stay so we could tend to his wounds, but he refused."

"Which way did he go?" Candy asked hopefully.

"North," the woman answered. "He was on foot, so you might be able to catch up with him."

Candy thanked the woman and continued at as brisk a pace as she could maintain.

The second day passed and she saw no sign of him, nor met anyone who had. Still she was convinced she was on his trail and kept pressing northward in spite of the cold and snow. Then, on the third day, she found a spot where she believed Gray Thorn had rested. There was a small amount of blood on the snow, and she was certain now she was closing in on her Michael.

Draco searched everywhere in Portston for Gray Thorn, but couldn't locate him or his body. Convinced Gray Thorn was still alive, he wanted to continue the search, but he was still weak from his wounds, and simply fell into exhaustion.

General Wilder and Miner too wanted to find their friend, but Wilder was busy trying to negotiate surrender terms with the remnants of the enemy army. Miner had been given the task of burying the dead and clearing the streets, which proved to be nearly overwhelming at the start. Falling Leaf was trying to do the search for Gray Thorn by talking to as many liberation troops as possible.

The inevitable surrender finally occurred in the dead of winter. Miner was able to re-establish some of the main thoroughfares of the city and even restore running water and occasional electricity. With some of his responsibilities now delegated to others, he too re-joined the search for his friend, but with no luck.

General Wilder, the Dragon, Miner, and Falling Leaf finally found time to plan a thorough search in mid-January. They met in the one undamaged building near the waterfront. They had listed endless possibilities when a young warrior appeared with a woman. She was tall and thin and wore a gray shawl over her head.

"My name is Barbara," the woman said. "I was told you are looking for the gray one."

"Yes," Miner answered excitedly. "Have you seen him?"

"Yes," the woman smiled. "He is travelling north. There is a woman following him named Candy. I treated the wounds of both of them."

"How long ago was that?" Draco asked.

"It's been days ago," Barbara replied.

"Did he say where he was going?" General Wilder queried.

"Not exactly," Barbara smiled. "He told me he was going home."

The group considered the word "home" and wondered where "home" would be for Gray Thorn.

"You knew him better than anyone, Miner," Draco said. "What do you think?"

"It can't be Capitol City," Miner mused, "Woodburne Mansion was destroyed in the first air raid." He forced his mind to work, then his eyes connected with Draco's stare.

"The Midland-Highlands!" Both men blurted at the same moment.

"Long Ridge to be exact," Miner underscored.

"Let's get going," Wilder suggested.

"I'll get a vehicle," Falling Leaf volunteered.

Chapter 27

The boat docked at a ruined pier in the ghost town of Riverview. A wounded warrior pulled himself out of the boat and onto the crumbling pier. "Thank you," the wounded man said.

"I wish I could do more for you," the boatman said.

"You have done enough," the warrior replied softly. He waved then slowly started making his way eastward.

Just a few miles south of Riverview, Candy cursed as her vehicle ran out of gas. She left the vehicle and began making her way northeast. A cold wind threatened to slow her, but she put her head down and surged into the wind with all her strength.

Sometime later, Candy came to the steep ridge that rose above the Midland-Highlands center. She only glanced at the steep slope before pushing ahead.

Gray Thorn rested against the base of a tree. Large, white snowflakes fell softly from the sky. He tried to recall how he had gotten here to Long Ridge. He didn't remember, but he was glad he was here; home. If he was going to die, he wanted to die here.

Falling Leaf, Miner, and Slug took turns driving as Draco cursed his useless arm. In spite of the eagerness of the searchers, it took nearly twelve hours to reach the wilderness. Heavy snow blocked the Old Road, and Falling Leaf stopped the vehicle.

"We should wait for daylight," Falling Leaf advised. "I don't think we can make it in the dark."

General Wilder nodded his agreement. "We need to sleep anyway. We'll need all our energy to walk through this stuff."

Draco and Miner couldn't disagree, and started passing out sleeping bags. There was no conversation as the tired people snuggled into the warmth of the insulated bags and quickly fell asleep.

The group awoke to a cloudy, snow covered vista the next morning. Falling Leaf looked at the smooth, undisturbed snow in front of her.

"How will I know where the road is?" She asked.

Miner leaned forward from his rear seat and peered through the windshield. "We'll have to assume that the road is the open space between the trees," Miner said.

Falling Leaf shot an angry glance at Miner thinking he was trying to be sarcastic. The sincerity on his face quickly calmed her. "You'd better buckle yourselves in," she suggested, then she started the engine. She heard the safety belts click in their locks then she put the vehicle in gear.

The trip up the Old Road was slow and treacherous. Several times the vehicle had to be winched up a steep incline or back onto the road surface. By nightfall, the travelers were still short of Long Ridge. They ate canned rations and melted snow for water. Then, they slept through the night.

It was snowing when they roused themselves the next morning. They stored their sleeping gear, and once again set out toward Long Ridge. The vehicle lurched, bumped and skidded through the deep snow while the occupants struggled to keep from bumping into one another. As mid-day approached, Miner spotted the road that ran up to Long Ridge. "There it is," he said "on the left."

Falling Leaf responded and guided the vehicle onto the narrow track that climbed the ridge. After a short distance, however, the wheels lost traction. Falling Leaf stopped the vehicle and Miner jumped out to secure the cable from the winch. He unwound a great length of cable, and then secured it to a sturdy oak. He waved to Falling Leaf who engaged the winch to slowly pull them out to a point where the wheels were functional again. Miner stayed ahead of the vehicle on foot while taking up the slack in the cable. Twice more he had to attach the cable before they came to the crest of the ridge.

Now Miner could see the cabin of his old friend's grandparents where they had spent a few days together so many, many years ago. He waved to the others, who exited the vehicle and joined him to march the remaining distance.

As they closed in on the old cabin, it became increasingly apparent that no one had been there. The snow was pristine and untouched. The hearts of the searchers fell into despair. They stood in silence while large snowflakes fell slowly all around them.

"What was that?" Miner asked. "I heard something." He walked a few steps toward the west and listened again. The others inched up to him. "Can you hear that?" Miner asked.

Again he walked forward; then, he spotted the ruts and footsteps in the snow. It appeared that one person was dragging another. There were also drops of fresh blood glistening upon the snow.

Candy kept repeating the same thing over and over as she drug her lover toward the hot spring. "Don't you die on me Michael! Don't you die on me, Michael! Don't you die on me, Michael!" She pulled, and pulled as she repeated her phrase. She would look over her shoulder to see how much further she had to go then continued pulling the limp man in her grasp. "Don't you die on me, Michael!"

The four friends drew closer and closer to the sounds. They could hear the voice of a woman. Finally, they saw them. The woman pulled Michael into the hot spring and embraced him. "Don't you die on me, Michael! Don't you die on me."

The sight of Michael's head slumped forward on his chest was more than Draco could stand. He collapsed into the snow sobbing uncontrollably. Falling Leaf went to ground with him trying to comfort him. General Wilder turned and pushed his face into his hands. Miner stared in disbelief. He stumbled forward while tears flowed down his face.

"Michael! Michael! Don't you die on me." Candy said with increasing speed and urgency. "Don't you die on me! Don't! Don't! Michael! Michael! Michael!" She screamed.

Miner was frozen by grief and the wild look on the face of the woman. He couldn't speak. He couldn't move. He couldn't look away. He couldn't think. The woman held on to Michael and repeated his name over and over and over.

The wind began to rush through the trees which creaked and groaned under the strain of the forceful air. The woman in the spring was unaware of the wind and continued her solitary lament. The wind grew stronger, and stronger. The snow began flying sideways and Miner was finding it difficult to stand up against it. Now, there was a roar coming from the west. Draco and Falling Leaf struggled to their feet to see what was causing the noise. General Wilder too, turned to see what caused the disturbance. They could no longer hear the cries of the woman in the hot spring. Then, they saw it.

A white, swirling vortex drove straight toward them. Tree limbs cracked and fell as the maelstrom approached. The snow cyclone moved steadily toward them then veered over the hot spring. They lost sight of the man and the woman in the spring, as the vortex seemed to pause over them. Then, the wind simply quit. The snow began falling straight down again. In the silence, they heard the woman again. But there was something different in her voice. The thing they heard in her voice was joy.

"Michael, Michael" she giggled through her tears.

"Candy," the man in her arms answered.

The four friends instantly began scrambling toward the spring. They slipped and fell in the deep snow and finally they plunged into the hot water and welcomed Michael back from the brink of death.

The next day, the weather cleared and a medical team arrived by helicopter. The old cabin had been re-opened and revitalized. There was warmth, hot food, comfort and above all – peace and camaraderie. Ivan Draco, General Wilder, Jane Linden, and Dudley Carpenter had all gathered in the living room listening to Dudley recount his visit to this cabin years before.

Dudley stopped his commentary when the doctor entered the room.

"Well, how are they?" Wilder prompted the doctor.

"They should both be dead," the doctor said, "but they're not."

"Good work," Wilder praised.

"I didn't have anything to do with it," the doctor admitted.

"I don't understand," Dudley said.

"Neither do I," the doctor responded. "Is there any whiskey around here?"

Ivan produced a bottle and the doctor took a large gulp. "Can we see them," Draco asked.

"Sure," the doctor answered as he handed the bottle back to Draco. "They're asleep or unconscious," the doctor continued. "I don't know which." He moved to the bedroom door and opened it.

Michael lie on his back with his left arm curled around Candy. Candy's head was on Michael's left chest and shoulder, and her left arm was drooped across his waist. Both appeared to be quite relaxed.

"Should they be together like that?" Wilder questioned.

"Try to separate them," the doctor challenged. "One of my nurses got a broken nose trying to do that."

Wilder nodded and everyone left the couple alone to rest.

"There's one more thing," the doctor announced, "the woman is pregnant."

"How wonderful," Jane blurted happily, "new life instead of death. It's wonderful. Is the baby all right?"

"As far as I can tell," the doctor confirmed.

Jane burst into tears and rushed out onto the porch of the cabin. Ivan limped behind trying to catch up with her and comfort her.

General Wilder let out an audible sigh. "I forgot," he confessed to the doctor.

"Forgot what?"

"I forgot that Jane was a woman, not just a warrior. I forgot that women want to be mothers and men want to be fathers. It is not natural for us to be warriors."

"We are what we need to be," the doctor observed. "That is what makes us strong; our ability to change to fit the occasion, to fulfill the need."

Wilder nodded in acceptance of the doctor's simple wisdom. "Will you be able to stay here with Michael and Candy?"

"No, there are others who need me. This young couple is immersed in forces I don't understand. I admit I would like to stay to see what happens next, but I am needed elsewhere."

"Then you feel that they will recover?" Wilder pressed.

"No doubt; they're just resting now. Let them sleep." The doctor started for the door then paused. "You know General, when I examined them and saw how they were healing I think I was seeing the work of God."

The General bit his lip thoughtfully then nodded. The image of the snow cyclone flashed through his mind. "Could be, doctor; could very well be," Wilder said softly.

Another day passed before Michael and Candy awoke. They were unable to take their eyes off each other or keep from touching each other. The two were only remotely aware that anyone else was there with them.

The next day they were able to sit up and have brief conversations with their friends. Both were much more aware and mentally alert than they had been. Still, they would frequently look into each other's eyes and drift off to a place where only the two of them could exist.

Slowly, the couple recovered. General "Slug" Wilder left Long Ridge to try to manage the rebuilding of the nation. Dudley, Jane and Ivan remained and waited on Michael and Candy as if they were royalty.

Finally, Michael and Candy were up and about and able to care for themselves. Reluctantly, Jane and Ivan left the wilderness to return National University.

Then the day came for Dudley to leave. It was difficult for him to do, but he knew he had to return to his dream before the war and manage Highet Industries.

"How do I thank you for your friendship," Michael asked his old friend.

"I was wondering about the same thing," Dudley laughed. "You have given all of us more than any one man should have to provide to a friend," Dudley acknowledged. "Now, it's my turn. I will rebuild the factories and foundries so men will have good paying jobs to care for their families. I will build an industrial base so strong, that our military will always be one step ahead of any potential enemy. This is my mission, my fate. I just hope I can endure the hardships along the way with the courage and commitment you had these past, horrible years."

The two men embraced, then, Dudley hugged Candy. "I'll be back to visit you," Dudley said.

"Yes, you must," Candy smiled.

"We insist," Michael added.

Dudley left. Michael and Candy looked into each other's souls. Their arms folded around each other and they went to that special place in their minds where they would dwell for the rest of their lives.

When Ivan Draco and Jane Linden arrived at the campus at National University they were met by none other than Doctor Henley. The professor greeted the two warriors with sincere warmth. "My god, I'm glad to see you both alive," Henley gushed.

"I'm surprised to see everything still standing," Draco admitted.

"Yes, we were most fortunate," Henley agreed. "We are hoping to re-open the university as soon as we find a new president," Henley went on. "Would you be interested in the job?"

Ivan Draco chuckled as he squeezed Jane close to him with one arm. "I have another priority right now," he said as he looked into Jane's face.

Henley smiled. "There is plenty of time to fill the university's needs," he grinned. "It can wait."

Dudley Carpenter returned to Capitol city and met with General Wilder. Dudley was told that he would keep his title of "general" during the imposition of martial law and was asked to stay on as Wilder's chief of staff. "I need you Dudley. I don't know where to start to rebuild this nation."

"Let's start with the leaders from the Midland-Highlands refugee camps," Dudley offered. "Ivan Draco says they're smart as hell."

"Great idea," Wilder agreed. "Will you contact them?"

"Sure," Dudley smiled.

After his brief meeting with General Wilder, Dudley walked through the streets of Capitol City. The destruction was already being repaired and the ruble being cleared. But sadness gripped Dudley and he didn't know why. He tried to recount events but his mind would not allow him to do so. In the end, he wandered aimlessly through the streets.

Finally, the sound of a bus rambling past him tore him from his thoughts. It was a military bus and it stopped a short distance from him at the local jail. Dudley continued walking toward the stopped bus as armed soldiers began off-loading prisoners. Dudley glanced at the hapless faces that stared at the ground. Then, a barefoot young woman in a poncho caught his attention. Her head had been shaved, but she looked familiar to Dudley. He drew closer to the prisoner and reached out to tilt her downcast face upward. The woman resisted a first, but then she cast a wary glance upward. Her lower lip began to tremble. She started to gasp for air and couldn't speak. Dudley threw his arms around her to comfort her.

Jane worked diligently to re-organize the library at National University while Ivan Draco and Doctor Henley spoke with the university's curators and board of directors. Both were happy in their civilian roles and eagerly plunged into their work. One day in early March, while Jane busied herself at the library, a young couple surprised her.

"May I check out this book?" The man asked

"Not yet..." Jane's jaw dropped open when she turned to see Dudley Carpenter. "Dudley!" Jane shouted as she grabbed him and hugged him across the counter. "And, Dianna Bartlett!"

"Dianna Carpenter." Dianna corrected.

Now Jane dashed around the counter to hug Dianna. When she released her grip she smiled broadly. "Ivan Draco and I were married last month."

"So were we," Dianna giggled.

"What brings you here?" Jane queried.

"We thought we would ask you and Ivan to join us to visit Michael and Candy in the Highlands. The old road should be open by now."

"Let's go find Ivan," Jane suggested.

Soon the two couples were driving down the old road through the wilderness. Most of the snow had melted and Dudley was particularly pleased to find that the road up Long Ridge was passable.

When the vehicle approached the small cabin, Candy was sweeping the porch. She watched as the car pulled up to the stairs. It only took an instant for her to recognize Dudley and Ivan.

"Michael! Michael! We have company!" Candy shouted in joy.

A moment later, Michael joined in the re-union. Next, he ushered everyone into the cabin to finish introductions.

"This is Dianna B..."

"Carpenter," Dianna finished.

"Congratulations," Michael smiled. "You two were together a long time before the war. I'm glad you found each other."

"Ivan and I are married as well," Jane disclosed. Ivan smiled but shuffled about nervously on one foot.

"I am so happy to see you," Candy said. "I'm so glad you're here."

Jane softly patted Candy on her belly. "When is the Baby due?"

"Sometime in June," Candy replied. "Oh, it's dinner time," Candy remembered. "Come help me, Dianna, Jane. We have venison and pheasant in the freezer. Michael, start a fire and get some drinks for Ivan and Dudley."

Michael smiled and seated his two friends near the fire place. Soon, the fire crackled and the whiskey flowed. The conversation was all small talk at first, then, Ivan asked the big question. "Do you think about it much; the war?"

"No," Michael replied.

"Same for me," Dudley chimed in.

"We need to document what happened," Ivan said. "We can't let the next generation grow up as ignorant and complacent as we were."

"All I want to do is keep Dianna pregnant," Dudley confessed. "I need to concentrate on the future."

"I just want to forget it all, Ivan," Michael echoed Dudley's sentiment. "There's no joy in remembrance."

Ivan could hardly contain his anger. "You two were the best students I thought I ever had," he began, "now, I realize you haven't learned anything. Can't you see how important it is to tell our stories? Do you only care about yourselves? If you share your suffering with the rest of the world you can lessen your own pain and make them aware of the potential threat they may have to live with. Our generation will sweep our bad memories under the rug, just as our grandparents did. I can't think of worst thing to do to future generations."

The room grew silent as Dudley and Michael considered Ivan's challenge.

The women in the kitchen were busying themselves with food preparation, but the conversation wasn't about food.

"Dianna, you are so beautiful," Candy smiled.

Dianna burst into tears.

"Oh," Candy recoiled, "I didn't mean to hurt you."

"It's o.k." Dianna recovered. "I guess you should know that it was only my looks that kept me alive during the occupation. I was a sex toy for the enemy officers," she finished as she burst into tears.

Candy embraced Dianna then Jane put arms around the other two.

"You lived through my worst nightmare," Candy disclosed. "You are much braver than I was."

Now Jane was in tears. "I can easily understand your need to survive," Jane said. "I don't know if any woman would have done anything else in your situation."

The tearfulness ended and a feeling of belonging and love flowed through the three women as they realized their good fortune.

Later when the couples sat around the dinner table, the conversation took on a light, buoyant air.

"So what did you men talk about while we were working to prepare this meal?" Jane asked with challenging tone.

"We talked about keeping you women pregnant," Ivan beamed.

"Wow," Jane cooed which brought laughter to the table.

"We also talked about the future," Dudley added.

"And," Michael continued, "that future includes us writing our memoirs; all of us."

The group grew silent. Suddenly, Michael got up from his chair and place one hand on Candy's bulging mid-section. With the other hand, Michael raised his glass. "To the future," he toasted.

It was the last day of spring, and the wilderness was in full foliage and flower. The spring morning was bright, but unusually quiet. It seemed as if the forest was holding its breath waiting for something special to happen. There was no wind. The birds were silent and the animals were still as they waited, watched and listened.

Finally, the moment arrived. The cry of a newborn infant echoed across the forest from the cabin on Long Ridge. The birds took up their songs, and the animals scurried about with joy. A light breeze tickled the leaves of the trees, and the sunlight ignited a dance of shadows.

The infant was a man-child. He had the bright red hair of his mother and the peculiar gray eyes of his father. His parents would call him Michael.

Two months later Ivana Draco came into the world. Six weeks after that Dianna Carpenter also gave birth to a daughter. She was named Deanna.

Ivan Draco was the first to finish his first book. It was titled "A History of the First War of Liberation". Jane Linden Draco was next to finish her tale as a military intelligence agent. Dudley and Michael were

The Last Day of the Last Spring

next with their treatises. Dudley's work "A Machine in the Wilderness" detailed the manufacturing capability hidden in the Midland-Highlands. Michael's tome was called "From Visions and Voices to Victory".

Candy Sylvan called her memoirs "Before the Mist Came to Portston" which proclaimed the valor of the children of that huge city. Finally, Dianna Carpenter offered her novel "Under Occupation" where she detailed her life of fear and survival in enemy held territory during the war. Dianna's book would become a best seller.

All the works were published by National University Press which was under the control of Jane Linden Draco, Dean of Library Science at National University.

Ivan Draco would not accept the job of President of National University. He appeared before the board of curators and made an impassioned plea for Doctor Henley to be the next president. Draco accepted the Vice-President title.

Being the sole heir to Highet Industries, Dudley Carpenter began living out his dream. His wife, Dianna, continued to manage the Bartlett Hotel business as re-construction caught fire in the new economy.

Michael Sylvan was promoted to Colonel and assigned as Commander-Tactical Training at the Military Institute. When he received the orders, a small, hand written note was also in the envelope. The note read, "If you can teach me, you can teach anybody." It was signed "Slug".

Candy Sylvan took over the administration of Woodburne Industries. She proved to be a very able and capable leader of the company and it prospered in the post war years.

The three couples' first re-union at the cabin on Long Ridge the following summer was bright and cheerful. Ivan Draco was heralded as the hero of the group for insisting they write about their lives during the war and free themselves of the hurtful burden that had silenced the previous generation. Everyone agreed that since writing their stories they felt that they could move on with their lives. But most of all they watched their babies play together in the lush grass that surrounded the cabin.

Local elections were held that fall, as General Wilder publicized his plan to return the country to civilian rule. Simultaneously, National University re-opened its main campus.

311

As for the Midland-Highlands; the vast woodland is silent now. Its hills, piled up on top of one another for countless miles, etch a jagged silhouette against the sky. Its valleys descend into deep mazes where sunlight never penetrates to cast a shadow. The mist is gone too, and in the winter, snow is permitted to stack up against the mighty wooden pillars that support the heavens above. But don't let the pristine image lull you into a sense of serenity. The place they call the Midlands, or Highlands, is simply at rest; gathering strength until it is needed again.

6463775R0

Made in the USA
Charleston, SC
28 October 2010